BEFORE YOU GO

Books by Jerome Weidman

NOVELS

I Can Get It for You Wholesale
What's in It for Me?
I'll Never Go There Any More
The Lights Around the Shore
Too Early To Tell
The Price Is Right
The Hand of the Hunter
Give Me Your Love
The Third Angel
Your Daughter Iris
The Enemy Camp
Before You Go

SHORT STORIES

The Horse That Could Whistle "Dixie"
The Captain's Tiger
A Dime a Throw

ESSAYS AND TRAVEL

Letter of Credit
Traveler's Cheque

A MUSICAL PLAY

Fiorello!
(with George Abbott, Jerry Bock,
and Sheldon Harnick)

BEFORE
YOU
GO

Jerome Weidman

RANDOM HOUSE
NEW YORK

FIRST PRINTING

For

CARL BRANDT

September 11, 1889—October 13, 1957

"*Soft you; a word or two before you go.*
I have done the state some service,
and they know it."
Othello

"*Always stick to the root of the matter,*
and the matter, as well as its roots,
will stick to you."
Benjamin Franklin Ivey

BEFORE YOU GO

1

Not until she arrived in London in the spring of 1943 did it occur to Julie Sarno, who weighed one hundred and eight pounds, that it was a fat girl's war.

"Back in Tulsa I'd still be dieting my head off and sitting home every night reading those columns in the evening paper on How to Hook a Man," Rita Merlin, who weighed one hundred and forty, had said when she met Julie at the boat train in bomb-scarred Paddington.

Julie, whose attention had wandered uneasily to the rather spectacular illustrations of the ravages of war by which she was surrounded and for which almost four years of American newspaper and magazine photographs had left her totally unprepared, had turned back and taken a look at Rita. She was still a trifle numb from the long, scary Atlantic crossing in convoy and a sleepless night in the sleazy hotel in blacked-out Liverpool, but her vision was unimpaired. What Julie saw, as she stared at Rita Merlin, was a girl of some thirty summers who was clearly at least ten pounds heavier than the jolly and then merely plump acquaintance to whom Julie had said good-bye—was it really no more than eight months ago?—in Washington. Only a sadist, however, could have said anything cruel, or even completely truthful, to anyone so kind and generous and basically innocent as Rita Merlin.

Six months later, on a morning when the increasing difficulties Rita had been having for several weeks with her girdle had clearly reached a crisis, Julie decided the moment of truth had arrived.

"It's possible, of course, that the air in this wonderful city has changed," she said as she spooned Nescafé into the two chipped coffee cups out of which they gulped all the breakfast Julie ever wanted and as much as Rita, who was usually hung-over, seemed to be able to get down. "It is also possible that your metabolism has changed, the way they say people's blood gets thin if they live in the tropics too long. But I wouldn't know about any of that." Julie recapped the jar of Nescafé and picked up the saucepan of boiling water from the hot plate. "What I do know is that if you tried staying home with a salad once in a while, instead of racketing around night after night in all those black-market restaurants where everything is cooked in Devonshire cream and the sauces are all as rich as Howard Hughes, you might get back to looking a little more like the neat little butterball from Oklahoma I met in the Board of Economic Warfare's Washington office a year and a half ago when we were both being processed for shipment overseas."

"No thank you," Rita said. "I had enough of that stay-home-at-night-with-a-salad routine back in Tulsa to last a girl a lifetime. Besides," the fat girl added as she whacked her massive hip, "Mac likes me this way."

As is the case with all incontrovertible facts, there was no arguing with this one. Mac, better known to his staff in one of the many buildings taken over by the American war effort on Grosvenor Square as Major General Crandall T. MacNeilson, was a man of simple tastes. These, so far as Julie had been able to observe in six months of a proximity she had not sought and did not particularly like, ran to rare steaks, straight bourbon, and Rita Merlin. Since the general's province was military government, and the Allied war effort in the early fall of 1943 had not yet reached a point where there was anything for it to govern, Crandall T. MacNeilson was able, while he waited in London for other branches of the service to breach the walls of Festung Europa for him, to devote a good deal of time to the indulgence of his simple tastes. This raised a problem for Julie Sarno. The war had come along at a moment in her life when, drained by an outpouring of emotions she had not yet learned how to guard against or control, she had grasped desperately at a job that took her away from the scenes of her troubled past. The fierce resolve never again to succumb to the spendthrift squandering of what little was left in her heart did not, however, exclude an elementary sense of loyalty to someone with whom through the accident of war she was sharing the same roof. For this reason Julie often found herself wishing that, to the public spectacle Major General MacNeilson made as he indulged his three simple tastes, Rita Merlin would not add an equally public demonstration of the embarrassing fact that she was the simplest.

"Yes, all right, granted, Mac likes you this way," Julie said as she worked her own way carefully back from the bathroom, around the bisected studio couch, and into the wings of the tuck-away kitchen. "But if you keep stoking yourself on starches and greases night after night, how long are you going to remain this way?"

Staggering out of the bathroom with her arms swaying aloft like the antennae of some gigantic beetle and her head hidden by the folds of a blue and white print dress she was trying to punch her way into, Rita mumbled something that sounded like: "Long enough."

"Long enough for what?" said Julie.

"Long enough for like maybe when this war is over," Rita said, her flushed face emerging from the folds of the dress. "Mac might be so used to me that he won't be able to do without me."

The simple, forthright statement—innocent as a child's request for the moon, and rooted in approximately the same grasp of the realities involved in granting the request—must have brought a look to Julie's face that her roommate construed as critical. At any rate, Rita's plump, flushed cheeks grew darker red with a rush of embarrassment.

"Oh, I know what you're thinking," Rita said with a touch of bitterness so uncharacteristic that Julie suddenly felt awful. "You're thinking that's pretty mean and cheap and calculating of me," Rita said, scowling as she yanked the dress into place over her tightly girdled hips. "You're thinking Mac is a married man,

5

with a wife and family back home in Springfield, and while he's over here, in the army, fighting a war, I come along and set a trap for him and try to get him to divorce his wife and marry me. Well, suppose it's true?"

With a gesture of defiance, Rita snatched up a lipstick from the litter of jars and bottles and packages of face tissue on the up-ended suitcase that served her as a dressing table.

"It's easy for you to adopt a high moral tone," she said. "You're young and you're pretty and you've got a beautiful figure and no matter what you eat, or how much, it doesn't show, and all your life you've had boys whistling at you, so you can afford to be snooty." Rita paused to trace, with savage thrusts of the lipstick, two smears of scarlet across her momentarily and, in the light of her words and frame of mind, ludicrously pursed lips. "But I'm not young," she said. "I'll be thirty-three next month. And I'm not pretty, and I've never had a figure, and nobody ever whistled at me until I came to London a little over a year ago. I can't afford to be snooty, and by God, I'm not going to be! This is my only chance, and I'm not going to miss it. If I go home without Mac, if this war ends without my landing him, I know I'll never get another chance. So stop looking at me that way and get those high and mighty thoughts out of your head."

"I'm not looking at you in any way," said Julie, which was not quite true, and she added, "You have no idea what I'm thinking," which was so distressingly true that she turned away and made a completely unnecessary fuss about rinsing the saucepan so that Rita, who like many slow-witted people had moments of surprising perception, would not, if this should happen to be one of those moments, be able to read Julie's thoughts.

They centered around what was for her the still puzzling question: *How can people be so dumb?* The answer, which was quite simply that they managed it with remarkable ease, was not very satisfying to Julie Sarno, who in her more depressed moments was only too well aware that in her own lifetime of twenty-seven years she had demonstrated time and again to her own unhappy satisfaction that she could be just as dumb as anybody else. Even so, in view of the known biographical facts about Major General Mac-

6

Neilson, it seemed to Julie that Rita Merlin was achieving a new high in the human animal's passion for self-delusion.

Crandall T. (the fact that the T. stood for Tecumseh was hardly, Julie realized, the general's fault) MacNeilson was sixty-two years old. What his life had been like up to the moment when the Japanese began to dump high explosive on Pearl Harbor could be read clearly, it seemed to Julie, in his beefy, florid face; in his small, cunning rather than intelligent, piglike eyes; in the enormous paunch he carried not with the dignity of a temperate man on whom the inevitable accretion of the years sat with a certain amount of portly grace but with the wheezing shamelessness of an insatiable slob who had never bothered to curb his animal appetites; in his ready, knowing, cackling laugh that brought into the most innocent conversation the uncomfortable, furtive echoes of complicated debaucheries; and in the snapshot which, when the general was in his cups—a state he could be counted on to achieve with dismal regularity somewhere between nine and ten o'clock every night—he would drag from his wallet and pass around for inspection and, his manner clearly indicated, approbation.

The picture had been taken in his Springfield living room several months after Pearl Harbor on the day Crandall T. Mac-Neilson, having resigned for the duration from the presidency of The Ohio Reliance Indemnity & Casualty Company, had received his commission. The newly minted general, resplendent in a band-box fresh uniform that fitted him with all the elegance of an inexpertly converted flour sack, was surrounded by the members of his family. These consisted of three sons, ranging in age from twenty-seven to thirty-six; their three almost belligerently undistinguished wives; eleven grandchildren, one of whom was pointing with grinning pride to the stars on Grandpa's shoulders; and the general's wife, a thin little woman with almost white hair who, even though clearly doing her best to obey the photographer's injunction to smile, managed to look terrified.

Julie Sarno, who since coming to London had seen the photograph more times than she cared to remember, understood that look. Her own father had been a never more than temporarily

7

solvent, and usually penniless, barber on East Ninth Street in New York. All his life, however, the big, handsome immigrant from Naples had been driven by the same appetites to the indulgence of which it was so plain the former president of The Ohio Reliance Indemnity & Casualty Company had devoted most of his sixty-odd years. The gap between the tastelessly expensive Springfield living room in General MacNeilson's snapshot and the shabbily functional three rooms above the barber shop on East Ninth Street, where Julie had been born and raised, was enormous. But the marks that the heads of both households had left on the faces of their wives were identical.

Julie had been bothered for a long time by the fact that Rita Merlin, whose wholesome decency frequently skirted the edge of simple-mindedness, should have thrown herself so completely into a relationship with a man like Crandall T. MacNeilson. Having once been forced by circumstances beyond her control to be her older sister's keeper, Julie was determined never to take on a similar burden again. Certainly not for a, if no longer total, nevertheless still accidentally met, stranger like Rita Merlin. Besides, she could understand, or until this moment Julie had thought she could understand, Rita's motives.

It was an axiom widely circulated, and perhaps even believed by those who found in it an excuse for their conduct, that everybody went slightly crazy during a war. Why, then, should the privilege be denied to a fat girl who, after a lifetime as a wallflower, was at last enjoying the heady experience of being led out onto the dance floor? Not until this awful moment, however, standing with her back to Rita, rinsing and rerinsing the spotless saucepan in their tuckaway kitchen, had it occurred to Julie that her roommate was taking Mac seriously. Suddenly she heard Rita's voice.

"Oh, now, Mac, you really are the limit! What a way to talk at this hour of the morning!"

Into the telephone, which had obviously rung while Julie was lost in her troubled thoughts, the fat girl from Tulsa was pouring the breathless little whimpers of ecstasy that always accompanied whatever words she happened to be uttering to the only man who had ever whistled at her.

8

"All right, I'll ask her, but only if you promise to behave," she said with a giggle that set every ounce of her now surely one hundred and fifty pounds aquiver. Rita waited, her large face suffused by a glow of happiness that Julie supposed every director who had ever staged the balcony scene hoped to elicit from the girl who played opposite Romeo, and Major General MacNeilson apparently came through with the promise. Rita nodded happily. "Hold it a sec, Mac," she said, and she put the mouthpiece to her ample shoulder. "Julie, what are you doing tonight?"

"Well," Julie said, and she hesitated. Not because she didn't know the answer, but because she knew, from her experience with several dozen of these morning calls from General MacNeilson, that the truthful answer would not protect her. An outright lie was the only shield. Julie said firmly, "I've got a date."

Rita's lips, so prettily shaped that they almost seemed a deformity in the large fleshy expanse of her face, came together in a small bud of disappointment.

"She's got a date," Rita said into the telephone and then, after several moments of listening, she put the mouthpiece back against her shoulder. "Mac wants to know with who?"

"And since when," Julie said as righteous indignation, rising swiftly like a soothing ointment, eased the slight laceration of conscience that telling the outright lie had left in its wake, "is it any of General MacNeilson's business who I go out with?"

"Oh, come on, quit it," Rita said with a cajoling grin. "This is important."

"Important to whom, may I ask?"

Rita giggled and said into the phone, "She's giving me the duchess act." Then, as the mouthpiece returned to her shoulder, "All Mac means, if it's not important, your date, I mean, couldn't you break it?"

"Why?"

"Well, Mac's got this friend, he just flew in from Washington—"

"No, I'm sorry," Julie said. "I can't break this date."

She had met quite a few of Mac's friends who flew in from Washington.

9

"No, she can't, Mac," Rita said into the phone and then, in surprise, "You mean it?" Apparently Mac did because, as the mouthpiece went back to her shoulder and she addressed Julie, the surprise lingered in Rita's voice. "Mac says why don't you bring him along?"

"Who?"

"Your date."

"Oh," said Julie, wryly trying all at once to remember a proverb her mother used to quote about the inevitability with which the only one who got caught by a lie was the liar himself: Julie's "date" for that night was the bottle of shampoo with which she intended to wash her hair while listening to the BBC's Home and Forces Program on which, for almost two months, a stupefyingly cultured voice had been reading one chapter each night from *Barchester Towers*. Julie said, "You mean Mac wants us to go out tonight like that? Five people?"

Rita rolled her eyes to heaven in quest of the patience she clearly felt was needed to explain the simplest facts of life to her beautiful and beloved but obviously dim-witted roommate.

"Look, Julie sweetie," she said. "Mac calls up and says he wants you to go out with us tonight, but you have a date. Mac says okay, he hasn't seen you for nearly two weeks, maybe more, what the heck, you've got a date you've got a date, why let that stand in the way? He can't have you alone, Mac says, he'll take you with your date. How about it?"

"But won't that make it a little embarrassing for this friend of Mac's from Washington?"

The point had obviously not crossed Rita's mind before, conceivably because Mac's friends from Washington, as Julie Sarno had observed them, were incapable of embarrassment.

"Oh," Rita said. Then, "Wait." And into the phone: "Julie says won't that make it a little embarrassing for this friend of yours from Washington? I mean, Mac, I'm with *you*, and Julie's with *her* date, the four of us we're paired off two and two, it sort of leaves Colonel Uxbridge—?"

The eager little attempt at clarifying the obvious, surrounded by its cloud of loving little whimpers, stopped abruptly. It had apparently run head-on into an explanation from the other end of the wire that, to judge by the look on Rita's face, was astounding. She turned with the phone, her eyes wide, and stared at Julie as though she had never seen her before.

"No kidding?" Rita said, a note of awe breaking through the incredulity in her voice, and then, in sudden excitement, across the mouthpiece, she said, "Julie, listen! Mac says this friend of his, this Colonel Uxbridge who just flew in from Washington, he wants—!"

What Mac said next was so clear, short, and forthrightly uttered that, even though the words were indistinguishable to Julie at the other side of the room, their meaning was unmistakable. Major General MacNeilson, whose manners and vocabulary were better suited to the playing fields of Bronx Park than those of Eton, had just told his beloved to shut her great big trap.

Rita obeyed, and kept it shut, shooting nervous glances at Julie and bobbing her head up and down dutifully while she listened to still another explanation from the man by whom, in the daydream fabricated out of her frustration and innocence, she saw herself after the war being led to the altar.

"Okay, yes," Rita said finally, her voice low, her face grave. "I understand, Mac. Yes, I've got it. Yes, Mac, I understand."

She put the phone back slowly, scowling with concentrated attention at her hand as she did it, giving to the small, mechanical act all the absorbed watchfulness she might have devoted to measuring out and then combining the many ingredients of a complicated recipe.

"All right," Julie said irritably. "Now what was *that* all about?"

The tone of her voice, intended to do no more than shake loose the nonsense with which Rita seemed to be surrounding what was to Julie a puzzling but thoroughly unimportant situation, had an astonishing effect. Rita's body jerked nervously and she took a step backward, as though she had been slapped. This, in the crowded room where any uncalculated movement was bound to spell disaster, brought the fat girl's calves sharply against the edge of Julie's half of the studio couch. Thrown off balance, Rita sawed wildly at the air, then, with a gasp of despair and a

11

thump that shook the room, she tumbled backward onto the couch.

Moving forward out of the tuckaway kitchen, with a laugh in which her momentary irritation had vanished, Julie stopped short. The ludicrous tumble, so long predicted in jest by both of them as they had schooled themselves to move about their tiny home with caution, was clearly not a laughing matter. Not to Rita, at any rate. With a feeling of shock followed promptly by a wrench of the heart she did not pause at the moment to examine, Julie saw that the fat girl was sobbing.

"Rita! Rita, for God's sake!" Julie reached the couch and sank to her knees. "Rita, darling, what's the matter?"

Rita's body, squirming as she worked herself over onto her face and buried it in Julie's pillow, heaved with harsh, dry, hacking sobs. They tore through her lumpy body like the coughing fits that long ago had finally shaken the life out of Julie Sarno's hard-drinking father. Julie remained for several moments on her knees beside the couch, raked by feelings that had for years remained buried with the terrible memories of which they were a part, patting Rita's shoulder with a sense of helplessness in which a bitter resentment stirred.

She didn't really know this girl. They were not friends as Julie Sarno understood the term. They had nothing in common beyond the many tendrils of household arrangements of which the thirteen pounds they paid each month to their landlady, was the central trunk. On guard against even minor involvements, Julie had stuck resolutely to her determination that the relationship should go no further. For eight months after they met in the BEW's Washington office—while Rita, who had been shipped out first, wrote glowing letters about life in London and the apartment in Old Quebec Street on which she had her eye and which Mac, by pulling the right strings, was sure he could get for her and Julie by the time the latter reached London—Julie had seen to it in her own letters that the relationship did not go any further. Nothing had happened during the six months they had shared the flat to make Julie feel the relationship *had* gone any further. Only a few moments ago, annoyed with herself for having inadvertently inserted an opinion into Rita's private affairs, Julie had been able to assure herself she had spoken out of nothing more than an elementary sense of loyalty to a roommate.

And yet here she was, on her knees beside this sobbing fool, racked by emotions as genuine as those that ten years ago had been torn from her by the despair of someone she had revered from the first moment Celia Sarno's extraordinary smile had been turned on her then baby sister. It didn't seem fair that the heart, which had been caught and sundered once by love, should be caught again by mere proximity.

With an effort that was clearly made more difficult by her weight, Rita pushed herself up from the pillow. Scraping at the tears with one hand, supporting herself with the other, her body bubbling up and down like the lid of a boiling pot, she gave Julie a look of agonized appeal.

"Mac says—I mean he told me *not* to say—" Rita's voice stopped. She shook her head desperately, as though to clear it of words she did not want to utter. "Julie, please, please, *please* don't ask me any questions," she said. "Just please, Julie, please come to dinner with us tonight. Please, Julie, please say yes?"

"But I just told you," Julie said slowly, speaking without thought, repeating automatically the remembered phrases of her trumped-up excuse. "I have this date that—"

Rita shook her head again, more desperately. "I know," she said. "We went through that. If you can't break it, bring him along. It doesn't matter, just so long as you show up. If you don't, Mac said if you don't—"

Her voice stopped again.

"If I don't?" Julie said stupidly. "What do you mean, if I don't?"

"Oh, it's not you," Rita said hastily. "He wouldn't do anything to you. It's just he said if I didn't get you to come tonight, he'd—" Once more the flow of words stopped abruptly, as though Rita had recognized, in the outpouring, samples of some she had been forbidden to utter. She drew a deep, painful breath. "Don't ask me any more questions," she said. "Please don't, Julie. Mac wants you to come to dinner tonight and meet this Colonel Uxbridge. That's all I know. I don't know who he is or what he wants. All I know is it's important to Mac. If you don't come, he said he'd, Mac said he and I, he said we— Oh, Julie, please, *please*? Please say you'll come to dinner tonight? You and your date? It's nothing to you, Julie, but it means an awful lot to me. If Mac walks out on me now I'll—I'll—"

"But what—?"

The question, part of a whole series erupting in her mind, each new one crowding its unanswered predecessors for attention, all jumbled together like angleworms squirming in a bottle, stopped on Julie's lips. The identity of Colonel Uxbridge, why and how it could be important to General MacNeilson that Rita's roommate should meet him, the dozen incredulously worded footnotes to both, all seemed suddenly unimportant. Thrusting them all aside, invading Julie's mind like an enemy who, after biding his time, had finally breached the walls of the past she had guarded so carefully even from herself, was the answer to the wrench of the heart that had brought Julie to her knees beside this preposterous stranger with whom she had been thrown together by the accident of war.

"All right, sure," Julie said wearily, and once more she paused, this time because the resentment at being trapped by a compassion against which she had tried to guard was being swallowed in a discovery she could scarcely credit: it did not seem possible that she should be feeling again, in this ridiculous key flat half a world away, on her knees beside this pathetic but foolish fat girl, what Julie had felt ten years ago in a Seattle hotel room on what was to have been her sister Celia's wedding day.

"If it means that much to you, Rita, of course I'll come along," Julie said quietly. "And don't worry about my date," she added as she stood up. "Breaking that won't be any kind of problem."

2

The entertainments provided by General MacNeilson for his friends who flew in from Washington were as primitive as Robin Hood's concept of the law of supply and demand.

In a war in which the American cause was allied with that of a nation famous for its tradition of soldier poets, there undoubtedly were fighting men in the ETO who in their moments of relaxation sought refreshment by reading Plato, viewing Gauguin, or discussing Schiller. The former president of The Ohio Reliance Indemnity & Casualty Company was not one of these. To the warriors with whom he relaxed from his arduous duties on Grosvenor Square, Major General MacNeilson served up the fare that between battles had sustained Hannibal and revived Attila: wine, women, and song.

The first of these took the form of an excellent 100-proof bourbon, a steady flow of which was maintained—between the distillery where it was made in Kentucky and General MacNeilson's suite at the Wyndham Hotel near Marble Arch in London—by an insurance company executive who, like his friend the general, had turned his back on private enterprise to give his all for the duration to the Air Transport Command. The women, who preferred to be called girls and frequently qualified for this designation, were supplied by Rita Merlin and the network of friends she had woven throughout the secretarial staffs of the BEW, OSS, OWI, and a half dozen other American war agencies with offices in London. The supply of song was less dependable. Not because General MacNeilson, who produced it himself on the harmonica he always carried in his pocket, was less generous with his music than he was with his whiskey. It was simply that, after his fifth drink, the general began to have trouble with his wind.

Julie Sarno could tell, as in answer to her knock Rita opened the door of the general's suite at seven o'clock, that things were still under control. From the far side of the room came the sound of music.

"Ssshhh while I take your things and make you a drink," Rita said in a happy whisper. "Mac is in the middle of 'Danny Boy.'"

She sounded as though they were the guests of Da Vinci and had arrived at the master's studio while he was putting the finishing touches to the Mona Lisa.

"Am I late?" Julie whispered as she slipped out of her coat. Hastily scanning the sitting room of the general's suite across Rita's shoulder, Julie could see only Mac himself. He was slumped down on his spine in the couch under the window that looked out on Hyde Park. His eyes were closed and his paunch heaved as he drew from the tiny instrument, which was almost completely concealed by the meaty red fists in which it was gripped, the surprisingly true notes of the lovely melody that, for some obscure reason, was to Crandall T. MacNeilson what the call of the muezzin at sunset is to the Mohammedan.

"No, right on the button," Rita said. "Matter of fact, you're a little early. This Colonel Uxbridge, he called a few minutes ago. He got held up in a meeting, but he's on his way now, and he—"

The music stopped.

"For Christ's sakes," General MacNeilson snarled. "How the hell yixpect a guy to play a song with all that yak, yak, yak—?"

The effort to lift himself higher on the couch, as well as out of the mood into which the general's music always thrust him, stopped abruptly. So did the unpleasant, angry complaint. The general, opening his eyes, had recognized Julie.

"Ah, there she is, the little gay deceiver herself," he said. The petulance creasing his florid face vanished in the crafty smile that always made Julie feel as though she needed a hot shower. "Come

16

on over here and give your Uncle Mac a great big kiss, you little devil, you."

Julie, who would sooner have kissed Quasimodo, moved reluctantly toward the couch.

"Hello, Mac," she said. "Don't let me interrupt the music."

"Interrupt?" the general said with a leer. He shoved the harmonica into his pocket and put out his other hand. "*You?*"

Julie reached out gingerly, intending to do no more than touch his palm in greeting. But the general, most of whose body was forced by its size and shape to the pace of a hippopotamus, could from the wrists up move like a cobra.

"I once read somewhere that even Cleopatra was a pain in the neck to Antony when she interrupted him in the middle of a song," Julie said, trying to tug free her suddenly imprisoned fingers. "And I'm no Cleopatra." She smiled to cover her feeling of revulsion. The general's palm was damp with what a stranger might have thought was perspiration. But Julie knew better. With every rendition of 'Danny Boy,' the general produced almost as much saliva as music. "And if you'll just give me back that hand, Mac," she said, "I'll take that drink Rita is poking at me."

"Take it with your other hand," said General MacNeilson. "I want to hold onto this one awhile. It's the prettiest thing I've touched all day, and you may not think you're Cleopatra, but Colonel Uxbridge sure does."

"Quit kidding a poor thirsty girl who has just given nine of the best hours of her life to the Board of Economic Warfare and is out on her feet." Julie tugged harder, but without success. "I've never seen Colonel Uxbridge, whoever he is, and if he's seen me, although I can't imagine where, and he thinks I'm Cleopatra, then he certainly didn't reach the rank of colonel because of his eyesight."

General MacNeilson laughed.

"You've never seen him, huh?" One of his small, hooded lids dropped in a conspiratorial wink. "How's about you quit kidding your Uncle Mac?"

Reaching with her free hand for the glass Rita was holding out, it suddenly occurred to Julie that a new dimension had been

17

added to her puzzlement. All day, from the moment in the morning when she had promised her weeping roommate she would join General MacNeilson's dinner party for his friend from Washington, Julie had been unable to get Rita's words our of her head. "I don't know who Colonel Uxbridge is or what he wants," Rita had sobbed. "All I know is that it's important to Mac." How, Julie had been asking herself all day, could it possibly be important to Mac? A colonel currying favor with a two-star general was an understandable situation, especially during a war. When the situation was reversed, however, it became incomprehensible, particularly during a war. The explanation for which Julie had finally, and somewhat uneasily, settled was that rank had nothing to do with this particular situation.

In the large gallery of General MacNeilson's friends who kept flying in from Washington, it had seemed to Julie reasonable to assume, Colonel Uxbridge undoubtedly occupied a special and favored place. A place he had earned long ago, before the war, when he and Mac, in the business world undoubtedly of equal rank—perhaps in Cleveland, perhaps in other cities where they met for business reasons—had after business hours been comrades in the indulgence of those simple tastes for which Crandall T. MacNeilson was so justly famed. Now, however, still trying without success to tug her hand free, Julie saw that her assumption was not so reasonable after all. Mac's words and questions, his leering wink, his knowing manner as he held her prisoner, clearly implied that he believed Colonel Uxbridge, completely unknown to Julie, was one of her old flames. Colonel Uxbridge, who obviously knew as well as Julie did that the belief was erroneous, could have set his old friend straight with a word. Why hadn't he done so? More important, and certainly more puzzling, how had the belief come to exist in Mac's admittedly dirty but far from witless mind?

"I don't want to kid anybody," Julie said, trying for Rita's sake not to sound exasperated as she made a renewed effort to free her hand. "All I want to do is sit down and enjoy my drink."

"Come sit by your Uncle Mac," the general said. He patted the

18

couch with his free hand. "And whisper in my ear what it is between you and Colonel Uxbridge."

"Go on, Julie," Rita said with a happy smile. "I'm dying to hear."

"You go make me another drink," General MacNeilson said to the fat girl. He chuckled roguishly as he began to haul Julie down on the couch beside him. "Rita's too young to hear this kind of stuff, hey, Julie?"

Outraged as much by the insulting implication of his words as by the indignity of being dragged toward him like a reluctant child, Julie managed, as she staggered forward helplessly, to plant her heel on the toe of the general's shoe. Three things happened simultaneously: all the creases of his roguish smile rearranged themselves abruptly in a startled expression of pain; he released Julie's hand; and he uttered a short, sharp yelp that reminded her of the sound her sister Celia used to produce when she pressed the black rubber bulb of the horn on the bicycle Julie's father had given Celia for her twelfth birthday.

"Oh, Mac, I'm sorry," said Julie, who couldn't have been more pleased. "I hope I didn't hurt you?"

"How, if I may interrupt with a perhaps foolish question, could a pretty girl hurt a major general of the United States Army?"

Turning quickly toward the strange voice, Julie had time to note that the expression of pain on Mac's face, vanishing as rapidly as the roguish smile, was being replaced by a smirk so clearly obsequious that Julie would not have been surprised to discover that the newcomer was Winston Churchill. What she discovered instead was even more surprising. In the open doorway, holding his hat, stood a tall, slender, handsome man with close-cropped white hair who, except for his beautifully tailored uniform, looked exactly like Mr. Tyler Crispin, the director of the Horace Judson Clarke House on Avenue B where Julie Sarno had been inducted into the Nature Club at the age of eleven. The resemblance was so startling that now, at the age of twenty-seven, Julie could suddenly smell again the harsh yet curiously pleasant odor of the disinfectant that went into the water with which the corridors

19

of the old settlement house on New York's Lower East Side used to be swabbed daily.

"If the heels of the shoes pretty girls are wearing these days get any sharper," Mac said as, with the help of Rita, he managed to get to his feet, "I think they'll put the whole damned army into the hospital." He limped hurriedly to the doorway. He seized the newcomer's hand and hauled him toward the couch. "Come on in, Colonel, and meet the girls."

The manner in which Colonel Uxbridge performed his part of this rite did nothing to dispel Julie's puzzlement. Bowing first over her hand, and then over Rita's, Colonel Uxbridge did not look at all—as the friends of General MacNeilson who flew in from Washington always did—like a man who, knowing he is standing on the threshold of an evening that will go down in the annals devoted to towns that have been painted red, can scarcely wait to dip his brush into the bucket. Colonel Uxbridge looked like the pastor of a fashionable church whose courtly manners forced him to conceal the irritation he felt on having been called out of his study, where he had been immersed in the preparation of next Sunday's sermon, to meet a couple of his teen-age daughter's jitterbug chums.

"This is a very great pleasure, Miss Sarno," he said. Perhaps it was, but a passer-by could have been excused for failing to draw that inference from the colonel's cool, detached, and completely unenthusiastic voice. "I am grateful to you for joining us."

The fact that here was an odd fish indeed to be included in the roster of Mac's friends who flew in from Washington must have impressed itself even on the slow-witted Rita. Or perhaps she, too, had caught the note of dislike in Colonel Uxbridge's voice as he addressed Julie. Rita stood there, not quite open-mouthed but close enough, absently rubbing the hand over which the colonel had bowed, staring at the newcomer as though they were fellow guests at a masquerade party and she had the uneasy feeling that, before granting his request for a dance, it might be wise to penetrate his disguise. Her confused ruminations were shattered by General MacNeilson's elbow which, catching Rita in the small of the back, sent her reeling toward the bar.

"Come on, baby," he shouted jovially. "Let's get the colonel wrapped around some bourbon and branch water!"

Three quarters of an hour later, when Mac was beginning to have trouble with his wind, Julie noticed that Colonel Uxbridge had wrapped himself around less than a half inch of his first drink, and the surreptitious glances he had been stealing at his wrist watch throughout General MacNeilson's concert were becoming less surreptitious and more frequent. He reminded her so much of Mr. Tyler Crispin on one of those nights when the director of the Horace Judson Clarke House had been forced to forsake his many other duties to attend a meeting of the Nature Club at which the members unveiled the newest collection of leaves or rocks or butterflies they had gathered in Tompkins Square Park, that Julie wondered anew what Colonel Uxbridge was doing here.

His mind, like Mr. Crispin's, was obviously elsewhere. His distaste for his host, his surroundings, and the other guests was now so obvious that even Rita, in spite of the load of bourbon she was carrying, seemed to notice that something was wrong. And if what Mac had said was true, namely, that Colonel Uxbridge had been anxious to see Julie, the visitor from Washington certainly had an odd way of demonstrating anxiety: after the barely polite murmur over Julie's hand when they were introduced, Colonel Uxbridge had not said another word to her. This silence, which puzzled Julie, was apparently considered by General MacNeilson as a tribute to his talents as a musician.

"What I like about you, Colonel," he wheezed, "I like a man when he's listening to music, he's not all the time like dames, yak, yak, yak. Try some of these olives, Colonel. They're really the money."

"Not right now, sir," said the visitor from Washington in a tone which implied clearly that he felt people who ate olives were on a level with heroin addicts. "Would you think me terribly rude, sir, if I suggested that we go on to dinner right now?"

Julie stared in astonishment at the alacrity with which a two-star general responded to the colonel's suggestion.

"You bet, Colonel!" Mac struggled out of the couch and, for a perilous moment, teetered helplessly on his feet. Rita's steadying arm arrived in time to keep him on them. "I got a table reserved at Nick's in Soho," the general said. "Wonderful guy, Nick. If you like Greeks."

"A certain fondness for Plato was instilled in me at school," Colonel Uxbridge said.

"Huh?" General MacNeilson said, and then his startled face contracted in a convulsive grin as he whacked Rita on the back. "You get that?"

Rita winced. "Yeah," she said nervously.

"Then why the hell don't you laugh?" Mac demanded. Rita laughed. Julie, watching Colonel Uxbridge's face, saw that for all his detached coolness, somewhere behind the impassive mask, thoughts involving murder were chasing one another. The general said, "Nick is a different kind of Greek, Colonel. Rationing or no rationing, if Nick likes you, you eat yourself silly. That's how Rita, here, she busted a cap on her front tooth last year." General MacNeilson, suddenly convulsed by the recollection, laid across his beloved's tightly girdled buttocks a wallop that would have sent a Percheron into a plunging gallop. "Rita says what busted her tooth was the crust on the fried turkey leg she bit into, but me, I say it's providence paying her back for eating a black-market gobbler." Mac winked at his guest from Washington. "That's why I ordered steaks for tonight. I hope you're a steak man, Colonel?"

"I am not unfond of beef."

"Wait till you stow away a hunk of Nick's," Mac said, staggering toward his coat. "You'll be fonder. For Christ's sakes, Rita, what are you trying to do? Give an imitation of a lamppost? Shake the lead out, kid. Can't you see the colonel is hungry? Where the hell is my hat?"

It proved to be on his head. This fact, when pointed out to him by Julie, sent the general into a paroxysm of mirth that kept him bubbling wheezily, like a lava bed, all the way out of his suite, down the elevator, across the Wyndham's crowded lobby, through the baffle that shielded the hotel's glass front doors from bomb blast, and across the blacked-out sidewalk to the olive-drab car provided by a thoughtful War Department to help two-star generals on active service perform their official duties more efficiently.

"You and Julie first, Colonel," Mac boomed grandly as his driver, who had saluted smartly and opened the rear door, held a flashlight beam on the running board. "Rita doesn't mind riding up front with the driver. She's done it before."

"She won't have to do it this time," said Colonel Uxbridge coldly. "I have a car of my own." With a short, neat, and to Julie unexpected, movement he took her elbow and said, "I hope you don't mind riding with me, Miss Sarno?"

It was hardly a question, but even if it had been, Julie would have been unable to gather the breath for a reply. Colonel Uxbridge, gently but firmly, was hustling her along as though the alert had sounded and he wanted to reach a choice spot in the nearest shelter before it became jammed. A few moments later, finding herself on the rear seat of another olive-drab car parked a few yards down the curb from Mac's, Julie wasn't quite sure how the slender, white-haired man with the prim face had accomplished the rapid transfer without hurting so much as her feelings.

"Hey, Colonel, we'll meet you at Nick's!" The general's voice came booming out of the darkness as though, in a dense fog, he was hailing an ocean liner from a rowboat. "Julie knows where it is! She'll tell your driver how to get there!"

Leaning forward toward the vague bulk under the garrison cap on the driver's seat up front, Julie said, "You go straight down Oxford Street to Marylebone Lane and turn left. On Marylebone you keep going until—"

"You needn't bother," Colonel Uxbridge said as he climbed into the car and sat down beside her. "I've already told the driver where to go."

Surprised, Julie said, "Oh, you know Nick's?"

"Not nearly so well as you do."

Colonel Uxbridge leaned forward, said, "All right, Sergeant," wound up the window that closed off the rear seat from the driver and, as the car started with a lurch, he said, "I'm sorry, Miss Sarno. I'm afraid I didn't catch that."

"I said," Julie repeated, "you can't possibly know how well I know Nick's to use that tone of voice to me. Will you please ask the driver to stop the car? I'd forgotten that the general's friends who fly in from Washington are all alike."

She gathered the skirts of her coat and started to get up. Colonel Uxbridge put his hand on her arm.

"I'm terribly sorry," he said. "If I've offended you, Miss Sarno, I would like to apologize."

"You needn't bother," Julie said. "The general's other friends never do."

"There seems to be some misunderstanding," he said. "I'm not one of General MacNeilson's friends. Until last night, when I arrived in London, I never heard of General MacNeilson." The colonel paused and then, dryly, he said, "I might add that, after the performance I have just witnessed, I would not be inclined to feel that fate had dealt me an irreparable blow if I never laid eyes on him again."

Julie sat there, in the blacked-out car, still poised for the indignant exit that now seemed a trifle ludicrous, trapped by her own confusion. The anger to which she knew she was not entitled, since it was nobody's fault but her own that Colonel Uxbridge had met her under circumstances which gave him a perfect right to assume she was no better than her host, had run head-on into the uneasy conviction that the man from Washington was speaking the truth.

"But Rita said, this morning when General MacNeilson called her, he told Rita you wanted to see me tonight. Me specifically. You'd asked for me by name."

"That is correct."

The quietly uttered reply was no help. Julie tried again.

"Rita and Mac, the general, he told Rita my going out with you tonight, he said it was important to him."

"When I introduced myself to General MacNeilson early this morning on the phone and asked him if he could arrange to have me meet you, I made it a point to leave him with that impression."

"You mean it's *not* important?"

"It is more important, Miss Sarno, than I have a right to tell you."

"Important to General MacNeilson?"

"No," Colonel Uxbridge said. "To your country and mine. Unfortunately, that is all I am at liberty to tell you." He leaned forward, toward the figure on the front seat, then stopped and turned back to Julie. "May I tell the driver to go on, Miss Sarno?"

Julie hesitated. Part of her months devoted to "being processed for overseas duty" in the Board of Economic Warfare's Washington offices had been spent at a series of lectures on security. Much of what she had been forced to listen to about spies and codes had seemed romantic nonsense to her at the time, and nothing in her experience since coming to London had caused Julie to alter that opinion. Nothing, that is, until this moment. Was it possible that her duties, which were almost unbearably dull, had actually without her knowledge brushed some aspect of the war effort which made her, in spite of her lack of awareness, a crucial figure in the schemes of high-ranking officers who flew in from Washington?

"Well, yes," she said finally, "I guess so."

"All right, driver," Colonel Uxbridge said. The man at the wheel nodded. The motor came to life, the car moved from the curb, and Colonel Uxbridge again wound up the window that cut off the rear seat from the front. "I really do want to apologize," he said as he sat back, "for anything unpleasant you may have read into my words when I said I did not know Nick's as well as you do. When it became my professional duty to ask General MacNeilson to arrange a meeting with you, I was unaware of the general's habits or the circumstances under which the meeting would take place. I make it a rule to try, although I must confess my attempts are not always successful, not to sit in judgment on my fellow men. Just the same, if I may resort to a phrase that I am certain you are tired of hearing, there's a war on. By and large, for most people, it's an unpleasant business. I could not help feeling, after a few minutes in General MacNeilson's presence, that this war is far from an unpleasant business for him. By extension, I am afraid I leaped to the assumption—"

"That it is not an unpleasant business for me, either."

Colonel Uxbridge shifted his spare figure slightly on the rear seat. "I could wish, Miss Sarno, that a certain puritanical streak in my nature, of which I am not particularly proud, reflected as much credit on me as your frankness reflects on you."

"I don't think either one of us, Colonel, is establishing any records for frankness."

The slender, white-haired man shifted his weight again. It occurred to Julie that Colonel Uxbridge was trying in the almost nonexistent light to get a better look at her.

"Not counting a small unpleasantness on the Mexican border when I was a very young man, this is my second war," Colonel Uxbridge said. "I have found that, when a nation takes up arms, its population can be divided into only two groups. There are those to whom war is a job that had best be finished as quickly as possible. And there are those to whom war is a great golden moment which they are not averse to having prolonged."

He paused as though, having paid Julie the compliment of assuming she belonged like himself to the former group, he wanted to give her a chance to say so. Julie didn't take the chance. Not merely out of loyalty to Rita. Remembering with reluctance the carefully guarded emotions that had burst loose that morning as she knelt beside her sobbing roommate, Julie realized all at once, and with astonishment, that she knew something this apparently ascetic, clearly intelligent, and probably very wise man had not, in a lifetime at least twice as long and perhaps even longer than hers, managed to learn. There was a third group of people: those to whom war was neither a job to be hurried nor a golden moment to be prolonged, but an anodyne to be gulped.

The fact that the anodyne had worked, at least until this morning, was her own business. She knew herself well enough to know that, with a little more application, she could make it work again. Some day, if she worked at it hard enough, the effort to forget would become forgetfulness itself. Some day, if the war lasted long enough, the agony of her sister Celia's fate would cease to haunt her. That was all Julie had wanted out of life for many years. It was all she still wanted. Colonel Uxbridge, whoever he was, didn't have to know about that.

The car stopped. The driver got out, came around, opened the rear door, and directed a weak flashlight beam on the running board. Colonel Uxbridge dipped down, got out, and turned to give Julie his hand. Reaching to take it, she saw in the faint glow of the driver's flashlight the gilded crest on the wooden baffle that shielded the front door of the building at the other side of the pavement. Julie put down her hand and dropped back on the rear seat.

"You can tell me something else," she said. "Why we stopped here."

Colonel Uxbridge turned, rapped out a few inaudible words to the driver, climbed back into the car, dropped onto the seat beside Julie, and pulled the door shut.

"Miss Sarno—"

"This isn't Nick's."

"No, we're at Claridge's."

"What are we doing here?"

"We're going in to see somebody."

"Who?"

"I can't tell you that, Miss Sarno. My orders are to bring Miss Julie Sarno to Claridge's."

"To do what?"

"I don't know."

"Now, look, Colonel—"

"Miss Sarno, I can imagine what you're thinking. It may help clarify your thoughts if I tell you that I am the father of two daughters, both approximately your age, and a grandfather three times over. Even if I shared General MacNeilson's tastes, habits, and tendencies, I assure you that my self-respect as a man, not to mention my respect for the uniform I have worn for thirty-three years, would preclude my employing the general's tactics to gratify those tastes. I give you my word of honor that my orders to find and bring you here to Claridge's for this meeting were issued by an authority you would yourself respect, in connection

27

with a matter of grave urgency to the security of our country, which might be irreparably damaged if you don't co-operate. Not only I, but a great many others, are counting on you, Miss Sarno."

Julie hesitated again. Not because she doubted Colonel Uxbridge's words or suspected his motives. She had handled enough of General MacNeilson's friends to feel certain she could, if it became necessary, handle this man who said he was not Mac's friend. What caused Julie to hesitate was the sudden uneasy feeling that what was in danger was not her virtue but her sanity. The forgetfulness she had sought for ten years, the capacity to erase the tragedy of her sister Celia, the pretense that none of it had happened, which the anodyne of war was making possible—all that, Julie suddenly felt, was about to be snatched from her. She didn't know how or by whom. She couldn't imagine what Colonel Uxbridge had to do with it. She knew only that some instinct of self-preservation was warning her not to do what he asked.

"When the general and Rita get to Nick's," she said, stalling for time, "and we don't show up, Mac will know something is wrong."

"He will also know enough to make no comment," Colonel Uxbridge said. "If the amount of bourbon General MacNeilson has consumed should make him forget that fact, he'll be back at his desk in Springfield wearing a sack suit at The Ohio Reliance Indemnity & Casualty Company before the week is out." The man from Washington reached for the door handle. "May I add that in his own way, by placing me in touch with you, General MacNeilson has rendered a service to his country which, even though he is totally unaware of it, is far greater than any damage he can cause by the continued indulgence while in uniform of his primitive and rather obnoxious habits. I ask you, Miss Sarno, to render a similar service by following me."

"Suppose I refuse?"

"That would be a matter of intense personal regret to me," Colonel Uxbridge said. "It would also, I am afraid, terminate your usefulness to the American war effort. You would be shipped home at once."

Colonel Uxbridge opened the door. Again he stepped out of

the car. Again he turned and leaned in to give Julie his hand. This time she took it.

On the sidewalk, while Colonel Uxbridge paused to give the driver some instructions about the car, Julie was swept by a cleansing wave of common sense. The instinct of self-preservation that, moments before, had warned her not to do what Colonel Uxbridge asked, now urged her to embrace his request, no matter where it might lead. She was, after all, her father's daughter. The optimism that, between drinking bouts, had for years kept alive Biaggio Sarno's pathetic belief that the ship he had never sighted in his native Naples would some day in his adopted America come in, now washed away the uneasiness that, beginning in the morning beside the sobbing Rita, had become for Julie near-panic in the darkened car on the seat next to the quietly insistent Colonel Uxbridge. She did not know who it was the white-haired man from Washington had been ordered to bring her to meet here at Claridge's. But Julie did know that if the meeting involved what Colonel Uxbridge had called "a matter of grave urgency to the security of our country," then it would certainly prove more absorbing than her routine duties as a member of the BEW's secretarial pool. If the war was the anodyne on which Julie Sarno counted to wipe out the past, what could be a better break for the addict who sought forgetfulness than the unexpected gift of an increase in dosage?

"Ready, Miss Sarno?"

"Yes," Julie said.

Colonel Uxbridge took her arm. "It is important that we attract as little attention as possible," he said quietly. "The presence here in London of the person who has asked to meet you is a military secret. If you see anybody who knows you, if you are greeted by anybody as we pass through the lobby or in the elevator, don't talk to them. On the other hand, don't avoid the meeting. Be as casual as you can. If possible, don't stop. A wave of the hand should do the trick. If you must stop, if the person who recognizes you comes toward us to greet you, we must avoid making the meeting even remotely memorable or odd to the greeter. He or she will expect you to introduce me. Do it without hesitation, using my name. That part of it will have no significance for anybody. Nobody in London knows who I am. If I say anything to you, don't reply, no matter how outlandish my remarks might seem to you. Is that all clear?"

"Yes," Julie said, aware of a small churning in her stomach. It was distressing, because moments of excitement were never for her free from the fear that she was going to throw up, but it was also pleasant because the anticipation of excitement, which had brought her to London, had not until this moment become a reality. She was reminded, in a flash of irrelevance that startled her, of the day when Katie Halloran, who lived with her mother and father—a policeman—in the apartment above the Sarnos, had come running into the barber shop carrying the letter from Mr. Tyler Crispin in which the director of the Horace Judson Clarke House, employing the formal, grown-up phrases which Julie and Katie found almost as thrilling as the news they conveyed, informed the two eleven-year-old girls that, after giving careful consideration to their proposal for the formation of a nature club in the settlement house, he had decided to arrange an appointment for the Misses Halloran and Sarno with Mr. Benjamin F. Ivey, associate director of the Horace Judson Clarke House, so that the practical details of such a move could be examined in more exhaustive detail. Now, a decade and a half later, on the blacked-out pavement in front of a world-famous hotel that at the age of eleven Julie had never even heard of, she could feel again, as she turned over in her mind the implications of Colonel Uxbridge's request, the long-forgotten emotion with which she and Katie Halloran, standing in Biaggio Sarno's barber shop on East Ninth Street, had turned over in their hands Mr. Tyler Crispin's letter: the door to a magic world, shadowy in outline but glowing with promise, was about to be opened. Julie said, "Yes, it's all clear."

Colonel Uxbridge gave her arm a small, reassuring squeeze. "All right, my dear," he said. "Here we go."

They went across the pavement, through the crested baffle, around the various groups of people in the crowded lobby, and into an elevator. It was empty.

"Two, please," Colonel Uxbridge said.

"Kyuh," the elevator operator said. As he started to close the door, a voice called, "Up, please?"

The elevator operator's hand shoved the door back. A British major, wearing on his lapels the red tabs of the General Staff, appeared from the left and stepped into the car.

"Thanks so much," he said.

"Notta tall, sir."

The elevator operator pulled the door shut. The British major moved to a position on Julie's right, behind the control lever, and fixed his glance on the back of the operator's head, as though unaware that there were other passengers in the car. When the car stopped, and Julie stepped out with Colonel Uxbridge, the major stepped out with them. All the way down a carpeted corridor, along which Colonel Uxbridge guided her without taking his hand from her arm, Julie was aware of the major just a few steps behind them. Once, turning her head slightly to see if Colonel Uxbridge realized they were being followed, she became aware of an increase in the pressure of his hand on her arm. Julie promptly turned her head forward. When they stopped in front of a door, Julie felt rather than heard that the man behind her had also stopped.

"What I'd really like to see," Colonel Uxbridge said to Julie in a casual, conversational tone, "is that Michael Redgrave production of *A Month in the Country*. I understand it's quite good."

As though his words were a signal, the door swung inward. Colonel Uxbridge, still holding Julie's arm, guided her through the door. As the door closed behind her, Julie saw that it had been opened by a short, bald man in a sweatshirt, who still gripped the knob, and that the British major had stepped in with them.

"All clear, sir," the major said quietly.

"Thank you," Colonel Uxbridge said and, to the bald man in the sweatshirt, "All right, Harry."

Harry nodded, opened the door an inch or two, peered out into the corridor and then, very quickly, pulled the door wide. The major, touching his finger to his forehead in an abortive salute, stepped through and was gone. Harry closed the door swiftly, but held the knob for several moments, twisting it slowly back into place as though the small mound of polished metal was something alive that fought back in desperate silence against the pressure of his hand. Finally, the catch clicked. The bald man released the knob and, just as slowly, turned the key in the lock.

"How is he?" Colonel Uxbridge said.

"Just about the same, sir," Harry said. "He keeps asking for the young lady."

"Well, we've got her," Colonel Uxbridge said. He turned to Julie. "Harry will take your coat, Miss Sarno."

"I think I'll keep it," Julie said. "If you don't mind?"

"As you like," Colonel Uxbridge said. "Won't you come this way?" He led her out of the foyer, through an archway, into a sitting room, where, for the first time since they had walked through the baffle on the sidewalk downstairs, the colonel released her arm. "If you'll wait here just a moment, please?"

"All right," Julie said.

Colonel Uxbridge nodded and went out through another archway at the far end of the room. Julie glanced at her wrist watch. It showed eleven minutes after eight. Two or three miles across the blacked-out city, at the table in the Soho restaurant that Nick always reserved for General MacNeilson, the military governor's consumption of bourbon would soon reach the point where Mac would begin showing Rita, and anybody else in his immediate vicinity, the snapshot of his family he always carried in his wallet. The contrast between that dismal performance, to which less than an hour ago she had been certain she would once again be subjected, and the excitement on the threshold of which she now stood, caused Julie's spirits to go up in a sudden, soaring leap. Turning to examine her surroundings, she saw that they included the small, bald man in the sweatshirt. He was standing in the archway that separated the sitting room from the foyer, his legs spread, apparently absorbed in the details of a story on the front page of the *London Evening Standard* about an RAF raid on Düsseldorf, but Julie noticed that he was rocking back and forth gently on the balls of his feet and neither his head nor his eyes moved.

There was something about the combination of his stance, the gray sweatshirt he wore, and his pleasant, knobbed, ageless, sun-tanned face that reminded Julie of Steve Shupka, the Horace Judson Clarke House athletic coach, at one of those moments when Steve used to rise on his toes to toss the basketball up into the air for the beginning of a game between the girls of the Nature Club and the girls of the Current Events Club. Even Harry's lips, though slightly parted, were partially pursed, as though they gripped an invisible referee's whistle on which he was about to blow the starting signal.

"May I sit down?" Julie said.

Harry looked up from his newspaper in surprise, as though he had never seen her before and couldn't, in this first startled moment of awareness that he was in the presence of another human being, imagine how she had got into the room.

"Certainly," he said, and then, as Julie dropped into an armchair, he asked politely, "Would you like something to read?"

He gestured toward a low, round table in front of Julie's armchair. Partially covering two ashtrays; a plate on which a small, gnarled apple sat crookedly, like a hunchback huddling into his coat for warmth; a portable typewriter with a sheet of paper rolled into it; and a tray with glasses, a siphon, and a bottle of whiskey, were scattered several London newspapers; copies of the overseas editions of *Time, Newsweek,* and *The New Yorker*; a number of small, colorful booklets that Julie recognized as publications of the OWI; a great many mimeographed sheets some of which, even from the distance of four or five feet that separated Julie's armchair from the table, she could see were stamped "For Immediate Release"; and somewhat surprisingly, since Julie had seen nothing but the flimsy overseas edition since she left home, a bulky, neatly folded copy of the *New York Times.*

From somewhere beyond the archway through which Colonel Uxbridge had disappeared, she heard faint sounds that could have been footsteps. Turning back to glance at the littered table, as though for another look at something her eyes had passed over too quickly the first time, she could see nothing that should have made her feel this. Julie took another look at her wrist watch.

Twenty after eight. At once, crossing her puzzlement about what it was that had drawn her glance back to the table, was a sense of surprise for the speed with which nine minutes had gone by.

"Did you mean that?" she said.

Harry looked up from his paper. "Beg pardon?" he said.

Julie gestured to the table. "About helping myself?"

"Absolutely," Harry said, tucking the newspaper under his arm and coming forward from the archway. "Be glad to make you one if you want?"

"Make me one?" Julie said, puzzled, and then, seeing the tray with the whiskey bottle and glasses, she said quickly, "No, not a drink, thank you. I meant something to read."

The bald man stopped short, poised on one foot, his body leaning forward, one arm spread out as though to help him maintain his balance, looking exactly like Steve Shupka peering through a knot of writhing players in one corner of the basketball court to see if anybody was being fouled.

"Sure," Harry said, coming to rest on both feet. "Anything at all."

He went back to the foyer archway. Julie picked up the *New York Times*, unfolded it, and noticed that it was dated two days ago. "Until last night, when I arrived in London," Colonel Uxbridge had said, "I never heard of General MacNeilson." Knowing as she did, from what the colonel had himself told her, that the necessity for hearing about Mac had arisen only in connection with what the colonel had described as his mission to locate a Miss Julie Sarno, she wondered if the mission had been assigned to him in the United States two days ago, when Colonel Uxbridge had apparently bought this copy of the *New York Times* before boarding his plane, or after he had arrived in London last night. Her eyes, as Julie tried to work out the possible significance of the moment in time when Colonel Uxbridge had been ordered to locate her, took in the first paragraph of a front-page statement made three days ago by Viscount Halifax before the Toronto Board of Trade to the effect that the United Kingdom, alone, could not claim equal partnership with the United States, Russia, and China. "The whole British Commonwealth and Em-

34

pire," Julie read, "must form a fourth great power to help the three others keep the permanent peace that it is the earnest hope of all free men will succeed the successful prosecution of this bloody conflict in which we are now—" Julie's head came up. Somewhere beyond the archway through which Colonel Uxbridge had disappeared she had heard a series of new sounds. She listened hard. There was a faint thud.

"Sure you don't want that drink?"

"Thank you, no," Julie said.

Harry smiled forgivingly, as though he were indeed Steve Shupka and he didn't want her to think there was anything personal about his feeling it necessary, in the interests of fair play, to give a member of the opposing team two foul shots because, even though he knew it had been unintentional, Julie had nevertheless been guilty of blocking.

"Well, if you change your mind," he said, "there it is."

"Thank you," Julie said.

She dropped the *Times* back on the table, wondering what it was that kept drawing her glance to the things on it, and she saw the sheet in the typewriter. Across the top, underlined and with spaces between each letter, was the single word: C O N F I D E N-T I A L. Julie hesitated, then sent another glance at the bald man in the foyer archway. Harry seemed to be absorbed in the front page of the *Standard*, and he *had* said she was welcome to read anything on the table. Crossing her legs and smoothing her skirt over her knees, Julie shifted her body in the chair so that she could see the sheet of paper in the typewriter more clearly. Under the word C O N F I D E N T I A L she read:

(Draft for second or third or God knows what ??? stage of conference—after agreement in principle has been reached with X —*if* agreement *is* reached!!!!—that he will co-operate)

SOLILOQUY OF REFORMATION

(I don't like this title—too poetic for the serious business in hand—but it's best I can think of at moment, and it does, poetic or not, get to the root of the matter)

THE IDEAL GERMAN: 194?

35

(This soliloquy—imaginary, of course—is an attempt to outline for X—whose mental processes our Intelligence indicates are rather primitive—in a manner he should be able to grasp—the way that most Germans should be thinking—if our propaganda as well as military effort are successful—by the time we want X to act. Naturally, unless the decisive moment of the war has been reached and passed, so that the initiative is ours, by the time we want X to act—a likelihood that as of this writing seems admittedly improbable—we cannot hope to generate all these thoughts in the minds of every German immediately. Here, however, is a rough attempt to picture for X our long-term goal—which, if the son of a bitch *gets* the picture, *should* make the little bastard willing to act)

Julie, without moving in the chair, sent her glance toward the foyer. The small, bald man in the gray sweatshirt had not moved from the archway. She wondered, as she watched him read or pretend to be reading his newspaper, if the sheet had been left in the typewriter deliberately, so that she could absorb its contents while she waited. If so, what did Harry, or whoever it was that had left the sheet in the typewriter, hope to gain by allowing her to read something surreptitiously that could just as easily have been handed to her? Was it some sort of test? Was she being observed, not only by Harry, but perhaps by others?

Julie's glance, moving slowly to the archway through which Colonel Uxbridge had disappeared, swept the walls of the sitting room. The only possible places of concealment for an observer were the heavy drapes that covered what she assumed to be three tall windows. Not knowing how deeply recessed the windows were, Julie supposed it was sensible to assume that somebody, or perhaps even more than one observer, could be and was even now concealed behind them. But this, in the light of the unobtrusive skill with which Colonel Uxbridge and the unidentified British major had managed the task of getting her into this room unobserved, seemed to Julie much too crude for serious consideration.

Shifting from the question of whether or not she was being

watched as she read, Julie turned her thoughts on the material in the typewriter. If there was any connection between the work she had been doing for the BEW and the work Colonel Uxbridge's attitude, if not his words, had implied she would be called upon to do, the connection must lie in what appeared on the sheet of paper in the typewriter before her. But what connection could there possibly be between her boring duties as a member of the secretarial pool in the BEW's London office and this strange document? Some of the letters that had been dictated to her by BEW executives during the past six months, and many of the reports she had typed, had dealt with bomb damage done to Germany by the RAF and the Eighth Air Force. But all this material had been so highly technical, and for security reasons couched in phraseology so cryptic, that Julie, who could remember none of it, felt certain neither Colonel Uxbridge, nor the man he had brought her here to meet, would be foolish enough to assume that she had any of it in her head.

The only other possibility that occurred to Julie was that her work at the BEW had been a proving ground, that all during the past six months, while she had been going through the tedious routine of the secretarial pool that had provided only in part the anodyne she had sought in the war effort, somebody had been observing her and, from such observation, had turned in a report which indicated, to the man Colonel Uxbridge had brought her here to meet or to whoever recruited this man's personnel, that Julie Sarno was equipped to handle more serious matters. The notion was so flattering that Julie, aware again of the small churning in her stomach, turned back to the sheet in the typewriter with the determination to absorb its contents before Colonel Uxbridge returned. She read:

(These, then, are the thoughts of the Ideal German as we want him to be thinking at the moment of X's co-operation—if X *does* co-operate:)

I am suffering now. I do not have enough to eat. The rooms where I live are inadequate. I grieve for members of my family who were killed in the war. I have few opportunities to

37

relax. I suffer because of the Nazis. They drove my country into war. They kept on fighting when the fight was lost and then they increased destruction and death. They lied to me from the very beginning. I hate Nazis. But I cannot forget the Nazis. I know now what the Nazis did. They blackened Germany's reputation throughout the world. They tortured and killed people everywhere including Germans. They ruined my country. They ruined me. Although I did not want war, although I did not want—

"Miss Sarno."

Julie's glance came up. Colonel Uxbridge was standing in the archway at the far side of the room.

"Yes?" she said.

"Would you come this way, please?"

Julie stood up and walked toward the archway. Colonel Uxbridge took her arm and guided her through it. They were, she saw, in a corridor that touched the end of the sitting room like the crossbar of a T. There were doors at both ends.

"I'm afraid the meeting will have to be held in his bedroom," Colonel Uxbridge said in a low voice as he led Julie toward the closed door at the left of the corridor. "Harry gave him a sedative a short time ago and he seems a trifle, well, tired. I don't mean that his mind isn't perfectly clear, but the effort of getting up might be a bit too—" Colonel Uxbridge paused, and he gave Julie a short, sidelong glance. "I trust that's all right, Miss Sarno?"

"You mean about meeting him in the bedroom?"

Colonel Uxbridge's lean, thin-lipped face was suddenly touched by a faint crimson glow, exactly the way Mr. Tyler Crispin's face used to glow when an accident during a basketball game made it necessary for him, as director of the Horace Judson Clarke House, to enter the girls' locker room for an inspection of the damage.

"Yes, that's what I mean," Colonel Uxbridge said and, after a pause, added, "I can probably arrange to remain with you throughout the meeting, if you like."

"That won't be necessary," Julie said. "Unless you or he, whoever he is, feel otherwise."

"My feelings are unimportant," Colonel Uxbridge said. "My role in this particular operation is purely that of a middleman, so to speak. My orders were to locate you and bring you here. Once you pass through this door," he said as he released Julie's arm and put his hand on the knob, "I will have completed my mission. Any further questions?"

"Yes," Julie said. "Who is he?"

Colonel Uxbridge's reply was a short, sharp twist of the knob and a short, hard thrust at the door. It swung inward.

"Hello, Julie," Ben Ivey said from a bed at the far side of the room. "I hope you'll forgive me for not getting up."

Her first thought—as, through the tumbling roar of shock and confusion that suddenly filled her head, Julie heard Colonel Uxbridge pull the door shut behind her—was that she mustn't think. Ben Ivey had always counted on that. You may not be as beautiful as Celia, he had once said to her, but you've got the better brain. If you give it half a chance, if you keep your emotions out of it, Ben Ivey had told her in Oregon, you'll always come up with the right answer. By that, Julie had at last learned bitterly, Ben Ivey always meant the right answer for him. But she was finished with finding the right answers for Ben Ivey. She had closed the door on that part of her life ten years ago. To open it now could mean only one thing: taking with clear knowledge of the inevitable result the same road that, when Celia had taken it, Julie's older sister had had no way of knowing would lead to destruction. *Don't think*, a voice inside Julie's head screamed above the tumbling roar of shock and confusion. *Don't think! Just turn and run!* But she couldn't turn, and she didn't run.

"I know what's buzzing around inside that pretty noggin of yours," Ben Ivey said.

Julie looked at him as though, in the dazed effort to recover from a blow that had hurled her to the ground, she had forgotten completely that she was still in the presence of her assailant.

"You do?" she said, and her voice showed no trace of the whirling confusion inside her head.

"You bet I do," Ben Ivey said, and the thin face under the tumbled yellow hair spread suddenly in the boyish grin that had broken Celia Sarno's heart and, Julie saw with a stab of terror, could still move hers. "I've always known what goes on under that crown of beautiful blue-black hair, Julie."

The quiet confidence in his voice saved her. It was as though Julie's head were a filing cabinet which had been seized by some giant hand that was shaking it like a dice cup, so that all the neatly lettered folders were being churned about inside, and all at once the cabinet had been set down and, one by one, as the folders slid back into place, she could read the lettering on the tabs. They explained the instinct of self-preservation that had warned her on the blacked-out sidewalk not to enter this hotel with Colonel Uxbridge, and they told her what it was that had drawn her puzzled glance back again and again to the littered table out in the sitting room: the label on the bottle of whiskey. Some members of the Mercerville group in Oregon had facetiously called "Uncle Ben's Blended" the poor man's Sani-Flush. Few had made any bones about the fact that they bought it only because, on a government salary, $1.60 a fifth was as much as they could afford for liquor. Only Ben Ivey had preferred "Uncle Ben's Blended" to decent whiskey. Or so he had said at the time. It was like him, now that he could afford the best, to continue drinking the rotgut he had been forced to drink when he could scarcely afford that. It was even more like him, Julie realized, now that he was not bound by the same restrictions that dictated how much luggage people of lesser importance could carry by air to a war theater, for Ben Ivey to carry to London bottles of "Uncle Ben's Blended" that he undoubtedly, since Julie had never seen it sold anywhere but in Oregon, still had to have shipped to his office in the White House from Portland. What was not like him was to give an opponent this pause at the critical moment in a struggle that enabled him, or in this case her, to rally the forces of a counterattack.

"If you know what goes on in my head, what I have to say next shouldn't come as a surprise to you," Julie said. "Good-bye, Ben."

She turned to reach for the knob and bumped her forehead against the door. She had not realized that, in the initial moments of shock and confusion, she had backed up against it.

"Julie, for God's sake!" Ben Ivey pushed himself up against the pillows. "Where are you going?"

She had another moment of shock. The thin body, on which clothes had always hung like pennants in a dead calm, had become so much thinner that the monogrammed blue pajamas— which Julie knew, from her recollection of his tastes as well as the expensive look of the material, had been tailor-made—seemed to have been cut for a man twice his size.

"I'm going back to New York," she said, refusing to acknowledge the tug of compassion evoked by the wasted body. "At any rate, I suppose that's where I'll be sent, if your Colonel Uxbridge's threats weren't just so much idle talk to get me up here."

The boyish face on the pillow creased in the quick frown she remembered so well, the frown that always reminded Julie of the two pictures on the wall of her father's barber shop. One, on the Catholic Aid Society calendar to the left of the big mirror in front of the chair near the door, showed a scene at the court of Ferdinand and Isabella in which Torquemada, appearing more regal in his unadorned black cassock than the bejeweled king and queen on the thrones before him, explained with disdainful arrogance to the rulers of Spain the nature of the Inquisition and how he intended to administer it throughout their domain under the authority invested in him by the Pope. The second picture, on a calendar distributed by Mark Eisner & Company, manufacturers of uniforms for the Boy Scouts of America, hung on the wall to the right of the mirror. This second picture showed a smiling, muddy-cheeked, yellow-haired young scoutmaster striding up the crest of a hill, leading into the sunlight a troop of happy, healthy boys whose scout uniforms were spotted, like the skins of chicken-pox victims, with merit badges and other insignia. The gap between the lean, dark, chilling face of Torquemada and the smiling, blond, open face of the scoutmaster was wider than the six centuries of time or the nature of the totally different dedications that separated them. And yet, whenever she saw Ben Ivey frown, it was as though in Julie Sarno's mind those two wall calendars out of her youth moved toward each other, meeting in the center of the mirror facing her father's barber chair, the face of Torquemada and the face of the scoutmaster merging into one another to create a completely new face, new and disquieting and irresistible, the face of Ben Ivey.

"Oh, that was just to get you here," Ben said. "It doesn't mean anything. I had to see you and I wasn't sure you'd come."

"You're so right," Julie said. "I didn't even suspect the possibility. Your presence in London, in case you've forgotten it, is a military secret."

The frown gave way to a quick grin. Ben Ivey shoved back from his forehead the yellow cowlick that no hair tonic had ever been able to keep in place. "How about that?" he said in a tone of delighted wonder, like a child displaying a prize it had not for a moment believed it had a chance to win. "Ben Ivey of the Horace Judson Clarke House on Avenue B, a military secret in London, England!"

"If Mr. Tyler Crispin were alive," Julie said, "I'm sure he'd be impressed."

"Aren't you?"

"I don't know anything about why you're here in London," Julie said. "And I don't want to know. I'm not doing anything for you, Ben. Never again."

He flicked the hair from his forehead with a short, sharp gesture of annoyance, but when he spoke his voice was untouched by emotion. It was cool, smooth, and functional, almost mechanical, as though the sounds were emerging not from a human throat but from a contrivance fashioned by some master of electronics to convey orders from a leader to his followers with a minimum of strain on the former and a maximum of clarity to the latter.

"I don't know why, Julie, at this crucial moment in history, when so much hangs in the balance and only clear-headed adults can be trusted with the task of trying to tip that balance in our favor, you have decided to act like a muddle-headed child. I do know that I must be back on my feet in four hours, and you're the only one who can put me back on them. If I am unable to be where in four hours I must be, the entire course of this war may take a turn that will cost us nobody can guess how many thousands of human lives. I don't intend to allow you to assume the

42

responsibility for that much blood on your hands. So you'll just have to quit acting like a muddle-headed child, and quit it at once. From here on in, I'm working on the assumption that I'm talking to the clear-headed adult I ordered Colonel Uxbridge to locate and bring here. You will please listen to me, and listen carefully."

Julie shook her head again. "No," she said. "Not any more. Never."

Ben Ivey moved his head on the pillow in a small arc of exhaustion. "Julie," he said quietly, "Julie, Julie, Julie, I'm sick." He drew a deep breath and, wearily, repeated the word, "Sick. It's the wrong time for me to be sick. We can't afford it. Not now. Not at this point in the war. Don't you understand that?"

Julie, who had never understood any of it and no longer wanted to, hauled blindly on the doorknob. "Get a doctor," she said.

"If doctors could do anything, this room would be crowded right now with the best England has to offer. Doctors can't do a damn thing for me, Julie, and you know it."

It was true, and because she did know it she hesitated, held against her will not by the force of his argument, or by his capacity to move the guarded corners of her heart, but by the strength of her own dream, the dream she hated but could not resist, the dream that no anodyne would ever dull and no facing up to hard fact could ever banish, the recurring dream that nothing had happened, that if you could only go back and start again it would all come out right, the dream of a second chance. Held by the dream, warmed by what her head knew could never be but what her heart so desperately wanted, Julie's mind, groping for help to support the dream, stumbled into Rita Merlin. Seen through the lens of the dream, the foolish fat girl didn't look so foolish after all. In the light of the dream by which they were all trapped, the shrewd and the stupid, the beautiful and the ugly, the lucky and the unfortunate, even Rita's loathsome Mac looked far from loathsome. Dreams, after all, had to be put together with bits and pieces of reality. Rita wanted what Julie wanted, a chance to go back and start again, to pick up what she had missed, to make it come out right. The things Julie Sarno saw in Mac did not change the one thing Rita Merlin saw, the thing Rita dreamed about, the thing Rita wanted: a second chance. If Rita could have it, why couldn't Julie? Why couldn't she forget the past? Why couldn't she pretend nothing had happened? Why couldn't she turn back, into this room, and start again? Why couldn't she do what Rita Merlin was doing, what Ben Ivey was pleading with her to do? Why couldn't she succumb to the dream? Why couldn't she take her second chance?

"Julie, look."

She turned back, toward the voice that had summoned her, and as her eyes followed Ben Ivey's pointing finger, Julie's heart leaped. On the dresser, standing out among the expensive toilet articles like a tramp at an embassy ball, was the battered old rectangular box covered with black imitation leather that Biaggio Sarno had brought from his birthplace in Naples to his new home above the barber shop on East Ninth Street. Julie took a step back into the bedroom, moving as though in a trance, and once again, unintentionally, Ben Ivey saved her: with a short, strangling gasp, he fell back against the pillows, and the dream fell with him, releasing her heart, turning it back to the bits and pieces of reality that could not be changed, no matter what lens you used, regardless of the skill with which the lighting was rearranged. There were no second chances. Julie pulled open the door.

"Colonel Uxbridge," she called.

He met her in the archway that opened into the sitting room. "What is it?"

Julie gestured toward the open door at the end of the corridor. "He—I think he's fainted."

Colonel Uxbridge stepped around her and hurried toward the open door. Julie looked after him, took a step back toward the bedroom, then realized what she was doing. She shivered slightly, pulled the collar of her coat up close around her neck and, holding her hands buried in the material, as though they were clasped in a prayer she didn't want anybody to know she was making, walked quickly across the sitting room to the foyer. Just as she was about to step through the archway, the small, bald man in the gray sweatshirt appeared in it. Julie stopped short. Harry did not move.

"Yes, ma'am?" he said.

"I'm leaving," Julie said.

"No, I'm sorry, ma'am."

He said it so gently that, for a moment, Julie wasn't certain she had heard him correctly.

"I said I'm leaving."

"I heard you, ma'am," Harry said, just as gently. "But nobody leaves here unless the colonel says so."

"All right, Harry."

Julie turned. Colonel Uxbridge had reappeared in the other archway.

"His breathing seems to be— I'm not quite sure, Harry. You'd better have a look."

"Yes, sir," Harry said, but he didn't move. Then Julie saw why. He was waiting for Colonel Uxbridge, who was coming toward them, to reach the foyer. When he did, Harry said, "The young lady said—"

"I heard her," Colonel Uxbridge said.

Harry nodded, ran swiftly across the sitting room, and disappeared through the other archway. A moment or two later, Julie heard the bedroom door open and close. Colonel Uxbridge, who had apparently been waiting for the sounds, cleared his throat.

"I heard Harry tell you that nobody leaves here unless I say so," he said. "That's not quite true, Miss Sarno. Or rather, it's true only technically. The point is that I can't say so unless I get my orders first from Mr. Ivey."

"Mr. Ivey won't keep me here against my will."

"Perhaps not," Colonel Uxbridge said.

"Perhaps?" Julie said, and then, hearing the echoes of her own startled voice, she felt her face grow hot. More slowly, trying to enhance the impression of calmness she did not feel by giving to her words a touch of sarcasm she did not enjoy, Julie said, "Would you be good enough to tell Mr. Ivey I'd like to leave, and ask him to give you the orders that seem to be necessary for the accomplishment of that simple matter?"

Colonel Uxbridge bowed slightly, the way he had bowed over her hand when she had been introduced to him a couple of hours ago in General MacNeilson's suite. "I'll be glad to tell Mr. Ivey anything you ask," he said. "But I'm afraid it's not as simple a matter as you think."

"Why not?" Julie said.

"Because while I don't know what happened at your meeting with Mr. Ivey, I do know that he is at the moment incapable of speech, and seems likely to remain that way for some time." Colonel Uxbridge gestured toward the sitting room. "Since we both have to wait," he said politely, "I think the waiting process will be a good deal easier on both of us if we do it in comfort."

3

It was not easier for Julie.

Returning to the armchair in front of the littered table proved simple enough, in spite of the suddenly released emotions hurtling around inside her without restraint or regard for one another, like so many progressive-nursery schoolchildren at recess. She sat down and picked up the copy of the *New York Times* that had accompanied Ben Ivey and Colonel Uxbridge across the Atlantic the day before. When the colonel offered her a drink, Julie nodded and even managed a fairly good imitation of polite interest in the way he mixed it.

"Thank you," she said, taking the glass.

"You're welcome," Colonel Uxbridge said.

Julie raised the drink to her lips, and at once all pretense of comfort fled.

"Uncle Ben's Blended," which had been held in such low regard by almost all members of the Mercerville group, possessed one quality that Julie realized could have meant nothing to, and probably was never even noticed by, most people who drank the cheap whiskey: faintly but unmistakably "Uncle Ben's Blended" smelled exactly like the oil Biaggio Sarno had used for years to lubricate the base pivots of the two barber chairs in his shop on East Ninth Street.

During all those strange weeks in and around Portland long before the war, a time Julie had never understood and now wanted to forget, she had never accepted a drink in any of the homes of the members of the Mercerville group to which she and Celia and Ben Ivey were invited, without remembering the day shortly after her eleventh birthday when Katie Halloran had come running into the barber shop with Mr. Tyler Crispin's letter. Julie, just home from school, had been sweeping the shop, and her father, on his knees between the two barber chairs, had been oiling the pivots. Now, sixteen years later, Julie hastily set down the drink Colonel Uxbridge had made for her. But it was too late. "Uncle Ben's Blended" had done its work again.

The odor was so strong, the memory it evoked was so vivid, that the years and her surroundings seemed to fall away like the pieces of a dream after a rude awakening, thrusting Julie back from the shapeless, threatening present into the clearly defined, troubling past. She was not a young woman of twenty-seven, seated in a London hotel room from which, Colonel Uxbridge had just informed her, she would not be allowed to walk out until Ben Ivey regained consciousness and gave the order to release her. She was eleven years old and Cockeye Katie Halloran, with whom only a few minutes ago she had walked home from school, had just banged open the door of the barber shop.

"Hey, Julie, look! Look what I just found in the letter box!"

Mr. Sarno, on his knees between the barber chairs, sat back on his haunches, the oil can in his hands. "Looka what?" he said sharply.

47

Katie, halfway across the store toward Julie, stopped short. She was a thin, ugly, precociously self-possessed little girl who, like the one-eyed man in the kingdom of the blind, had early grasped that the ugliness which made her an object of derision in the world of her contemporaries gave her a considerable advantage in the world of adults. Most men and women, secretly ashamed of the fact that they find a child revolting, and too cowardly to admit it to one another, will go out of their way to pay such a child special attention. Katie Halloran, understanding instinctively the motivation behind these favors, took a savage pleasure in repaying them with malice. Her appearance helped. She wore glasses that were either improperly fitted or contained in the cheap metal alloy of the frames some element to which Katie's pale, freckled skin reacted in protest. The nosepiece, cushioned by a strip of dirty adhesive tape, always rested on a small, angry-looking inflamed area between her eyes. Katie's almost constant efforts to poke the glasses straight were just as constantly frustrated by this sore spot. It was not, however, because the glasses, sitting crookedly on her nose, gave her a malevolent and slightly demented look that she had earned the derisive nickname Cockeye Katie. The nickname was an attempt on the part of the kids of East Ninth Street to repay the insults which Katie's sharp tongue hurled at everybody on the block. The only person on Ninth Street for whom Katie seemed to have any respect was Julie's hot-tempered father. It was, however, a respect not for age but for retaliatory striking power. When the drink was on him, the last thing in the world that would stay Biaggio Sarno's ready fists was the age of whoever happened to cross his path.

"I said looka what?" he rapped out.

"Nothing," Katie said coldly, shooting a quick, annoyed glance at Julie, who was aware that her friend's annoyance was directed at Katie herself. It was clear to the watching Julie that Katie, knowing Mr. Sarno's tendencies, felt she should also have known better than to come barging into the shop like this. Which meant in turn that the news Katie was bringing must be exciting indeed, if it had made Katie forget momentarily how to handle Mr. Sarno. She said, "I just wanted to show something to Julie."

48

"Wanna show Julie what?" Mr. Sarno demanded with mounting annoyance. His reactions to the little girl with the crooked glasses always reminded Julie of the picture in her school reader of a bull snorting with rage and pawing the ground in helpless fury as the nimbly circling picador stabbed him with the lance at will.

"I just told you," said Cockeye Katie contemptuously. "Nothing."

She thrust the envelope behind her back and, with her other hand, poked at the nosepiece of her glasses as she began to edge slowly toward the door. At the same time, with short, sharp jerks of her head, she signaled Julie to meet her out in the street.

"Nothing, hah?" Mr. Sarno said.

He heaved himself to his feet. Julie, her hands frozen to the broom, could tell, from the low roaring sounds as the air pumped slowly in and out of her father's massive, heaving chest, what she had not noticed when she came into the store a few minutes ago and found him squatted on the floor with the oil can: Mr. Sarno had already started the day's drinking.

"Lemme see whatsa nothing."

He advanced on Katie, who, though clearly regretting her impetuous entry, was not upset by its consequence, and continued skillfully to back away. Beyond the mirror, under the Catholic Aid Society calendar that showed Torquemada facing Ferdinand and Isabella, the thin little girl, who had outmaneuvered Mr. Sarno before, turned to make the move for which practice told her the moment had come: the run for the door. Julie's father, however, was not yet as drunk as on other such occasions he had been. His large, muscular, beautifully shaped hand, darting like an adder, caught Katie Halloran's shoulder.

"Pa!" Julie cried. "Pa, don't—!"

"Shattap," Mr. Sarno rasped.

He snatched the envelope from Katie and released her shoulder. Almost any other little girl would have seized the opportunity to bolt. Not Cockeye Katie. She stood there, flat against the wall under Torquemada and the rulers of Spain, breathing through her open mouth, poking delicately at the lump of adhesive tape that was supposed to ease the inflammation on the bridge of her

49

nose, watching tensely not so much for the lumbering blow, which she obviously believed she could duck, as for the next opening through which she could send a barbed insult to torment this man she loved to bedevil. Julie, who was frightened by physical violence, understood that much of Cockeye Katie's audacity was due to the fact that Mr. Halloran was a policeman and his ugly little daughter lived with the secure knowledge of what that imposing fact about her father meant to everybody on Ninth Street. Just the same, Biaggio Sarno, whose charm for members of the opposite sex had more than once brought Katie's father into action to stop some irate husband from attempting to break up the barber shop as well as its owner's good-looking head, was at the moment an angry and therefore unpredictable mountain of adult towering over a skinny little girl. Wishing Katie would turn and run, Julie nevertheless admired the fact that her friend didn't, as Mr. Sarno pulled the sheet of paper from the envelope.

He stared at it, breathing hard, his dark, handsome face scowling with the effort to bring the typewritten lines into focus and, at the same time, make sense of the words written in a language that, after so many years in America and even when he was cold sober, the lusty, ambitious, frustrated immigrant from Naples still considered a personal plot against him.

"Aaah," he said in an abrupt explosion of disgust as he shoved the letter back at Katie. "What it say?"

"Can't you read?"

The mocking question sent the blood surging into Biaggio Sarno's face. "You bitch," he said, pulling back his fist. "I read when I wanna. I ask a question. What it say?"

Katie cringed slightly, like a fighter taking up a defensive stance, but she held her ground. "Nothing," she said.

"Nothing!" Julie's father roared. "A whola page—words! words! words!—like a summons, come to the court!—the copsa daughter, she says itsa nothing!"

"If you'd stop yelling," Katie Halloran said with the supercilious note in her adenoidal voice that Julie, who unlike Katie was thrown into confusion by the antagonisms and irrationalities of the adult world, admired so much in her friend, "I'll be glad to explain it to you." Making a last attempt at setting the glasses straight on her nose with a disdainful poke of her forefinger, Cockeye Katie took the sheet of paper in both hands. Thrusting it straight out in front of her at eye-level, keeping her arms stiff, like the town crier in a movie about the Revolutionary War reading a proclamation from General Washington to the assembled townspeople, she declaimed: " 'Dear Misses Halloran and Sarno. In answer to yours of the twenty-first instant, please be advised that, after giving careful consideration to your proposal that, to the other activities already in existence at the Horace Judson Clarke House, a nature club be added, I have decided to arrange an appointment for both of you with Mr. Benjamin Franklin Ivey, our associate director, so that the practical details of such a move may be examined in more exhaustive detail. If you will be good enough to meet with Mr. Ivey on June 4th at 8:30 in the evening, in his office here at the Horace Judson Clarke House, I trust the matter can be moved forward to the satisfaction of all concerned. I beg to remain, yours sincerely, Tyler Crispin, Director.' "

Cockeye Katie lowered her arms, refolded the sheet of paper, and replaced it in the envelope as though she were rolling up a parchment scroll.

"What it means?" Biaggio Sarno said.

"I thought you understood English?" Katie said.

"You shattap the rotten dirty mouth and answer me the question, you copsa daughter, you! What it means?"

"Just what it says," Katie said with an arrogant toss of her small head. "Julie and I, we decided to start a new club, so we wrote to Mr. Crispin, asking him—"

"You wrota, hah?"

"Yes, we wrota, haha," Katie said, mimicking the big man's broken English. "Since when is writing a letter against the law?"

"The law!" Biaggio Sarno roared. "You cockeye copsa daughter! You rotten bastids with the law!"

"You better close your great big mouth," Katie said. "Or my father will close it for you."

Mr. Sarno's reply was a quick, swooping lunge at the little girl.

51

Cockeye Katie, whose feet were as quick as her tongue, ducked around the barber chair. This, while placing her momentarily beyond his reach, also put Mr. Sarno between her and the door.

"I showa you!" he panted. "I showa you who closa whosa mouth!"

As he moved up on the barber chair, the breath roaring noisily in and out of his chest, his long arms spread wide to prevent Cockeye Katie's escape from either side, the skinny little girl's eyes darted to right and left. Through the terror that kept her frozen to the broom handle, Julie was aware of a renewed stab of admiration for her friend. Katie didn't even seem to be upset, much less terrified, by the trap that was closing around her. The darting eyes seemed to be hunting with confidence for something that would shatter the trap before it could close.

"What's the matter?" Katie suddenly cried, and Julie could tell from the jeering lift in her friend's voice that whatever it was those darting eyes had been hunting, they had found it. "One of your crazy get-rich-quick schemes go wrong?" Katie dipped down, snatched something from the floor near the base of the barber chair, and, as she hurled the object at Mr. Sarno, shouted, "Is *this* why you're boozing it up so early today?"

The object, catching Julie's father in the chest, seemed to hang there for a long, long moment, so that she had time to see what it was: a bundle of white kid gloves, one of two hundred similar bundles Biaggio Sarno had bought three weeks before at a jobber's auction on Canal Street with every penny he had managed to save and borrow since his last financial disaster. Then, as Biaggio Sarno with an enraged grunt tumbled backward, the bundle of white gloves slid with him to the floor. Cockeye Katie laughed contemptuously and started around the barber chair toward the door. Waving the letter from Mr. Crispin triumphantly above her head like a soldier who has snatched the enemy flag from its standard on the walls of a fortress he and his comrades have just successfully stormed, she yelled at Julie, "Don't forget our appointment tonight with Mr. Ivey! Mr. Crispin says—"

What Mr. Crispin said, or rather Katie's attempt to repeat it, was a mistake. It gave Mr. Sarno time to roll over and, the breath whistling crazily in his chest, grab her ankle.

"I showa you!" he gasped as Katie, with a scream from which all the triumph and contempt had vanished abruptly, tumbled headlong. "I showa you!" Biaggio Sarno panted, rising to his knees without releasing his grip on the kicking little girl's ankle. "I showa you!" he grunted, crawling slowly toward his tormentor. "I showa you, once and for all I showa you, you cockeye copsa daughter with the snake's tongue!"

Katie's second scream, a jagged, completely uncontrolled sound Julie had never before heard from that self-possessed little throat, shook Julie out of her frozen terror.

"Pa, no!" Julie said, dropping the broom and running forward to grab his shoulder. "Pa, don't!"

The touch of her hand seemed to take Biaggio Sarno by surprise. He paused to blink up at his daughter, as though he had not realized until this moment where he was or what he was doing. It was a very short moment, but it was long enough. With a whimper of terror that changed on its way out of her throat to a cackle of victory, Katie wriggled free, scrambled to her feet, worked her lips back and forth, spat the lump of saliva full in Biaggio Sarno's face, and ran out of the store.

For several long moments the big man sat there, squatted on his haunches, his body heaving, the air roaring in and out of his great barrel chest, his lower lip hanging slack, his eyes blinking slowly at nothing in particular, as though he were trying to work his lids free of some gummy substance that interfered with his vision. All at once the blinking stopped. He seemed to bring Julie into focus. For several even longer moments Biaggio Sarno stared at his youngest daughter. Then, with great care, as though working himself out of a cask in which like Ali Baba he had been hiding, he pushed himself up onto his knees, rose to his feet, drew a deep roaring breath, and wiped his face with the back of his hand. He paused for another moment to look down at the result of this tidying process, as though the smear of Cockeye Katie's saliva on his skin possessed a significance he wanted to absorb

53

fully. When he did, Biaggio Sarno swung the hand back and up, gently, like a conductor calling for a special effort from his orchestra, held the hand poised for a few seconds, and then, with a grunt, brought it down in a long, hard, smashing slap. He did not wait to see the result.

When Julie's head struck the wall and she slid to the floor in a crooked sitting position, feeling the blood begin to ooze from her broken lips, her father was halfway across the barber shop toward the cluster of witch-hazel and hair-tonic bottles, under the Mark Eisner & Company calendar, in one of which Biaggio Sarno kept his camouflaged supply of cheap whiskey.

By the time this particular supply was exhausted, he was snoring drunkenly in one of the barber chairs; Julie had finished sweeping the shop; the pain in the back of her head and along the side of her jaw had settled down into a dull, throbbing ache, no worse than others with which Biaggio Sarno had presented her in the past; her lips had stopped bleeding; and a heavy rain had begun to fall on Ninth Street. Julie liked that. The rain added a special touch to what had become for her during the past few months the part of the day to which she looked forward eagerly.

Until the previous June, when Celia Sarno had graduated from Fenimore Cooper High and found a job as a stenographer with a law firm on Twenty-third Street, her kid sister's world had been a neatly contained physical unit almost every square inch of which Julie knew intimately from personal contact. She was aware, of course, that some sort of life went on in the mysterious area beyond her immediate world, in the shapeless, exciting place known as Uptown, but this awareness was based entirely on secondary evidence: conversations Julie had heard among customers in the barber shop; Cockeye Katie Halloran's highly colored accounts of her father's adventures as a policeman; things Julie had read; and fantasies she had put together from drunken fragments dropped by Biaggio Sarno after his return from those periodic get-rich-quick forays that always ended in disaster.

After Celia Sarno went to work, however, Julie had a personal contact with the great, mysterious land beyond her own world, an ambassador who six mornings a week set out from East Ninth

Street, spent the day Uptown, and in the evening stepped out of the Tenth Street trolley car at the corner of Avenue B to present Julie not only with a detailed report of life in the exciting, unexplored terrain but also, or most evenings at any rate, with some souvenir of the way that life was lived. Julie could see by the Seth Thomas on the barber-shop wall that the time had come for the daily meeting with her beloved ambassador.

She tiptoed to the rear of the shop, set the broom in a corner, and picked up the umbrella. It was the only one left of twenty-seven dozen Biaggio Sarno, with a hundred dollars of borrowed money, had bought sight unseen four years ago at a bankruptcy auction on Avenue A. He had heard about the auction while cutting the hair of a man who had just been fired from his job in the umbrella factory because the firm, which was in financial difficulties, was being liquidated by a committee of its creditors. Perhaps, if he had listened harder, Biaggio Sarno would have heard more. Enough, perhaps, to save him from yet another disaster. But he had not listened. He never did, once the seed of an idea for a financial killing took root in his mind. He had seen it all so clearly, as he always did: the bright, bright ship laden with gold, coming in for him at last. All he had to do was put his hands on a few dollars, buy up as much of the bankrupt firm's stock as the borrowed money would pay for, then sit back and watch the money roll in as his customers, who came to the barber shop for shaves and haircuts, snapped up the bargain-priced umbrellas at a dollar each, or perhaps even two dollars, or why not three?

That was all Biaggio Sarno had to do, and that was all he did do. Until he unpacked the cartons in which the twenty-seven dozen umbrellas were delivered to the barber shop. Then he did two other things. First, he got drunk, and then, when he sobered up sufficiently to hear the mocking laughter of his neighbors, Biaggio Sarno started destroying his purchase. It was a slow process, partly because he chose to do it alone, bit by bit, late at night, when his neighbors were asleep. But mostly because the umbrellas, purchased sight unseen, were not umbrellas at all; they were dainty little pink and white parasols with fine steel shafts for which, as the manufacturer they had driven into bankruptcy could have told Biaggio Sarno, there was no market. Certainly not among the men of East Ninth Street who came into the Italian immigrant's barber shop to get their hair cut.

What Julie had got, when her father discovered she had saved one parasol from the holocaust, was not much different from what she had just received for preventing Biaggio Sarno from beating the jeering taunts down Cockeye Katie's throat. After Mrs. Sarno had dyed the frivolous pink and white a sensible black, however, Biaggio Sarno had allowed his daughter to keep it. Julie was glad now, as she tiptoed past her sleeping father, that he had. When she stepped down from the Tenth Street crosstown, Celia was always pleased to see her kid sister. She would be especially pleased this rainy evening to see that Julie had come to meet her with the only thing resembling an umbrella the Sarno family owned.

"Where you going?"

Julie's heart jumped as she turned in the doorway. Her father, twisting his body with lumbering thrusts into a more comfortable position in the barber chair, was watching her with bloodshot eyes.

"To meet Celia," she said.

"You tella her I hit you," Biaggio Sarno said hoarsely, "I hit you again, worse."

His oldest daughter Celia was the only human being for whose good opinion the drunken barber seemed to care. Julie, who understood absolutely nothing else about her father, understood that. If you loved someone, it was only natural to want that someone to think well of you, and how could anybody help loving Celia?

"I won't tell her," Julie said.

She was in a hurry, but she remained in the doorway, waiting, because she knew what was coming next. It would not mend her broken lips. It would not ease the dull throbbing ache in the back of her head or the side of her jaw. But it would mean something to her father. Just what, Julie didn't know, because she had no feeling for him, not even hatred, and without some sort of feeling she was incapable of making even an attempt at comprehension.

But Julie did know, because she had lived with this almost total stranger all her life, what was expected of her. She waited for the inevitable apology.

"I sorry," Biaggio Sarno said sullenly. "I no mean it. That cock-eye bitch, that copsa daughter with the rotten mouth, she make me go crazy."

"All right, Pa," Julie said.

"I said I sorry," Biaggio Sarno repeated, his hoarse voice rasping angrily. "You hear me?"

"Yes, Pa," Julie said, trying not to sound impatient, thinking nervously about the rain and Celia on the Tenth Street trolley. It ran on storage batteries and was just as likely to be early as late. "I hear you."

"You tella Celia," the big man in the barber chair shouted, "I killa you!"

"I won't tell her," Julie said patiently. "I promise, Pa."

"Then why you stand there? Why you no go? You wanta Celia getta wet, catcha cold? Go! Go, quick!"

Julie went, up Ninth Street to Avenue B, then turned right, hurrying past the Horace Judson Clarke House, keeping the dyed parasol tipped forward, not because at this angle it provided a better shield against the rain, but because she didn't want to meet anybody's eye and have to pause for even so much as a greeting. The bright moment of the day when she met Celia coming home from work was something Julie didn't like to accept as though it was a present, something to be taken without effort. She liked to feel she had earned it.

She always built toward the big moment, adding in her mind as she walked from the barber shop to the trolley stop lesser but nonetheless extremely pleasant moments of anticipation, piling one on top of the other, fashioning a stepladder of happiness that brought out more fully the sweetness of the ultimate moment of joy waiting for her at the top.

The rain, which had added a special touch to her daily ritual, had also, Julie saw as she approached the corner of Tenth Street and Avenue B, placed the construction of her secret stepladder in jeopardy: half a dozen people were waiting with umbrellas on the scrap of pavement that Julie had come to regard as her own. Dismayed by the possibility that one or more of them might distract her with conversation, she stopped on the outskirts of the group, examined its members furtively from under the edge of the parasol, and saw with relief that, while she knew them all, the group did not include Cockeye Katie, the only one to whom Julie would have had to speak. A moment later, as the relief was followed by a twinge of guilt for this disloyal thought about her best friend, the trolley car came clanging into view. Julie's mind, forcing its way up the last rung of the ladder, was swept clean of everything but the moment for which the ladder was each day built anew.

Rising on her toes, peering through the rain from under the edge of her parasol, she absorbed the familiar sight: the trolley slowing down for the Avenue B stop; the few passengers gathering newspapers, purses, and parcels as they got to their feet; the jerky, shuffling movement of the tired homecomers toward the front door of the car. Then Julie's mind, cleared and ready for the sweet stab of love, was unexpectedly flooded instead by a harsh wave of fear: something had gone wrong!

Always, at this moment, behind the shapeless, shuffling knot of tired men and women, appeared the tall, slender, clearly defined figure of Celia, holding herself proudly erect, her bright red hair gleamingly alive, like a fluttering pennant above the colorless inferiors with whom an infuriating accident of economics forced her to share this lowly vehicle. The ugly and the stupid were born rich. Celia Sarno was born on East Ninth Street.

If she had as yet, at the age of eighteen, been unable to do anything about correcting the injustice, she could do quite a few things to indicate to the world her awareness that the injustice existed. One of those things was not, at the end of her day's work in the uptown offices of Ellentuch, Prohst & Wadsworth, to come shuffling off the trolley like a beast of burden plodding back with the herd to the stable at the end of a day in the fields. Celia Sarno came off like a princess who had spent the day choosing fabrics for a coronation gown and was about to have a refreshing cup of tea with her ladies in waiting.

She moved unhurriedly, with regal grace, maintaining between herself and the shuffling passengers up front the gap that even the motorman, whom she thus delayed by a few seconds from reaching his own dinner, could see was proper. He never clanged the bell impatiently, as he did if any other passenger dragged his or her feet in getting off. He always watched with admiration and approval, the way everybody watched when Celia Sarno moved.

The motorman was not watching now.

It was this fact, Julie realized as she struggled with the wave of fear, that had told her something was wrong: the tall, slender, beloved patrician figure with the bright red hair was missing from the familiar scene.

For Julie, to whom the scene meant nothing unless it was built around Celia, time seemed to stop. She remained there, stunned, clutching the steel shaft of her dyed parasol, watching while the tired passengers descended, were greeted by waiting mothers and brothers and sisters, and moved off in huddled groups under the shelter of sensible umbrellas. Her mind, struggling with the question of what had gone wrong, couldn't seem to do more for Julie than keep her glance riveted on the open door of the trolley car. Celia came through that door every day. She had to come through now. She *had* to. But she didn't. The door slid shut. The folding step came up. The motorman, as the trolley started across Avenue B, tramped a clanging warning. The bell shook Julie out of her trance.

"Wait!" she cried, starting after the trolley car on the run. "Wait!"

She didn't get very far. Half a dozen steps from the curb Julie heard behind her a sudden screaming of brakes. She stopped and spun around. The parasol, scooping rain and air like an ineptly raised sail, pulled her off balance. Staggering, Julie saw with astonishment that a cab had pulled up at the curb from which she had just leaped. Her astonishment was not caused by the sight of a taxi, although they were rare enough on Avenue B to attract attention under any circumstances. Julie was astonished because this cab was a Luxor. The gleaming white vehicles, equipped with thick flexible silver pipes that snaked excitingly in and out of mysterious holes in their low hoods, had appeared on the city streets only a few months before. Katie Halloran's father, coming home from his beat somewhere uptown, had been the first to bring news of them to East Ninth Street. Soon after the first one showed up in the neighborhood, the foreign-looking cars became the center of a rite practiced by every boy and girl on the block: on catching sight of a Luxor, the viewer stopped dead, spit into his or her left palm, touched the damp spot with the right thumb, and followed through with a hard, smacking punch of the right fist. If the ritual was completed before the cab disappeared from view, the performer earned the right to make a wish, and this right was worth a good deal because the wish always came true. Julie knew. It was only because she had seen a Luxor last Friday on the way to school, and had succeeded in tapping and punching her damp left palm before the silver and white cab turned the corner and vanished, that she had got a passing mark on Mrs. Koenig's arithmetic test in reducing compound fractions. Not ordinary fractions. *Compound* fractions, a subject that for weeks had made the short walk to P.S. 64 a daily horror for Julie.

Instinctively, only partially aware of what she was doing, she now tucked the parasol shaft under her arm, spit into her left palm, tapped the damp spot with her right thumb, and smacked it home with her fist. But Julie did not get a chance even to think of a wish, much less to make one. Out of the cab, raising a folded newspaper to shield her beautiful red hair from the rain, stepped a familiar figure. Julie's heart leaped.

"Celia!" she cried.

Her sister turned, saw Julie, and then, instead of coming toward her, Celia did something so curious that Julie, who had started forward with the parasol outstretched protectingly, was even more astonished. Celia's lovely face, which should have spread in the warm, wonderful smile of recognition and affection that every day lighted up this moment to which Julie looked forward so eagerly, seemed instead to contract with puzzlement. It was as though Celia had been hailed by a total stranger and even though her mind was on other and more important matters she felt, because of the intimacy of the greeting, she should make at least some token effort to identify the owner of the unfamiliar voice.

Apparently she did, but the result was even more curious. Celia's puzzled look gave way to something that Julie's suddenly hammering heart refused to acknowledge: annoyance. It's a mistake, she told herself desperately, Celia couldn't look at me like that. And indeed it did seem to be a mistake because Celia's face cleared and she made a warning gesture with the folded newspaper, as though Julie were approaching her across a bridge over a dangerous river and Celia from her side could see what her kid sister couldn't: the bridge was beginning to give way. Julie stopped short. Celia, apparently satisfied that Julie would not resume her forward movement, dipped down and spoke hurriedly through the open window to somebody on the rear seat of the taxi.

Julie heard a man's strong, unhurried voice say quietly, "You're sure?" Celia nodded hastily, and Julie clearly heard her sister say, "Yes, positive." Then a large tanned hand with a thick gold ring on the small finger appeared in the open window and touched Celia's small white hand in two short, reassuring pats. The same unhurried voice inside the cab said, "See you tomorrow," or something that to Julie sounded like "See you tomorrow," and Celia Sarno straightened up to watch the cab pull away from the curb. She stood very straight in the rain, one hand holding the folded newspaper gracefully over her head, looking like the picture in Julie's history book that showed a grave Pocahontas moving through the tall grass, supporting effortlessly on her head the bowl of fruit she is carrying to Captain John Smith shortly after saving his life.

Then the Luxor disappeared around the corner into Avenue B, and Celia Sarno turned, and she saw her kid sister.

"For crying out loud, Julie," she said, "what are you doing here?"

In the silence that followed, the only thing that kept Julie from bursting into tears was the conviction that she could not possibly have heard correctly.

"I—I—I came to meet you," she managed to say, and then,

because the simple, stammered statement was so unnecessary that it sounded foolish, she added, "The way I do every day."

The addition helped. It brought Celia's mind back from whereever it was roaming to the scrap of sidewalk on which her kid sister did indeed meet her every day, and at once the daily miracle happened: the lovely face spread in the warm wonderful smile of recognition and affection.

"I must be going cuckoo," Celia said. "I mean asking a dopey thing like that, what are you doing here?" She laughed and dipped down and gave her kid sister a swift little hug and kiss. Julie, taken by surprise, had no time to steel herself. She winced. Celia, her mind clearly poised to take wing again, was caught by the gesture. She looked more closely at her kid sister and then, in a shocked voice, said, "What happened to your face?"

Julie, annoyed by this irrelevance which detracted from the pleasure of meeting Celia, shook her head quickly. "Nothing," she said. "I was just—"

"Nothing?" Celia's voice rose sharply. Her fingertips, damp with rain, walked delicately, like the legs of a grasshopper feeling its way cautiously across a broken leaf, from the clot on Julie's split lip to the discoloration along the side of her jaw. Celia's own lip quivered. Tears came up in her eyes. She said savagely, "The dirty rotten drunken—" The words stopped. Celia caught her breath, dipped down again, and said quietly, "Why did he hit you?"

Julie's annoyance increased. What difference did it make why her father had hit her? Why couldn't Celia stick to the point? Why didn't she get on with the exciting business of telling Julie what had happened uptown that day?

"He didn't hit me," Julie said. "Honest. I was just—"

"Does it hurt?"

"No," Julie said impatiently. "Honest, Celia. I was just coming along the street, with Cockeye Katie, and I sort of, I mean I, *you* know, the rain, I slipped and I—"

"You poor kid." Celia's fingertips explored Julie's bruised face again, and for a few silent moments, in spite of Julie's eagerness to hear the latest adventures of her ambassadress in the great mysterious world known as Uptown, Celia's worry about the unimportant bruise brought the eleven-year-old and the eighteen-year-old sisters so close that Julie felt a small wave of gratitude to her drunken father for having inadvertently provided her with this dividend of happiness. "You listen to me," Celia said. "If he ever hits you again, I'm going to—"

"He didn't, Celia. Honest to God. It was only I slipped. In the rain. You can ask Cockeye Katie. I was in a hurry to come meet you. On account of the rain, I mean, and—"

Julie's voice stopped. Celia, catching her lower lip in her teeth, had turned to look back across her shoulder in the direction of the vanished Luxor. Julie heaved an inward sigh of relief. All this distracting nonsense was over. The promise she had given her father would be kept. Celia's mind, Julie could see, was finished with its momentary interest in her kid sister's bruised face. It was plain to Julie that Celia Sarno's mind had returned to wherever it had been roaming when the taxi disappeared. This was fine. Julie knew from experience that when Celia's mind roamed, it did so not in the dull, commonplace world of East Ninth Street but in the shining, exciting world of Uptown.

"I was good and worried," Julie said, rising on her toes to keep the parasol over Celia's head. "I mean the trolley stopping, and me waiting, and everybody gets out. But you, gee, Celia, you weren't—"

"Huh?" Celia said, turning back.

"You're getting soaked," Julie said, tipping the parasol a few inches to the right. "I was waiting for you, and everybody, they got out of the trolley car. But you, Celia, gosh, you didn't get out, so I was worried. I mean I thought, gosh, what's happened? Every day I come to the trolley, you're the last one out, but today, with the rain and all, you—"

"Yes, well, now, look." Celia tucked the wet newspaper under her arm and took the parasol from Julie. Tipping the steel shaft to keep the dyed silk over both of them, Celia put her other arm around her kid sister's shoulder and pulled her into a loose hug as they moved down Avenue B toward Ninth Street. Julie walked along in the bend of her sister's arm, feeling so wonderful as she inhaled the sweet smell of Celia that she was only dimly aware of the sounds Celia was making until Celia gave her shoulder a short, sharp shake and said, "You're not even listening to me."

"Sure I am," Julie said.

"What did I say?"

"You said," Julie said, and her hand went to her mouth. "Gosh, I—"

Celia laughed and pulled Julie close in another hug. "All right, now, but really listen. When we get home, I don't want you to say anything about the taxi. Okay?"

"About the taxi?"

"Julie, what's the matter with you? The taxi I just got *out* of."

"Oh."

"When we get home I don't want you to say anything about it. Understand?"

"Oh," Julie said again, and it was only as the small bubble of disappointment came to the surface of her happiness that she realized she had been planning unconsciously, ever since the white and silver beauty hove into sight, to tell Katie Halloran not only that she had *seen* a Luxor but, wonder of wonders, her sister Celia had been *in* it!

"What's the matter?"

The edge in Celia's voice caused Julie to look up quickly. "Nothing," she said.

"The way you said that 'oh' it didn't sound like nothing to me."

"I only meant—"

But Celia didn't seem to have time for what her kid sister meant. It was as though the words explaining what *she* meant had been entrusted to her as a loan, with the understanding that the words would be forfeited unless she used them before a specified deadline, and Celia, aware that her time was running out, was anxious to meet the condition.

"You see, what happened," she said, smiling down on her in a way that bothered Julie. There was something mechanical about the smile, as though Celia was trying to remember not only the borrowed words but also the lender's advice that they would be more effective if delivered in a casual, reassuring manner. "Mr.

64

Prohst had this examination before trial, and he asked me to come along to take the testimony, because his regular secretary was tied up with, well, never mind that. She couldn't leave the office, Mr. Prohst's regular secretary, so he took *me*, and this examination before trial, it was all the way downtown, John Street, in this other lawyer's office, and it ran longer than he thought. The *other* attorney made it run longer, not Mr. Prohst, asking a lot of questions that didn't have anything to do with the case, just to be mean, Mr. Prohst said. Mr. Prohst, if it was up to him, an examination before trial, he just sticks to the facts, and it's over very quickly. But this *other* attorney, well, we didn't get out until almost six o'clock, and it was raining, and Mr. Prohst said there's no point going all the way back uptown to our office on Twenty-third Street. I mean all it would mean, it would mean turning right around again, for me, I mean, and coming home, so Mr. Prohst said he was going home in a cab anyway, he lives up on Central Park West, he said he'd drop me. So, well, anyway, that's what he did. I mean that's how it happened."

Celia stopped, ostensibly to look both ways, because they had reached the Ninth Street corner and now had to cross from the west side of Avenue B to the east. But Julie, who had been staring up into her sister's face all during Celia's explanation, noticed as they stood side by side on the curb that while Celia's head did move in a dutiful arc from left to right, as though in quest of threatening vehicles, her eyes remained fixed on Julie. This may not have been the best way to guard against being hit by a truck while crossing Avenue B, but it was the only way Julie liked to receive her ambassador's daily report: knowing that Celia was just as absorbed by the telling as her sister was in the listening.

"John Street," Julie said. "What's it like?"

Celia looked puzzled. "What?" she said.

"John Street," Julie said. "You said this thing, where Mr. Prohst took you, you said it was on John Street."

"That's right," Celia said. "What about it?"

Julie hesitated. Almost every word Celia uttered in these daily reports was for Julie the equivalent of snapping open a pigeon-coop door: the questions came swarming out like impatient birds

65

after a long imprisonment. What was an examination before trial? Who was Mr. Prohst's secretary? What was the name of the other lawyer? Where was Central Park West? Did the name mean there were four Central Parks, East, South, and North, as well as West? What was testimony? How did you "take" it? These and the many other questions that raced through Julie's happily excited mind could not, however, be asked. Not all of them. Julie had made this discovery months ago, soon after Celia landed the job with Ellentuch, Prohst & Wadsworth, and Julie started meeting her sister at the trolley stop. When Celia got off that trolley she was tired and hungry and, now that the warm weather had set in, she was also hot. While she loved her sister, and she didn't really mind answering Julie's questions, Celia was only human. This was the phrase she had herself used when she apologized for the outburst of temper with which she had met Julie's first barrage of questions. There had never been another outburst. Not a real one, at any rate. Julie had seen to that, just as she was seeing to it now: by reducing the large number of questions she wanted to ask to the few she felt it was safe to ask.

"I was wondering what it's like there on John Street," she said. "With tall buildings, like Twenty-third Street, the way you said, high like this? Or like, say, here on Avenue B, with—?"

"It's just a street," Celia said impatiently. "Now stop asking dopey questions and listen. I don't want you to say anything in front of Ma and Pa about the taxi. Understand? So far as they're concerned, you went to meet me at the Tenth Street crosstown, the way you meet me every night, and you *met* me at the Tenth Street crosstown, the way you do every night. Understand?"

"Sure," Julie said, and she wondered, as Celia's odd request began to shove aside the many questions about Celia's day Uptown that were tumbling through her mind, if she might risk the very small question: *Why?* A short sidelong glance up at Celia, who was looking down at her kid sister with puzzling but unmistakable anxiety, convinced Julie that the question would be a mistake. Not so much because it might provoke one of Celia's outbursts of temper, but because to ask for an explanation would diminish the pleasure it gave Julie to do something, anything for

Celia. If Celia wanted her to shut up about the Luxor, okay, Julie would shut up about it. She said firmly, "I never even saw the darn taxi."

Celia grinned and, with a sudden, carefree swoop, as though her kid sister's hand were a baton she was snatching in a relay race, Celia dragged Julie from the curb and hauled her on the run across the street. They jumped up on the opposite curb side by side, plopping their feet down on the wet sidewalk in front of the Horace Judson Clarke House like a couple of kids landing in a hopscotch box and, as they paused for breath, Celia looked down at Julie and Julie looked up at Celia. Their eyes met and they suddenly doubled up in a fit of shrieking giggles.

"Okay, okay, okay, come on before we get like dishrags in this darn rain," Celia gasped finally, moving around the corner, still holding Julie's hand. As they made the turn into Ninth Street, and the barber shop came into view, the delicate little final bubbles of the giggling fit vanished from Celia's throat. She cleared it, gave Julie's hand a sudden squeeze, and said, "John Street isn't exactly like Twenty-third Street, but a little. I mean it's a business street, office buildings mostly on both sides, but the street isn't so wide, and the office buildings are taller, or maybe they just seem that way because the street's so narrow, and, well, what else? Well, the offices, mostly they're lawyers and insurance companies and like that. This office where we had this examination before trial, for instance. On the ground floor, the street, there was this insurance company. Then upstairs, the offices, when we got out of the elevator, they were like this one I went in with Mr. Prohst, lawyers mostly, and—" Celia's voice stopped. They had reached the barber shop. Her lips twisted thin as she looked at the locked door. "Did he get a chance to cut any hair today?" Celia said. "Or was he too busy between his witch-hazel bottle and counting those stupid white kid gloves he bought last week?"

"No, he's all right," Julie said quickly, trying, even though she knew it was impossible, to hold onto the good feeling. It always slipped away when her father came into the conversation. She couldn't understand why Celia hated him. Biaggio Sarno never put a hand on his oldest daughter. He never even had an unkind word for Celia. Everybody on Ninth Street knew the big barber was crazy about the slender red-headed girl. Celia knew it, too. The knowledge only seemed to increase her contempt for him. To Julie—whose feelings for Biaggio Sarno were not unlike her feelings for compound fractions: a nuisance she had to live with; something Mrs. Koenig, who addressed her classes in neat little Uptown phrases, would have called a necessary evil—Celia's hatred for their father was not only puzzling. It got in the way. It interfered with the reports of Julie's ambassadress to the world of Uptown.

Knowing as she did every night at this time that the effort was wasted, she nevertheless tried to recapture the feeling that was compounded of Celia's smile of recognition, and the swooping run across Avenue B, and the fit of giggles on the sidewalk in front of the Horace Judson Clarke House, and the description of John Street. Very quickly, too quickly to make her attempt at casualness convincing, Julie said, "He was working hard all afternoon when I got back from school. He really was. Celia, what's an examination before trial?"

"Hard, huh?" Celia said. "On what? The witch-hazel bottle?"

She dropped Julie's hand and climbed the three gray stone steps of the stoop next to the barber shop. Celia pulled the parasol shut and with her shoulder pushed open the heavy street door, which, because of its thick plate-glass panel and the two protective layers of black wrought-iron scrollwork on the inside and outside, moved with the ponderous slowness of the door to a bank vault.

"Is it like a doctor's examination?" Julie said, pushing past the door into the vestibule behind her sister. Celia had dipped down to peer through the grilled brass front of the panel of letter boxes. "There's nothing," Julie said helpfully. "I looked."

Celia straightened up. "Sure there's nothing," she said. "Who's there to write letters to Celia Sarno, 292 East Ninth Street, Garbage Grove, near Sewer Pipe Hill, on Ash Can Acres, in the great stinking Lower East Side of the City of New York?"

With a sudden, vicious swing that sprayed raindrops all over Julie, Celia slammed the parasol against the panel of letter boxes. In the slowly fading hum that filled the vestibule, the red-headed girl stared for several moments into her sister's troubled eyes, and then Celia Sarno's face broke in a crooked little smile.

"Don't mind me," she said, patting Julie's cheek. "I'm just sweating like a pig and dog-tired and worn out and I'm hot and hot and *hot*, God damn it, *hot*. I'll be all right in a few minutes, or a few years, or maybe a century or two, if I live that long in this damn cesspool."

The smile grew straighter, smoothing the distorted creasings of pink and white cheek into the familiar, faintly shadowed dimples, making Celia look more like Celia.

"You're a sweet kid," she said. "And I'm a bitch on skates to take out my God knows what to call it on you. Here, look, I brought you a little present." She held out to Julie the soggy folded newspaper with which Celia had protected her hair from the rain when she stepped out of the Luxor. "It's not much, but I didn't have time to get anything else," Celia said. "I mean, Mr. Prohst deciding to drop me off by taxi, there was no time to—"

"That's all right," Julie said, getting the words out with difficulty past the sudden lump in her throat. "This is fine, Celia." She stared at the square of damp newspaper as though it was the Rosetta stone. "This is fine," Julie repeated. "It's fine."

It was better than that, but there were no words, none that Julie Sarno knew at any rate, to express what she felt. In spite of the heat, in spite of the rain, in spite of whatever it was she'd had to do for Mr. Prohst at the thing she'd called an examination before trial, Celia had not forgotten her kid sister.

"I'll try to do better tomorrow," Celia said. "Not just a rotten old newspaper. I'll get something real nice."

"No, this is fine," Julie said, knowing that as long as she lived she would never forget the feel of that damp wad of newspaper or the headlines that spread across the top in bold black letters: *Clarence Chamberlain and Charles A. Levine Set New World Non-Stop Record Colombia Arrives Safely in Saxony Germany 3,905 Miles from New York in 43 Hours.* "This is fine," Julie said again. "Thanks, Celia."

"Forget it," Celia said, and then, archly, resting the heel of her palm on Julie's head and tapping the damp black hair with her middle finger as though it were a woodpecker's beak: "But don't forget about the taxi. I mean *do* forget it. You never saw it. I got off the Tenth Street trolley. Right?"

"Right," Julie said, and both girls exploded in another fit of giggles as Celia took Julie's hand, shoved open the vestibule door, and started up the grooved stone stairs. At the first landing Celia's giggles trickled away. She released Julie's hand and laced her fingers together. Then, like a nurse applying the ether cone to a patient in an operating room, Celia clapped her two cupped palms over her cute little upturned nose in a gesture from which all the humor was drained by the fury of the words that accompanied it: "Phew! Those damn Hallorans. Him a cop, with a steady salary, every week the pay check is there, that dopey Irish slob he's married to, can't she cook anything else but cabbage?"

Even if an answer had been expected, and Julie knew in her sinking heart that the question was rhetorical, she couldn't have made it. Celia, supplying her own answer in an explosion of disgust and rage, had vanished up the stairs. Julie followed more slowly, hoping what was about to happen would not happen, knowing it was foolish to hope, wondering dully what form the explosion would take tonight. A few moments later, pushing open the door covered by a prudent landlord with sheets of tin painted brown, she found out.

At the end of the long dark hall that led from the front door of the Sarno apartment to the kitchen, silhouetted against the light from the small areaway window over the sink, stood the three members of Julie's family. As always at this moment, she made in her mind a last stand, refusing to accept the inevitable ugliness which each evening at this time sucked up and destroyed the happiness Julie had put together from the bits and pieces of her daily trip to the Avenue B trolley stop. For one stubborn hopeless moment Julie managed to pretend it was not her mother and father and sister she was seeing at the end of the hall. Then Julie heard the screaming voices, and the moment ended with the inevitable plunge back into reality.

"What I said?" Biaggio Sarno roared. "What I said that it's so terrible?"

"Can't you remember?" Celia shouted. "What are you? Too drunk to remember?"

"All right, all right, all right," Mrs. Sarno moaned, banging out the words in Italian, repeating them over and over again, doggedly, patiently, adding nothing to the scene but noise, as though she had somehow managed to get hold of the clapper of a bell and she hoped, by drowning out the screams of the antagonists, to make the fight itself disappear. "All right, all right, all right."

"Shut up!" her husband bellowed in Italian. "I'm trying to talk!" He swung back to Celia, reverting to English, as he always did when he addressed his children, even though the reversion placed him at a disadvantage. "Tell me what I said that'sa so terrible! My daughter she comesa home from work! Itza hot! I say go take a bath before you eat! The tub izza clean! I wash it out for you! I let the water in for you!"

"I don't want a bath!" Celia yelled. "I'd rather be hot and dirty than get into that rotten old tub! Why can't we have a shower? Like decent people?"

"We getta the shower!" Biaggio Sarno roared. "We getta!"

"When?" Celia cried. "When you sell those damn-fool white kid gloves you bought last week? Don't you know you got stuck again? They're all right-hand gloves! There isn't a pair in the whole two hundred dozen! That's why you got them for a hundred dollars! You'll have to throw them out the way you threw out the umbrellas!"

"All right, all right, all right," Mrs. Sarno intoned, swaying slightly between her daughter and her husband. In one hand she held a ladle. In the other, a black iron frying pan. Her arms were spread wide, the ladle pointing at Celia, the frying pan pointing at the big barber. It was as though the kitchen utensils were swords with which the gray-haired woman was trying to keep the antagonists apart. "All right, all right, all right!"

"We getta the shower!" Biaggio Sarno shouted across his wife's head. "We getta the shower!"

"That's what you said six months ago!" Celia screamed. "When you bought those stupid umbrellas! That's what you said a year ago! When you bought those crazy rubber boots that were going to make you rich! That's what you've been saying for years! We getta the shower! We getta the shower!" Celia's lips twisted savagely as she mimicked her father's accent. "But we're still stuck with that stinking tub! We're still living down here in this rotten—!"

"Izza not stinking!" Biaggio Sarno shouted. "Izza clean! I wash it myself for my daughter!"

"What am I supposed to do?" Celia cried. "Get down on my knees and thank you? Or maybe send you a medal? He washed it himself! Hooray for him!"

"You come-a home from work, you hot, izza better a bath than notta bath! You come-a home from work, the father wantsa his daughter should have—"

"The father! Some father! If you were a real father, if you cared about your children, I wouldn't have to go to work! I'd be going to college now, like the other girls! I'd be able to hold my head up! I wouldn't be living in a garbage can like this! I'd *be* somebody! A real human being! Not a cheap little stenographer! Making sixteen dollars a week! Trying to pay for my lunches and buy my clothes on eight because the other half, the other eight, my father needs it for booze!"

"All right, all right, all right." Mrs. Sarno's shrieking chant grew louder. "All right, all right, all right."

Biaggio Sarno snarled, "Get out of my way, you lousy rice eater!" and Julie's heart leaped with terror. The fact that his wife had been born in Milan was to the immigrant from Naples even more infuriating than his disastrous business ventures. Julie didn't understand why. She had learned, however, that when her father, a spaghetti eater from the south of Italy, began to refer to her mother as the rice eater from the north, the next step was physical violence. Biaggio Sarno shouted in Italian, "I'm talking to my daughter, not to you!"

With the last word he brought his fists down, side by side, as though he were driving a stake into the ground. Mrs. Sarno grunted. The ladle and the frying pan hit the floor and then went clattering dully across the worn linoleum. Celia screamed a last incoherent insult as she lunged forward and caught her tottering mother's shoulders. They staggered together across the kitchen locked in each other's arms, following the crazily skipping path of the ladle and the frying pan, as though they and the kitchen utensils were part of a game. The jutting wooden cover of the gray cement washtubs, which met the chipped white enamel sink at right angles, stopped the game. Mrs. Sarno grunted again, and this time the sound ended in a whimper of pain. Celia straightened up, pushed her mother behind her, into the corner, and stepped forward. Two strands had come loose from the net that bound her hair in a neat red cap. Beads of sweat hung and slithered on her forehead like bearings from a broken skate wheel rolling in the sun. Her face was chalk-white except for two bright red circles on her cheekbones. Julie's mind, numb with fright, nevertheless recorded the fact that her sister had never looked more beautiful.

"You dirty rotten drunk!" Celia Sarno said to her father. "You cheap, disgusting booze hound! That's all you're good for, isn't it? Hitting women!"

"Celia, no!" Biaggio Sarno cried, dropping back again into English. "Celia, no say that!"

"What else should I say? It's the truth, isn't it? What else are you good for? Hitting women, that's all!"

"No! I no hit her! I just—"

"You just what? Gave her a love tap? The way you gave Julie?" Celia dashed into the hall, grabbed Julie's arm, and hauled her forward into the kitchen. "Look!" Celia tipped her sister's chin up. "Look at this and tell me you didn't do it! Go ahead, tell me! You big dirty disgusting filthy slimy lying drunk!"

Biaggio Sarno stared down at Julie's chin, the breath roaring in and out of his chest, the tip of his tongue licking nervously at the corners of his mouth, the rage in his eyes turning slowly to surprise. It was as though a prisoner in the dock, making a spirited defense which in the heat of the moment he has come to believe will win him an acquittal, had suddenly been confronted with unexpected evidence which even he could see established his guilt. Then his glance moved from the clotted lip and the bruised jaw, and Biaggio Sarno's eyes met Julie's, and she knew that what was going to happen next was just.

It would hurt, of course, but that was unimportant. She was accustomed to being hurt by this man with whom she had to live. What she was not accustomed to, what impressed her even as she waited for the blow, was the sudden knowledge that she deserved it. To Biaggio Sarno, who lived for the good opinion of his daughter Celia, his other daughter had made a promise. The fact that Julie had kept her promise did not change the fact that on Biaggio Sarno, at this moment in his degradation, the effect was the same as if she had broken it. Celia must not know what he had done. But Celia did know. Somebody, therefore, had to pay.

Closing her eyes to receive the payment, Julie found her numbed mind suddenly flooded by the bright vision of the Luxor, the beautiful silver and white vehicle from which Celia had stepped only a few minutes ago at the corner of Avenue B and Tenth Street. Julie's eyes blinked open with sudden hope. She had spit into her palm. She had tapped the damp spot with her thumb. She had punched it home with her fist. She had done all that before the white and silver taxi had disappeared from view. She had met the conditions set by fate. She had earned the right to make a wish.

"Please, God," Julie prayed with sudden excitement, silently, inside her head, enunciating the soundless words clearly so God would not misunderstand what she wanted. "Please, God, I wish Pa and Celia should stop the fight. It should stop, the fight, God, please stop the fight, please stop—"

The words slithered to a halt in Julie's head. She had heard a sound behind her. She turned. Celia turned with her. The sound was repeated: a short, sharp knock on the door.

"Yes?" Celia called.

The door opened. A thin young man with yellow hair tumbled forward on his forehead was standing on the threshold.

"I beg your pardon," he said through a smile that suddenly made him look familiar. "Does a Miss Julie Sarno live here?"

4

Six years later, in Oregon, while driving to a party at the home of Arnold Brahmin, the leader of the Mercerville group, Ben Ivey suddenly mentioned that first meeting on East Ninth Street. Julie was sitting between Celia and Ben, on the front seat of the beat-up old Pierce-Arrow convertible he loved so much, listening to Ben draw a parallel between Arnold Brahmin's talents as an administrator and Neville Chamberlain's talents as a national leader, when all at once, as Ben swung the car around a loaded hay wagon, Julie realized he was quoting Wordsworth.

"*Look for the stars,*" Ben intoned in the slightly resonant midwestern voice that always grew more resonant and, to Julie, more attractive when it shifted from ordinary conversation to quotation, "*you'll say there are none; look up a second time, and, one by one, you mark them twinkling out with silvery light, and wonder how they could elude the sight!*"

"What's that got to do with it?" Celia said, leaning forward to look across her sister at Ben. "You were just talking about Arnold Brahmin and Neville Chamberlain. Wasn't he, Julie?"

"That's what it sounded like to me," Julie said. "Before I suddenly found myself knee-deep in Palgrave's *Golden Treasury.*"

"The connection is obvious," Ben said. "Arnold Brahmin and Neville Chamberlain both lack one of the most important qualifications for true leadership: the ability to take that second look

75

Wordsworth talks about. Either of you two charmers know the name of the poem, by the way?"

"No," Celia said, "and don't change the subject."

"I'm not changing the subject," Ben said. "It's 'Calm Is the Fragrant Air.' Not the old maestro's greatest effort, perhaps, but one of my favorites. The second look, that's the thing that counts. Plus the ability to see, of course. That second look will do you damned little good if you're myopic or astigmatic or just plain cockeyed, which is exactly, I'm sorry to say, what both Mr. Brahmin and Mr. Chamberlain are. If dear old Arnold had twenty-twenty vision and he took a second look at yesterday's directive from the Secretary of the Interior, he'd understand what the boys in Washington are about to do to him, just as if dear old Neville had even one eye in his head as sound or at least as prominent as his many buck teeth, and he had the ability to turn that eye on the most commonplace and routine AP and UP reports coming out of Berlin and Rome, he'd grasp at once what is going to hit him if he is fool enough to go and sit down at a table with those boys at this meeting they're cooking up in Munich. It's like that night in 1927 when I first met the Sarno family."

"What?" Celia said, clearly startled.

Ben chuckled, the quiet little rumble of appreciation for a point well made, for a bit of unusual verbal dexterity whether his own or somebody else's. Ben's chuckle always sounded to Julie not so much like laughter as the movement of well-oiled tumblers in a beautifully made piece of machinery functioning with the perfection that the designer had hoped for when he first sketched it on his drawing board. Ben was obviously pleased by the effect he had created on the front seat of the convertible.

"You heard me," he said. "It's like that first night I met you girls, six years ago, almost seven. In that crummy flat over the barber shop on East Ninth Street."

Celia leaned forward again, to get a better look at Ben. It occurred to Julie that her sister did that quite often. It was as though Celia was constantly forgetting what Ben looked like.

"You really mean that?" she said. "That there *is* a connection?"

"I certainly do," Ben said.

"I wish you'd tell me what it is," Celia said. "I mean I don't quite grasp—"

"Because you're at the other end of the telescope, so to speak," Ben said. "Forget yourself for a moment. Think of me for a while. The way I was six years ago, that night when I first met you and Julie and your parents. What was I? Who was Benjamin Franklin Ivey on that particular night?"

He paused, perhaps because he wanted to concentrate on guiding the car around another hay wagon, but Julie suspected the pause was intended to underscore Ben's next words with a touch of drama. There was a good chance, Julie knew, even though it sounded paradoxical, that the intention was completely unconscious. She had noticed long ago that, tucked away in the arsenal of his many talents, Ben had the born actor's flair for timing.

"I'll tell you who I was on that particular night six years ago," he said. "A frustrated, disappointed, troubled, almost frantic young man of twenty-two, that's what I was, that's what Benjamin Franklin Ivey was on that historic night when our paths crossed."

"Well, you certainly didn't look *any* of those things," Celia said. "Standing there in that door, wearing a great big Rotarian's grin on your face, you looked—"

"To *you*, yes," Ben said. "Because you were at the other end of that telescope I just mentioned. But to me, the way Benjamin Franklin Ivey saw himself, uh-uh. Try to look at me the way I was looking at myself. Put yourself in my shoes. They may pinch a bit, but stay with it just long enough to get the picture. You're standing in my shoes six years ago. Okay?"

"Ben," Celia said, "will you please—?"

"No, I'm serious," he said. "Are you standing in my shoes?"

"Go ahead," Julie said. "Stand in his shoes."

Ben rewarded her with a quick grin. "Better do as your kid sister says," he said. "She always gives good advice."

"All right," Celia said impatiently. "I'm standing in your shoes."

"So standing there, six years ago, in my shoes, who are you?" Ben said. "Why, you're a young squirt of twenty-two who was born and raised in Cleveland. You're the only son of a fire-and-

77

brimstone Methodist minister whose great tragedy was that his poor eyesight, so poor that it amounted to legal blindness, had prevented him from going off as a youth to the far ends of the earth, China, Africa, Tibet, any place, so long as it was far away, to convert the heathen. If you're a kid raised in that kind of town, in that kind of an atmosphere, by that kind of a father, what do you live with all the years you're a kid? Simple enough for anybody even casually acquainted with our modern shorthand jargon of psychiatry.

"Why, all the years you're a kid you live with your father's frustrated ambition. That's elementary, isn't it? Dr. David Ivey couldn't go off to Timbuctoo to convert the heathen, so he's damn well going to fix it that you, his son, will go off to do what he didn't get a chance to do. Unfortunately, fate decides to throw a monkey wrench in the machinery. When you're in your last year at the state university, and you're understandably and wholeheartedly living all your father's plans to go to the seminary before taking off for the far horizon and the as yet unconverted heathen, your father drops dead one day in the pulpit, leaving you not only with a satchelful of his own unfulfilled ambitions but, surprisingly enough, with an unsuspected desk drawer full of more unpaid bills than you would have thought a parsimonious and scrupulously honest Methodist minister could accumulate. What do you do?

"Why, if you're a kid raised in that kind of an atmosphere by that kind of a father, there's only one thing you *can* do: assume the obligation of your father's debts as though they are your own. By the time a series of back-breaking after-school and summer jobs has done the trick, and your dead father's financial slate is wiped clean, you're not only good and pooped, you're also a little critical of the plans your father has made for you.

"All of a sudden you realize that for a couple of years now, ever since your father died, you've fallen into the habit of thinking for yourself, and as habits go, this is one you sort of like. Applying your own thinking, therefore, to the plan your father thought up for you all those years ago, it suddenly occurs to you that after the four years you've just put in at the state university, the prospect of wading and working your way through four more years of the seminary doesn't exactly make your heart leap up the way Wordsworth's did when he beheld that rainbow in the sky, and besides, all of a sudden you're asking yourself something else: what's so wonderful about spending your life in Timbuctoo converting the heathen?"

Ben chuckled again, and he sent another of those swift glances down the front seat of the car to see if Julie and Celia were listening. Julie didn't know about Celia, whose mind had a tendency to take wing even in the midst of one of Ben's most entertaining explanations, but Julie knew about herself. She was listening. She had learned long ago that, when Ben Ivey got going, there was very little else she could do.

"I remember it was on my twenty-first birthday that I asked myself that question," he said. "Before I was twenty-one years and one day old, I had the answer. I wanted to quit all this studying, all this sitting in lecture rooms and having people talk at you, telling you how things are done. I wanted to get out and *do* something. But what? I could have found any one of a dozen jobs easily enough. Delivering newspapers. Pumping gas. Weaving raffia baskets. Teaching tennis. Smoking eels. Or to quit the kidding, something nice and white-collar. Selling bonds, maybe. Or the traditional Horatio Alger clean-cut American-boy job in a bank. Why not? I was what they call personable, I had a college education, and this was 1926. So, girls, would you like to know why not?"

"If it leads to that night we first met on East Ninth Street," Celia said, "I certainly do."

"Like a homing pigeon to its roost it leads there, sweetie," Ben said. "So I will tell you why not. Because while the leopard can change his mind, his point of view, his direction, and even his pants, if he happens to be a pants-wearing-type leopard, the one thing he can't do is change his spots. So it has been written, and so it is. I found that out, because while I no longer wanted to go where my fire-and-brimstone Methodist preacher father had raised me to want to go, namely, Timbuctoo and the unconverted heathen, I still wanted to convert. The itch had been planted in me too early and too deep to be either overlooked or yanked out. Putting it in its bluntest terms, not because I want to, but because I know if I don't, one of you two sardonic beauties will put it in those terms for me, I discovered that I was a do-gooder, and a do-gooder I would remain to the end of my days. Now, then, class, those being the conditions, I will now pose the question: what sort of job did young Mr. Benjamin Franklin Ivey take?"

"A job," Celia said bitterly, "in which people like the Sarnos could be studied under a microscope."

"What's wrong with that?" Ben said. "If you're an American do-gooder by instinct or training, and if you don't want to go to Timbuctoo, there's only one place in America to which you *can* go: New York's Lower East Side. That small island within an island, that strip of congested, steaming, multilingual pavement occupies an absolutely unique place in our American culture. Not only because it is the breeding ground from which have sprung some of the most distinguished leaders in every walk of American life—the arts, finance, politics, whatever you choose or can think of, just name it, and up at the top of each list you'll find a whole clutch of ex-East Side boys—but also because those few acres of tenements and garbage cans are the *training* ground for an entirely different but equally important group of leaders: the movers and shakers who were not *born* in the melting pot but learned the tricks of moving and shaking by serving their *apprenticeship* in the melting pot."

"That's why you came to East Ninth Street?" Celia said slowly, the corners of her eyes crinkling as though all at once, instead of taking another look at Ben, it was her own words as they issued from her mouth that she wanted to see clearly. "You chose it deliberately? The way you'd choose a college? Because it offered a curriculum you had a special interest in?"

"More or less," Ben said. "Except for that word deliberately. It sounds too, too, oh, hell, you know, Machiavellian. A kid with an itch to, say, paint or sculpt or whatever the word is for hacking away at marble, a kid like that instinctively heads for Paris. A kid with an itch to convert or do good, call it what you will, heads for New York's Lower East Side. It isn't as sinister as the 'word 'deliberately' implies, nor is it as difficult, even if you're practically penniless, which I sure was. Just as there are regular drops for dope addicts, word of which gets around by dope-addict grapevine, there are also all sorts of things like foundations for kids who want to go to Paris but haven't got the fare, and there are sort of unofficial but effective clearing houses for do-gooders.

"Less than a week after I made up my mind I wanted to go to New York, six days to be precise, and I *will* be precise, I had a call from a man in the administrative office at the Cleveland Y. He said he'd heard there was a job open as associate director of a settlement house on a street called Avenue B in New York and it was mine, he thought, if I wanted it. Boy, did I want it! I don't know how I lived through the two weeks—no, I'm not going to let my passion for precision go by the board—not two weeks; fifteen days. The fifteen days it took for the letters to be exchanged. You know, applications filled out and sent to New York, that sort of thing. It took fifteen days.

"How I lived through them, I don't know. The terror that my qualifications might not be adequate, that somebody at the Horace Judson Clarke House, somebody in charge, I mean, might not like the photograph I'd sent along, or that the director himself, this faceless creature named Tyler Crispin, might object to having an assistant who came from Cleveland or because his name began with the letter I or because his hair was blond, or a million other becauses, all equally silly, of course, but all equally capable of striking terror into the heart of a twenty-one-year-old who wanted that job the way Abélard wanted Héloïse.

"I've read some pretty steam-heated descriptions of that gentleman's emotions when he finally got the girl, but you have my assurance that Abélard's feelings at that particular moment were as nothing by comparison with the feelings of young Benjamin Franklin Ivey when, traditional cardboard suitcase clutched in hot hand, he finally climbed aboard the bus in Cleveland that was to carry him to his job in the Horace Judson Clarke House on Avenue B."

Some fragments of those feelings were apparently still rattling around in their owner's slender frame because, even though the stretch of road pasted like a ribbon across the gathering Oregon dusk from the convertible's windshield to the horizon was as empty as a desert landscape, Ben suddenly hit the horn button several times with the heel of his palm, as though sounding a warning to a whole string of invisible vehicles that he was about to pass.

"The quintessence of biography, the whole damn story of any man's life, is a handful of moments, high or low," he said. "Just a handful of moments. That's all. Take anybody. Napoleon? Okay, Napoleon. No five-volume work says it better than five simple words: Eylau, Austerlitz, Elba, Waterloo, and St. Helena. Moses. Bernhardt. Shakespeare. Bismarck. Name anybody. It's still the same. Each life can be told in a handful of moments. Nobody has yet bothered to tell the life of Benjamin Franklin Ivey, and maybe nobody ever will, but if anybody does take on the job, and if I'm still around, I think I'd warn the biographer that no matter what his subject accomplished, no matter how far he went or how long he lived, nothing that ever happened to Ben Ivey was ever as shiny and bright as that moment at the age of twenty-one when he sat shivering with the sweet, sweet, *sweet* ecstasy of anticipation in the bus that was carrying him from Cleveland to Avenue B." Ben held his hand on the horn button for a long, hard blast that reminded Julie of the herald in a pageant sounding his trumpet to announce the entry of a prince. Then Ben took his hand from the horn and, in the curiously hollow silence that suddenly filled the car, he said quietly, "I was Dick Whittington setting out for London. I was Julien Sorel on his way to Paris. I had my foot on the first step of the ladder to glory."

His voice stopped and he leaned forward across the wheel to peer through the windshield with a small frown, as though trying to pick out of the rapidly deepening Oregon dusk that moment of brightness.

"I still don't see the connection," Celia said. "I mean between all that, and the night you first met the Sarno family."

Ben laughed and leaned away from the wheel. "The Sarnos gave me back a piece of that feeling I'd had on the bus." He sent another of his quick glances along the front seat of the car. "You didn't think you were in a giving mood, did you? That moment, six years ago, when I opened the door of your flat?" He laughed. "No, you certainly were not in a giving mood," he said. "But I was in a taking mood, even though I wasn't exactly aware of it. At that moment I was, after all, as I've said, a frustrated, disappointed, troubled, and almost frantic young man."

"About what?" Celia said. "That's what I don't understand. What were you frantic about?"

"My life," Ben said. "What else is anybody frantic about at that age? It's a time when only big things are important. Kids never worry about hangnails. They worry about the cosmos. It's only when you're old that hangnails become important, that you fret about little things like your health. I didn't give a damn about my health. I lay awake nights in my top-floor room at the Horace Judson Clarke House worrying about my life. I could see it slipping away before my eyes, unused, pointless, getting nowhere, a long, long freight train clickety-clacking away, rushing like crazy to the horizon, but all the boxcars were empty. You see, the Lower East Side had let me down."

"In what way?" Celia said.

"There weren't any heathen," Ben said, and he must have been certain of the effect his words would have, because the rumbling chuckle of appreciation had started before he could have caught the startled look on Julie's face. "I'd turned my back on my father's dream of Timbuctoo because New York's Lower East Side seemed a quicker way to glory," Ben said. "I arrived on Avenue B with the do-gooder's itch sticking out all over me like goose pimples. I was all primed to tussle with dens of iniquity, stamp out cesspools of vice, and drain pools of poverty. Congestion, squalor, disease, malnutrition, all were waiting to be destroyed by the skinny young knight from Cleveland. Or so I thought.

"Very soon after I arrived on Avenue B, I began to suspect I'd come to the wrong place. I didn't see much champagne and caviar, true. But I never saw any natives dying of starvation on the streets, either. As a matter of fact, the people who lived on the streets in the immediate vicinity of the Horace Judson Clarke House seemed to eat a hell of a lot better than my father and I used to eat in Cleveland. There wasn't much room for swinging cats or installing bowling alleys in the tenement flats they lived in, but everybody seemed to have as much elbow room as they wanted. Now and again somebody would break a leg or an appendix would burst, but the Bellevue ambulance always seemed to arrive in plenty of time, and the incidence of beriberi, or any other colorful disease that a brilliant and fearless young social worker could lick single-handed after it assumed epidemic proportions, was nonexistent. Even the few local members of the world's oldest profession that I felt pretty sure I had managed to identify not only looked healthy and prosperous, but the young ladies seemed positively happy in their work.

"In short, kiddies, for young Benjamin Franklin Ivey it was a hell of a note. I soon began to feel a little like Stanley, thinking he has arrived in darkest Africa in full jungle hunting regalia to locate Livingston, and finding instead that he has somehow or other been set down in Scarsdale, where his quarry is contentedly sitting in a rocker on a shaded porch sipping iced tea and working out the crossword puzzle in the morning paper. I was, in other words, nonplused, frustrated, and in a nice juicy troubled state of mind. And then, by the end of my first year as associate director of the Horace Judson Clarke House, when the dreams of glory with which as a twenty-one-year-old infant I'd come to New York had vanished, and I was a twenty-two-year-old frantic graybeard in whose mind thoughts of suicide had begun to pop up, I opened the door one night of a flat over a barber shop on East Ninth Street and, well, there you all were, exactly what Dr. Do-Gooder had ordered, or, as Wordsworth put it," and Ben's voice became resonant as he repeated: *"Look for the stars, you'll say there are none; look up a second time, and, one by one, you mark them twinkling out with silvery light, and wonder how they could elude the sight!"*

Ben's voice stopped and after a few moments, during which he seemed to be waiting for the echoes of Wordsworth's words to die away, he said, "I didn't realize at the time that I had the ability to take that second look Wordsworth talks about, but I did take it, and that's how I saw that by coming to New York's Lower East Side I'd come to the right place after all."

"You saw that by looking at us that night?" Celia said. "The Sarno family?"

"Absolutely," Ben said.

Celia shook her head. "I don't get it," she said. "What did you see?"

"What a social worker *expects* to see when he comes to the Lower East Side," Ben said. "A family torn by strife. A group of human beings shaking themselves to pieces as a result of the economic conditions in which they are forced to live. If you'll just think back to that first night, and take a look at yourselves as I first saw you, you'll understand what I mean. Here's what I saw: immigrant father screaming at first-generation American oldest daughter, who is screaming back at him; immigrant mother screaming at both of them in hopeless effort to restore peace; first-generation American youngest daughter cowering in hallway, clearly terrified by the snarling battle, which starts with a simple exchange of insults over fact that family lacks adequate bathing facilities, and soon fans out over the more deeply rooted resentments, such as—"

"You couldn't have known all that at the time," Celia said quickly. "I mean, all you could know from that first glimpse of us, all you could take in—"

"Was a picture," Ben said. "Almost a stylized photograph, that could have been used as an illustration in a textbook on *How to Become a Social Worker*, a picture that might have been captioned 'A Typical Situation in the Slum Dweller's Home.' That's the picture you presented that night to the discerning eye capable of taking that second look. That's the picture I absorbed, and with the absorption all my frustration and worry and disappointment in the Lower East Side fell away. In its place came back enough of the glow of anticipation with which I'd set out a year before from Cleveland to make me grasp at once that I'd taken a new lease on life. Benjamin Franklin Ivey, aged twenty-two, was back on the right road to glory."

Julie, who was suddenly wondering if the car was on the right road to the home of Arnold Brahmin, snuggled down on the front seat between Celia and Ben. He had asked them to take a look at that six-year-old moment through the other end of the telescope. And Julie, who had taken the look, was surprised by what she had seen. The feeling was nothing, however, by comparison with the surprise she had felt six years ago, when she was still looking through her own end of the telescope, so to speak, at that extraordinary moment when, apparently in direct response to the silent but desperate plea she had made to God, the door had opened and the slender young man with the blond hair had looked into the Sarno apartment.

Julie's first thought was that this business of spitting into your palm and punching it home when you saw a Luxor taxi was even stronger stuff than she'd come to think it was. Julie's next thought, as the young man on the threshold stared with interest at the four Sarnos, was that God chose some pretty tricky ways to pay off His obligations.

He had answered her prayer that the fight between Celia and her father be stopped, sure. But the minute this young man in the doorway opened his mouth and revealed why he was here, the result would be an even bigger fight, and this time Julie didn't see how she could blame her father for exploding. After all, a month ago, when the first young man showed up, Julie had promised her father that she and Katie Halloran would stop sending away for catalogues. Julie had kept her promise. But it was clear now that Cockeye Katie hadn't. This was understandable, too. Not only because it was an exciting game, but because Katie had invented it.

For months she and Julie had pored through the magazines in the reading room of the Tompkins Square Park Branch of the public library, surreptitiously snipping out and then mailing off the coupons from every ad that urged readers to send for free descriptive literature. For months the mailbox downstairs in the vestibule had been a source of continuing excitement. Every day brought a new surprise from the great world beyond East Ninth Street. Over the months the two girls had accumulated a treasured collection of multicolored folders and booklets, in various shapes and sizes, extolling the virtues of cold creams, air rifles, Caribbean cruises, radio sets, banking services, outboard motors, delivery trucks, calculating machines, floor waxes, fish pastes, portable electric drills, headache cures, cameras, motor oils, draughtsman's equipment, vacuum cleaners, denicotinized cigarettes, and products identified by their manufacturers as brake linings and steel casters that neither Julie nor Katie quite understood but both enjoyed reading about.

It had never occurred to them that the advertisers who urged readers to clip and mail in these coupons had any motive in sending out their handsome brochures other than the entertainment of two eleven-year-old girls. Julie discovered her error one hot night when, in the middle of the regular evening battle between Celia and her father, there was a knock on the door and the startled Sarnos found themselves facing an even more startled young salesman for the Crawford Cruiser Corporation.

The young man's list of prospective customers had been compiled for him by a clerk in the Crawford Cruiser Corporation's offices from the names of people who had sent for copies of the company's beautifully illustrated catalogue. A few moments after he opened this particular prospective customer's door, the young man apparently understood that his chances of selling a seventy-five-thousand-dollar pleasure boat to a slum-area barber were not very good. It took the young man, who was clearly so well trained in all the usual gambits of successful salesmanship that he was almost totally incapable of handling an unusual situation, a good deal longer to make his escape.

By the time he did, Julie's father, who had not fully grasped the meaning of the embarrassed exchange of explanations between the young man and Julie until just before the salesman left, decided that the whole thing was a plot on the part of Cockeye Katie and his youngest daughter to humiliate him with a dramatic and mocking illustration of his poverty. The fight that followed had set a new mark in the unwritten but vividly remembered annals of Sarno family quarrels.

Now, a month later, staring at this new young man in the doorway, Julie saw that there was a good chance the four-week-old mark would be surpassed. The fact that this young man, like the first one, carried no sample case indicated clearly that the product his company manufactured was, like that of the Crawford Cruiser Corporation, large. The fact that it was not Julie who had sent for his company's catalogue could not possibly be established before her father exploded and, even if that fact could be proved, Julie knew her father would hold her responsible for the fact that her friend Cockeye Katie, by sending for the catalogue in Julie's name, had set the stage for another humiliating demonstration of Biaggio Sarno's financial failure.

"I beg your pardon," the young man in the doorway repeated. "Does a Miss Julie Sarno live here?"

"Who'sa want her?" Julie's father demanded.

"My name is Ivey," the young man said, and the smile, which under other circumstances Julie would have found attractive, now merely puzzled her again because, even though she knew she had never seen him before, it made him look familiar. "Ben Ivey," he said. "I'm the associate director of the Horace Judson Clarke House around the corner." Julie's heart, thudding along dully as she waited for her father's explosion of rage, leaped. She stared at the young man who was not a salesman after all. Frightened, she remembered what had happened in the barber shop that afternoon when Cockeye Katie came in with Mr. Tyler Crispin's letter, and wondered what this man who had been mentioned in that letter was doing here. He said, "I hope I'm not intruding, but I did want—"

"Wanta what?"

Biaggio Sarno's truculent manner and sullen voice, which made Julie's flesh crawl with shame, merely caused Mr. Ivey's cheery smile to expand across his thin features.

"In point of fact, what I want is a chat with Miss Julie Sarno's father," he said. "Would that be you, sir?"

The big barber's dark face flushed darker. Biaggio Sarno, whose grasp of English was never more than adequate, thought he understood the language only too well when it was being used to mock him.

"I her father," he said, hitching up his belt and coming forward in a slow, threatening lunge. "I ask whadda you want?"

"I've told you," the young man said pleasantly, and all at once Julie understood why the smile made him look familiar: the associate director of the Horace Judson Clarke House looked exactly like the ruddy-cheeked young scoutmaster on the Mark Eisner & Company calendar in the barber shop downstairs. "I understand you have recently purchased at auction some two hundred bundles of white kid gloves," Ben Ivey said. "I would very much like, Mr. Sarno, to talk with you about them."

Julie's father stopped moving. One hand continued to fumble nervously with his belt. The other came up to rub slowly across his lips. It was clear that he couldn't quite believe he had heard correctly. Julie didn't blame him. Many people had made fun of Biaggio Sarno for his crackbrained financial schemes which inevitably ended in disaster. Always, however, the mockery had been carefully concealed behind the big barber's back. Nobody had ever dared laugh at him to his face. Was it possible that this skinny kid with yellow hair had come here to do what people twice his size had thought it wiser not to attempt? If so, why? What satisfaction or profit could this total stranger get out of it?

Julie could tell that it was these questions, tumbling rapidly through a mind not very well equipped to deal with the unexpected, that gave her father his suddenly troubled look of indecision. She could also tell, from the way her sister suddenly drew in her breath, that Celia had seen the look and was angry with the young man who had brought it to her father's face. Celia Sarno loathed her background. She detested the place where she had been born and still lived. She resented the man she held responsible for what she was. But this hatred was a private matter. It was something between herself and her father. Nobody else had the right to dilute it. Least of all a stranger from the world beyond East Ninth Street, which Mr. Benjamin Franklin Ivey clearly was. Celia stepped between him and Biaggio Sarno.

"My father does not speak English very well," she said coldly, rolling her *r*'s just a little longer than usual in a way that Julie always thought about as her sister's Uptown voice. "I'm afraid he doesn't understand what you mean. Perhaps, if you explained to me—?"

"I'll be glad to," Mr. Ivey said, and the smile, rearranging itself on his face for the new speaker, seemed to grow even wider. "This would be Miss *Celia* Sarno I have the honor of addressing, wouldn't it?"

"You know a great deal about our family," Celia said. "I find that rather puzzling."

Julie gave her sister another quick look. When Celia used the word "rather" she was really reaching hard for the fancy touch. Why, Julie wondered, should her sister be so anxious to impress this Mr. Ivey?

"There's really nothing very puzzling about it," he said cheerfully. "I've been at the Clarke House for almost a year and, well, naturally, I've come to know quite a good deal about the families in the neighborhood. That's how I happened to learn, by the way, about your father buying these two hundred bundles of white kid gloves."

"What do you want to talk to him about them?" Celia said, and apparently she didn't like the sound of her own remark, because very quickly, so quickly that Julie knew her sister was flustered, Celia added, "I mean you said you'd come here to talk to my father about these gloves?"

"That's right," Mr. Ivey said. "I was wondering if he had any plans for disposing of them?"

Celia exchanged a quick glance with her father. Biaggio Sarno's flushed face grew a trifle darker. His English was good enough for him to grasp the significance of the young man's question.

"How do you mean?" Celia said. "Plans for disposing of them?"

"Well, I'd been given to understand that Mr. Sarno bought the gloves at a bankruptcy auction for speculative purposes," Mr. Ivey said. "He bought them in bulk, that is, with the intention of reselling in smaller quantities at a profit. That's correct, is it not?"

"Yes," Celia said.

"I was given to understand further that it was only after Mr. Sarno's purchase arrived at his home, when he'd already paid for

90

the two hundred bundles of gloves and couldn't possibly get his money back from the auctioneer, that he made his regrettable discovery."

Celia and her father exchanged another glance. She put her hand on his arm, a short touch of reassurance or warning, Julie couldn't figure which, as Celia turned back to Mr. Ivey.

"What regrettable discovery?" she said.

The young man in the doorway shoved the yellow hair up from his forehead in a gesture of surprise that pulled his eyes wide. Julie noticed for the first time that they were light blue.

"They did all turn out to be right-hand gloves," Mr. Ivey said, the surprise moving down into his voice, "did they not?"

Celia hesitated and then, squaring her shoulders just a trifle, she said defensively, "What about it?"

"Why, this about it, Miss Sarno. I gathered that making this discovery about his purchase was pretty distressing to your father, as indeed it would be to anybody, and in his, well, shall we say distress, in his distress I was given to understand he was seriously considering destroying all those two hundred bundles of right-hand kid gloves, which is why I came hurrying up here tonight."

"To help him do it?" Celia said acidly.

Mr. Ivey gave her a quick, startled look and then, as though the meaning of her words had just caught up with their sound, which had reached him first, he threw back his head, the way Julie had seen Art Acord do it in the movies when one of his cowboy pals made a joke, and laughed with shoulder-shaking delight.

"No, no," he cried. "Not to help him destroy them. I came up here to help your father get his money back and perhaps even make some of that profit he was hoping for."

Julie, staring at the young man in astonishment, saw out of the corner of her eye that her father and Celia were doing the same thing. They did not do it long, because Biaggio Sarno suddenly exploded in a series of hurried whispers to Celia, who nodded rapidly and whispered something back in his ear before she looked up again at Mr. Ivey.

"You've come to buy the gloves?" she said.

"No, I'm afraid I couldn't do that," he said, allowing the

laughter to simmer down into the smile which Julie, now that she no longer had to worry about why it made him look familiar, had time to note was one of the nicest she had ever seen. It made her feel good to watch Mr. Ivey. "For one thing," he said, "as the associate director of a settlement house I could hardly afford to buy two hundred bundles of gloves, and for another, even if I could afford to buy them, I'm afraid I wouldn't have much use for them. But I do know who would, which is why I'm here."

"You have a customer for the gloves?" Celia said.

Mr. Ivey, still smiling, shook his head, and the yellow hair came tumbling down again over his forehead. "Not quite," he said. "But I know where a customer, or rather several customers, can be found."

"Where?"

"Elevator operators," Mr. Ivey said.

"What?" Celia said, startled.

"Elevator operators," Mr. Ivey repeated, clearly pleased by the effect his words had created. "I understand, Miss Sarno, you are employed by a law firm somewhere uptown. I don't know the building you work in, but if it has an elevator or several elevators, you may have noticed that the men who operate them wear gloves. What you may *not* have noticed is that an elevator operator wears only one glove, on the hand with which he works the controls. I've made a few judicious phone calls to office and hotel supply houses, just to check my facts, and I find that they are not only correct, but almost any one of these supply houses, certainly the ones who sell uniforms to office buildings for the use of elevator operators, will be glad to buy as many right-hand gloves as they are offered. I jotted down the names and addresses of the two outfits which, I thought, offered the best prices." Mr. Ivey thrust a hand into the inner depths of his brown tweed jacket, clawed about in the breast pocket like a Tompkins Square Park sparrow scratching for seed, and came up with a slip of paper. Holding it out to Celia, he said, "There we are."

Celia took it slowly, read the few scrawled words with a small scowl, then looked up at Mr. Ivey. "This is really very nice of you, Mr. —?"

"Ivey. I, v, e, y. Not at all. It's my job to keep things running smoothly in the neighborhood serviced by the Clarke House, or at any rate as smoothly as I can help make them run, and it doesn't seem to me to be too broad an interpretation of my duties to see them as extending to the relief of a close neighbor who, through no fault of his own, seems to have got himself in a bit of a financial jam. If your father will ring up these people whose names are on that slip, or better still, if he drops around to see them tomorrow, I'm sure all will be well."

"I still want to say it's very nice of you to have done this," Celia said.

"All right, you may say so," Mr. Ivey said cheerfully. "And now, if you'll excuse me for this intrusion—"

His words trailed away like cigarette smoke as he turned toward the long hall that led to the door.

"It's no intrusion," Celia said. "We're very grateful to you, Mr. Ivey. I wish there was something we could do for you in exchange, something to show our appreciation."

"Well, as a matter of fact," the young man said, turning back, "there's one thing you *can* do for me. Or rather, it's something your father could do."

"What's that?" Celia said.

"We're adding a nature club to our other activities at the Clarke House," Mr. Ivey said. "I'd consider it a personal favor if you could induce Mr. Sarno to give your sister Julie permission to join."

5

The permission was granted. This was neither surprising nor puzzling. At least to Julie. To emerge from one of his financial schemes with a profit was the dream of Biaggio Sarno's life. In justice to her father Julie had to admit to herself that to achieve this dream he might have hesitated before selling his youngest daughter to a glue factory. Since this, however, exhausted the list of things at which Julie felt he would have drawn the line, giving his permission for her to join a nature club could hardly be described as a surprising concession. What she did find surprising, what puzzled Julie so much that she mentioned it to Celia, was why Mr. Ivey should have gone to so much trouble to obtain the concession.

"I don't agree that it's surprising, and I assure you it was no trouble at all," he said to Celia several weeks later when, at Mr. Ivey's invitation, Julie's older sister had come to the Clarke House one evening to see some of the Nature Club's work. "Is there anything surprising about your going in to take a letter when Frank Prohst rings for you?"

"Of course not," Celia said. "That's my job. It's what I get paid for doing."

"My job is associate director of a settlement house," Ben Ivey said. "I get paid for seeing to it that the activities of the settlement house function smoothly. Why should you be surprised merely because I do my job?"

"It's that word merely," Celia said. "What you did doesn't seem to be merely."

"In what way?"

"This Nature Club was not a part of the Clarke House's activities when you came to see us a few weeks ago," Celia said. "It wasn't even in existence. It was just an idea that Julie and her friend Katie Halloran had cooked up. Because they'd received a seed catalogue or something like that from one of those companies whose advertisements they're always answering. Two eleven-year-old kids wrote a letter, that's all."

"Not quite all," Ben Ivey said. "It was a letter that both Mr. Crispin and I thought had a great deal of merit. If you were in our shoes, I think you would have thought so, too. Stand in my shoes for a moment and consider. What is a settlement house? Answer: a business like any other. Why shouldn't it be run properly? A man who manufactures let's say widgets, such a man cannot be said to be running his business properly if all he does is sit back, wait for orders to come in, and then fills them. If he's doing his job properly, he should be spending at least part of his time in research, looking for new ways to make better and cheaper widgets, hunting for new places and markets where widgets can be sold.

"A director of a settlement house cannot be said to be running *his* business properly if all *he* does is sit back and watch his allocated funds running out, checking to make sure each area of activity gets the proper amount, so much for gymnasium activities, so much for music classes, so much for the boy scouts, so much for adult citizenship instruction, so much for janitorial services, and so on. A settlement house director worth his salt should be looking for *new* ways to spend money, *new* activities to improve the neighborhood in which his settlement house is located. The people uptown, the men and women who are on the board, the people who appropriate the money or have to go out and get it, the way to attract the attention of those people is not to run your settlement house within the budget they provide for you, but *outside* your budget.

"If they give you a hundred thousand dollars a year to spend, and you spend ninety-nine thousand nine hundred ninety-nine dollars and ninety-nine cents, they don't know you're alive. But if you spend one hundred thousand dollars and one cent, so that when they get together for one of their official meetings they're faced with a deficit and the problem of finding that extra cent to meet the deficit, they'll sit up and say what goes on down there on Avenue B? Who is this boy that's causing us all this trouble by not staying within his budget?

"If the boy who is causing them all this trouble can show that the extra one cent was spent on something the settlement house should have been doing long ago but never did because the man in charge had no imagination and was merely coasting along, if this boy can at the same time say in effect not only have I spent that extra cent over my budget in a proper fashion, but I serve notice on you here and now that I intend to spend many more extra cents on many more new activities, so that next year you're going to be presented with a much bigger deficit, and I don't care where you get the money for me, so long as you get it, because—" Ben Ivey paused and his thin features spread in the quick, boyish grin. "I can tell, Miss Sarno, from the way your eyes are wandering, that I've said too much."

"On the contrary," Celia said. "You haven't said enough." What her remark did to the expression on Ben Ivey's face caused Celia to laugh. "You remind me of something they say in our office about Mr. Ellentuch, our senior partner," she said. "He's a very fine lawyer, and quite old now, with a passion for thoroughness that sometimes gets a little out of control. He's so thorough that he can be, well, please don't think I'm rude, Mr. Ivey, but in our office they say with Mr. Ellentuch, you ask him what time it is, and next thing you know you're in bed with an elephant. Oh, gosh, I guess I *have* been rude."

"No, no," Mr. Ivey said. "I see your point. Here I am, gassing away about the philosophy of running a settlement house, and you, you're still surprised at my showing up in your home unexpectedly several weeks ago."

"Frankly, yes," Celia said.

"Well, you needn't be. The letter your kid sister and Katie

Halloran sent to Mr. Crispin was bumped along to me. Most things here at the Clarke House involving new activities come to me, and I could see at once that this was a good one. We've got home economics classes, current events clubs, basketball teams, first aid courses, all the standard items on the curriculum of any settlement house, but the one thing we haven't got, I saw right away, the one thing we *should* have in a slum area, is some activity devoted to helping the slum citizen make contact with what is so completely lacking in a slum, namely, God's green earth. After all, hasn't Wordsworth told us: *One impulse from a vernal wood may teach you more of man, of moral evil and of good, than all the sages can?*

"All this I saw in a flash, as soon as I read that letter cooked up by those two eleven-year-old girls, so I asked Mr. Crispin to answer the letter and set up a date for me to meet the girls. Late in the afternoon of the day the meeting was to take place, one of them, Katie Halloran, came into the Clarke House in quite a state of excitement and reported that Mr. Sarno was, well, she told a rather lurid story about what happened when she came into the barber shop with Mr. Crispin's letter, a story the details of which don't matter except that Katie did say your father had absolutely forbidden your sister Julie to join the club. This seemed to me unfortunate, particularly since Julie was one of the originators of the idea, and even though I'd been at the Clarke House for a year and had never met Mr. Sarno, I'd heard a good deal about him. From what I'd heard it seemed to me unlikely that he could be induced to change his mind merely by asking him, so I decided to do something concrete in the way of persuasion. The most concrete thing I could think of was to do something about the financial jam he'd got himself into with that purchase of gloves and about which so many jokes were being made on East Ninth Street, and well, you saw how it worked out, so I guess I've answered your question, haven't I?"

"Except for one point," Celia said.

"What's that?"

"How do you know my boss's name is Frank Prohst?"

Mr. Ivey looked startled. "Do I know that?" he said.

"A few minutes ago, when I told you I was surprised at your coming to see us," Celia said, "you asked *me* if there was anything surprising about *my* going in to take a letter when Frank Prohst rings for me. I can understand your learning from people here in the neighborhood that the local barber's oldest daughter works uptown in a law office, and I can even see how somebody might know and tell you the name of the firm she works for is Ellentuch, Prohst & Wadsworth. But how you could learn that my boss in the firm is named Frank Prohst, that's what I don't understand."

"Neither do I," Mr. Ivey said.

It was Celia's turn to look startled. "I beg your pardon?" she said.

Ben Ivey laughed. "I said I don't understand any more than you do how I picked up that particular bit of information, but it shows how much one *can* pick up without even being aware of the picking-up process if one keeps one's ears open, and even though I've been keeping mine open ever since you honored us by your arrival this evening, Miss Sarno, I have still not heard the nine words I've been hoping to hear."

Celia's eyes crinkled at the corners. "Nine words?" she said.

"I think they add up to nine," Mr. Ivey said. "Let's count and see." He held up his left hand and began ticking off the words on his fingers. "Mister, that's one. Ivey, that's two. Won't, is three. You, four. Come, five. To, six. Dinner, seven. Some, eight. Night, that's right, nine." He dropped his hand and grinned. "Mr. Ivey, won't you come to dinner some night?"

Speaking slowly, the crinkles at the corners of her eyes growing tighter, as though she were repeating a phrase in a foreign language she had learned phonetically but did not understand, Celia said, "Mr. Ivey—won't—you—come—to—dinner—some—night?"

"I certainly will, thank you," he said promptly. "What night would you suggest?"

Julie, who was standing nearby, pretending to be at work on her paste-up of the Large Tooth Poplar or Trembling Aspen page for the club's Leaf Book, saw Celia's face flush.

"Oh, I didn't mean—" She paused and tried again. "I mean I was merely repeating what you—" Celia paused once more and then, with a nervous smile, said, "Why do you want to come to our house to dinner?"

"If you've been living on settlement-house food for a year, Miss Sarno, you begin to think about a home-cooked meal the way Jason thought about the Golden Fleece. May I come tomorrow night?"

"Well," Celia said, scowling worriedly, "I'm afraid that's a little—"

"The following night?"

"Well—"

"The night after that?"

"I'll tell you what," Celia said. "I'll talk to my mother and then let you know."

"You won't forget, now?"

"No, of course not."

"Good," Mr. Ivey said. "I look forward to this with pleasure. It should be great fun."

Julie couldn't imagine why he would think so. After all, the first time he opened the Sarno front door Mr. Ivey had hardly walked into a block party. On the other hand, it was true that by the time he walked out, the people on whom he had dropped in so unexpectedly were in a more cheerful frame of mind than Julie could remember her family having enjoyed for years. Perhaps, she reflected as she set aside the Large Tooth Poplar or Trembling Aspen page and started to mount the sugar-maple leaves she and Katie Halloran had collected in Tompkins Square Park that afternoon, perhaps when Mr. Ivey observed that his second visit to the Sarno home should prove to be great fun he was merely reflecting confidence in his capacity to bring fun with him, no matter where he went, the way Luxor cabs brought luck. He certainly seemed to have brought it to the Horace Judson Clarke House.

Until Katie Halloran had been struck by the notion of starting a nature club and had induced her friend Julie to help compose the letter to Mr. Tyler Crispin, Julie's relationship with the Clarke House was not unlike her father's relationship with the bank on the Tenth Street corner of Avenue B: a convenience to be used with caution, when such use became necessary or desirable, but never to be completely trusted. Just as Mr. Sarno never went to the bank unless he could get nobody else to lend him the few dollars he needed to swing one of his financial schemes, so Julie had never gone to the Clarke House unless all other forms of entertainment suddenly failed her.

Under normal conditions the big brick-and-sandstone building, known in an area not particularly partial to the pronunciation of the letter *r* as the Clock House, was to Julie what it was to most kids on East Ninth Street: an outpost of the Uptown world planted in their midst, an oasis founded and operated by strangers for reasons never quite understood or trusted by their beneficiaries.

The people who ran the Clock House insisted they had no ulterior motives. It was true enough that they provided certain conveniences and amusements absolutely free of charge. But there was always a catch to it, a catch that somehow canceled out the fun. Sure, on Hallowe'en, if you came in off the street, you got a paper bag of fruit and cookies, and at Christmas you were handed a sack of hard candies that held their design all the time you sucked them, right down to the wafer thin end when they disintegrated on your tongue. Along with the goodies, however, you were forced to take a dreary lecture, illustrated with slides that turned even Julie's pretty tough stomach, on the importance of using a toothbrush at least twice a day. There was no doubt that you could come in at almost any hour for a game of basketball, but along with the thrill of sinking a foul shot you had to comply with Steve Shupka's rule that nobody could leave the locker room without taking a hot shower.

The arrival of Mr. Ivey changed all that. Nobody knew just how. You still had to pay for your basketball game by taking a shower and for your gumdrops by staring at the slides that depicted the horrors of dental caries, but, somehow, after Mr. Ivey showed up in the Clock House, taking a shower became a painless activity and the terrifying slides became the springboard for a whole series of jokes. Walking into the lobby from Avenue B stopped being for Julie an interval during which she had to drown out a small inner voice that warned her she was a fool to put herself within the grasp of these mysterious Uptowners and she still had time to turn and run. Even the smell of the disinfectant that went into the water with which the Clock House corridors were daily swabbed, an odor that had always tightened Julie's stomach with the sudden fear that she was walking into the nurse's office in P.S. 64 for another dose of the Schick test, even this odor became pleasant to Julie soon after the Nature Club under the leadership of Mr. Ivey became a regular part of her life.

The most impressive demonstration, however, of the yellow-haired young man's talent for spreading sunshine did not take place in the Clock House, where Mr. Ivey lived and worked and as a result had time to give his talent free rein, but in the Sarno family, which he had visited only once.

Julie was aware, of course, that much of the lasting effect of that visit was due to its financial result: the information Mr. Ivey had brought with him about elevator operators and their need for single gloves had proved accurate. As a result, Biaggio Sarno had not only recouped the money he had invested in the two hundred bundles of up-to-that-moment-useless white kid gloves but, for the first time in his hitherto disastrous financial career, the big immigrant from Naples had emerged from a venture with a profit. It was true that much of this profit had gone into replenishing his camouflaged witch-hazel bottle down in the barber shop. And it was equally true that Biaggio Sarno was spending more time somewhere uptown, apparently on the prowl for the raw material of a new financial killing, than he was spending on East Ninth Street cutting hair.

But at least the screaming fights with Celia when she came home from work had stopped. And in the three weeks since Julie had joined the Nature Club her father had hit her only twice, both assaults being in Julie's mind completely understandable since they had followed immediately after Cockeye Katie and her barbed tongue had crossed Biaggio Sarno's path.

All in all, Julie decided, soon after Celia issued her reluctant invitation, that Mr. Ivey was probably justified in feeling his second visit to the Sarnos should be, as he put it, great fun. By the time she went to meet Celia, on the day Mr. Ivey was due for dinner, Julie had reason to believe he was right.

"Papa hasn't come home yet," she said as soon as Celia kissed her. "He's been away all day. Somewhere uptown, I guess."

"Good," said Celia, and Julie was pleased with herself.

All the way to the trolley stop she had been turning over in her mind the various bits and pieces of the day's news, trying to choose from the many things that had happened on Ninth Street since her older sister had gone off to work in the morning the one thing that it would please Celia most to hear first, and it was obvious from the quick smile of relief on her older sister's face that Julie had chosen correctly.

"If only you knew how I've been worrying about him all day," Celia said, shaking her head as she set out briskly down Avenue B toward the Ninth Street corner. Julie, trotting along beside her, did know. Celia's screaming fights with her father may have stopped, but her contempt for Biaggio Sarno had not in any way diminished. Certainly not in any way that was reflected in Celia's voice when she mentioned their father in Julie's presence.

"All the things I've had on my mind about this darn dinner," Celia said, "I need only that, *him* ruining everything with his big drunken mouth."

Julie understood some of the things that were in Celia's mind about this darn dinner. Not all, but some, especially why to Celia it was a "darn" dinner.

The main reason was that the event, in its relation to the Sarno family, was not unlike the relation between Isaac Newton's head and the apple: a revolutionary encounter. Nothing like it had ever happened before. On East Ninth Street the consumption of food was a private rite. People did not eat dinner or anything else at other people's houses. They ate their meals in their own homes, with the members of their own families. Once in a while, when Julie and Katie were mounting butterflies or sorting out the day's collection of Tompkins Square Park rocks, Mrs. Halloran might give the girls a glass of milk or Mrs. Sarno would let each of them have a piece of fruit, depending on whose flat they were working in. But Julie had never eaten an entire meal at any table other than her own and nobody but she, her parents, and Celia had ever eaten a meal at the Sarno table.

Furthermore, the Sarno table was not what, to judge by the advertisements Julie had seen in magazines, was known in the Uptown world as a dinner table. It was a three feet by six feet rectangle, made of cheap pine, covered with worn blue and white checked oilcloth, which stood against the kitchen wall, taking up most of the floor space not given over to the sink, the stove, and the washtubs. On it, when the Sarnos were not eating, Julie did her homework, Mrs. Sarno did her ironing, Mr. Sarno did the primitive bookkeeping involved in his financial deals, and Celia laid out the dress patterns she was constantly clipping from newspapers with the intention of increasing her wardrobe.

When the Sarnos *were* eating, their four chairs took up so much more of the kitchen floor space that only a narrow lane of free space was left. Fortunately, this lane ran in a straight line between the stove and the table, so that Mrs. Sarno's task of conveying food from her pots to her family's plates was a simple one. That this task would not be simple with an additional mouth to feed was at the center, Julie knew, of Celia's worries about the evening.

"You put one more chair in that darn kitchen and there's no room to take even a deep breath," she said. "If we lived uptown, somewhere where they build houses for human beings not sardines, we'd be able to invite a guest into the house without—" Celia paused and, looking down on Julie, said sharply, "When did he go uptown?"

"I don't know, exactly," Julie said. "The barber shop was closed when I got home from school. Ma says—"

"You can skip what Ma says," Celia said. "When she isn't lying down on the floor to make a doormat out of herself so he can wipe his shoes on her, she's looking the other way not to see how he's boozing it up or chasing every slob in a skirt from here to Delancey Street. If he'd only get himself good and drunk somewhere uptown, and not come home until tomorrow or next year or better yet never—" Celia sighed and blew out her breath in a

sharp little hiss of annoyance. "But he won't. Since he got him off
the hook with those darn-fool gloves he thinks Mr. Ivey is J. P.
Morgan. He'll be here tonight, shooting off his great big drunken
mouth about buying the Brooklyn Bridge or something, and how
in God's name we're going to get five people around that table
in that darned kitchen is something I—"

"Celia."

"What?"

"I don't have to sit at the table," Julie said. "I mean, I could
eat earlier or later, and I could sort of, *you* know, help Ma carry
the stuff from the stove, so it wouldn't look—"

Celia stopped walking. "That's an idea," she said slowly, her
eyes crinkling as she examined the idea. "In that way we could—"
She paused and shook her head. "No," Celia said, moving on
more briskly. "Mr. Ivey is coming to eat with our family and
you're part of the family. If we're a little crowded, and he gets
himself squeezed a little, that's just too bad. He's the one who
wanted to come. He practically hit me over the head to get himself invited. So let him be squeezed a little. Besides, the way I've
worked it out, I think there'll be room enough. Did Ma cook
the chicken?"

"I think so," Julie said. "The house smelled like—"

"When doesn't it?" Celia said. "All I hope, I hope that disgusting Mrs. Halloran, for once, just once, I hope she isn't cooking that rotten cabbage of hers."

Celia's hope proved vain. The moment she shoved open the
heavy door, even before Julie could follow her sister into the
vestibule, the familiar odor wrapped itself around them like fog.

"Oh, God!" Celia groaned, rolling her eyes to heaven in disgust. "She's at it again!" She dipped down to peer into the letter
box. "Of course," Celia said, straightening up. "Empty. Naturally. What else?" She shoved open the vestibule door and started
up the stairs. "Some day I'll look in that darn box and there'll
be a letter addressed to Celia Sarno and it'll say under separate
cover we are sending you a magic carpet, our new special model
for people who are up to here and overflowing with living in
sewers. Just climb on and make a wish and the next thing you

know you'll find yourself living on Central Park West in an apartment with two showers, neighbors who don't cook cabbage, and a dining room, a real room to eat in, so when you invite somebody to dinner you don't have to eat in the kitchen and there's enough room so that you don't have to hope one member of your family will get drunk somewhere and not show up and crowd the others up against the—"

The bitter monologue stopped. It had carried Celia up the steps to the fourth floor, through the brown tin-sheathed door, and into the long dark kitchen passage. Julie, rising on her toes to peer around Celia and see what had stopped her older sister in her tracks, saw a boiled chicken sitting on a plate in the center of the oilcloth that covered the kitchen table.

"Ma!" Celia called.

Mrs. Sarno came out of the bedroom. She was tying a clean white apron over her black bombazine skirt. The two high tortoise-shell combs studded with bits of glass, which she always wore on ceremonial occasions, were tucked into her thick gray hair.

"Yes, Celia," she said. "I'm here."

Julie looked sharply at her mother. There was a note in Mrs. Sarno's voice her youngest daughter had never heard before.

Celia pointed at the boiled chicken. "What's that?"

Mrs. Sarno turned slowly, moving her whole body with great deliberation, like a big gun swiveling around on a battleship in the newsreels, and she stared at the chicken while her nimbly moving fingers fashioned from the ends of her apron strings a neat rosette. Julie had noticed before, of course, that the air of sardonic regality her mother had inherited from her northern Italian forebears deserted her only in the presence of her drunken husband, but even so Julie sensed there was something in her mother's exaggerated movements now that matched the odd note in her voice.

"To me it looks like a chicken," Mrs. Sarno said finally, and she swiveled back to face Celia. "What does it look like to you?"

Celia started to say something and then, apparently struck by the curious tone and manner that had struck Julie, she closed her mouth and gave her mother a long glance.

"Are you trying to drive me crazy?" Celia said finally. "Ma, it's almost half past six. Mr. Ivey will be here at seven-thirty. I told you when I went to work this morning—"

"You told me to cook a chicken," Mrs. Sarno said. "I cooked a chicken. What else, please?"

"What else?" Celia cried. "What good is a boiled chicken sitting there on a plate like that? Chicken *salad*. That's what I told you we're going to have. Not a boiled chicken. To make chicken salad you've got to boil the chicken first, sure, but any boob knows—"

"Any boob except your mother," Mrs. Sarno said. "I'm not a chicken-salad maker. I cook chicken the way my mother taught me. It was good enough for her children. It ought to be good enough for mine. If it isn't, if my children like chicken prepared in some other way, all right, they can prepare it themselves."

"That's fine. That's wonderful. That's just marvelous. My own mother, instead of helping me, she—she—" Celia's words seemed to get tangled in a series of choking gasps of rage as she slammed down on the table her purse and the armful of paper sacks with which she had come off the trolley car. She did it so hard that the chicken jumped. "Why can't something go right for a change?" she said. "Why does it always happen to me?"

"Because you're not what you are," Mrs. Sarno said, very calmly. "You're what you *think* you are. You're not a barber's daughter on Ninth Street with a job uptown to make money to live. No. You're a duchess, too good for Ninth Street, swimming around in crazy ideas like onions in a stew, ideas about palaces where you think you belong. You want to invite people to come here to eat? Good. Fine. You want to feed them what I know to make? Good. Fine. I'll make. You want to feed them like a duke's daughter? Sorry. Good-bye, duchess. You'll make it yourself."

Mrs. Sarno turned, marched back into the bedroom, and slammed the door. Celia glared at the door for several moments while Julie struggled with two emotions: sympathy for Celia, whose plans had gone awry, and a reluctant admiration for her mother, whose uncharacteristic stand and extraordinary articulateness somehow made sense to the uneasy Julie.

"I might have known I'd have to do it all myself, anyway," Celia said finally as she snatched up her purse. "Why don't I ever remember? Why do I always like a dumbbell think next time it's going to be different? Julie, sweetie, here, be a doll. Run down to Pechter's and get me a small bottle of sweet cream." She shoved the fifty-cent piece into Julie's hand and then said, "Wait." Julie waited while Celia poked among the paper bags she had dumped on the table, muttering hurriedly to herself as she pulled them open, peered in, and shoved them aside: "Tomatoes, biscuits, cottage cheese, mayonnaise, pineapple, ginger squares, where's the —? Darn it. Julie, also a bunch of chives. Okay?"

"Sure," Julie said. "Anything else?"

"No, sweet cream and the chives, that's all, and shake a leg, sweetie, will you? I don't know how I'll get it all done."

Pechter's did not have chives, and Julie had to go to three stores before she found one that did. By the time she got back, Celia had worked such a transformation in the dingy little kitchen that Julie stopped short at the end of the passage and stared. Celia, who was opening a small bottle of cherries at the sink, turned, saw the look on her kid sister's face, and her own tense scowl gave way to a quiet smile.

"Nice?" she said.

"Oh, Celia!" Julie breathed. "It's *beautiful!*"

The scuffed old oilcloth had vanished. The kitchen table was covered with an orange and yellow crepe paper tablecloth in the center of which stood a platter heaped high with a mound of chicken salad as big as a basketball. Around the edge of the platter, circling the chicken salad like a guard of honor, ran a necklace of bright-red tomato slices on each one of which sat a small lump of snow-white cottage cheese, each lump wearing, like a tiny green plume, a sprig of parsley. Ranked like squads of soldiers on both sides of the central platter were smaller platters on which rested, in cunningly arrayed patterns, little round white biscuits that Julie had never seen in the bakeries on Avenue C; rich brown squares of ginger cake sitting on slices of pineapple; rectangles of butter leaning against one another like dominoes; long slivers of raw carrot thrusting out like wheel spokes from a central hub in the form of a mound of green olives stuffed with bits of red pimiento; a glass pitcher of golden iced tea in which slices of lemon floated lazily; cardboard knives and forks, laid out like a display in the window of Mr. Slatzman's jewelry store on Avenue B, on one side of a pile of cardboard plates and, on the other side, folded trickily to support one another in an airy bridge, a line of orange and yellow paper napkins that matched the crepe paper tablecloth.

The whole thing reminded Julie so much of one of those colored advertisements in *The Saturday Evening Post* for Pillsbury's Flour or Heinz 57 Varieties or Dole Pineapple at which she and Katie Halloran liked to stare, that she felt there must be a coupon in the lower right-hand corner of the tablecloth which could be cut out, filled in, and mailed off for a catalogue.

"The sweet cream," Celia said. "Come on, quick."

"Gee," Julie said, coming toward the sink. "I never knew you could—"

"Neither did I," Celia said with a laugh. "Until I tried it." She set down the bottle of cherries, snatched the paper bag from Julie, tore it open, saw the look on her sister's face, and laughed again. "It *is* nice, isn't it?" Celia said. She gave Julie a quick kiss and then, before her sister could reply, Celia dragged the bottle of sweet cream from the torn bag and, snatching the open bottle of cherries, said, "There's no time to whip the darn cream, but I think this will be all right. Bring the chives, sweetie."

Julie brought the chives and stood at one side, watching with awe as Celia poured a trickle of cream over each square of ginger cake, deftly set a bright red maraschino cherry in the center of each little white pool, disposed of the empty cream and cherry bottles, and snatched up the chives. Celia was sprinkling them over the little hills of cottage cheese that, mounted on their tomato platforms, guarded the mound of chicken salad, when the door at the end of the passage banged open. Even before she turned, Julie knew it was her father. She could smell the whiskey.

"I bringa the guest!" he shouted jovially, and then Julie saw Mr. Ivey. He was smiling his pleasant, wholesome, boy-scout-calendar smile as the big barber drew him forward into the kitchen, chanting, "The guest, the guest, I bringa the guest!"

"Good evening," Mr. Ivey said to Celia. "Your father was good enough to drop in at the Clarke House and pick me up—" His words stopped. Julie, following Mr. Ivey's glance, saw that he was staring at the beautiful table. "Good God!" he said. "What's that?"

Julie, who was puzzled by the tone of Mr. Ivey's voice, saw that it had brought two red spots to Celia's cheeks.

"We're rather crowded for space," she said, and Julie recognized the danger signal of the rolled *r*'s and that "rather." "Instead of a sit-down dinner," Celia said, "I thought we'd have a buffet."

Mr. Ivey gave the table a long look, during which the pleasant, wholesome, boy-scout-calendar smile changed slowly to a dry, sardonic grin. Then he looked down at something in his hands. Rising on her toes to peer around her father, Julie saw that Mr. Ivey was holding a small, straw-covered wine flask.

"I wish I'd known that," he said. "I wouldn't have wasted my money on this stuff."

"I beg your pardon?" Celia said, bearing down so hard on the last *r* that the word emerged as a growl.

Mr. Ivey shook his head slowly, as though amazed at something that had just crossed his mind. "I was looking forward to, oh, I don't know, cannelloni, chicken cacciatore, a paillard, at least a plate of spaghetti. A bottle of Chianti, I thought, would be just right."

He stepped up to the table and, very delicately, as though he were lowering the final piece into place in one of Mr. Slatzman's window displays, Mr. Ivey set the bottle of wine beside the platter of ginger squares covered with cream and maraschino cherries. He stepped back, cocked his head to one side, folded his arms across his chest, and stared at the table for several moments through the sardonic grin.

"My God!" he said. "What a sight!"

"That's what you came for, isn't it?"

The grin slid from Mr. Ivey's thin face. It was replaced by a look of surprise as, turning to Celia, he repeated her words: "I beg your pardon?"

"I said that's what you came for, isn't it?" Celia said bitterly. "To see a sight? As though you were going to a zoo or a side show to look at the animals and freaks? We don't live in cages, but it's the same thing, isn't it? These filthy tenements? Full of dumb Italian immigrants? Who don't know how to serve an American meal? A bunch of filthy spaghetti eaters? Something for a person like you to stare at, and make fun of, and feel superior to? Well, go ahead and stare all you want, Mr. Ivey. I hope you have as good a time as you expected when you asked me to invite you to this side show!"

It was only after she heard the slam of the door at the end of the passage that Julie realized what had happened. Mr. Ivey seemed to realize it at the same time.

"Miss Sarno!" he cried, starting down the passage after her. "Miss Sarno, please! I didn't mean—!"

The second slam of the door stopped Julie from learning what it was Mr. Ivey had not meant.

"He wants something from us."

Julie turned. Her mother was standing in the bedroom doorway.

"What did you say?" Mr. Sarno said in Italian.

"That young man with the smile that comes so quick, and the yellow hair that makes him look so innocent," his wife said. Mrs. Sarno shook her head slowly and then, as though the movement had loosened one of the rhinestone-studded combs, she tapped the piece of tall tortoise shell back into a safer anchorage in her thick gray hair. "I don't trust him," Mrs. Sarno said. "He wants something from us."

"From us?" her husband said in Italian. "What can a man like that, an American, a college graduate, what can he want from a barber, an immigrant?"

"I don't know," Mrs. Sarno said. "But the first time he came here it was the same as now. When I saw him my corns started to hurt."

"You and your God-damn corns," the big barber said.

"My corns never lie," his wife said. "They hurt when you bought those umbrellas, and they hurt when you bought the gloves—"

"How about when I *sold* the gloves?" Biaggio Sarno said sarcastically. "At a nice profit? Because this Mr. Ivey told me where to take them? Did your corns hurt then?"

"They hurt now," Mrs. Sarno said. "It's always a warning. This young man with the smile and the yellow hair wants something from us."

"You stupid rice eater," Biaggio Sarno said. He strode to the table, snatched up the Chianti bottle, and began to claw at the tin foil around the cork. "You frightened rice-eating fool," Julie's father snarled at her mother. "What can a man like that want from people like us?"

6

The following Sunday Julie found out.

What she never found out was what happened between the moment when Celia, chased by Mr. Ivey, banged out of the Sarno flat and the moment, several hours later, when Celia came tiptoeing into their bedroom. Julie sat up on her side of the big brass bed she shared with her older sister.

"Celia?"

"Ssshhh," Celia whispered. "Go to sleep."

Julie's head dropped back on the pillow. She had turned off

the wall gas bracket over the bureau before getting into bed, but the window was open to the warm night. The faint yellow glow from the lamppost on the Avenue B corner, four stories below, came oozing up softly through the bars of the fire escape outside the window, penciling on the bedroom wall a pattern of long, thin vertical stripes through which Celia, slipping out of her clothes, moved like a dancer on the Loew's Delancey stage in one of those musical numbers involving a trellis in the moonlight. Julie waited until Celia eased herself down onto the bed beside her and the spring stopped squeaking.

"Celia."

"I told you to ssshhh," Celia said softly.

"I just wanted to ask—"

"Not now," Celia said. She turned on her side, so that her back was to Julie, and said, "Good night, baby."

"Good night," Julie said and, as she did every night, added, "Sleep tight."

Celia didn't say what *she* said every night, "I will." Not for a while, anyway. Julie was just beginning to doze off when her sister's whispering voice cut through the delicious fuzziness into which she was sinking: "Julie?"

"What?"

"You awake?"

"Yes."

"What are you doing Sunday? I mean the Nature Club?"

"We're going on a hike to the Palisades," Julie said. "To get flint."

"To get what?"

"Flint," Julie said. "We're making flint and steel sets. The steel is easy. Mr. Ivey got three old files from the Clarke House janitor and broke them in small pieces so we each have a piece. But flint is hard to get. Except over there, the Palisades, they're building this bridge over the Hudson River, and Mr. Ivey says any place where they're blasting rock, like they're blasting over there for this bridge, any place like that there's plenty of flint lying around, he says. Pieces from the blasting. Why do you ask?"

"I'm going with you," Celia said.

She did, too, much to the disgust of Katie Halloran.

"I thought this was a flint-hunting expedition," she said on Sunday morning when Julie arrived at the Clock House with her older sister. "Not a necking party."

"A what?" Julie said, startled. "What the heck you talking about?"

Cockeye Katie, poking at the piece of dirty adhesive tape on the nosepiece of her glasses, looked at her friend witheringly. "What do you *think* I'm talking about?" she said. "The price of polly seeds? Just take a look at those two, dopey."

Julie turned to take a look. On the sidewalk at the other side of the Clock House front door, right next to Jennie Javitz, who was repacking the lunch in her shoebox, and Chink Lezinski, who was fixing the elastic in her bloomers, Celia Sarno and Mr. Ivey were bent over a small notebook in which the associate director of the Clock House was making swift little check marks with a pencil as he talked to Julie's older sister.

"They're checking the attendance," Julie said. "Who's here and who didn't show up yet. What about it?"

"Boy, oh, boy, why don't you grow up?" said Cockeye Katie, who was exactly nine days older than Julie. "Since when does it take two people to check the attendance for a club that's got eleven members?"

Julie took another look at Mr. Ivey and her sister. "She's not checking the attendance with him," she said irritably. "I mean the two of them aren't—"

"No?" Katie said. "Then what *is* Celia doing?"

It was, Julie realized uneasily, difficult to describe. Celia was just standing there watching Mr. Ivey make his little check marks, and yet the word "just" seemed wrong. Celia, who was doing absolutely nothing, seemed to be more actively engaged than Mr. Ivey, who was doing it all.

"She's stuck on this guy, dopey," Katie said, and the leering little wink with which she accompanied this startling statement changed her slightly demented look to a demoniacal grimace. "And from the way it looks to me, it looks to me like he's stuck on her, too," Katie added. "All the flint we're going to pick up on this hike, you'll be able to carry it back home in your locket, dopey, you wait and see."

Julie, who could scarcely do otherwise, did wait. But all she saw, as the club, two abreast, with Celia and Mr. Ivey in the lead, set out for the Astor Place subway station, was that Katie Halloran's remarks had spoiled the day for her even before it had begun.

It was as though Katie's words were a lens through which Julie, who could not get them out of her head, was now forced to look at her sister. From the moment four nights ago when Celia, lying in her bed beside Julie, had announced she was coming along on the hike, Julie had been so delighted that it had not occurred to her even to wonder, much less ask, why her sister should do such an astonishing thing. Even during her visit to the Nature Club at which Mr. Ivey had wangled the invitation to dinner, Celia Sarno had not been able to conceal completely the fact that her interest in the club's activities was no more than a polite pretense, which she was going through because she did not want to hurt the feelings of either her kid sister, whom she adored, or the leader of her kid sister's club, who was adored by its members. None of this, so far as Julie could see, had changed.

All the way over to Astor Place, all the way uptown in the subway to Dyckman Street, all the way across the Hudson on the ferry, and then all the way on foot up the Jersey shore to Alpine, as she watched her sister through the lens of Cockeye Katie's remarks, it seemed to the troubled Julie that Celia was still pretending. Maybe the other kids didn't know, and maybe Mr. Ivey didn't, but Julie could tell. When Mr. Ivey plucked a sumac leaf from a bush, or picked up a limestone sliver, and everybody gathered around to hear him point out the distinguishing features of the specimen, Julie could tell, because she knew Celia so well, that Celia was not as interested in the impromptu lecture as she pretended to be.

This would have been as all right with Julie today as it had been the night Celia visited the club in the Clock House. It was not a condition of Julie's love for her sister that Celia love all the things Julie loved. It had always been a joke between them, for example, that Celia couldn't stand the sight of all those catalogues for which Julie and Katie were constantly clipping and sending away coupons. What made it not all right today, what this morning changed the joke of Celia's boredom with leaves and rocks to something vaguely unpleasant, were the words Katie Halloran had uttered on the sidewalk in front of the Clock House.

Five hours later, on a pebbly scrap of Jersey shore, where the club had camped for lunch, Cockeye Katie uttered a few more.

"Get a load of those two," she said, nodding toward Celia Sarno and Mr. Ivey as she peeled a hard-boiled egg.

"Oh, shut up," Julie said.

"Me?" Katie said in amazement. "What did *I* say?"

"Just shut up," Julie said, shoving things around in her shoebox as though hunting for something to eat.

"All I said, I said get a load of those two," Cockeye Katie said. "We came all the way to the Palisades to find flint, but instead of flint what we get, we get a free show—"

"If you don't shut up!" Julie hissed, her face hot, her eyes fixed on the shoebox at her feet.

"Shut up about what?" Katie said innocently as she took a bite of egg. "All I said—"

"They can hear you!"

Katie's eyes, distorted by the lenses sitting crookedly on her nose, spread wide. She turned to look down the beach toward the rock on which Celia Sarno and Mr. Ivey were squatted side by side, munching sandwiches and talking quietly.

"Them?" Katie said with mock astonishment. "Why, Julie, dopey, those two love birds, they couldn't hear—"

"Ssshhh, you crazy! They've heard you! He's—he's—"

Julie, who was even more ashamed than she was frightened, couldn't get the word out. Mr. Ivey and Celia, apparently having indeed heard, had turned to look toward Julie and Katie. Then, as Julie watched with mounting horror, Mr. Ivey and Celia turned back toward each other, laughed conspiratorially, rose, dusted their backsides, and came sauntering toward Julie and Katie.

"I hope you two don't mind our breaking in on your little

chat," Mr. Ivey said through his boyish smile. "But Celia and I wanted to give you a piece of good news." Julie's numbed mind, noting the significant fact that Mr. Ivey had referred to Celia by her first name, recorded the even more significant fact that he was holding her sister's hand. Gently, dipping down over Julie and Katie like a courtier in the movies greeting a queen, Mr. Ivey said, "Celia and I both feel that you two should be the first to know, because if it hadn't been for you two, why, the Nature Club would never have come into existence and, well, Celia and I would never have met. That's true, isn't it?"

Julie couldn't even nod, but Katie bobbed her head up and down vigorously.

"Absolutely, Mr. Ivey," she said and then, with an insolent little poke at the tape on her nose, Katie said sweetly, "What's the good news, sir?"

"Why, I simply want to announce," Mr. Ivey said, beaming at Celia as he lifted her hand and gently placed his other one on top of it, "that Celia has consented to take over my duties as director of the Nature Club."

7

It was possible, of course, that there existed somewhere in the world institutions of which it could be said, at the age of under six months, that they were drenched in tradition. If so, Julie Sarno, at the age of eleven years, had never heard of them. It was even possible that some of these institutions, in addition to being at that tender age already drenched in tradition, also happened to be children's clubs located in slum-area settlement houses. Julie Sarno, at whatever age she happened to be when later she looked back on the incident, doubted it.

She saw no reason at the age of eleven, therefore, to think her reaction was odd when she found herself startled on learning that Mr. Ivey intended not only to make a formal ceremony of handing over the Nature Club leadership to Celia, but he apparently brought to his concept of the ceremony approximately the same point of view that the British Crown applied to the durbars at which were invested new viceroys of India.

"We could do this without any fuss at all," he said to the eleven members of the Nature Club when the girls assembled in the Clock House for the special meeting he had called for the day following the flint-hunting expedition to the Palisades. "I could simply have asked Miss Sarno to come to this meeting tonight, and after showing her the work we've been doing, I could have said okay, it's all yours, from here on in you're the leader of this club, and that would have been that. There certainly would be nothing wrong with such a crude and cavalier handling of the matter. There certainly is plenty of precedent for doing it that way, not only in most settlement houses, but particularly here in this one. That's how it's been done here at the Clarke House for years. Somebody new comes in for one reason or another to lead the Adult Citizenship Group or Troop 224 of the Boy Scouts, and the old leader says pretty much what I've just indicated. He introduces the new leader to the group or the club or the troop, wishes them all luck, and then disappears out of their lives, off on some new business of his own. I don't want to do it that way with the Nature Club because, well—"

Mr. Ivey paused to send his glance around the room, taking his time, touching with the smile that Julie found so attractive and so disturbing each of the eleven small faces turned up to his.

"I don't want to do it that way with the Nature Club," Mr. Ivey said quietly, "because I don't want to disappear out of your lives."

He slipped off the table on one corner of which he had been

sitting casually, his long thin fingers laced around his crossed knees, and he walked slowly to the window. He stood there, his back turned to the eleven small girls, and Julie for one was glad Mr. Ivey had turned it. There was a lump in her throat.

"No, I don't want to disappear out of your lives," he said slowly, addressing the dusk that, beyond the window, was settling on Tompkins Square Park. "These last few months, this comparatively small space of time that has elapsed since the Nature Club came into being, it has meant a great deal to me. Much more than until this moment even I have realized. I've been here at the Clarke House a little more than a year, and while I have no complaints, while I can honestly say I've enjoyed every minute of it, I would be less than honest if I didn't also say that it was not until this club came into active being, not until you and I began to meet regularly here in this room, with our leaves and rocks and insects and flowers, not until we began to put together out of our common interest in God's green earth the intangible bond that an inadequate language calls friendship—"

Mr. Ivey paused again, and he slipped his hands into his pants pockets, and his narrow shoulders hunched forward slightly as, turning back from the window and lifting his eyes to some invisible point on the wall over the door, very quietly, his voice growing more resonant, he said, "*Come forth into the light of things, let nature be your teacher.*"

His voice stopped, but his glance remained fixed on the invisible point over the door. Finally, with a small, embarrassed shrug, and an even smaller, embarrassed smile, Mr. Ivey turned back to the eleven small girls.

"A great poet wrote that," he said. "A man named William Wordsworth, and since he was an English poet, perhaps I should take back what I just said about the inadequacy of our language, because Wordsworth's words, which I have just quoted, are not only adequate but a beautifully precise expression of what I feel, what being here in this room with you these past months has meant to me, and why, now that other considerations and pressures make it necessary for me to hand over the torch, as it were, of active leadership of this club, I don't want the handing-over process to be unworthy of the happiness this club has given me and the happiness which, since as I have said I have no intention of disappearing out of your lives, I intend to keep on drawing from what we have built here together."

Mr. Ivey's hands, coming up out of his pants pockets with the abruptness of a couple of startled birds, met in front of his face with a crackling slap that brought Julie and her fellow Nature Club members up straight in their chairs.

"Now, here's what I had in mind," Mr. Ivey said. "I thought we'd lay out a little, well, a little ceremony you might call it. Nothing very pretentious or complicated, but something that Miss Sarno will be pleased by, something that she'll remember, something that we'll *all* remember, so that no matter how far this club goes, and I for one think it will go beyond anything that's been seen in the Clarke House before, none of you will forget that what got it on its way, what helped set the club on its feet, was the hand of a skinny little chap with yellow hair and a rumpled tweed coat who did indeed come forth out of Cleveland into the light of things and had enough sense to let nature, in the form of eleven East Ninth Street little girls, be his teacher."

This time, when Mr. Ivey paused, Julie thought her swelling heart would burst and her brimming eyes would overflow and the lump in her throat would explode in a shameful cascade of noisy sobs. Perhaps Mr. Ivey thought the same thing, because he gave her a soothing smile, and perhaps he thought the other ten little girls were in similar danger, because he took the time to turn the soothing little smile on all of them, one at a time, the way an efficient fireman, armed with a hose, might turn it on eleven bonfires, calmly, methodically, one at a time.

"Now for the ceremony," Mr. Ivey said, pulling a piece of paper from his pocket. "I've got it all worked out, and with one or two practice sessions, say tonight and tomorrow night, I don't see why on the big night it shouldn't all work out beautifully."

Julie didn't see why, either, until on the big night, just as Mr. Ivey gave the signal, and Celia rose from her chair at the back of the room and started forward, the meeting-room door banged open. Celia stopped and turned. So did Mr. Ivey and the eleven Nature Club members. In the doorway stood Mr. Tyler Crispin.

"I trust," he said in what seemed to Julie a funny voice, "I'm not interrupting anything?"

Julie, who for no reason that made sense to her had turned at once from the tall, slender, handsome old man with close-cropped white hair in the doorway to the tall, slender, handsome young man with unruly yellow hair at the front of the room, saw something that caused the breath to catch in her throat: Mr. Ivey frowned, and it was as though in Julie's mind the two wall calendars in her father's shop had moved toward each other, meeting in the center of the mirror facing the barber chair, the face of Torquemada in the Catholic Aid Society calendar and the face of the scoutmaster in the Mark Eisner & Company calendar merging into one another to create a completely new face, new and disquieting and irresistible.

"Not at all," the new face said. "You're not interrupting a thing."

"Good," said Mr. Crispin. "Then I'm sure you won't object to my coming in."

The white-haired man came in, moving with a springiness that Julie had never before seen Mr. Crispin display, and he closed the door. It seemed to Julie that he made more noise doing this than was necessary.

"I won't object to your coming in, no," Mr. Ivey said. "I will, however, ask, if I may, why you have come here tonight?"

"I happen to be the director of the Horace Judson Clarke House," Mr. Crispin said. "Do you consider that a sufficient answer?"

Mr. Ivey hesitated, sent a short glance at Celia, then turned back to Mr. Crispin.

"No," Mr. Ivey said, "I'm afraid I don't consider it a sufficient answer."

"I don't think you're afraid," Mr. Crispin said. "If you were, you wouldn't try to pull this stunt behind my back."

"What stunt?"

"Let's dispense with the little deflecting questions and the looks of injured innocence," Mr. Crispin said. "You know damned well what stunt, Ivey, and—"

"I'd like to call your attention, sir, to the fact that there are children present."

"And I'd like to call yours to the fact that their presence is my responsibility, not yours."

"I'm going to have to disagree with that," Mr. Ivey said.

"You can disagree all you damn please. It won't do you a bit of—"

"I warn you again, sir, that that sort of language in the presence of impressionable young girls—"

"Ivey, I'm too old a bird to be thrown off by smoke screens, and if you haven't managed to learn that during your year here, you're not nearly so smart as you and those people in Cleveland who recommended you for the job think you are, so you'd better learn it now and just answer my question: what's going on here tonight?"

"Nothing," Mr. Ivey said.

"Nothing, eh?" Mr. Crispin turned to Celia. "Who are you, miss?"

Mr. Ivey stepped forward, placing himself firmly as a shield between Celia and the director.

"I said nothing is going on here," Mr. Ivey said to Mr. Crispin. "Nothing that would interest you."

"Your grasp of what does or does not interest me is clearly as inadequate as your grasp of the ease with which I can be bamboozled. Are you going to tell me what's going on here, Ivey, or shall I turn for my information to these impressionable young girls for whose delicate ears you have, I am interested to learn, such a deep concern."

Mr. Ivey sent another glance at Celia and then, as the glance moved on to sweep the faces of the eleven watching girls, Julie saw another surprising thing. The frown left Mr. Ivey's face and, at once, in Julie's mind, the two faces from the wall calendars in her father's barber shop seemed to separate, so that the completely new face vanished, and once again she was looking at the boyishly smiling Mr. Ivey she had known.

"When I said nothing is going on, sir," he said, "I meant only that nothing important is going on. We're just inducting a new leader for the Nature Club, that's all."

"That's all?" Mr. Crispin said.

"That's all," Mr. Ivey said.

"Just inducting a new leader?"

"That's right, just inducting a new leader."

"What's the matter with the old leader?"

"Why, nothing," Mr. Ivey said.

"Then why does this club need a new one?"

"No special reason."

"The old leader tired, perhaps?"

"Certainly not."

"The work too difficult for the old leader?"

"Of course not."

"Or perhaps the old leader is bored with the Nature Club?"

"That's a lot of—"

"Watch your language, Ivey. Remember the tender ears of these impressionable young girls."

"I wish *you'd* remember, Mr. Crispin, that this form of crude third degree in the presence of children does not help with our overall disciplinary problem. If you have any questions to ask me—"

"I have one, Ivey, but you don't seem to have any desire to answer it. If the present leader of the Nature Club is not tired, and the work is not too difficult for him, and he's not bored with the club's activities, why does the club need a new leader?"

"It doesn't."

Mr. Crispin's eyebrows went up in an exaggerated pantomime of astonishment. "Indeed?" he said. "If the club doesn't need a new leader, why are you inducting one?"

"Miss Sarno volunteered her services."

The director took a step to the right, so he could look around Mr. Ivey at Celia. "You are Miss Sarno?" he said.

Mr. Ivey also took a step to the right, cutting off Mr. Crispin's view. "She has absolutely nothing to do with this," Mr. Ivey said.

Mr. Crispin's white head came whipping back to Mr. Ivey. "Of the many remarkable statements you have uttered in this room tonight," the director said, "I consider that the most remarkable."

Mr. Ivey's face did the most incredible thing Julie had ever seen it do. Mr. Ivey's face flushed bright-red. "I meant—"

"I know what you meant," Mr. Crispin said. "More clearly than you could possibly have imagined I would know when you embarked on this little scheme. Now let me tell you what *I* mean, I as director of the Horace Judson Clarke House. Are you listening?"

"Yes, sir," Mr. Ivey said.

"The director of the Horace Judson Clarke House is perfectly satisfied with the present leadership of the Nature Club," Mr. Crispin said. "If you are bored with the work, or if you find it is too much for you, or if for any other reason you would like to drop it, just let me know and I will have Steve Shupka take over."

"I spoke to Steve, and—"

"You did, eh?"

"Well, I mean—"

"I told you I know what you mean, Ivey, so let's not waste any more time in *that* direction. Did you speak to anybody else on the staff?"

"No, sir."

"Good. If I were you, I wouldn't. To get back to the leadership of this club. If you want to drop it—"

"I don't, sir. I've told you that. It's just that Miss Sarno volunteered her services. She doesn't expect to be paid for her work. She volunteered. Not only because her younger sister is a member of the club, but also because she's interested in the work. The study of nature is a lifelong passion with Miss Sarno. She's very anxious to—"

"Since you seem determined to prevent me from talking to Miss Sarno directly, you can after I leave tell her that while I sympathize with her anxieties, and few things would please me more than to provide an outlet for her passion, I am afraid I cannot indulge either my sympathy or pleasures at the expense of a reflection on my capacities as director of this institution. We have what I consider a perfectly adequate staff, all salaried. To accept unpaid volunteer workers would be an admission that my staff is not adequate. I refuse to make such an admission. Is that clear?"

"Yes, sir," Mr. Ivey said. "Perfectly clear."

8

Julie wondered if it was. It certainly was not clear to her.

"What was *that* all about?" she said to Katie Halloran on the sidewalk after the meeting.

"I don't know." Cockeye Katie looked thoughtful as she stared down the street. Following Katie's glance, Julie saw her sister Celia and Mr. Ivey going into Bloom's Bakery, which remained open every night until after the last show at Loew's Avenue B for the convenience of theatre patrons who liked a cup of coffee and a piece of Mrs. Bloom's apple strudel before going home to bed. Cockeye Katie said, "Why don't you ask your sister Celia?"

"How would she know?" Julie said.

"Maybe Mr. Ivey told her."

Julie thought that over for a couple of moments, then shook her head. "No," she said, "I don't think so."

"Why not?" Cockeye Katie said.

"If Celia knew, she wouldn't have been surprised when Mr. Crispin came in," Julie said. "Celia was just as surprised as the rest of us."

"I'm not so sure," Katie said.

Neither was Julie, but she couldn't tell anybody, not even her best friend, what was really troubling her: a feeling that was so new to Julie that she hated herself for even thinking about it, a feeling that had first crossed her mind the previous Sunday, during the flint-hunting expedition to the Palisades, an uneasy suspicion that, for the first time in their lives, Celia was concealing something from her.

"Well, *I'm* sure," Julie said irritably. "I ought to know my own sister."

"Ought, sure," Katie said. "But *do* you?"

"Aah, you make me sick."

Cockeye Katie put one hand on her hip, extending the small finger in a burlesqued imitation of elegance, and with the thumb and forefinger of her other hand she pantomimed a monocle through which she ogled Julie as she said through a malicious grin, "Did you know before tonight that the study of nature is a lifelong passion with Celia? That she volunteered to take over Mr. Ivey's job because she's so anxious to—?"

"Why don't you shut up?"

"Why should I?" Cockeye Katie said. "Who started this club, anyway?"

"So what do you want? A medal?"

"I want to know what's going on."

So did Julie. Hours later, when Celia came tiptoeing into their bedroom, Julie decided Cockeye Katie had been right. There was only one way to find out.

"Celia?"

"My God, are you still awake?"

"I can't sleep."

"Well, you better. It's late."

"Celia?"

"What?"

"Did you really volunteer?"

There was a pause, during which Julie could suddenly hear the ticking of the alarm clock on the icebox out in the kitchen.

"Well," Celia said finally, "yes, sort of."

"Because of what he said? That the study of nature is a lifelong passion with you? And you wanted—?"

Unexpectedly, Celia giggled. "You know better than that," she said. "God, when he gets wound up, he either starts quoting that darned Wordsworth or he drags out pieces of his father's old sermons. The *words* he uses! My lifelong passion for nature! God! I can't tell a rock from a leaf, practically."

"Then why'd you want to become head of the club?"

"I didn't really," Celia said, and she paused, holding up the wire hanger on which she had been about to put the dress she had just taken off. "I mean," she said, and Celia paused again. In the light from the street Julie could see that Celia was scowling, as though trying to remember something. Then she shrugged and began slipping the dress over the hanger. "I don't mean that I *didn't* want to become head of the club," she said. "He said it would help him a lot if I did—"

"Who?"

"Ben."

"Oh," Julie said, and the uneasy feeling that Celia was concealing something from her grew just a little stronger and just a little more uncomfortable. She had not known until this moment that her sister referred to Mr. Ivey as Ben.

"Oh, what?" Celia said sharply.

"Nothing," Julie said.

"Then stop sounding like it's something," Celia said. "What happened, Ben said it would help him a lot if I stepped in and took over the club, because it would leave him free to get on with some other things he wanted to do, and the club was taking up the time he needed for these other things, so I said sure. That's all there's to it. I didn't know that old boob Mr. Crispin would have any objections, and Ben didn't, either. But since he does, Crispin, I guess I'm not going to be running the club after all, which is probably just as well, since I'd be rotten at it anyway, all those rocks and leaves and bugs, for God's sakes, the thing you and that Cockeye Katie and your other nutty pals think is fun, my God, well, it's over, so now will you please stop

126

the cross-examination and go to sleep, because that's the end of the whole foolish business."

It wasn't, of course, but neither Julie nor, she supposed, Celia had any way of knowing that at the time. The next day, as Julie and Katie were coming home from school, they met Mr. Ivey. He was walking up Ninth Street from Avenue C toward the Avenue B corner, moving with those long swift strides, his arms pumping up and down, which Julie had come to recognize as characteristic of him and which always made her think of a man running inside his skin. From the way his face brightened when he saw them, Julie thought for a moment that Mr. Ivey had been waiting for them, but this seemed so silly that she dismissed it from her mind.

"Say, look, you two," he said. "I just remembered something Celia happened to mention the other day. She said you've never been to a Broadway movie. Is that true?"

Julie was so startled by the question that she found herself temporarily incapable of putting together the words of a reply, but Cockeye Katie was never startled. She certainly was never at a loss for a reply or anything else that involved words.

"Julie, it's true," she said. "But me, not. I been twice, Mr. Ivey. Once the Hippodrome, my father took me, I forget the name but Lew Cody was in it, and the other time the Capitol, my mother took me, *Ben Hur*."

"They've got this talkie now," Mr. Ivey said. "I'm quite anxious to see it. People on the screen actually talking. Would you two girls like to go with me?"

"Say!" Cockeye Katie said, and she undoubtedly said a good deal more, monosyllabic comments not being her forte, but Julie didn't hear any of it. She didn't even hear her own words of acceptance and thanks, although she must have uttered them. The fact was, however, that between the moment when Mr. Ivey issued his surprising invitation and the moment two days later, on Saturday afternoon, when the social worker came to fetch the two girls, Julie had to make a special effort to hear anything.

She was locked away in the soundproof chamber of her own emotions. The prospect of paying a visit to the mysterious world known as Uptown was something that had crossed her mind many times, just as the prospect of sailing west to the Indies had undoubtedly crossed the mind of Columbus many times. Until Mr. Ivey issued his invitation, however, the journey had been to Julie just that, a prospect, something to think about at idle moments, a glowing but shapeless event floating about in that timeless haze known as the future, so that, for all the excitement the event was capable of arousing in her mind, it nonetheless had no reality.

Now, however, it had become intensely real, just as Columbus' prospect must have become real with the assurance that the necessary money was being placed at his disposal, and Julie found the contemplation of the reality a little frightening. At one moment she would be raking through all the daily reports her ambassadress had brought her during the months Celia had been working uptown, wondering excitedly which bits and pieces of life in the new world she would encounter on her first visit, and the next moment Julie was wondering desperately how she could get out of the invitation. When Mr. Ivey finally did arrive to pick her up there was one awful moment when Julie, perhaps like Columbus just before he set foot on the *Santa Maria,* wanted to turn and run. The fact that she didn't was probably due as much to Katie Halloran's ceaseless chatter as to Mr. Ivey's casual manner about the whole thing.

"Instead of going across town on the Tenth Street trolley and then uptown in the subway," he said as they walked away from the barber shop, "I thought in this nice weather it would be fun to travel in a way that would not interfere with our vision."

Even if Julie had been capable of absorbing his words, she could not possibly have understood what they meant. When, at the Avenue A corner, Mr. Ivey stopped and raised his hand to something or somebody in the distance and Julie, wondering vaguely what he was doing, saw a white and silver vehicle come surging toward them, and all at once the meaning of Mr. Ivey's words reached her, she felt as though her knees had suddenly been filled with hot soup.

From then on, from the moment Mr. Ivey helped her in and she sat down on the squishy leather and Julie accepted the incredible fact that she was actually riding in a Luxor cab, she became conscious of only two things: a burning sensation in her eyes, as though sand had been flung into them, and her own voice, as though coming from a phonograph record on which the needle was caught in a groove, shrieking inside at her, over and over again, "There's something you must remember! There! There! There! Look at that, fast, before you forget!"

She never forgot. Julie did remember, clearly, for the rest of her life, as though, with no attempt at coherence, in response to the shrieking inward voice that drove her burning eyes this way and that, her mind had recorded a series of indelible snapshots.

Julie remembered that all the people looked taller; and everybody seemed to be on the verge of breaking into a run; and the warm October sun, coming in through the open top of the taxi, caused the leather of the seat to grow hot and give off a smell that made her stomach quiver with nausea. Julie never forgot that the name of the movie was *The Jazz Singer*; and the seats were so soft and big that she had to sit on her knees to see the screen; and there was a little tin box on the back of the seat in front of her out of which, when Mr. Ivey inserted a nickel and turned the knob, came a round bar of chocolate. She remembered that, when Al Jolson moved his lips and the sound of words came from the screen, her heart jumped the way it did when her father slapped her; and when they came out into the street there were so many more people on the sidewalk than there had been when they went in that she was afraid of being crushed; and the feeling of disappointment when Mr. Ivey raised his hand again and, instead of a Luxor cab, what drew up at the curb was an ordinary yellow taxi, the kind you saw every day on Avenue B; and the feeling as the cab turned into Ninth Street, and she realized it was all over, that she wanted to cry.

Julie never forgot any of that, but what she remembered most clearly, what that night after she went to bed she found herself turning over and over in her mind more often than any of the snapshots her mind had recorded, was what Mr. Ivey said as the yellow cab crossed Avenue A and headed toward the Avenue B corner.

"Did you have a good time, girls?" he said.

"Yes, sir," Katie said. "Thank you very much, Mr. Ivey."

Julie made an attempt to say the same thing, and she must have succeeded, not only because of her mother's training in politeness, but also because Mr. Ivey smiled and nodded and then he said, "We could have lots of good times like this if I remain as head of the Nature Club."

Julie didn't know what to say to this, but Cockeye Katie, as usual, had no such difficulty.

"*If* you remain?" she said.

"Mmm-hmm," Mr. Ivey said, and he chuckled, as though the look of sudden concern on Katie's face amused him. "Oh, I *want* to remain, and I have every *intention* of remaining, but one never knows in this world," Mr. Ivey said. "Things happen over which one doesn't always have the control one would like to have. You were both present the other night when Mr. Crispin—"

Mr. Ivey paused, and the smile sank into his face like spilled soup into a tablecloth as he stared earnestly first into Katie's eyes and then into Julie's.

"Suppose," he said quietly, "suppose Mr. Crispin were to do more than just come barging into our meeting room and make a scene. Suppose he fixed things in such a way that it was up to the members of the club to vote on who they'd like to have as their leader, and suppose the choice was between Mr. Crispin and me." Mr. Ivey paused again and then, quietly, he said, "How would you girls vote? For which one, Katie?"

"I would vote for you, Mr. Ivey," Cockeye Katie said firmly, as though she were answering one of Mrs. Koenig's questions in compound fractions, an answer about which she had no doubts because she had looked it up in the back of the arithmetic book before coming to school.

"Thank you," Mr. Ivey said with a new kind of smile. "And you, Julie?"

Julie hesitated, not because she couldn't decide on an answer, but because there was something about Mr. Ivey's new kind of smile that made her feel ashamed for him. Katie poked her with an elbow.

"You, sir," Julie said quickly.

"You really would vote for me?" Mr. Ivey said, as though the news had taken him by surprise. "Both of you?"

"Absolutely," Katie said.

She poked Julie again.

"Yes, sir," Julie said hastily.

"Well, then," Mr. Ivey said as the taxi pulled up in front of the barber shop, "I guess Ben Ivey doesn't have anything to worry about."

As a guesser, Julie was to learn during the years that followed, Ben Ivey had few equals. That first time, however, he guessed wrong.

Julie began to suspect as much two days later when, passing the Clock House on her way to meet Celia at the trolley stop, Mr. Tyler Crispin suddenly materialized in front of her. There was no other way to describe it. Julie had been walking along, her eyes fixed on the pavement, avoiding the glances of passers-by to whom she might have to speak, piling up in her mind, one on top of the other, the pleasant moments of anticipation, fashioning as she always did the stepladder of happiness that led to the day's bright moment, the moment when Celia stepped out of the trolley, and suddenly the ladder was kicked out from under her.

"Julie," a strange voice said, "I wonder if I could speak to you for a moment?"

Julie looked up from the mental wreckage and, astonished, saw that she was facing Mr. Crispin. For a puzzled moment she did not understand why his appearance reminded her of the way Mr. Ivey had looked several days ago when the yellow-haired social worker had intercepted her and Katie on their way home from school. Then Julie remembered her odd feeling that Mr. Ivey had been waiting for them, and she had the feeling again: Mr. Crispin must have been waiting for her. He had the look of a man who far in advance had worked out a problem in timing and was now pleased by the way his calculations had come off.

"Sure," Julie said, because there was nothing else to say. She had never in her life exchanged a word with the director of the settlement house. That the dignified, white-haired Uptowner should be so anxious to exchange words with *her* that he would lurk behind the Clock House front door, peering out until she came by so he could step into her path, was a notion for which she had no reaction except disbelief. Yet there he was, right smack in front of her, smiling that Uptown smile that always made Julie feel a little nervous. Then she remembered the ladder of happiness Mr. Crispin had shattered, and she said, "I mean, sir, I'm just going to meet my sister at the trolley—"

"Will she be carrying anything?"

"Huh?"

"If you should be a few minutes late, or if you should miss her entirely—?"

"No, I couldn't," Julie said quickly. "No, no. Celia expects me. Every day I—"

"I know you do. I merely mean that if you *should* be late, not that you will be, since what I want to talk with you about won't take but a moment, but if you *should* be just a mite tardy, it won't mean your sister won't be able to carry home something you were supposed to help her carry, will it?"

"Well," Julie said cautiously, "I don't think so." What did this curious old man think Celia brought her every day? Cobblestones? The book of matches from the restaurant in which Celia had eaten lunch, or the stamp from a foreign envelope that had been received in the Ellentuch, Prohst & Wadsworth offices, or any of the many other souvenirs Celia brought home to her kid sister from the Uptown world—did Mr. Crispin really think Julie went to meet Celia every day to help her *carry* these things? Julie said, "It's just that my sister expects me to meet her, and if I'm not there she might think—"

"She won't get a chance to think anything if you're there to meet her on time, and I'm sure you will be if we just pop right in and get our little talk over with, shall we?"

It was hardly a question, because Mr. Crispin, without waiting for an answer, took Julie's arm and, gently but firmly, led her up the three sandstone steps, shoved open the large double doors, steered her across the white marble vestibule, past Steve Shupka's check-in board, and through the brown door on which, in gold leaf, was painted the word "Director."

"Ladies and gentlemen," Mr. Crispin said. "I would like you to meet my friend, Miss Julietta Sarno."

Julie's surprise, which for the past moments had been circling nervously around the irrational but comparatively simple fact that the director of the Horace Judson Clarke House should want to see her at all, now exploded into so many fragments of astonishment that her mind began to make snatching darts in all directions, like a player trying to recover a dropped armful of tennis balls.

Since when had she become, to a man she had believed until this moment was unaware of her existence, "my friend"? How had Mr. Crispin learned that Julie's name, which nobody ever used, was actually Julietta? Why had she never suspected that this room, of which she had never before seen anything but the forbidding closed door with the single golden word painted on it, looked like the secret hideaway of the Chinese smugglers' chieftain in the Jack Mulhall serial about the San Francisco waterfront that she and Katie Halloran were following at the American Theatre on Third Street? And who were these "ladies and gentlemen"?

"Don't be frightened, little girl," one of them, a woman in a black frying-pan hat, said with a smile. "We won't bite you."

The others laughed in a manner that they obviously considered reassuring, because, in the wake of the sounds directed at Julie, they directed small congratulatory nods at one another, as though complimenting themselves on the speed with which they had struck the right tone in a difficult situation.

"We certainly won't," Mr. Crispin said. "Here, Julietta, you sit here."

He didn't exactly shove her into the straight-backed golden oak chair, which was the only thing in the room that matched the outside of the closed door. Yet Julie had the feeling that any

attempt to sit elsewhere would not only have been contested vigorously but would have earned her some of those bites about
which the lady with the frying-pan hat had been so reassuring.
While Mr. Crispin moved toward the high-backed chair behind
the big glass-topped desk, both of which were made of rich dark
wood eroded by carvings of monstrous serpents writhing symmet-
rically around tiny coolies pulling rickshaws laden with plump little mandarins, Julie sat up straight and worriedly examined the
"ladies and gentlemen."

There were eight of them, five male and three female, not
counting Mr. Crispin, and they all had his Uptown look.

There was absolutely nothing wrong or spectacular about their
clothes: dark dresses with high necks; dark suits with white collars.
They were simply the kind of clothes nobody on East Ninth Street
wore. There was absolutely nothing wrong or threatening about
the way they sat in the carved chairs that obviously were supporting pieces of the "set" dominated by Mr. Crispin's desk: the ladies
with both feet planted firmly on the oriental carpet and fingers
interlaced on the sensible black purses resting on their laps; the
gentlemen with legs crossed and arms folded across their chests. It
was simply that no eight citizens of Ninth Street had ever sat
like that in one room. There was nothing wrong or memorable
about their faces: clean-shaven jowls on the men, faint mustaches
on the women. They simply looked like the etching on the wall
in Mrs. Koenig's classroom called: "The Jury."

"Perhaps, Julietta, before we begin," Mr. Crispin said with a
smile that Julie thought he had copied from the grinning Chinese
face that dominated the complicated bronze inkwell on his desk,
"I'd better explain that these ladies and gentlemen are all members of the Board of Governors of the Horace Judson Clarke
House. They really run this institution, not in the sense that they
supervise the day-to-day functions, but in the sense that they
select the director who is answerable to them for the performance
of those day-to-day functions, and they provide the wherewithal
that makes the performance of those day-to-day functions possible.
In other words, they are the real, how shall I put it so that you will

134

comprehend, yes, I know, they are the real *bosses* of the Clarke House. Do you understand, Julietta?"

"Yes, sir," said Julie, who understood nothing but sensed that Mr. Crispin was talking not so much to her as across her head to the Uptown ladies and gentlemen in the room, a fact that was even more puzzling than the way he kept calling her Julietta, since Mr. Crispin had obviously been with these people in this room before he went bounding out to Avenue B to grab Julie, so why hadn't he told them then whatever it was he was trying to tell them now? Julie said, "Please, Mr. Crispin, could you ask me whatever you want to ask me? My sister Celia—"

"Of course, my dear," said Mr. Crispin, and he sent the oriental smile across her head toward the fingers-laced, arms-folded Uptowners sitting in a semicircle around Julie's golden oak chair which, she suddenly realized, must have been brought in from Steve Shupka's office for this occasion. "Julietta has an older sister named Celia whom she meets every evening at the trolley stop when Celia comes home from work."

"How sweet!" said the lady with the frying-pan hat. "What a wonderfully sweet gesture!"

Julie was bewildered. Sweet was a word she had always associated with things you ate or drank, and while she wasn't too sure about the word gesture, she had always thought it was something you did with your hand or arm.

"I promised Julietta that we would not make her late for her regular meeting with her sister," Mr. Crispin said. "So perhaps I'd better begin." The eight heads nodded, and the eight faces took on small smiles that involved nothing but the eight sets of lips, and Julie's stomach tightened with apprehension. "We understand, Julietta," Mr. Crispin said, "or perhaps I should say that I understand, yes, that's better, Julietta, I understand that you are quite friendly with our associate director, Mr. Ivey. Is that correct?"

Julie stared at him. Was *this* what Mr. Crispin had dragged her in off the street to ask?

"Julietta," the director said gently, "I asked a question."

135

"Yes, sir," Julie said quickly. "I—we—"

"You needn't be afraid, my dear," Mr. Crispin said even more gently. "Nobody is going to harm you."

"Yes, sir," said Julie, wondering what was the matter with him.

"Yes, sir, what?" Mr. Crispin said. "That you're friendly with Mr. Ivey?"

"Well—"

"You're not going to retract, are you? You just did admit you're friendly with him, didn't you?"

"Well, friendly, yes, sure," Julie said. "I mean Mr. Ivey, he's the head of the Nature Club, and I'm a member—"

"Please don't confuse the issue, Julietta. We know Mr. Ivey is the head of the Nature Club and we know you're a member. What we want to find out is whether or not you and Mr. Ivey are friendly?"

"Why?"

The smile, which had never looked as though it had a very convincing hold on Mr. Crispin's face, now lost its grip.

"Julietta," he said. "You want to get to that trolley car to meet your sister, and we want to get the answers to some simple questions. Both ends will be achieved much more quickly, I assure you, my dear, if you let me ask the questions. May I?" Julie nodded and Mr. Crispin said, "Are you or are you not friendly with Mr. Ivey?"

"I think so, yes."

"You think so? Don't you know?"

"Well, friendly, it's a word—"

"Julietta, I must insist—"

"Mr. Crispin."

Julie turned toward the new voice. It belonged to the woman in the frying-pan hat.

Mr. Crispin said, "Yes, Mrs. Webster?"

"May I take over for a moment?"

"Of course," the director said.

"Julietta," the woman said as the small smile dug in around her lips for what was clearly going to be a major effort at ingratiation, "I think you're a little afraid of us. Is that true?"

"Well, no, not exactly," Julie said. "It's just that—"

"That what?" Mrs. Webster said.

"Well, my real name, what everybody calls me, they call me Julie."

A trickle of low, controlled laughter, not unlike the sound of potatoes rolling across a table, swept through the room. Mrs. Webster contributed her share to it.

"All right, Julie," she said. "I don't blame you for being put off. Julie is a much nicer name than Julietta. If I call you Julie, will you answer my questions?" Julie nodded. "Good," Mrs. Webster said. "My first question is: what do you understand by the word friendly?"

"It's like, well," Julie said, "it's like me and Katie Halloran."

"Katie who?"

"Halloran. Some people call her Cockeye Katie, the kids mostly, on account of her glasses. She wears glasses, but her father is a policeman. She lives upstairs, over us, Katie and her mother and father, and she's my best friend. We go to school together and we, well, she tells me things and I tell her things and, *you* know, she's my *friend*."

"Of course I know," Mrs. Webster said. "That's exactly what I also mean by the word friend. Would you say that your relationship to Mr. Ivey is similar to your relationship with Katie Halloran?"

Julie stared at the woman in astonishment. "Me and Mr. Ivey like me and Katie?"

"Yes," Mrs. Webster said.

"Oh, no!" Julie said.

"Just a minute!" Mr. Crispin's voice, rapping out the three words like buckshot pinging against a window, caused Julie to jump on the hard chair. He said, "You just said—!"

"*Mr. Crispin!*"

He swung a quick, worried glance at Mrs. Webster, and then sank back against the carved serpents and coolies crawling across the back of his high chair.

"Sorry," the director muttered.

"Now, Julie," Mrs. Webster said. "You say your relationship

with Mr. Ivey is not the same as your relationship with Katie Halloran. Very well. Would you say that your relationship with Mr. Ivey is in any way different from your relationship with any other—wait, I know. Do you belong to any other clubs at the Clarke House?"

"No, ma'am."

Mrs. Webster nibbled thoughtfully at her lip without affecting the let's-be-buddies smile.

"Teachers, Edna," the bald man on her right said in a low voice. "Schoolteachers."

Mrs. Webster's nibbling stopped. Her face brightened. "Thank you, Paul," she said to the bald man, and then, to Julie, "What is your teacher's name? In school, I mean?"

"Mrs. Koenig," Julie said.

"Do you like her?"

"Yes," said Julie, who frequently wished, especially on Fridays, when the weekly arithmetic test was given, that Mrs. Koenig would drop dead.

"Would you say that your relationship with Mr. Ivey is in any way different from your relationship with Mrs. Koenig?"

"Oh, yes."

"In what way?"

"Well, Mr. Ivey doesn't give us tests."

The rattle of controlled laughter swept through the room again.

"I can see where that would be quite a big difference," Mrs. Webster said, and for the first time it seemed to Julie that the woman was really smiling, from the inside, the way real people smiled. "If I understand you correctly, then, Julie, you feel about Mr. Ivey more friendly than you do to Mrs. Koenig, but not as friendly as you do to Katie Halloran. Is that correct?"

"Yes, ma'am."

"Could you tell us, Julie, how much more friendly you feel toward Mr. Ivey than toward Mrs. Koenig?"

Julie hesitated. "Well—"

Mr. Crispin leaned forward again. "You invited him to your house for dinner, didn't you?"

"No, I didn't."

"That's a lie!"

"It is not!"

"I happen to know he was there!"

"*Mr. Crispin!*"

The director, his face flushed, sank back against the serpents and coolies. "Sorry," he mumbled to Mrs. Webster.

"I should think you would be!" she said coldly and then, with a new and not-quite-so-nice-to-look-at smile, she turned back to Julie. "I don't think Mr. Crispin meant to call you a liar. He meant only that he has evidence that Mr. Ivey did go to your house for dinner—"

"Sure he did, but I didn't invite him," Julie said indignantly. "He invited himself."

"He *what?*" Mrs. Webster said.

"He invited himself!"

"You see?" Mr. Crispin said, his voice rising in triumph. "What did I tell you, ladies and gentlemen?"

"We know what you told us," the bald man said dryly. "We're gathered to hear what this child has to tell us."

"Thank you, Paul," Mrs. Webster said.

"Sorry," Mr. Crispin said.

"Julie," Mrs. Webster said.

"Yes, ma'am," Julie said.

"You say Mr. Ivey invited himself to your house to dinner. I wonder if you could tell us about that?"

Julie did, starting slowly and awkwardly, but when she began to sense that she had their complete attention, that they were really interested in what she had to say, she found not only that the words came more smoothly but also that she enjoyed uttering them.

"Now, then," said Mrs. Webster. "Are there any other occasions when Mr. Ivey forced his attentions on you and your family?"

"Forced his attentions?"

"You know, invited himself along to be with you or—?"

"He took us to a movie last Saturday. To Broadway, a talking picture, Al Jolson."

"Your whole family?"

"No, just me and Katie."

Mr. Crispin's thin body came forward once more. "Just the two of you?"

"Me and Katie, yes."

"Just you two little girls?"

"Katie isn't little, and me, I'm—"

"I withdraw my reference to size. Just you two girls went with Mr. Ivey?"

"I said me and Katie, that's right."

"Did he do anything unusual?"

"What?"

"How did you go to this movie?"

"How did we go? We went. Mr. Ivey took us."

"I mean what sort of vehicle, what method of transportation, how did you—?"

"Oh," Julie said. "A taxi."

"Where did Mr. Ivey sit?"

"Where did Mr. Ivey—? In the taxi, with us."

"I mean where in the taxi?"

"On the seat. In the middle. Katie at one side and me in the other."

"Did he try any funny stuff?"

"*Mr. Crispin!*"

Julie stared from the red-faced Mrs. Webster to the red-faced director and then back at Mrs. Webster. The red, Julie decided, did nothing for Mr. Crispin's dried old crepe-paper face, but it made Mrs. Webster look more like a person who might live on East Ninth Street.

"I would like to remind you," she said icily, "that I and the other members of the board consented to this method of inquiry only on condition that the utmost tact be used."

"All I'm trying to do," Mr. Crispin said, "is get at the facts."

"In order to get at them," Mrs. Webster snapped, "I see no reason for compounding in the mind of a child what may already be an irreparably damaging emotional shock."

"Sorry," Mr. Crispin said.

"Please prove that you are by refraining from further interruptions," Mrs. Webster said, and she turned back to Julie. "When you were in the taxi with Mr. Ivey—"

"Or in the theatre, Edna," the bald man said quietly.

"Thank you, Paul," Mrs. Webster said and, to Julie, "When you were in the taxi with Mr. Ivey and then when you were in the theatre with him, did he do anything that you thought was unusual?"

"Unusual?" Julie said.

"Odd? Curious?"

"Familiar, Edna," the bald man said even more quietly.

"Thank you, Paul," Mrs. Webster said. "Familiar, Julie? Did he do anything familiar?"

"Familiar?" Julie said.

"Did he put his arm around you, perhaps?" Mrs. Webster said. "Or—?"

Julie never heard the rest of Mrs. Webster's question. Looking around from face to face, wondering what these Uptowners wanted her to tell them, her swinging glance stopped on the window back of Mr. Crispin's head. Framed in it, moving across the pane of glass in the direction of Ninth Street, Julie saw her sister Celia's profile. She didn't see it very long, because Celia's profile was moving fast, but it was long enough for Julie to see that Celia was angry, and Julie didn't blame her. For the first time since Celia had gone to work at Ellentuch, Prohst & Wadsworth, Julie had failed to meet her at the trolley stop. With a cry of dismay, Julie pushed herself off the golden oak chair and ran out of the room. On her way across the white marble vestibule she saw Steve Shupka, who was thumbtacking some additions to his check-in board, look up and she heard him call to her, but Julie didn't stop. She kept right on going until, at the Ninth Street corner, she caught up with Celia.

"Gee, I'm sorry," Julie said breathlessly. "That crazy Mr. Crispin, I was coming to meet you, and he jumps out in front of me, and he grabs me, and next thing I know—"

"Julie," Celia said, "what's wrong with Ben?"

"With Ben?" For several moments, hearing the surprise in her own voice, Julie found it difficult to grasp what was apparently the incredible fact: Celia had not missed her at the trolley stop! Julie said, "You mean Mr. Ivey?"

"Of course I mean Mr. Ivey," Celia said. "How many Bens do you know?"

"What about him?"

Celia stopped hurrying along the sidewalk just long enough to give her kid sister a suspicious glance. "Are you trying to be funny?"

"Me?" Julie said, and then, worriedly, "Celia, what's the matter? What happened?"

Her worried tone seemed to erase the suspicion from Celia's face.

"How should I know?" she said irritably. "I've been uptown all day, working." She resumed her swift movement down Ninth Street and Julie hastily fell in beside her. Celia said, "How does he feel?"

"Who?" Julie said.

Celia, stopping again, said angrily, "Julie, are you trying to drive me crazy?"

"I'm not doing anything," Julie said, fighting back the sudden tears. "I was going to meet you, the way I do every day, and you jump on me like I—"

"Oh, God!" Celia said, addressing the early-evening sky, and then she gave Julie's shoulder a swift little pat of reassurance. "Don't bawl, please."

"I'm not bawling!"

"Good," Celia said. She took Julie's hand and again started down the street. "The reason I sound like this, and I'm sorry, but the reason is Ben called me this afternoon at the office and he said he had to see me right away. I asked what about, but he said he couldn't tell me on the phone, and with Mr. Prohst and everybody else around, I couldn't do much talking, either, so I said I'd see him when I came home and he said fine, he'd meet me at the house."

"You mean *our* house?"

"That's what he said. He'd be waiting for me at home. He sounded sick to me. Sort of, oh, I don't know. He just sounded sick. That's why I asked you what's the matter with him."

"I don't know," Julie said. "I haven't seen him."

"You mean he's not in the house now? Waiting for me?"

"He wasn't there a little while ago, Celia. When I went to meet you. Ma was there, and Katie was there before, right after we got back from school, the arithmetic test for tomorrow, we studied a while, but when I left to get you, Celia, nobody was in the house except Ma, and she didn't say anything about—"

A sharp rattling sound caused Julie's words to stop. She turned. They had reached the barber shop. Inside, tapping a coin on the glass with one hand and beckoning them toward him with the other, was Mr. Ivey.

"For God's sake," Celia said. "What in the world—?"

Julie didn't hear the rest. Celia was hurrying into the barber shop. Julie followed. Mr. Ivey, who had pulled the door open for them, shoved it closed and turned to put his shoulders to it, sinking back against the jamb with a little tired plop.

"Ben," Celia said, "you look awful."

"No, no," he said, "I'm fine."

It didn't seem to Julie that anybody who looked as white as that could be fine.

"What are you doing here?" Celia said.

"Waiting for you," Mr. Ivey said and, as Celia turned to look into the store, he added, "Nobody's here. Your father went out a little while ago."

"Where did he go?" Celia said.

"Oh, I don't know," Mr. Ivey said impatiently. "What difference does it make? I'm trying to—" He paused and drew a deep breath and said quietly, "I'm sorry. I'm afraid I'm being rude as well as irrational. Maybe I'd better—" He paused again, and he put his hand up to his forehead, and then he said, "I think I'd better sit down."

He moved toward the barber chair and Celia moved with him, bending over him slightly but not touching him, as though she

143

were poised to catch him if he fell. He didn't, but getting into the chair seemed to take a lot out of him. He leaned back against the black leather headrest, breathing heavily, and closed his eyes.

"Ben, you're sick," Celia said. "I knew it when you called this afternoon. I could tell from the sound of your voice on the phone. You'd better—"

"No, no, no," he said, rolling his head from side to side on the little padded square of black leather. "I'm all right, I tell you."

Celia put her hand to his forehead and said sharply, "All *right?* My God, you're on fire! Julie, run get Dr. Zuckerberg! Come on, Ben, let's go upstairs! You can't stay here like this! You'll—"

"Will you please, please, *please* stop acting like a hysterical woman?" he snapped. "*Julie!*" Julie, on her way to the door, stopped. "Stay right here!" Ben Ivey ordered. "I thought I was among friends," he said bitterly, his eyes closed tight, one fist rubbing back and forth across his forehead. "I seem to have landed instead in a nest of idiots. Between your father and his insane commercial schemes—"

"What's my father got to do with the way you look and feel and the way you're acting?" Celia said. "Either crazy or close to it, if you ask me."

"I'm not asking you a damned thing. I called you this afternoon because I wanted to *tell* you something, but you were too damned busy taking dictation from that Mr. Frank Prohst to—"

"He's my *boss*, for heaven's sake! I'm his secretary! I can't leave the office in the middle of the afternoon just because somebody calls up and says come on! I came as quickly as I could. Now that I'm here, instead of screaming and insulting everybody, you could at least tell me what it's all about!"

"My neck is what it's all about! That son of a bitch Crispin has gone to the Board of Governors, that's what he's done! He's accused me of plotting behind his back to destroy him so I can move in and take over the Clarke House as director!"

"Isn't that what you want?"

Mr. Ivey's eyes, coming open, reminded Julie of a pair of window shades snapping up on their rollers.

"Do you believe that's what I want?" he said to Celia.

"Well, plotting and destroying, no," Celia said uncomfortably. "Those are, you know, that's terrible language. But when you asked me to take over the Nature Club because you had other things you wanted to do, I assumed—"

"That I wanted free time to *plot* and *destroy* Tyler Crispin?"

"Oh, Ben," Celia said, "will you stop putting words in my mouth? All I said was—"

"That you believe what that bastard Crispin is going to tell the Board of Governors. That when they call on you to give your side of the story—"

"Me?" Celia said. "When they call on me for what side of what story?"

"Why do you suppose I telephoned you at the office this afternoon? Because I enjoy playing with Mr. Bell's little invention? They've scheduled this meeting for tonight. *Crispin's* scheduled it. And God knows what he's *already* told them, if he's been able to round them all up on such short notice from their various brokerage houses and banks and offices and wherever else members of settlement house boards of governors spend their time when they're not summoned to crucify the innocent victims of a terrified, worthless, vindictive, pooped-out old *status quo* boob like Tyler Crispin. My only chance is to have you go in and tell the truth."

"The truth about what?"

"The Nature Club. That you volunteered to—"

"Ben, you know I didn't volunteer."

It seemed to Julie that Mr. Ivey's thin face grew thinner as he stared at Celia Sarno for several long, silent moments.

"Do I?" Mr. Ivey said finally. "Perhaps you wouldn't mind refreshing my recollection on what did happen? Go ahead, Celia. Tell me *your* version. I'm all ears. You have my complete, total, and undivided attention."

"Oh, for heaven's sake, you and that tone of voice. There's no version. There's just the truth. You told me first, that night you came to dinner and I ran out and you chased me, you told me you needed help, and then on Sunday, that time we went to the Palisades, you said if I come in and take over the club it would be just the help you needed, so I said sure, if that's what you want—"

"Isn't that volunteering?" Mr. Ivey said. "What do you call that, if you don't call it volunteering?"

"All right, Ben, all right," Celia said. "I call it volunteering."

"Do you? Or are you just saying it because that's what you think I want you to say?"

"*Think* you want me to say? You've just practically *told* me that's what you want me to say!"

"You know, Celia, the more I contemplate his offspring, the more I begin to understand the mental processes of that great financial genius, Biaggio Sarno."

"Now what has my *father* got to do with your battle with Mr. Crispin for control of the Clarke House?"

"There is no battle, Celia. There is an attempt on the part of Crispin to ruin my character, and get rid of me because he feels I'm a threat to his long-entrenched position. There is no question of controlling the Clarke House, since that is done by the Board of Governors. And even if there *were* a battle, which there isn't, and even if it *was* a question of control, which it is not, it wouldn't be *my* battle or *my* attempt at control, but Crispin's. So there, in one innocent statement, you have made three major errors, any one of which is in itself sufficient to blacken the character of a perfectly innocent man. Very few people could achieve so much by saying so little, but it surely is not surprising that one of those few should be the daughter of a man who is firmly convinced that the way to make John D. Rockefeller turn green with envy is to buy a carload of shovels without handles."

"Ben," Celia said. "For God's sweet sake, what *are* you talking about?"

"Your father, who has been driving me out of my mind all the time I've been here waiting for you."

"Shovels without handles?" Celia said.

"Surely you wouldn't expect a man who buys two hundred bundles of white kid gloves, all of them right-handed, to buy a carload of shovels *with* handles?"

"Ben, I can't *stand* this! Unless you start making sense, I'm going to—"

"I can't stand it, either," Mr. Ivey said. His voice suddenly sounded so weary that Julie thought he was going to burst into tears. "I'm sorry, Celia," he said. "I know I'm acting badly, but I can't help myself. It's been awful, so awful that you can't begin to imagine what I've been through. Crispin broke the news of the meeting to me late in the afternoon, just sprung it on me the way you'd spring a gallows trap, and it's only because Steve Shupka is a friend of mine, and he was willing to risk his job by tipping me off, that I was able to learn what line of attack Crispin is going to use tonight. I went out to the drug store to call you right away, but when you couldn't meet me, I decided to come over here to wait for you. I couldn't face going back to the Clarke House until I was ready to face the meeting, so I thought I'd just sit here in the barber shop and think, but your father had just come back from swinging this preposterous deal of his.

"I know it sounds insane, but he's done it. Every penny he pulled out of that glove thing he's sunk into these shovels, and I'm just the man he's looking for because I come from out west, where there are a lot of farmers, and so I'll know how to unload all these shovels without handles for him at a huge profit, and he went on and on and on about it, hammering away with his wild plans and how I was going to help him realize them, until my head was ringing like a blacksmith's anvil but I couldn't stop him, even though every moment counted and I had to have some peace and quiet in which to figure out my defense for tonight, but I couldn't do that until you came home, and if he hadn't finally gone out to get something he said was important, I think I would have—"

The rush of words stopped, and Mr. Ivey looked at Celia as though she had just come into the barber shop, and then all at once the thin face seemed to fall apart and Julie saw with horror that Mr. Ivey had burst into tears.

"Celia," he said hoarsely, his thin body shaking with sobs, "Celia, I can't, I can't. I'm sick. I can't do it, Celia, I can't. I can't—"

Celia stepped to the barber chair and put her arms around the thin shoulders and, as she pulled Mr. Ivey toward her, she spoke quietly across his yellow hair: "Julie, go get Dr. Zuckerberg, fast!"

It was the way most people went to get Dr. Zuckerberg, but it was rarely the way he came.

Dr. Zuckerberg was a short, plump man with a Vandyke beard who wore a tailcoat and lived in the last of a row of six brownstones near the Avenue C corner. They were known as the "stoop houses," and while all the people who lived in the stoop houses were financially a cut or two above the Ninth Street average, Dr. Zuckerberg was generally conceded to be the richest man on the block. He was also generally conceded to be as slow as an undertaker. Since he had made every penny of what was considered to be a substantial fortune out of his medical practice, Julie had wondered for a long time why he was so slow to respond when he was summoned. After all, it wasn't as though he was being asked to come for nothing. Everybody on the block knew that, when you sent for the doctor, you had to be prepared to say goodbye to a dollar.

One day, when Julie and Katie were walking home from school with Ida Zuckerberg, who was in their class, they passed Ida's father, little black bag in hand, moving majestically up the street, putting one foot in front of the other with so much cautious deliberation that he reminded Julie of a man trying to conceal his movements across a snow-covered sidewalk by treading in the footprints of a previous passer-by. Katie, who had made plenty of caustic remarks about Dr. Zuckerberg in the past, took this occasion to make another one.

"Look at him," she said. "Moving like he's got raw eggs in his pockets. Some day somebody is going to send for that father of yours because they got a cut throat or something, they're laying there bleeding, and the way he takes his time, he'll be in plenty of trouble with the cops for getting there too late."

Ida Zuckerberg shook her head. "In this neighborhood my father says no doctor can ever get to anybody too late," she said. "By the time people around here get ready to spend a dollar to call the doctor, it's already too late, so what's the rush?"

Dr. Zuckerberg did not, of course, use those words to Julie when, in answer to her ring, he opened the door at the top of his stoop and, breathless from her run down the block, she told him Mr. Ivey was sick and her sister Celia wanted the doctor to come to the barber shop right away. Judging by the way he acted, however, it seemed to the frightened Julie that Dr. Zuckerberg was *thinking* "What's the rush?"

"He's very sick," Julie repeated in a worried voice. "My sister said—"

"I know," Dr. Zuckerberg said calmly, "I know."

He sighted down the crease of his pearl-gray fedora as though he were aiming a gun, blew some invisible dust out of the dent in the felt, then set the hat carefully on his head. In the mirror on the wall near the umbrella stand he checked the result, adjusted the angle of the brim by a fraction of an inch, and with several swift upward thrusts of his fingers combed the Vandyke to a jaunty point.

"He couldn't hardly breathe," Julie said desperately. "Like in his chest there was—"

"I know," Dr. Zuckerberg said in the same unhurried voice. "I know." He took the small black bag from the hall table and, with a backward glance across his shoulder, he checked in the mirror the drape of his tailcoat. Apparently satisfied that he looked the way the people of East Ninth Street were entitled to have their only medical practitioner look in public, Dr. Zuckerberg said, "So let's go."

They went, it seemed to the almost frantic Julie, like a dog act she had once seen at Loew's Delancey, in which a tiny, yapping terrier tried to hurry a huge, placid St. Bernard across the stage. Julie would run forward up the street a few yards, hoping with her haste to set Dr. Zuckerberg a good example. She would then pause, look back, note with a sinking heart that the plump man in the gray fedora was apparently unaware of her existence, and wait impatiently for him to come plodding up to her. Then she would run up the street another few yards and the cycle would be repeated. By the time they reached the barber shop Julie felt as though she had carried Dr. Zuckerberg all the way up the block on her back. Perhaps that was why, for a few moments after she opened the door and held it wide for the doctor to precede her into the barber shop, she did not see her father. Then Julie smelled the whiskey and, as she closed the door behind Dr. Zuckerberg, she saw Biaggio Sarno.

He was standing beside Celia, his breath roaring with the wheezing rasp that always told Julie just as much about what her father had been doing during the past few hours as the way he smelled. The big man was staring down at Mr. Ivey in the barber chair, which, since Julie had left the shop, had been tipped back into the shaving position. When the door clicked shut, Biaggio Sarno lifted his head and Julie saw with a small stab of shock that her father looked scared.

"Whatsa the matter witha him?" he said hoarsely. "Whatsa he got?"

"How do I know?" said Dr. Zuckerberg. "I just got here."

"I don't know how long he's been like this, Doctor," Celia said helpfully. "I don't mean unconscious. I mean—"

"How do you know he's unconscious?" said Dr. Zuckerberg, putting his bag on the white marble ledge under the mirror where Biaggio Sarno kept his case of razors.

"How do I know?" said Celia, startled. "Why, a few minutes ago, after I sent my kid sister to call you, he closed his eyes and sort of collapsed, so I let down the chair to make him more comfortable, and I, well, I'm not a doctor—"

"In that case we can disregard your diagnosis," said Dr. Zuckerberg as he removed his fedora, using both hands to do it. He looked around the shop with obvious distaste. "Is there any place I can put this where it won't get dirty?"

"Certainly," said Celia, reaching for the hat, but Dr. Zuckerberg swung it out of her reach. She looked even more startled, then said, "I was going to hang it on one of those pegs."

"Hats as good as this don't get hung on pegs," said the plump man. "Here." He thrust the hat at Julie. "Hold this and don't drop it."

"Yes, sir," Julie said.

She took the hat and Dr. Zuckerberg turned to the barber

chair. For a few moments he stared down at Mr. Ivey, scowling slightly at the thin white face as, with delicate, probing fingers, he checked the fastenings of his large, square gold cuff links. Then, just as slowly and deliberately as he had come up the street, Dr. Zuckerberg went to work. The only instruments Julie recognized were a stethoscope and a thermometer, but Dr. Zuckerberg used several others, including a small funnel-shaped object with a light inside that the doctor poked into Mr. Ivey's ears, and a flat gray hose he wound around the social worker's arm before inflating it by pumping on a rubber bulb. Finally, the plump man straightened up and began, at the same maddeningly slow pace, to replace his instruments in the small black bag.

"Whatsa the matter witha him?" Biaggio Sarno asked hoarsely. "Whatsa he got?"

"Nothing," Dr. Zuckerberg said, folding his stethoscope.

"Huh?" Biaggio Sarno said.

"I said nothing is the matter with him," Dr. Zuckerberg said, putting the stethoscope into the bag as though, having reached the crucial stage of a religious rite, he were placing an offering on an altar.

"I'm afraid we don't understand," Celia said. "He's sick, isn't he?"

"Not according to my diagnosis," Dr. Zuckerberg said, and he turned to Julie. "My hat, please."

Julie gave him the hat, which Dr. Zuckerberg set on his head, again using both hands to do the job, and then he checked the result in the mirror.

"If your diagnosis shows nothing is wrong with him," Celia said slowly, "then why is he unconscious?"

"Did I say he was unconscious?" said Dr. Zuckerberg.

"No," said Celia with a worried frown, "but—" She paused, looked down at Mr. Ivey, then up at Dr. Zuckerberg. "But he is, isn't he?"

"I don't think so," said Dr. Zuckerberg. He snapped shut the catch of the black bag and said, "One dollar, please."

"Oh, I'm sorry," said Celia. "Of course." She took her purse from the marble shelf, pulled out a dollar, and, as she handed it to Dr. Zuckerberg, said even more slowly, "If he's not unconscious, then what—I mean what—what *is* he, Doctor?"

"Faking," said Dr. Zuckerberg. He drew a wallet from his breast pocket and, as slowly as he had done everything else, he added the dollar to a comfortably thick batch of bills inside the leather fold. He slid the wallet back into his breast pocket, tapped the bulge it made in his coat, and said, "His temperature is normal, his pulse is normal, his blood pressure is normal, there is no congestion in the chest, and no sign of anything that would prevent him from running a race with this Mr. Paavo Nurmi I am reading about in the papers. If he prefers to lie there like a herring with his eyes closed it is because he has his reasons. Since as a doctor his reasons don't interest me, I can only as a doctor repeat my diagnosis. He is faking."

"But that's ridiculous!" Celia said.

"I agree," Dr. Zuckerberg said and, as though bowing to a royal personage, he dipped his plump body over the barber chair and said, "You're not fooling anybody, young man, so take my advice and get up."

But Mr. Ivey did not take the advice. Neither did he get up. For several moments after Dr. Zuckerberg left, Celia and her father and Julie stood in a semicircle, staring down at the young man stretched out in the barber chair. Julie's mind, trying to make some sense of the senseless events by which she had been engulfed for several hours, fastened on Dr. Zuckerberg's statement that there was no congestion in Mr. Ivey's chest. It didn't seem possible that the doctor was right. Nobody would be making the sounds Mr. Ivey was making if his chest was all right.

"He's a *gotta* be all right!" Biaggio Sarno said finally. "He's a gotta!"

The touch of desperation in his voice reminded Julie that, when she came back into the barber shop behind Dr. Zuckerberg, she had been shocked to see that her father looked scared.

"Shut up!" Celia snapped at her father, and then, quietly, to the figure in the barber chair, "Ben? Ben, what is it?"

"I counta on him!" Biaggio Sarno said, the desperation in his voice honing down to the sharper edge of hysteria. "Withouta him

I lose-a everything! I already pay-a for the shovels! I gotta have-a him to sella them! Withouta him I go broke-a! Withouta him—!"

With a short, angry thrust, Celia sent her father staggering to the other side of the barber shop. "Get away from here, you drunken fool!" She turned back to Mr. Ivey. "Ben," she said gently. "Ben, what is it?"

"I don't know."

Julie caught her breath. Mr. Ivey had opened his eyes.

"I don't know," he said again, very quietly, so quietly that he seemed to be whispering. "But what the doctor said is not true, Celia. I'm not faking."

"I know you're not," Celia said.

The thin, terrifyingly white face broke in a small, crooked smile. "No, you don't," Mr. Ivey said. "But you're sweet to say so."

"Ben," Celia said again. "What is it?"

"It's a shame," he said. "That's what it is."

"Ben," Celia said, "I don't understand."

"Neither do I," Mr. Ivey said. "Look at me!" His head came up an inch or two, creasing the flesh under his chin into a series of narrow ridges, so that he could look down the length of his long, thin body. "Helpless! Like Gulliver, waking up on his first morning in Lilliput! Helpless as a child! Staked down to this preposterous barber chair as surely and helplessly as Gulliver was staked down by those thousands of tiny people any one of which, any *hundred* of which, he could have swept out of his path like so much dust if—" The bitter voice stopped and Mr. Ivey repeated the word: "*If!*"

"If what?" Celia said.

"If God were on my side," Mr. Ivey said. "But I guess He isn't." The thin young man paused again, and then, with a curious little break in his voice, Mr. Ivey repeated, "I guess He isn't," and Julie, aware of a sudden sick feeling in her stomach, saw that Mr. Ivey was crying again. "He's not," the white-faced young man said as the tears, running out of the corners of his eyes, moved crazily in little bouncing leaps to the lobes of his ears and then shattered themselves noiselessly in small wet pools on the black leather headrest. "He's not, He's not, He's not."

153

"Ben," Celia said desperately. "Please, for God's sake—!"

"Yes, for God's sake," he said. "That's what we all kid ourselves into believing. That we're doing it for God's sake, when the truth is that all the time it's really for our own sake, for ourselves, to feed our vanity, our ego, our insane ambitions." He paused to let Celia dab at the wet corners of his eyes with a crumpled handkerchief. "Thanks, Celia," Mr. Ivey said, and then, "You were right, of course."

"About what?" Celia said.

"My plotting to destroy Tyler Crispin."

"I didn't say that, Ben."

"You should have," Mr. Ivey said bitterly. "Because it's the truth. Of course I've been plotting to destroy him. The moment I got here from Cleveland, as soon as I settled into the job, I knew he had to go. The way the old trees, no matter how sentimental we may be about them, if they can no longer bear fruit must make way for the young saplings. What counts is the common good. What matters is the vision."

Mr. Ivey paused, and he rolled his head helplessly from side to side, and Julie saw that the tears had started again.

"The vision," Mr. Ivey said brokenly. "The vision." The head moved once more and then it was still. "Celia," he said, looking up at her, "Celia, don't you hear it?"

"Hear what, Ben?"

"*The still, sad music of humanity,*" Mr. Ivey said, and Julie could tell, from the way his voice changed, that he was quoting poetry. "I've heard it all my life," he said. "Ever since I was a kid. I suppose that's one of the penalties of having a Methodist minister for a father, except that I've never considered it a penalty. To me it's been what *the sounding cataract* was to Wordsworth at Tintern Abbey: *an appetite; a feeling and a love, that had no need of a remoter charm.* I've listened to that *still, sad music of humanity* every hour of my waking life, but I never knew what to do about it until I got here, to the Clarke House, to East Ninth Street. I was like a musical instrument, a violin that's been lying useless in its case ever since it was made, picking up sounds, hints of what it had been made to do, but unable without the help of a player to do them. The very first morning after I got here from Cleveland, just walking around these crowded streets, I knew that the violin was coming out of its case at last, I knew I was going to stop picking up sounds, as I'd been doing all my life, and I was about to start making music. I knew it, I felt it, I was certain of it, and yet I couldn't figure out how. The 'how,' the way to do it, the direction, that continued to elude me. For a year I kept looking and hunting, and for a year it kept eluding me, and then one day, after I'd been here almost a year—"

The voice stopped and Mr. Ivey squeezed his eyes shut so hard that two tears came swelling through the tight-pressed lids.

"No!" he said, and even though the voice was no stronger than it had been when Mr. Ivey began to speak, Julie could feel the sudden explosion of passion go humming through the barber shop. "It's *not* for my own sake! I was *not* feeding my vanity! My ego had nothing to do with it! Insane ambitions or ambitions of any kind were not involved! It was the vision, that's all. Just the vision. I saw it clearly and I tried to follow it. To an old fool like Crispin it's just a settlement house, just a job, a chair to sit in until by merely sitting he's earned himself a pension. But to me, to anybody who can hear the *still, sad music of humanity* it's a world in microcosm, the opportunity to change a world, the chance to *begin* changing it. In order to begin, Crispin had to go. Suppose in order to make him go, a certain amount of plotting had to take place? So what? Is it more important to play the game by the stupid rules that crafty chair-warmers like Crispin have themselves dictated into the rules book? Or is it more important to follow the vision, to bring to the many what now is the privilege of only a few, to change the world? Go on, tell me. Which is more important?"

"Ben," Celia said worriedly, "I don't know what you're talking about."

"Of course not," he said, and the gentleness in the tired voice was now as apparent as a few moments earlier the passion had been. "How could you know? You haven't seen the vision. You haven't heard that *still, sad music.* Some day, if you do, you'll know what Ben Ivey was talking about. And some day you'll wonder, as I'm wondering now, why God should have cast his lot with Tyler Crispin rather than with Ben Ivey."

"God has nothing to do with it," Celia said.

"No?" Mr. Ivey said. "You heard what Dr. Zuckerberg said. There's nothing wrong with me. Pulse, temperature, blood pressure, everything medical science can check on is normal. Everything except Ben Ivey, who can't move a finger, who is lying here paralyzed, as helpless as—"

The weary, bitter words stopped as Biaggio Sarno, breathing hoarsely, appeared beside the barber chair.

"I fixa," he said. "I putta him onna feet."

"For heaven's sake, will you go back to your witch-hazel bottle and keep out of this?" Celia said angrily. "What can *you* do?"

Biaggio Sarno held up the battered old rectangular box covered with black imitation leather that, along with his case of razors, he had brought from his birthplace in Naples to the fragment of the New World in which for so many years he had been trying without success to make his fortune.

"I fixa," he repeated. "Take off hizza shirt."

"Oh, for God's sake!" Celia said in disgust. "Haven't we got enough trouble without your drunken—?"

Her father, whom she was trying to thrust aside, made a short, hard sweeping motion with the leather box. Celia staggered away from the barber chair.

"I said I fixa," Biaggio Sarno repeated. "You no take off hizza shirt, okay. Julie!"

She jumped nervously. "Yes, Pa?"

"Take off hizza shirt!"

Julie looked desperately at Celia, who had recaptured her balance and was closing in again on the barber chair.

"Pa, that won't do any good," Celia said. "We've got to get another doctor."

"No doctors," Biaggio Sarno said. "He gotta be onna feet help sella my shovels. I fixa."

"Celia," Mr. Ivey said. "What does he want to do to me?"

"Oh, it's nothing painful or dangerous," Celia said. "It's just stupid, that's all."

"Izza not stupid," Biaggio Sarno said. He set the black leather box on the white marble ledge that Dr. Zuckerberg had used for his black leather bag. "I fixa. Julie, I say take off hizza shirt!"

"You keep Julie out of this," Celia said.

"Then *you* take off the shirt."

Celia hesitated.

"What is it?" Mr. Ivey said in his weak, tired voice. "What does he want to do?"

"A preposterous peasant superstition he's brought with him from the slums of Naples," Celia said. "Little glass cups. He puts them on your chest by creating a vacuum or a suction with a small flame and they're supposed to draw out the poisons that are making you sick. It's idiotic and stupid. It's—"

"Izza not stupid," Biaggio Sarno said. "Izza way to fix, put him back onna feet. You take offa the shirt, or Julie?"

"Celia," Mr. Ivey said. She turned toward the barber chair. Mr. Ivey said, "You say it's not dangerous?"

"Of course not," Celia said impatiently. "He does it all the time to the other superstitious peasants in this filthy neighborhood who are as idiotic as he is and would rather give their fifty cents to a drunken barber than a sober doctor."

"Let him try it," Mr. Ivey said.

"Ben," Celia said, "I'm embarrassed about this. I can't help it if I have to live down here, but I'm certainly not going to let you or anybody else think I believe in these remedies out of the Dark Ages that my distinguished sot of a father has—"

"Celia, let him try it," Mr. Ivey said.

She looked down at him, chewing her lower lip, and then finally, with an angry shrug, she turned to Julie. "Lock the door," Celia said. Julie ran to the door and locked it. Celia said, "The shades, too."

Julie pulled down the wide green shade over the window and the narrower one over the door. When she finished, Celia was unbuttoning Mr. Ivey's shirt and her father was opening the black leather box. The four walls of the box, which were lined with red velvet, bristled with the small glass cups. These were held in place, and kept from smashing against one another, by tiny brass clamps fitted into the velvet. From the narrow free space in the bottom of the box Biaggio Sarno brought out the vial of alcohol and the buttonhook. The curved end of the buttonhook was wrapped in a small wad of surgical cotton fastened to the metal with a twisted hairpin. The big barber, breathing hoarsely, uncorked the vial with his teeth, thrust the buttonhook into the alcohol, held it there for a few moments, until the wad of cotton was thoroughly saturated, then withdrew the buttonhook and rammed the cork back into the vial with his teeth. He returned the vial to the box, struck a match, and touched the yellow flame to the end of the buttonhook, which instantly became a flickering bit of pale blue, transparent, dancing light.

"Holda the box," he said to Celia, who had peeled back the flaps of Mr. Ivey's unbuttoned shirt and rolled the undershirt up under his neck so that the young social worker's chest was bare. Celia took the black leather box. Her father said, "One at a time."

Working swiftly, and with surprising accuracy for a man who was carrying a not inconsiderable load of cheap whiskey, Biaggio Sarno took the little glass cup Celia handed him, held it mouth-down an inch or two from Mr. Ivey's chest, poked the buttonhook with the dancing blue flame into the glass, held it there for a moment, and then, as he jerked the flame free with his right hand, with his left he set the rim of the glass against Mr. Ivey's chest. At once, as Biaggio Sarno's hand went back for the next cup, which Celia was holding out to him, Mr. Ivey's skin under the first cup, held firmly to his chest by suction, began to rise in a low hill about the size of a fifty-cent piece.

When the last cup had been attached, and Mr. Ivey's chest looked as though twenty or thirty unlighted ten-watt electric bulbs had been screwed into the skin, Biaggio Sarno with a tired grunt blew out the dancing blue flame. He dropped the buttonhook into the box and walked heavily to the rear of the store, where, without bothering to conceal what he was doing, he took a long swig from the witch-hazel bottle. He stood there for a while, breathing hard and staring at the bottle, as though waiting for the whiskey to take hold. When it did, he replaced the bottle in its nest of hair tonics and dandruff cures, and came back to the barber chair.

"Holda the box," he said to Celia.

She took it from the marble ledge. Biaggio Sarno bent over Mr. Ivey. Working even more swiftly, the big barber with his left hand took hold of one of the inverted glass cups stuck to Mr. Ivey's chest and, with his right forefinger, pressed Mr. Ivey's flesh near the base of the cup. There was a small hiss as air rushed into the cup and, as the cup came free, Biaggio Sarno handed it to Celia. She slipped it under one of the clamps and reached for the next cup her father was holding out. When all the cups were back in the box, and Mr. Ivey's bare chest was covered with twenty or thirty fifty-cent-piece-size bright-red welts, so that his skin looked like a piece of white polka-dotted cloth, Biaggio Sarno made another trip to the rear of the store.

"All right," he said, wiping his mouth. "Now up onna feet."

"Pa," Celia said, "he can't—"

"Biaggio Sarno say he can." The big barber came forward, carrying the witch-hazel bottle. When he reached the barber chair, he said, "Up onna feet!"

Julie didn't realize she had been holding her breath until, seeing the tremor that suddenly shook Mr. Ivey's body, she heard her chest deflate itself like a punctured tire. The sharp hiss caused Mr. Ivey, who was staring down at his legs, to look up. His eyes, catching Julie's, were wide with wonder. Then, as though her startled exhalation was a signal, in a sudden flurry of movement that reminded Julie of the way Steve Shupka during calisthenics class flung himself lightly from the high leather horse in the Clock House gym, Mr. Ivey's body bent up in the middle, like the two arms of an outstretched nutcracker snapping up into a right angle; both hands, palms down, slid under his buttocks and pressed hard, lifting the slender body two or three inches from the black leather seat; and then, with a dip of the elbows that ended in a crisp, hard shove, Mr. Ivey came up and away from the barber chair in a jaunty little arc that landed him upright, feet planted together, in front of Celia, where, like an acrobat announcing the end of a difficult turn, he snapped one palm across the other in a sharp punctuating slap of finality.

"V*oilà*," he said.

"Good God!" Celia said.

From Mr. Ivey's throat came a low sound that was part happy laughter and part nervous incredulity. "He *is* good, isn't He? He's on my side after all!"

"Here," Biaggio Sarno said, holding out the witch-hazel bottle. "Take a drink."

"I don't need it," Mr. Ivey said, flexing his arms gingerly. "I don't need a thing."

"Take a drink," the big barber said. "Izza good."

Mr. Ivey grinned. "Whatever you say, Doctor." He took the bottle, put the neck to his mouth, and tipped it up. Fascinated, realizing she had never seen him at this angle, Julie watched Mr. Ivey's Adam's apple bob up and down. "Wow!" he said as he took the bottle from his mouth. "Wow-*wee!*" he gasped, and then, with a laugh, holding the bottle out to Mr. Sarno, he said, "It's not good, but it feels great!"

The big barber grinned. "This"—he patted the bottle—"and this—" he patted the black leather box—"they always fix! Now you sella my shovels, hey?"

"I will not only sell them," Mr. Ivey said. "I will personally arrange for every farmer west of the Mississippi to make an annual contribution to the Biaggio Sarno Fund for Putting Social Workers Back on Their Feet!"

He threw his arms around Julie's father and, with an astonishing display of strength for a man who moments before had been flat on his back, Mr. Ivey lifted the big barber off the ground, whirled him around in a wild little dance, and set him down in the barber chair with a thump.

"But first," Mr. Ivey said, laughing and gasping for breath, "I've got to polish off some unfinished business with a certain Mr. Tyler Crispin!"

He ran to the door.

"Ben!" Celia said. "You've got to have something to eat!"

"Later," he said, hauling on the knob. "We'll celebrate in Bloom's! I'll take you all out for coffee and strudel! What the hell is the matter with this damned thing?"

"It's locked, silly!" Celia ran up to him, her face working oddly in a way that Julie knew meant her sister wanted to hold onto her anger but couldn't prevent it from giving way to laughter. "You're crazy," Celia said, twisting the key in the lock. "You really are!"

"Of course I am!" Mr. Ivey said. "Who wouldn't be? I'm on my way at last! *Sensations sweet, felt in the blood, and felt along the heart!* God, that Wordsworth! What *didn't* he know? Now, look, baby. Crispin said that board meeting is scheduled for eight o'clock in his office." Mr. Ivey glanced at his wrist watch. "It's almost seven now. Five of. Okay. We'll surprise him. You go get yourself something to eat and then meet me in the Clarke House lobby at a quarter to eight. Okay?"

"Of course, but—"

"Better make it twenty of. I want to rock that so-and-so back on his heels but good. Twenty of?"

"Of course, yes, anything you want," Celia said. "But what am I to *do* at this meeting? What do you want me to say?"

"The truth! Always the truth! Your version of what happened. How you volunteered to take over the Nature Club. We'll flay him with the truth right in front of his own Board of Governors! What a show! How I wish I could watch instead of being relegated to the dull role of participant! *Milton! Thou should'st be living at this hour!*" With a sweeping gesture, as though he were waving a pennant, Mr. Ivey dipped down, kissed Celia's cheek, laughed happily, stroked the place he had kissed and, as he hauled open the door, said, "Twenty of eight!"

For a few moments after the door closed behind him, while the barber shop seemed to hum with the echoes of his ringing words, Julie and Celia and their father stared at the green shade. Then Baggio Sarno laughed.

"Some boy!" the big barber said. "You wait, you see, comes a day, thissa country, that boy, he own the whole thing!"

161

"Hey!" Celia said. "Where you going?"

"I just remembered something," Julie said. "I forgot to tell Mr. Ivey—"

She didn't finish the sentence because she was out in the street. She caught up with him at the Avenue B corner, not because she had been running, but because Mr. Ivey had been stopped by Cockeye Katie. From the way he was bent over the small girl with the crooked glasses, from the way he was holding his thin body, as though he had run head-on into a wall in the dark, Julie could tell something had gone wrong.

"Are you sure?" Mr. Ivey was saying.

"Am I sure?" Katie said, her voice rising. "Mr. Ivey, I just told you, I just came out of Mr. Crispin's office. He dragged me in off the street. You don't believe me, ask Julie."

"Julie?" Mr. Ivey turned to scowl down at Julie, as though trying to figure out where she had come from. "What's Julie got to do with it?"

"The same as me, sir," Cockeye Katie said brightly. "Mr. Crispin said they had Julie in there a little while ago, the office, the same people, asking her the same questions they asked me."

"What sort of questions?" Mr. Ivey said.

"Well, like did you ever put your hand up under my skirt," Katie said thoughtfully, squinting up at the sky in what Julie knew was an act her friend put on when she was giving a grownup a particularly bad time, "and did you ever take me up to your room in the Clock House, and did you ever—" Katie stopped and turned and said, "What else, Julie?"

Mr. Ivey ran the back of a hand across his lips. "Julie," he said in a tight little voice, "is this true?"

"No," she said desperately. "I don't mean Katie is lying. I mean—"

"Julie!" Katie said reproachfully. "I'm just saying what Mr. *Crispin* said. And these people in his office."

"Julie," Mr. Ivey said. "What *do* you mean?"

"They—they—they didn't ask me *those* kind of questions!"

"Julie," Mr. Ivey said slowly, "what kind *did* they ask?"

She told him, managing to get the words out somehow, in spite of the hammer strokes inside her chest, staring down at the sidewalk as she talked.

"Well, what did I say?" Cockeye Katie said when Julie finished. "It's the same thing, isn't it?"

Mr. Ivey ran his hand across his lips again. Julie had the crazy feeling that he had gone away from them, that what was standing there on the sidewalk in front of her was only his hollow skin.

"Yes," he said slowly. "For Mr. Crispin's purpose, it's the same thing."

"I beg your pardon, sir?" Katie said, her eyes wide as she looked up at him in a way that suddenly made Julie, who didn't usually mind her friend's malicious tactics with grownups, want to punch Katie in the nose. "Mr. Crispin's purpose?"

"What?" Mr. Ivey said and then, like water pouring into a bottle, he seemed to come back into his skin. "It's nothing important," Mr. Ivey said, straightening up. "I, uh, I wonder if I could ask a favor of you, Katie?"

"Me, sir?"

"Yes, please."

"Anything, Mr. Ivey. You know that, sir."

"Thank you, Katie. What I'd like you to do isn't much, but it's very important to me. There's going to be a meeting in Mr. Crispin's office at eight o'clock."

"About what, sir?"

"Administrative matters, Katie."

"What's administrative matters, sir?"

"I don't have the time to explain now. Running the Clarke House. That sort of thing."

"Is anything wrong, sir?"

"No, nothing, Katie. It's simply that I've got to prepare some material for this meeting, and since it's seven o'clock now, a few minutes after, in fact, I won't have time to do anything about this other matter."

"What other matter, sir?"

"Cut it out!" Julie said, finding relief in her anger, as though, in the wildly tossing events by which she had been surrounded since Mr. Crispin had dragged her into the Clock House earlier in the evening and about which she understood nothing except that they might destroy her, she had at last managed to grasp something solid to which she could cling. "You hear me? Cut it out!"

"Cut what out?" Katie said. "Gee whiz, the way everybody is all of a sudden—"

"You cut it out!"

"It's all right, Julie," Mr. Ivey said. "Thank you."

"What are you thanking Julie for, sir?"

"I don't have time to explain that now, either, Katie. All I have time for now is this thing I'd like you to do for me, which you said you'd be happy to—"

"Sure I would, sir. If there's any trouble, Mr. Ivey, and I can help—"

"There's no trouble, Katie, but you *can* help."

"In what way, sir?"

"By not saying anything about these questions until after this meeting."

"What questions, sir?"

"The questions you just told me Mr. Crispin asked you."

"And these people in his office, too, sir. Eight of them. Five men and three women. From uptown. They asked, too, sir."

"Yes, I know, Katie. Will you promise not to repeat those questions until after this meeting?"

"Gosh, Mr. Ivey, who would I repeat them to, sir?"

"I don't know, Katie. All I'm asking now is that you do me this favor. Will you?"

"Gee whiz, sure, Mr. Ivey, you know that, sir."

"Thank you, Katie."

"What about Julie? She got asked the same questions, sir."

"They were *not* the same!" Julie said furiously. "I just explained—"

"It's all right, Julie," Mr. Ivey said, and to Katie, "I'm sure I can count on Julie."

"You mean you think you can't count on me, sir?"

"No, Katie. I mean I'm sure I can count on both of you."

"In that case, sir—"

"If you don't shut up," Julie said through her teeth, "I'm going to—"

"No, you're not," Mr. Ivey said, stepping between them. "I said I'm sure I can count on both of you, and I am."

He started up Avenue B, toward the Clock House.

"Mr. Ivey!" Julie said.

He stopped and turned back. "What?"

"The date with Celia? You said she should meet you in the lobby at twenty minutes to eight?"

"Oh, that, yes," Mr. Ivey said. "Of course. What about it?"

"Can I come?"

"What?"

"Me?" Julie said. "Can I come, too?"

"Of course."

"What about me?" Cockeye Katie said. "If it's something about the Nature Club, sir, I helped start it, isn't it fair for me, too?"

"Certainly," Mr. Ivey said. "All of you. The Clarke House lobby. I'll meet you there at twenty to eight."

The fact that he was late did not bother Julie for a while. Mainly, she realized when it was all over, because it did not occur to her to check the time. This in itself, she also realized later, should have warned her. It was difficult to pass the settlement house without being aware of the two enormous black clock hands, as big as broomsticks, that dominated this section of Avenue B, and it was certainly impossible, unless you came in off the street with your eyes closed, to enter the Clarke House without making at least an unconscious note of the exact time. Julie, who came in off the street with her eyes wide open, missed the clock completely. Cockeye Katie, who was standing on the front steps when Julie came along with Celia, undoubtedly had a good deal to do with the omission.

"Something is wrong," she said.

"What do you mean something is wrong?" Celia demanded.

"Gee whiz," Katie said, "I can't say anything without right away everybody jumps down my throat."

"If you didn't have it wide open all the time, making nasty remarks about people, nobody would jump down into it."

"Nasty remarks?" Katie said. "What nasty remarks? I'm just standing here waiting for you, that's all I'm doing."

"Go on home and do it there," Celia said. "Nobody wants you around here tonight."

"Oh, yeah?" Katie said, making another of her unsuccessful attempts to poke the crooked glasses straight on her nose. "Mr. Ivey happens to want me around here tonight, in case you want to know. Ask Julie."

Celia looked at Julie, who nodded and said uncomfortably, "I forgot to tell you. He said Katie should meet him, too."

"Why?"

"On account of these questions—" Katie began.

"You shut up!" Julie said fiercely. "You promised!"

"Promised what?" Celia said. "What are you two nutty kids talking about?"

"Mr. Ivey," Julie said, glaring at her best friend. "He said on account of Katie was one of the founders of the club, she wrote the letter to Mr. Crispin at the beginning, he wants her here, too."

"He must be out of his mind," Celia said.

"Oh, yeah?" Katie said.

"Can't you say anything else?" Celia snapped.

"You don't let me," Katie said. "I'm trying to tell you something is wrong."

"*What*, for heaven's sake?"

"How should I know?" Katie said. "It's just I was in there." She jerked her head toward the lobby behind her. "And it's like that night, remember, when your father was drunk, and Mr. Wytrikush, the one has the fruit pushcart on Avenue C, he found him in the cellar with Mrs. Wytrikush, and my father, it was lucky he was off duty, he had to come running with his gun to stop—"

"All right, all right, all right," Celia said, pushing past Katie. "I wish my kid sister would try making friends with somebody who shut up once in a while."

Following her sister and her friend into the lobby, Julie sensed at once what Katie had meant. The Clarke House lobby in the evening, when the Citizenship Club and other adult-education classes got under way, was always a busy place, just as all of

Ninth Street in the evening, when the men who had come home from work had finished their suppers and were sitting out on the sidewalks and stoops with their wives, always seemed noisier and more alive than during the day.

Except on the night Katie's father stopped the fight in the Avenue C cellar between Mr. Wytrikush and Biaggio Sarno. Julie remembered the uneasy silence that, before Mr. Halloran found her father and Mr. Wytrikush rolling around on the cellar floor, had hung over the block like heavy, invisible rain clouds, a silence during which the people sitting out on the sidewalk and the stoops had been strangely silent, apparently sensing that something terrible was happening or about to happen, something they did not dare discuss because to mention the unseen horror aloud might mean becoming involved in it.

Coming into the Clarke House lobby now, Julie with a stab of fear sensed the same thing. Men and women were hurrying across the white marble floor, carrying their textbooks and musical instruments, and the doors leading to the gym and the meeting rooms kept opening and closing, and Steve Shupka, in his gray sweatshirt, was busy at his check-in board, taking down notices and thumbtacking up new ones. But the sounds made by the shuffling feet, and the squeaking doors, and the muted screech of chairs being dragged into place, seemed to be strangely isolated, as though something that held them together, something that gave them their familiar unity, was missing. Then Julie saw Steve Shupka, who always had a cheery greeting for her and Katie, send a quick, nervous glance in their direction and, even more quickly, turn back to his check-in board, and Julie knew what was missing: the voices.

Nobody was talking, the way nobody had been talking on Ninth Street that terrible night when Mr. Halloran had saved Mr. Wytrikush from death, and her father from committing murder, by clubbing them both unconscious with the butt of his revolver.

"See what I mean?" Katie whispered.

"Shut up!" Celia said venomously.

"Gee whiz, what did I say?"

"Shut up!"

"All I said—!"

"Shut up!"

Katie shut up, and they stood there, a small tight group in the middle of the white marble floor, like explorers on an icy waste who, having lost their bearings, were huddling uncertainly together for warmth until they could reach some decision about their next move. Julie didn't realize how long they had been standing there until the dark brown door, on which was painted the single word "Director," opened and Mr. Crispin came out. Then, as he came toward them, her eyes leaped to the big clock on the wall, a duplicate of the one set in the limestone arch over the entrance outside, and she saw, as a small sick feeling began to worm its way up out of her stomach, that it was almost eight-thirty.

"You are Miss Sarno, of course?" Mr. Crispin said politely to Celia.

"Yes, sir."

"I regret that the unfortunate events of the other evening prevented us from being introduced," the director of the Horace Judson Clarke House said. "My name is Tyler Crispin," he said with a small bow. "I'm very pleased to meet you."

"Thank you," Celia said, and Julie could tell her sister was rattled. "I'm very glad to meet you."

"Is there anything I can do for you, Miss Sarno?"

"For me? No. I was—I mean, no, thank you."

Mr. Crispin's eyebrows, which Julie noticed for the first time were black even though his hair was white, went up to the middle of his forehead.

"Are you sure?" he said.

"Am I sure?" Celia said. "I'm afraid I don't understand?"

"It seems simple enough," Mr. Crispin said. "If there isn't anything I can do for you, why have you come here tonight?"

"Oh, that. Well, uh, well, Mr. Ivey asked me to meet him here."

Mr. Crispin's eyebrows, which Julie would have thought couldn't possibly move in any direction except down, did the impossible: they rose another inch.

"He did?" the director said.

"Yes," Celia said with more confidence. "Mr. Ivey asked me to meet him here at twenty minutes to eight." And then, as though to lend weight to the statement, she added, "My sister and Katie Halloran, too. Didn't he?"

"Yes, sir," Katie said brightly. "He told us to meet him here in the lobby at twenty to eight."

"How odd," Mr. Crispin said, but to Julie it was not his words but what he did that seemed odd: with the huge clock on the wall facing him, so that only a blind man could have been unaware of the exact time, the director slowly pulled out his watch and stared at it for several moments. "How very odd," he said, as though talking to himself. "How very odd indeed."

"Why?" Celia said. "What's odd about it?"

Mr. Crispin replaced the watch in his vest pocket as though he were sliding a dangerously sharp dagger into its sheath. "I find it very odd, Miss Sarno, that Mr. Ivey should have made a date to meet you and these young ladies here in this lobby at twenty minutes of eight when, a full half hour before that, at ten minutes after seven to be precise, he left us."

"Left us?" Celia said.

"Yes," Mr. Crispin said. "The Horace Judson Clarke House."

"I—I don't understand?"

"I can hardly blame you, Miss Sarno. However, if you will tell me what it is you don't understand, perhaps I can clear things up for you?"

"I don't know what you mean by, well, by left?"

"You're quite right. That *is* my fault. I should have used a more explicit verb. What I meant to say was that at ten minutes after seven tonight Mr. Ivey resigned as associate director of the Horace Judson Clarke House. Does that clear things up, Miss Sarno?"

"Yes, it—" Then, more quickly, Celia said, "No. I mean, where is he now?"

Mr. Crispin's austere face broke in the smile that Julie felt he had copied from the Chinese figure on the bronze inkstand that dominated his desk.

"I have no idea, Miss Sarno, and I might add that I couldn't care less. He left us bag and baggage. There wasn't much of it. Just the one cardboard suitcase with which he arrived from Cleveland a year ago, but I did see to it that he carried that with him."

"Where?"

"I beg your pardon?"

"I mean where is he now?" Celia sounded frightened. "Where did he go?"

"I haven't the remotest idea," Mr. Crispin said. "Back to Cleveland, I guess."

9

It was a bad guess. But even now, sixteen years later, in this London hotel suite from which Colonel Uxbridge had informed her she would not be allowed to walk out until Ben Ivey regained consciousness and gave the order to release her, Julie did not see how Mr. Crispin could have been expected to make a better guess. Ben had come to New York from Cleveland. It seemed reasonable to assume that, on leaving New York, he would go back to Cleveland.

"Colonel Uxbridge?"

The two words, quietly spoken, with no more emotional underpinning than an elevator operator might supply for calling out the number of a floor, nevertheless had a surprising effect. Colonel Uxbridge, sitting in the chair that faced Julie's across the littered table, let out a small gasp. That the sound was involuntary, and that the colonel regretted having made it, was clear from the sharp glance he directed at Julie before he turned toward the archway at the far end of the room.

In it stood Harry, looking calm and unconcerned, or trying to look like that. There was nothing calm or unconcerned about the way the short, bald man was rubbing his hands up and down the front of his gray sweatshirt, as though his palms were damp with perspiration. Steve Shupka, Julie remembered clearly, had been doing the same thing sixteen years ago when she and Cockeye Katie Halloran came into the Clock House lobby on the night Ben Ivey disappeared.

"Yes, Harry?" Colonel Uxbridge said.

"See you a minute, please?" Harry said.

Colonel Uxbridge stood up, started toward the archway, stopped, turned, and gave Julie another sharp glance. She supposed he was trying to assess the effect his surprising little gasp had had on her. Julie hoped there was nothing in her face to indicate that the effect had gone beyond surprise: her heart was racing with a sudden sense of impending disaster.

Colonel Uxbridge turned again, moved on to the archway, and stopped when he reached Harry. The short, bald man started to step back, into the hall that touched the top of the room like the crossbar of a T, and Colonel Uxbridge started to follow. Something made both men change their minds. They stopped moving back into the hall. They remained in the archway, face to face, very close together, while they held a whispered consultation. They looked, Julie thought with a stab of irrelevance, like a couple under the mistletoe at a Christmas party arguing heatedly, but in low voices so the host would not overhear, about whether the man had actually earned the right to the kiss he was demanding. Finally, Colonel Uxbridge turned.

"Miss Sarno," he said, "I'd like to go into the bedroom for a few minutes. I mean I'd like to go in with Harry. Both of us." He nodded down toward the archway at the other end of the room. "The front door is locked and bolted. So are the windows. You couldn't possibly get out, but you might think you could if you made enough noise by hammering on the door or something like that, to attract the attention of the hotel staff. I assure you it would do absolutely no good. This entire floor, all the rooms and suites on either side as well as above and below, has been sealed off as a security zone by the British military, the members of which would pay no attention to your screams or poundings or other attempts at attracting attention. I tell you this only because it would distress me personally if you made such an attempt. I know you won't."

He was gone, and Harry with him, before Julie could reply. A moment later she heard the bedroom door open and close. Julie stood up, not quite understanding why, and then she realized that she could no longer bear the wild racing of her heart. She started to walk up and down the room slowly, making a conscious effort to calm herself, torn between the foolish desire to make a run for the door, which she knew would be wasted effort, and an even more foolish pride in the fact that Colonel Uxbridge seemed to have a good enough opinion of her intelligence to be certain she wouldn't make the attempt.

The fourth or fifth time she passed the littered table, her eye was caught by the sheet of paper rolled into the portable typewriter. Julie stopped, and once again she read: "SOLILOQUY OF REFORMATION (I don't like this title—too poetic for the serious business in hand—but it's the best I can think of at the moment, and it does, poetic or not, get to the root of the matter)." She was wondering why, on first reading those words less than an hour ago, she had not realized at once that they had been written by Benjamin Franklin Ivey, when she heard the bedroom door open and shut again.

As soon as she saw Colonel Uxbridge reappear in the archway, Julie knew her sense of impending disaster had been justified. In the few minutes that had elapsed since Harry had summoned him to the bedroom, the colonel seemed to have placed a dozen birthdays behind him.

"Miss Sarno," he said, "I am going to have to make a decision in the next few minutes that I am not at all sure I have the right to make. Since you are vitally involved, indeed since the decision cannot be made without your consent, I am going to tell you a number of things that come so close to being breaches of security that they may well justify my being court-martialed in the event the decision I make proves to be wrong."

"I don't want to hear them," Julie said.

Colonel Uxbridge shook his head irritably and wagged two fingers back and forth several times, quickly, as though wiping a peephole for himself on a fogged windowpane.

"What you want or don't want is completely irrelevant," he said.

"Not to me," Julie said, aware that her voice was shaking. The meeting in Ben Ivey's bedroom, arranged by Colonel Uxbridge, had taught Julie more than the fact that there was no anodyne, not even a war, that could blot out the past. What Julie had just learned, what was making her heart race with terror, was the discovery that her enemy was not the past but the future. She could handle what had happened. She had enough strength left for that. She had no reserves to fall back on for handling what might still happen. She said, "I don't want to hear another word. I didn't ask to come here. You threatened to have me sent home if I didn't come. You practically kidnapped me. All your fancy talk about security and patriotism and service to my country by coming with you, it's all just talk. I don't believe any of it. I don't believe my being here is going to change the course of this war. I don't believe anything I do or say or don't do or don't say is going to save any lives. I think it's all crazy. I don't want to have anything to do with it. I want to get out of here. If that means being shipped back to New York, that's all right with me, too. All I want is to get out of here. I want to get out!"

In the sudden silence, which hung in the room like a solid, tangible presence, the look of irritation on Colonel Uxbridge's face slowly vanished.

"Miss Sarno," he said very quietly, "for whatever it is worth, you might as well know this: I don't like being in this hotel suite with Mr. Benjamin Franklin Ivey any more than you do."

It proved to be worth quite a lot. At least to someone trembling on the edge of hysteria. Drawing back from the edge, Julie saw herself as she must have looked to Colonel Uxbridge during the past few minutes, and at once her face grew hot.

"I'm sorry," she said, talking to a point slightly above and beyond the colonel's right shoulder. "There's no reason for you to believe me when I say that I don't usually act this way, but too much has been happening that I don't understand."

"I do believe you," Colonel Uxbridge said. "And it is because I don't understand a good deal of it myself that I thought I had better chance a court-martial by trying to clarify some of it for both of us, before I make my decision. May I?"

"Of course," Julie said. She risked a small smile, not so much to win back his good opinion, which it surprised her to discover she wanted, as to reassure herself. "I promise not to scream again."

"I wish I could say as much for myself," Colonel Uxbridge said. "Before this business is over and done with, screaming may well be the only recourse left to me. Until then, I can give you the facts as I know them. An hour or so ago, in the car that brought us here to Claridge's, I remember telling you that until earlier this evening, when I walked into his hotel suite at the Wyndham Hotel, I had never clapped eyes on General MacNeilson, who introduced you to me. You were surprised, and I could not blame you. I won't blame you now for being surprised when I tell you that until three days ago, or twenty-four hours before I boarded the plane with him in Washington that brought us to London yesterday, I had never clapped eyes on Benjamin Franklin Ivey. I see you *are* surprised."

"Well," Julie said, "he's not exactly a newcomer to the Washington scene, and even if you hadn't told me you come from Washington, I would assume any American who's been reading the papers during the past seven or eight years—"

"I have been doing that, along with most people," Colonel Uxbridge said. "So of course I know about Mr. Ivey. Just as I know about Winston Churchill and Mahatma Gandhi. I even knew, from friends and associates who had had dealings with him, that much of his reputation is deserved. Without touching on the various roles he played during the early days of the New Deal, sticking only to his activities since this war began, it seems to me that, aside from the President himself and the Chief of Staff and perhaps half a dozen of the leading military figures, no name is better known to the American people as being part of the war effort's central directing team than that of Ben Ivey. You can imagine my surprise, therefore, when three days ago, quite early in the morning, as a matter of fact while I was having breakfast with my wife in our house in Arlington, the phone rang and I was asked—no, to be frank, I was *told*—to report to Mr. Ivey's office in the White House within the half hour. When I got there, no time was wasted on polite introductions before he got down to business. This consisted of a single question. Was it true, Mr. Ivey wanted to know, that I speak all the Scandinavian languages?"

Colonel Uxbridge paused, and it was possible that he needed the pause to catch his breath, but it occurred to Julie that perhaps the colonel's brief association with Ben Ivey had begun to rub off on him just a little. The pause at crucial moments in a recital had always been one of Ben's most effective histrionic tricks.

"Scandinavian?" said Julie, almost automatically, the way she used to respond to one of Ben's carefully placed pauses.

"Scandinavian," Colonel Uxbridge said and, perhaps because he was not as experienced as Ben at this sort of thing, he ruined the moment by adding what did not have to be added: "Odd," the colonel said, "isn't it?"

"Yes, I suppose so," Julie said. "Although I don't really know why."

"The number of officers with the rank of colonel or higher who happen to be on the General Staff and know all the Scandinavian languages happens to be limited to one. Me."

Colonel Uxbridge paused again, and this time Julie suspected the pause was not calculated. She could tell, from the suddenly narrowed eyes and the slightly furrowed brow, that the colonel, who obviously preferred simplicity, was rendered momentarily speechless by the same thing that had bothered her from the moment they had met: the contemplation of a complexity that seemed pointless.

"As soon as I admitted to him that, yes, it was true, I did speak those languages," Colonel Uxbridge said, "Mr. Ivey gave me my orders. I was to meet him the following morning at the same time in the same room with a packed bag. I was to tell absolutely nobody, not even my wife, that I had seen him or that I was going anywhere with him. I could tell *only* my wife that I would be away for a few days, perhaps a week, but if I told anybody else, and indeed if my wife told anybody else, my thirty-two-year army career would end as abruptly and ignominiously as, and I use Mr. Ivey's own phrase, that of a New York police commissioner reduced to walking a beat in Flatbush."

Colonel Uxbridge permitted himself a small, wintry smile in which Julie was surprised to sense a touch of genuine amusement.

"I would like to make clear at this point, Miss Sarno," he said, "that the fact that I obeyed Mr. Ivey's orders implicitly is a tribute not to his stature in Washington, which we both know is considerable, but to his personality, about which you undoubtedly know a good deal but which took me by surprise. Civilians, no matter how important they are, do not talk like that to full colonels with thirty-two years of honorable service on their records. Not if they expect their orders to be obeyed, that is. The army man of rank and experience can always rely on his superior knowledge of what we might as well reduce to the simple word channels, although there is a good deal more to it than that, to frustrate, obstruct, and even turn the tables on the highest-ranking civilian in the land, and that goes, even though you may think I'm exaggerating, for the President himself. My first instinct, when Mr. Ivey issued his orders to me, was to utter some suitably profane version of the traditional suggestion that he jump in the lake. The fact that instead I followed his orders to the letter, is the tribute to his personality that I mentioned earlier. From the moment I walked into his presence, I never doubted his sincerity. I liked him at once. I don't mean like merely in the sense of an absence of dislike. I mean something much more positive than that. I can't quite say what caused it. Perhaps his thin, reedy frame, which makes him look so helpless. Or perhaps it's that astonishingly boyish smile, which brings out all one's paternal instincts. Whatever it is, almost at once, immediately, I was swept by a very real feeling of affection for him, a genuine desire to help him, no matter what he asked. Does that make any sense to you, Miss Sarno?"

"Yes," Julie said. "A great deal."

The tone of her voice caused him to look at her sharply. Their eyes met, and Julie could feel her face grow hot again.

"I discovered, when I reported the next morning to Mr. Ivey's office in the White House, that I was not alone in this feeling," Colonel Uxbridge said. "A man named Harry, the man in the sweatshirt who is in there—" the colonel nodded to the archway at the far end of the room—"with Mr. Ivey right now, was waiting with him when I arrived. During the almost thirty-six hours that elapsed between our departure from the White House and our arrival here at Claridge's, I gathered that Harry, who is not a doctor, nonetheless functions as the approximate equivalent of a personal physician to Mr. Ivey. I did not think it odd, I might add, that Mr. Ivey told me nothing about our trip, not even where we were going. Security is a curious business. To some, especially civilians, it isn't a business at all, but rather a sort of screen of mumbo-jumbo invented by the military to conceal their mistakes or venality from the world at large. And while I daresay it is used often enough for those two lamentable purposes, the fact does remain that it serves an extremely important function, certainly during a war, and I have been involved with it for enough of my adult life to assume I understood the reason for Mr. Ivey's silence and to approve of that silence: the beans you don't know, an old CO of mine once put it, you can't spill. I was perfectly content to wait until we arrived at our destination before Mr. Ivey told me what he wanted me to do. This contentment lasted for a little less than half an hour after we arrived here."

Colonel Uxbridge paused again, walked up to the archway at the top of the room, and stood there for several silent moments, apparently listening for sounds from the bedroom into which Harry had disappeared to be near Ben Ivey.

"Even though the plane in which we had traveled had been hastily fitted with a few conveniences that are not standard equipment in the average army bomber, it was still a fairly rough means of transportation, and it had become pretty clear to me, if only from the way Harry kept such close watch on him all during the trip, that Mr. Ivey was not in the best of health. I felt pretty worn out when we got here. I could imagine how he felt. I was not surprised, therefore, that the first words Mr. Ivey spoke to me after our departure from Washington should be the suggestion that I have a wash and a nap. I assumed that Mr. Ivey would be doing the same in his bedroom. My assumption was wrong."

Colonel Uxbridge bent down over the littered table and twisted the knob of the typewriter carriage until the sheet of paper came up a couple of inches. For several moments he stared down at the paragraphs under the word CONFIDENTIAL, as though he had forgotten what he wanted to say next and he thought the words B.F.I. had typed might refresh his recollection. Finally, twisting the sheet back to its former position, Colonel Uxbridge looked up.

"I took a bath and shaved," he said, "and I was just about to lie down for my nap, when I heard a curious sound out in this room. I hurried out and found Mr. Ivey lying there."

Colonel Uxbridge pointed to a spot on the floor two or three feet to the right of the chair in which Julie had just been sitting.

"A moment later Harry came running out of the other bedroom and spoke his first words to me since we had met thirty-six hours earlier in Washington. *Grab his feet*, he said. Harry took him under the arms, and we carried him into his bedroom, where Harry spoke his second words to me. *Okay, Colonel*, he said, *you can beat it now*."

Colonel Uxbridge sent another glance at the typewriter, but apparently his recollection needed no further refreshment, because he went right on.

"I don't like to be talked to like that, and I had barely opened my mouth to put Harry in his place with a few words carefully chosen for their caustic content, when Mr. Ivey, who had been lying motionless on the bed, exactly as we had placed him, still fully clothed, opened his eyes and in the tiredest voice I have ever heard issue from a human throat, he said: *Please do as Harry says, Colonel*."

Colonel Uxbridge walked back up to the archway and then turned to face Julie.

"I did as Harry said," he said, coming down the room toward her as he spoke. "I beat it. Exactly forty-eight minutes later, Harry came out to join me, and that's when you entered the picture."

"Me?" Julie said.

"You," Colonel Uxbridge said.

"In what way?" Julie said.

"Harry said that Mr. Ivey wanted me to locate and bring to this suite, as soon as it was possible to do so within the framework of the security plan under which we were operating, a Miss Julie Sarno. Harry knew only what Mr. Ivey had told him, and Mr. Ivey had clearly told Harry all he knew. Miss Sarno was American, worked as a secretary in the London office of the Board of Economic Warfare, and lived in a flat on Old Quebec Street with another BEW secretary named Rita Merlin."

"How did you find out about General MacNeilson?" Julie said.

"I'm going to be asking you for some information very soon," Colonel Uxbridge said. "You might be reluctant to give it to me, but you might be willing to swap."

"I have absolutely no information that can possibly be useful to you," Julie said. "I assure you, Colonel Uxbridge, there's nothing—"

"Wouldn't it be more sensible to withhold your assurance until you know the nature of the information I want?"

Julie's face grew warm again. "I'm sorry," she said, and she was. On the unwritten assessment sheet that Colonel Uxbridge was probably compiling in his mind, her score had undoubtedly gone down a notch.

"I told you earlier this evening," he said, "that locating you and bringing you here, Miss Sarno, would end my official interest in you as a person. This was true until a few minutes ago, when Harry came out of that bedroom and asked me to go in with him. During those few minutes, Miss Sarno, the situation has changed completely."

"In what way?" Julie said.

"Mr. Ivey's ailment, the nature of which Harry did not explain to me, has taken a new and disturbing turn. I gather that Mr. Ivey has been the victim for some time of an illness that at recurring intervals causes him to suffer sometimes partial and sometimes total physical paralysis for periods of varying length. According to Harry, these periods are usually quite short, sometimes a matter of minutes, rarely longer than one hour. During all of these seizures, Mr. Ivey always retains consciousness, although in order to get through them he usually closes his eyes as though in sleep, and he never loses his powers of speech, hearing, taste, and touch. The seizure that struck Mr. Ivey last night differs from all previous seizures in two important respects."

"I would prefer not to hear them."

"You said that a few minutes ago," Colonel Uxbridge said. "You promised not to scream again."

"I didn't scream. I said—"

"Having allowed me to come this far down the road toward a potential court-martial, Miss Sarno, I find any interruption, even if whispered, the equivalent of a scream."

"I'm sorry," Julie said.

"Very well, then," Colonel Uxbridge said. "First, this seizure has lasted longer than any other of which Harry has any knowledge."

"Why didn't you send for a doctor?" Julie said. "It's been almost twenty-four hours. It seems to me shocking that you should let—"

"I don't think it does, Miss Sarno."

"I beg your pardon?"

"I don't think it seems to you shocking," Colonel Uxbridge said. "I think you know why we didn't send for a doctor. I will, however, pretend you don't know and tell you. Several times today, while I was waiting to go over to the Wyndham Hotel for the date with you that General MacNeilson had promised to set up, Mr. Ivey assured me, and Harry corroborated this assurance, that doctors are useless. They have tried many times in the past, proving only by their attempts that they cannot do anything for

Mr. Ivey when he has one of these seizures. Furthermore, his presence in London is a military secret. To bring in a doctor or several doctors, army or civilian, would merely enlarge the area of security risk that Mr. Ivey feels is already too large for the safety of our mission. We now come to the second way in which this seizure differs from all the others Mr. Ivey has ever had. The second difference occurred a few minutes ago. For the first time since Harry's contact with these seizures began, Mr. Ivey has lost consciousness. Even though he is not a doctor, Harry assures me he has had sufficient training and he has been in charge of Mr. Ivey long enough for me to accept his assurance that Mr. Ivey's unexpected lapse into unconsciousness has placed him in no danger. His pulse, his breathing, his blood pressure, all are normal. Harry checked them all. Mr. Ivey is not, I repeat, in any danger. What is in danger, Miss Sarno, is something so much greater than the life of any one man, that I have felt it worth risking a court-martial to speak to you in this fashion."

This time, when Colonel Uxbridge paused, Julie was reminded of a swimmer who has reached the far end of a pool and, before shoving off for the return lap, takes time out for an extra-long breath. It seemed a good time to say something that had been forcing its way to the top of her mind for several minutes.

"I hope you won't interpret this as screaming," she said. "And I also hope you won't think I'm being frivolous about something that is obviously to you very serious, but I honestly don't see how anybody could give you a traffic ticket, much less court-martial you, for what you've just told me. You really haven't told me anything. I already knew Mr. Ivey is in London. He'd sent for me. I spoke to him in the bedroom a little while ago. He must have come here from somewhere, and since he's front-page news out of Washington almost every day, it's not a sign of spectacular brilliance on my part to have assumed, even before you told me, that he'd come here *from* Washington. In fact, Colonel Uxbridge, the only thing you told me that might be described as something I didn't know before you told it to me is that you speak several Scandinavian languages."

The slender, white-haired man nodded. "Precisely," he said.

Julie shook her head. "You're going to have to do a lot better than that," she said.

"I intend to," Colonel Uxbridge said. "I told you that I am going to ask you for certain information which you might not want to give me but that you might be willing to swap. Very well. Would you tell me what you and Mr. Ivey talked about when you were in his bedroom a little while ago?"

"No," Julie said.

"Is there any information I have that you would like me to give you in exchange for telling me what went on between you and Mr. Ivey in that bedroom?"

"No," Julie said.

Colonel Uxbridge nodded, almost to himself, as though to indicate for his own satisfaction that this was the reply he had expected. "In that case," he said, "I will do what any man who has tried a bluff and failed should do. If he has any sense, that is. Miss Sarno, I am in no position to swap information with you. I am completely at your mercy."

"I don't want you to be," Julie said. "I mean, I don't want to feel—"

"Miss Sarno, you're screaming again."

"I don't think that's fair."

"I am abandoning fairness," Colonel Uxbridge said. "I told you I am at your mercy. Harry thinks I can persuade you to do whatever it was you failed to do when you were alone in that bedroom with Mr. Ivey."

"Harry is wrong," Julie said.

"Am I also wrong?" Colonel Uxbridge said.

"About what?"

"My belief that you are not the sort of person who would allow her personal feelings, whatever yours toward Mr. Ivey might be, to interfere with the performance of her duty."

"Colonel Uxbridge, you started talking about duty downstairs in the car, on our way over here, and it seems to me you haven't stopped. You might as well know here and now that it means absolutely nothing to me. It's just a word, two syllables, so far as I'm concerned, that people who want you to do something for them are fond of using, as though it is part of a prayer or a mysterious password, something you must respond to without any question. I know I must sound like someone trampling the Stars and Stripes in the dust, or even worse since there is a war on, but the word duty gets no more response out of me, Colonel Uxbridge, than the word auto or apple or phony. No, I'm not telling the truth. It does get a response out of me. It makes my stomach turn. I am sick and tired of it, Colonel Uxbridge. I have had the word duty pushed down my throat for so long that the mere sound of it makes me gag."

"I see," Colonel Uxbridge said quietly, "that I am correct about one of my guesses at any rate. You *have* known Mr. Ivey for some time, haven't you?"

Julie caught her lower lip in her teeth and held it. Anything further she might say would only intensify the feeling of regret for what she had said already. She had begun to like this slender, white-haired man too much to have given herself away like that.

"Very well," Colonel Uxbridge said. "I am beginning to see my problem more clearly. Not as a duty, then, but as a gesture of politeness I probably have no right to ask you to make, would you let me show you my position?"

Julie did not answer.

"Thank you," Colonel Uxbridge said. "It is this. I know absolutely nothing about the nature of my mission here in London. Mr. Ivey, as I told you, explained nothing before we left Washington. I assumed, as I also told you, he would give me whatever information I needed when we reached our destination. He has not done so. I thought it odd that all day today, while he was in bed but conscious and able to talk, he did not tell me. I can only conclude that he saw no reason to push ahead the moment of revelation because he fully expected to be put back on his feet by your visit. He hasn't, and now that he has lapsed into unconsciousness, it is too late for him to tell me. I could, with a reasonably clear conscience, accept this failure on Mr. Ivey's part to reveal the nature of this mission as no fault or responsibility of mine. I could, in short, sit it out. If I prefer not to, it is because I have discovered that a conscience which is only reasonably clear is a pretty irksome piece of luggage to carry around. You see, Miss Sarno, even though Mr. Ivey has told me nothing, I know a good deal. I cannot close my conscience to knowledge I have acquired merely by using my eyes and ears."

Colonel Uxbridge turned and walked back to the table on which the portable typewriter sat among the litter of newspapers and magazines.

"I know, to begin with, that I was chosen for this mission because of my Scandinavian background," he said. "I know, also, what the entire world knows, namely, that the Allies are preparing to invade occupied Europe at some time in the not too distant future, and I know that all of Scandinavia is part of occupied Europe. I know from this document"—he dipped down and touched the sheet of paper in the typewriter—"on which Mr. Ivey was working when he collapsed and which I assumed he had no objection to my reading since he allowed it to remain out here all day—I know from this document that the nature of Mr. Ivey's mission is some sort of meeting with somebody identified as X in connection with our invasion of occupied Europe in the near future. And I know that the meeting is scheduled to take place in" —Colonel Uxbridge looked at his wrist watch—"approximately three hours, because one hour ago Mr. Ivey told you he had to be back on his feet in four hours."

Julie gave him a sharp glance.

"How do you know that?" she said.

"Harry told me," Colonel Uxbridge said.

"How does Harry know what Mr. Ivey said to me?"

"He was listening at the keyhole, Miss Sarno."

"What else did he tell you?"

"Do you trust me to give you an honest answer?"

"Yes," Julie said.

"Absolutely nothing else," Colonel Uxbridge said. "Harry justified his eavesdropping on the ground that it was his duty under the circumstances to learn anything he could, but apparently the only time that anybody raised his or her voice enough for Harry to hear what was being said was when Mr. Ivey made his remark to you about having to be back on his feet in four hours."

Colonel Uxbridge took his hand from the sheet of paper in the typewriter. He straightened up and came forward.

"This, then, is my position," he said. "I can sit here in this hotel suite and wait for Mr. Ivey to regain consciousness. If he does so within the next three hours, he will, of course, make the decisions, whatever they may be. If he does not recover consciousness within the next three hours, he will not be present at the meeting for which he came from Washington. It is Harry's guess, based on his long experience with his boss's condition, that Mr. Ivey will not regain consciousness within the next three hours unless something is done for him. Assuming nothing is done for him, I must then face the fact that Mr. Ivey is going to miss the meeting for which he came here. If I knew who X is, or what was going to happen at this meeting, I would not have to make a decision. However, since I do *not* know, but can only guess, I *must* make a decision. Because my guess is that if Mr. Ivey is not present at this meeting, the course of this war may take a turn that may cost us nobody can possibly guess how many thousands of human lives."

Julie gave the colonel another sharp glance. Ben Ivey had used almost exactly the same words. Had Colonel Uxbridge used them independently? Or was he quoting Ben? If he was quoting, then everything the white-haired man had said since coming out of the bedroom was suspect.

"Which brings me to my decision," Colonel Uxbridge said. "I can break the security pattern within which we are operating in order to seek help in getting Mr. Ivey to that meeting. The consequences of such an act on my part, especially if any link in the chain of deduction and guesswork I have put together in order to reach my decision should prove to be wrong, are so potentially dangerous, not only to me but to the forces that could save those thousands of lives I have just mentioned, that I will not even attempt to describe them. I am perfectly willing to face those consequences, one of the least important of which would be the court-martial I have already mentioned, because I am convinced that the gravity of the situation demands it. I am not convinced, however, that the risk must be taken. I don't mean the risk to me, a matter of minor importance. I mean the risk to the thousands of lives that would be affected. There is a simple alternative. Unfortunately, it is not within my power to act on it. You are the only one who can do that, Miss Sarno."

"In what way?" Julie said.

"You can do what Mr. Ivey asked me to bring you here to do and what you apparently refused to do when you were in there with Mr. Ivey an hour ago. You can put him back on his feet in time to attend that meeting under his own power."

Abruptly, as though the movement was an instinctive leap away from some sudden physical threat, Julie turned her back on Colonel Uxbridge. She did not want him to see what she was certain her face reflected: the feeling of helplessness that had been creeping up on her for some time and by which she now felt completely overwhelmed.

"I am no longer asking you to do this out of a sense of loyalty to a concept such as patriotism," Colonel Uxbridge said quietly. "I am being much more unreasonable than that. I am asking you to do it as a favor to a total stranger: me."

Julie kept her back turned. Churning up through the helplessness she did not want him to see was the bitter knowledge Colonel Uxbridge had not yet had time to acquire for himself: when Ben Ivey wanted something it did not matter that he was not himself available to ask for it; there was always somebody ready and willing to step in and work to get it for him.

"I don't want to pry into your relationship with Mr. Ivey," Colonel Uxbridge said. "Whatever it was, I have no doubt your feelings about him are justified. I would like to remind you, however, that not everybody shares your feelings. May I read something to you? It is an editorial from the *Journal-Courier*, a newspaper in St. Paul, Minnesota. It appeared on December 8, 1941, the morning after Pearl Harbor. Harry gave it to me a few minutes ago. I'm sure he felt it might help to persuade you."

Julie turned and saw Colonel Uxbridge holding a piece of newsprint, from which he read aloud: "*In this moment of our nation's peril, we Americans can thank God that among the men in the control tower of the national effort we have one of the most selfless, devoted, and gifted servants this country has ever known —a man who has never held public office, but for a decade has held something infinitely more precious: the public confidence—* Mr. Benjamin Franklin Ivey."

Colonel Uxbridge looked up.

"What paper did you say that was from?" Julie said.

The question seemed to puzzle the colonel. "The *Journal-Courier*, St. Paul, Minnesota," he said. "Why?"

"I have a friend who lives across the river, in Minneapolis," Julie said, picking up her purse. "I haven't seen her for a long time, not since she got married and went out to Minneapolis to live, but we used to go to school together, and she met Mr. Ivey at the same time I met him." From the wallet in her purse, Julie took the now badly creased and partially faded clipping that Cockeye Katie Halloran had sent her a year and a half ago. "This is an editorial from the Minneapolis *Herald-Clarion*," Julie said. "It also appeared on December 8, 1941, the morning after Pearl Harbor. My friend thought I'd be interested in it. It says," Julie said, and she read aloud: "*When the definitive history of our country in this desperate time is finally written, the responsibility for its most degrading pages will be lodged at the door of that malevolent, corrupt, mysterious man who for almost a decade has been known to his fellow Americans with bitter accuracy as 'Poison Ivey.'* "

Julie looked up. Colonel Uxbridge tapped the piece of newsprint in his hand and nodded toward the piece she held in hers.

"They can't both be right," he said, "can they?"

"No," Julie said, "they can't."

"As long as there is any doubt," Colonel Uxbridge said, "is it asking too much to resolve the doubt in favor not of the devoted or the corrupt public servant, but in favor of the sick human being lying helpless in that bedroom?"

It was so much too much that, even to avoid seeming a heartless monster in the eyes of this man she liked, Julie did not see how she could put it into words.

"Of course," Colonel Uxbridge said, "I can imagine what you must be thinking—"

The look of astonishment on Julie's face exploded so suddenly, and was so total, that it stopped the words in Colonel Uxbridge's throat.

"Can you?"·she said.

"Why, yes, I— No. I mean I *thought* I could, but quite obviously I'm wrong. That is—" Colonel Uxbridge's uncharacteristic floundering came to an abrupt halt and he gave Julie a highly characteristic look of totally absorbed interest. "Would you mind telling me?" he said. "I very much want to know. What *were* you thinking when I said that?"

"Nothing that would make much sense to you," Julie said. "I was thinking of a day in 1933, the day the banks closed."

10

She didn't know, of course, when the day began, that the banks were going to close. Or indeed, as it later turned out, that when the alarm clock blasted Julie awake at seven o'clock, the banks had already been legally closed for two and a half hours: Governor Lehman's declaration of a bank holiday, Julie read in the *Times* the following morning, when the information could no longer do her any good, had been issued in Albany at 4:30 A.M.

At 7:00 A.M., when the information might have changed her

whole life, Julie was aware only, as she had been aware almost every morning since the Sarnos had moved to the Bronx, that all those people who in novels and plays sold their souls to the devil had driven excellent bargains: at seven in the morning Julie would have parted with hers for ten extra minutes of sleep.

Her fumbling fingers found the button on the alarm clock, clicked it off, and the next thing of which she became aware was a feeling of outrage that the clock should have chosen this moment to go out of order: the bell continued to ring.

"Oh, God," Julie groaned, heaving herself into a sitting position as the fumbling process started again, this time for the switch on the lamp between the beds. A moment later, in the brightness splashed by the lamp, Julie said again, but with more feeling, since she was that much closer to wakefulness, "Oh, *God*."

There was nothing wrong with the alarm clock. Nothing, at any rate, that had anything to do with the continued sound of ringing. The telephone out in the hall was doing that.

Staggering toward it on her bare feet, Julie noticed that the kitchen light at the far end of the hall was on, which was not surprising, since Mrs. Sarno always rose at six-thirty to make sure her two daughters had a hot breakfast before they went off to the subway that carried them to their jobs downtown. But the bathroom light at the other end of the hall, Julie noticed as she reached the phone table, was also on, and this was very surprising indeed, since Celia was still asleep, as she always was until Julie shook, cajoled, and practically dragged her out of the other bed in their room, and Mrs. Sarno would no more leave a light on in a room nobody was using than she would allow anybody in her presence to utter an unkind word about the deceased husband of whom, during her six years of widowhood, she had managed completely to forget she had once been terrified.

"Hello?" Julie said into the phone. The oilcloth runner in the hall was icy underfoot, and the cold receiver, touching the ear she had just dragged from its luxuriously warm nest in her pillow, made Julie wince.

"Celia?"

"No, it's not Celia. Who's calling, please?"

"Who does it sound like? Bebe Daniels? It's Katie. What's the matter with you?"

"Oh, hi," Julie said to the best friend whom, now that they were both seventeen, she no longer dared call Cockeye Katie. "What's the matter with me is people who drag me out of my warm bed to answer the telephone at this hour of the morning. I am freezing."

"Why don't you turn on the heat?"

"In *this* house? Katie, we don't have the kind of landlords *you* have down on Kelly Street. Up here on Daly Avenue, our Mrs. Pyser doesn't believe in providing her tenants with anything so commonplace as *heat*."

"What was that?" Katie asked.

Julie moved toward the noise, carrying the phone three feet down the hall to the window that looked out on Bronx Park.

"The camels, I guess," she said, and then, "No, wait." She took another look, out across Bronx Park South, toward the steel fences and the naked trees that, when spring exploded them into huge swaying mushrooms of green leaves, managed to conceal a great part of the zoo. "Yes, I guess it *is* the camels," Julie said into the phone. "They look sort of upset. I think a llama, anyway it *looks* like a llama, he's just come wandering around from back of the Small Mammals House, and the ships of the desert seem to resent it. I can hardly blame them. A llama yet, in this weather. Katie, my feet are like *ice*."

"Why don't you sue that Mrs. Pyser? After all, you work in a law office."

The touch of bitterness in Katie Halloran's voice, which was unmistakable, was also understandable. Katie had never quite forgiven her best friend for the fact that, eight months ago, when she and Julie had graduated from Fenimore Cooper High into the middle of what everybody was calling the Great Depression, Celia Sarno had managed somehow to get her kid sister a job in the offices of Ellentuch, Prohst & Wadsworth. However, even though her father was a policeman, which had seemed for a time to give Katie a small leg up on some sort of civil service job, the best

Katie had been able to do was office helper and general assistant to a resident buyer on Seventh Avenue.

Julie suspected that what Katie resented was not so much the intellectual gap between typing briefs for a well-known law firm, and being, in Katie's own phrase, chief cook and bottle washer to a totally unknown man who made his living by buying in wholesale lots everything from rubber heels to hair tonic for customers all over the country. Julie was certain what bothered Katie was the reversal in their positions.

On East Ninth Street, where both girls had been born and raised, there had never been any doubt about which was closer to the top of the social heap: the family of an American-born Irishman whose job as a policeman was the personification of law and order, or the family of an immigrant barber whose disorderly habits brought him into repeated conflict with the law. Julie knew it didn't seem fair to Katie that the death of the barber—which, by the yardsticks of virtue Julie was certain the Halloran family employed, was richly deserved—should have lifted his survivors to a position above their former betters. Although Biaggio Sarno's demise had made it necessary for Julie to forget about college and go to work, her salary and Celia's, though neither was large, together added up to more than the sum of Cockeye Katie's earnings and her father's retirement pension.

As a result, the best the Hallorans could afford, on leaving the Lower East Side for greener social pastures, was a four-room flat on Kelly Street with a clawfoot bathtub and a fine view of the Intervale Avenue subway station, which in that part of the Bronx, a borough of paradoxes, ran overhead. The surviving Sarnos, on the other hand, while also limited to four rooms, could get from the windows of all of them a clear view of the borough's great park and its world-famous zoo as well as the aardvark and kudu with which, apparently to Katie Halloran's chagrin, the Sarnos were privileged to live cheek by jowl. Julie, whose notions about privilege were somewhat different from Katie's, had assured her best friend over and over again that her duties in the steno pool at Ellentuch, Prohst & Wadsworth were no more elegant than

Katie's duties in the office of Howard L. Karp, but the assurances had done no good.

Katie Halloran still made cracks about people who worked in law offices.

"Working in a law office and suing a landlady are two different things," Julie said. "And if I don't get off this darned oilcloth in my bare feet, I'll have pneumonia, so what can I do for you?"

"Would you tell Celia I can't deliver the suitcase to your office this morning, the way I promised, because Mr. Karp has this rush order for hats from this store in Toledo, and I didn't know about that when I told Celia yesterday I'd deliver the suitcase—"

"What suitcase?" Julie said.

"The suitcase Celia asked me to get for her. What suitcase did you think? For Albert Einstein maybe? I thought I'd be doing a glassware order from Terre Haute this morning, which would have made it a cinch, since so many of the glassware showrooms are down on Twenty-third Street, right near your office, but Mr. Karp just called me at home here a few minutes ago. He's going to do the glassware order himself. He wants me to do the hats for Toledo, and the millinery district is further uptown, Thirty-eighth, Thirty-ninth, Fortieth, up there, so here I am with this suitcase—"

"You mean a suitcase for *Celia?*" Julie said.

"Julie, darling, what type law do they have at this Ellentuch, Prohst & Wadsworth? Sanskrit or something? I am talking English, kid. Celia asked me yesterday if I can get her a nice buy on a suitcase, and if I could, would I pick it up for her. I said not only I could, but I went and I did, and then I called her and said I'd be practically in her building tomorrow morning, that's today morning, now, because I had to do this glassware order for Terre Haute, so I'd deliver it to Celia in your office on my way. But now that Mr. Karp has changed the signals on me, slipping me this millinery job, I'm calling to ask Celia what she wants me to do about the suitcase, because when she called about it yesterday she seemed in a hurry—"

"What does Celia want with a suitcase?" Julie said.

"You know, kid, it's either those legal briefs or maybe it's living with all those llamas and camels, but *something* is slowing you up, Julie. How do I know what Celia wants a suitcase for? She's *your* sister. Why don't you ask her?"

"Hold on a minute, Katie, will you?"

Feeling the beginnings of an uneasiness that made no sense to her, Julie put down the phone, walked back to her bedroom, and then abruptly forgot all about the uneasiness in a sudden flood of surprise: Celia's bed was empty.

"If you don't stop standing around with your mouth open, you'll catch more flies than Lou Gehrig."

Julie turned toward the voice behind her, and had another surprise: Celia was completely dressed. No surprise, however, could dull the small delicious thrust of the heart that was for Julie a part of each morning's first glimpse of her sister. It was as eagerly awaited and as indispensable a part of the life of Julie's seventeenth year as it had been down on Ninth Street when, as a child of eleven, she would in her mind build the ladder of happiness at the top of which every evening she met Celia coming home from work at the Tenth Street trolley stop. If there had been any danger that for Julie the never-ending wonder of Celia's radiance might pall because they now both worked in the same office, and every day they traveled to that work together, the threat had been eliminated before Julie had even had a chance to become aware of its existence. The eliminating factor had been for Julie an even greater wonder. What had been perfection in the mind and heart of a child had gone beyond perfection in the mind and heart of a near-adult. At eleven Julie Sarno had never for a moment doubted that the most beautiful thing in all the world was her sister Celia. At seventeen, when Julie's knowledge of the world had expanded considerably, it seemed to her that Celia was growing more beautiful every day. She had certainly never looked more beautiful, Julie thought, than she did on this cold, puzzling morning when, instead of being sound asleep in the bed from which Julie had been about to drag her, Celia was standing fully clothed in front of her.

"Where have you been?" Julie said.

"The bathroom," Celia said. "Where would I be?"

"Well, this sure is not my morning," Julie said. "Where else

193

you'd be is there." She pointed to Celia's bed. "Out of which I have to haul you every morning, fighting every inch of the way, like one of those deep-sea fishermen landing a tarpon in the newsreels. But this morning, since for some reason I don't have to drag you out of bed, you'd better answer your own phone calls. My feet are as cold as—"

"What phone calls?"

"Celia, what's the matter with you this morning? All I said was Katie Halloran's on the phone. She wants to know what to do about your suitcase. She said—"

What Katie had said seemed completely unimportant to Celia. Or perhaps she preferred to hear it from Katie's own lips. In any case, before Julie could give her sister any part of Katie's message, Celia had given her a quick little push up the hall, toward the bathroom, saying hurriedly, "Keep the prosecutor out of my hair for a minute, sweetie, will you?" Snatching the phone from the small table, Celia took it into the bedroom, kicked the cord into the groove on the threshold that allowed the door to fit snugly, and pulled it shut.

"Who's on the phone?" Mrs. Sarno called from the kitchen, and then, as Julie approached on her way to the bathroom, Mrs. Sarno appeared in the kitchen doorway, holding a grapefruit knife.

"It's Katie," Julie said. "She wants to talk to Celia."

"About what?"

"I don't know, Ma. She said she wants to talk to Celia, so I put Celia on."

"Since when did Celia and Cockeye Katie become friends?"

"You know how she hates that name, Ma. I wish you'd quit using it, and just because they're talking on the phone doesn't mean they're friends."

"Let her hate the name or love it, she's still cockeyed," Mrs. Sarno said. "If they're not friends, why does Celia have to take the telephone into the bedroom and close the door to talk to her?"

"I don't know, Ma," Julie said, wishing that her mother would not try so hard to live up to the nickname Celia had invented for Mrs. Sarno: the prosecutor. "If you'll stop the cross-examination, I'll be able to go into the bathroom and start getting dressed."

"Why weren't you in the bathroom first, the way you are every morning?"

"Because Celia got up first, Ma, that's why."

"Why did she suddenly today get up first?"

"I don't know, Ma, but when she gets off the phone you can ask her. Now please let me get into the—"

"Because the duchess doesn't talk to her servants, that's why I won't ask her," Mrs. Sarno said. "Besides, I did ask her, a few minutes ago. What's the rush, up a quarter to seven, are you sick? Only of your questions, she said, and disappears into the bathroom with a bang on the door. Fried, boiled, or scrambled?"

"I don't think I want any eggs this morning, Ma. Just orange juice and—"

"No oranges today. Grapefruit. Nine cents a dozen he wanted for oranges. I said, Mr. Coteletti, my daughters work too hard for me to throw away nine cents of their money on oranges that aren't worth three. I'll take grapefruit. You've got to put something down into your stomach besides fruit in the morning or the day has nothing to stand on. If your father, may he rest in peace, had taken better care of himself, and eaten a good, solid breakfast every morning, that wonderful man would still be with us today. Fried, boiled, or scrambled?"

"All right, Ma, fried. And just one, please."

"Spaghetti eaters have one egg," Mrs. Sarno said. "We Milanese eat two or none at all. Where are your slippers? You'll be eighteen next month. Do I still have to tell you that the surest way to an early grave is walking on cold oilcloth with bare feet? Your father, the poor man, look what happened to him."

Julie looked, instead, at her mother. It was one of those moments of unexpected revelation in which the familiar, the commonplace, and the dull suddenly become strange, unique, and even terrifying. It was as though an elevator operator, into whose car people have stepped every morning for years, and about whom their knowledge is limited to an awareness of a vague, almost inhuman shape that is part of the machinery of getting to their daily tasks, suddenly becomes—when one morning he un-expectedly turns for a moment to face his passengers—a human being in whose eyes can be seen at a glance the disturbing signs of passion and sorrow.

For the first time since Biaggio Sarno's death, Julie realized that her mother, who used to display her rhinestone-studded tortoise-shell combs only on ceremonial occasions, now wore them con-stantly, like a diadem, in the thick gray hair piled high in an old-fashioned manner. All at once, for the first time in her life, Julie had a glimpse of what the hot-blooded, handsome, penniless spaghetti eater from Naples who had been her father must have seen when he first clapped eyes on the slender, red-headed, patri-cian rice eater from Milan who was to become Celia's mother. Somewhere, in the years between that first glimpse in Italy and the drunkard's death on a Lower East Side dock, that proud Mila-nese figure had vanished. Somehow, in the six years between that moment of ignominious extinction and this moment of as-tonishing revelation, the woman that patrician girl was destined to become had fulfilled her destiny.

"Julie!"

She turned toward Celia at the far end of the hall. "What?"

"Come here a minute."

"She hasn't been in the bathroom yet," Mrs. Sarno called. "You'll be late for work."

"Ma, you're not addressing a grand jury and asking for an in-dictment," Celia called back. "I want to talk to Julie for a min-ute."

Julie started down the hall.

"Get your slippers on the way," Mrs. Sarno said. "If you won't think of yourself, think of your poor father."

Julie tried, for a fleeting moment, to do this. But the image of Biaggio Sarno as she remembered him, walloping a child of eleven across the floor of the East Ninth Street barber shop, re-fused to mesh with the image of a Neapolitan Galahad her mother had reconstructed. Besides, before Julie had even reached the telephone table, Celia had grabbed her arm, pulled her into their bedroom, and shut the door.

"Look, sweetie, do me a favor, will you?"

"Sure," Julie said. "What?"

"On your way to work, get out on the Intervale Avenue station. Katie will be waiting for you there. If she's not, give her a few minutes. She promised it won't be more than a few minutes, and after she gives you the suitcase—"

"What suitcase?"

"The suitcase she bought for me yesterday," Celia said. "Bring it down to the office for me, will you?" There was a pause and then, the impatience lifting her voice to a note not very far removed from anger, Celia said, "Why are you staring at me like that? Haven't I been talking plain English?"

"Sure," Julie said quickly. "I'm sorry. Of course I'll do it. I was just wondering—"

"Wondering what?"

"Well, we both—I meant what—?" It seemed ridiculous to be unable to make the simple statement that, since Julie and Celia went to work together every morning, getting out on the Intervale Avenue station platform to meet Katie was something Julie would be doing in Celia's company, and therefore all these instructions from Celia made no sense. Julie said, "I was wondering about you, Celia. Where will *you* be?"

Celia's face cleared. "I get dumber every day," she said with a smile. "I forgot to tell you. I'm not going down with you by subway. Louis is giving me a lift to work in his car."

"Oh," Julie said, and she was suddenly freed from the uneasiness by which she had been plagued ever since she had answered the phone. In fact, all at once the day, which had started so threateningly a few minutes ago, looked bright with promise. Louis Vinutti was not only the most persistent of Celia's many admirers. He was the handsomest and the nicest, which was why Julie liked him, and he was by far the richest, which was why Mrs. Sarno considered him the most desirable. How Celia considered him was something of a mystery to Julie, but the fact that Celia was accepting a lift to work from him seemed to indicate that at the moment she was favorably disposed toward Louis, and even more important, at least from the standpoint of the Sarno family's emotional climate, it meant that Mrs. Sarno would be in a good mood at breakfast. Julie said, "I'll be glad to pick up the suitcase for you. What do you need it for?"

"I don't really need it," Celia said. "Not now, anyway. But I *will* in the summer, when vacation times comes around, the way I always do, and every time that happens, you try to buy a suitcase, prices are way up to here. This time, when Katie told me she could pick up this beauty cheap, because it's sort of off season, I decided I'd beat the market for once, and get my summer suitcase in March. One other thing, sweetie."

"What?" Julie said.

"Don't say anything about the suitcase to the prosecutor, will you?"

"Sure," Julie said.

"You know how she is about spending money," Celia said. " 'Suitcases in March? Are you crazy? Think of your poor father, that wonderful man who gave his life for you!' God!" Celia said. "The fairy tales she's made up for herself about that drunken, stupid, cruel—"

"Celia."

"What?"

Julie hesitated. "Nothing," she said. "I was just going to say I'll keep my mouth shut about the suitcase, but I realized I've already said that, so I'd better get started on my teeth."

She was brushing them vigorously when all at once she saw her eyes, in the bathroom mirror, spread wide, as though she had just made a startling discovery. Julie had. And the discovery brought with it a new wave of the uneasiness with which the day had begun. Katie had said on the phone that Celia had called her the day before and asked Katie to find a suitcase because Celia needed one immediately. But Celia had just said in the bedroom that it was Katie who had initiated the project. They couldn't both be telling the truth, but why would either her best friend or her sister lie to Julie? And while it was entirely possible that what was involved was an error rather than a falsehood, how could either Katie or Celia possibly make a mistake about a thing like that? Julie wondered uneasily if she should ask Celia, but when next

Julie saw her sister, Celia was at the breakfast table, over which Mrs. Sarno's presence loomed with all the dominating authority of a presiding justice on the bench. It was the wrong place for anybody to ask questions. For anybody, that is, except Mrs. Sarno.

"Why is it such a hard question to answer?" she was saying as Julie came in and sat down across the table from Celia. "It seems to me it's as simple as ay, bee, see."

"Please, Ma," Celia said. "I don't want to discuss it."

"I know you don't," Mrs. Sarno said. "You're not telling me anything new. But I want to discuss it." She brought the neatly cored grapefruit from the white enamel counter and set it in front of Julie. "It seems to me I have a perfect right to discuss it," Mrs. Sarno said. "I'm a widow. I have two daughters. One is still too young for such questions, although eighteen isn't all *that* young, but the other is twenty-three. You'll be twenty-four in three months, Celia."

"I suppose that makes me an old maid," Celia said.

"Not exactly, and God forbid that should happen," Mrs. Sarno said. "But the trouble with being twenty-three years old, and saying sarcastically to your mother I suppose that makes me an old maid, is that nobody remains twenty-three forever, and if that's the only answer you can make to your mother when she raises the subject, I can tell you this: you'll be an old maid before you know it, God forbid. What are *you* thinking, Julie?"

"Nothing much," Julie said. "Just why we can't have breakfast once in a while without all this talk about age."

"I can answer that," Mrs. Sarno said, pouring Julie's coffee. "Because to a woman it's the most important subject in the whole world. What she does with her life depends completely on how she handles herself at the right age. You, for instance, at your age, going on eighteen, if you came to me and told me you wanted to get married, even if it was to somebody as nice and as rich as Louis Vinutti, I'd say no. You're too young. Other mothers might not agree. They might think grab what you can get when you can get it, take anything, just so long as you don't miss the boat, but I disagree. I think until she's twenty a girl can't really miss any boats. Unless, of course, she's ugly or crippled or something like that, God forbid, which I'm happy to say neither one of my daughters is."

"Good," Celia said. "Hooray. First complimentary word out of the prosecution this morning. Is there any more coffee?"

"Have I ever let you go to work without there being enough coffee for both my daughters?" Mrs. Sarno came around the table to pour another cup for Celia. "Please don't try to change the subject. If somebody like Louis Vinutti wanted to marry Julie, I'd be willing to risk losing him by making him wait until she was twenty, because in exchange for the risk you could get a lot. He'd get a little impatient, maybe, that's true—"

"And go find himself some other chick," Celia said.

"That's true, too," Mrs. Sarno said. "That's the risk I was talking about. But at eighteen a girl can afford that risk. If he won't wait the two years, then it's not really right, and there would have been trouble later, after the marriage, and I'd say as a mother that my daughter is well out of it, especially since at eighteen the chances are that there will be others. If he *does* wait till she's twenty, then you've got two years of impatience that can be made to work for you, so that in the end—"

"What I'd like to know," Celia said, "I'd like to know how that point of view is any different from plain, ordinary, simple black-mail?"

"You can be as sarcastic as you like," Mrs. Sarno said. "If what a mother does for her daughter is in your mind blackmail, then I say keep the label if it makes you happy, but do whatever it is, so long as it gets the result you want for your daughter. This result changes when a girl passes twenty. She moves into a different class. She's no longer a young girl. She's now just a girl. She's still got plenty of chances, in fact it's the time when she has her best chances, especially if she's beautiful, which thank God my daughters both are, but they're different kinds of chances. One section of the race track is already behind her, you could say, and the section that's in front of her, the part from after she's twenty-five, that part is not so good, so she's got to make up her mind to act and act fast when the opportunity comes, and I know what I'm talking about, because that's what *I* did when *I* was your age."

"Oh, sure," Celia said. "That was quite a prize you chose for yourself."

"I'm not going to get angry," Mrs. Sarno said as she brought Julie's eggs from the stove. "I know you're trying to change the subject by getting me angry, but I'm not going to fall into your trap, Celia. I'm going to remain calm and continue this discussion in a calm way, because your whole future is what we're discussing, your life, what you're going to do with it, and what you're going to be, but even when I'm calm, and without falling into your traps, one thing we might as well get clear: there will be no bad talk at this table, or in any other part of this house, about your father. He was a wonderful man, who gave his life for his children and his wife, and if he were here today I would not have the trouble with you that I'm having. I have a fresh jar of strawberry jam if you'd rather for the toast?"

"No, thanks, Ma," Julie said. "This raspberry is fine."

"The seeds get in my teeth," Celia said.

"Would you like the strawberry?" Mrs. Sarno said.

"No, just silence," Celia said. "So I can drink my coffee in peace."

"You can drink your coffee in peace after you're married," Mrs. Sarno said. "And if your children are daughters, I advise you to drink it fast, when they're young, because once they start growing up it's not peace you'll get from them but worries and headaches and smart remarks—"

"Smart remarks?" Celia said. "Did anybody hear any smart remarks? I know *I* didn't. All I've been hearing since I came in and sat down—"

"Is a simple question that you won't answer," Mrs. Sarno said. "Why won't you marry Louis Vinutti? He's tall. He's handsome. He's crazy about you. He's got a business of his own—"

"Some business," Celia said. "Cigars and cigarettes."

"But wholesale," Mrs. Sarno said. "Louis Vinutti doesn't run a cheap little candy store on a street corner. He's a jobber, with a warehouse and an office and delivery trucks and a bookkeeper and people working for him—"

"He's still selling cigars and cigarettes," Celia said.

"And John D. Rockefeller sells oil," Mrs. Sarno said. "What difference does it make what a man sells, so long as he owns his own business and makes money out of it and he's crazy about a girl—"

"I've heard some pretty wild remarks in this kitchen, Ma, but comparing Louis Vinutti with John D. Rockefeller takes the cake." Celia glanced at her wrist watch and said to Julie, "What time you got?"

Julie glanced at her own watch. "Twenty-five to eight." She looked up at the alarm clock on the refrigerator. "It's right, too."

"This darned watch," Celia said.

She pulled out the winding stem and made an adjustment.

"If you marry Louis Vinutti," Mrs. Sarno said, "you won't need a watch. The way that man feels about you, he'd hire somebody to follow along behind you just to tell you the time whenever you wanted to know."

"I'd be a nervous wreck in two days flat," Celia said. "I don't want people following me, thank you."

"What *do* you want?" Mrs. Sarno said. She sounded calm and reasonable. There was no change in the inflection of her voice. Yet the small kitchen was suddenly charged with tension, as though the preliminaries in an evening of prize fights had been completed and the main bout was about to begin. "When we lived on Ninth Street, you made every day a living hell for your poor father, screaming at him over and over again, every day, that you were a duchess and it was his fault you were forced to live in a sewer like the East Side. The minute that wonderful man died, you made us take every penny of the insurance and come running up here to the Bronx where you could *be* a duchess."

"Your ideas of what a duchess is, and mine," Celia said, "I'm afraid are very different, Ma."

"All right, don't be afraid, tell me," Mrs. Sarno said. "I want to know. We've been living here next to lions and tigers and those tall ones, whatever they're called—"

"Giraffes," Julie said.

"Thank you," Mrs. Sarno said. "Giraffes. We've been living next to them for six years. I don't say what we live in is a palace, but by comparison with what other people are living in these days, including the Hallorans on Kelly Street, this is practically Park Avenue."

"Practically," Celia said. "That's some word, Ma."

"Say a more sensible one," Mrs. Sarno said. "I'm listening. Is that what you want? Park Avenue?"

"Oh, Ma, for heaven's sake, let's cut this out."

"Why?" Mrs. Sarno said. "For six years I've been asking a question, and for six years, when I think I'm getting close to an answer, you say let's cut it out. I'm not complaining that we spent every penny of your dear father's insurance money on furnishing this place. You were sick of living in a sewer. You wanted something fancy. All right, so here we are. On Daly Avenue. And the investment makes sense. Because here, on Daly Avenue, something happened that didn't happen when we lived on Ninth Street. Here you met Louis Vinutti. He wants to marry you. Why won't you marry him? Because you want to live on Park Avenue? It's crazy. People on Park Avenue are starving and jumping out of windows because they can't pay the rent. But if that's what you want, all right, I'll tell you something. If you marry Louis, you can live on Park Avenue. He told me so."

For a moment, in the silence that filled the room, Julie did not quite grasp what was happening. Then she saw Celia's face, and Julie knew her mother had gone too far.

"Do you mean to tell me," Celia said, her voice flat and hard, "that you've been bargaining with Louis Vinutti over me?"

"I don't bargain," Mrs. Sarno said. "I listen. When a man like Louis Vinutti, a man with a business of his own, a warehouse, an office, a bookkeeper, delivery trucks, a payroll, when such a man comes to me and asks me why my daughter won't marry him, do you expect me to throw him out of the house?"

"I expect you to have the simple intelligence, not to mention the common ordinary decency, to treat me like a human being and not a chattel!"

For several moments, during which Julie could hear Celia stalking down the hall, pausing in their bedroom for her coat, and then stalking to the front door, Mrs. Sarno remained motionless. Then the front door slammed and Mrs. Sarno began to clear away Celia's dishes.

"A chattel," she said. "What's that?"

"It's a legal word for a thing," Julie said. "A house or a piece of land, that's real estate. But something you can move or carry, a fountain pen, an automobile, that sort of thing, that's a chattel."

"She's too old to carry," Mrs. Sarno said at the sink. "But maybe, if I keep working, I'll move her out of those crazy ideas she lives in. Louis Vinutti won't wait forever."

Julie didn't suppose he would, merely because forever was a concept that had no meaning for her, but it occurred to her, as she finished her coffee and went down the hall to get her coat and purse, that Louis Vinutti's patience, which Julie had for so long taken for granted, might indeed some day run out. She didn't really believe it. Julie couldn't imagine any man giving up the attempt to capture a creature as lovely as Celia. But the possibility that he might, a completely fresh idea that Mrs. Sarno had just planted in Julie's mind, was disturbing. She had known for a long time, of course, that Celia was indecisive about Louis. But Julie had never doubted how the decision would go, once Celia straightened out in her mind whatever it was that was making her postpone saying yes to Louis.

Now, as she said good-bye to her mother and left the apartment, Julie suddenly had very grave doubts. She had not realized, until this moment when the doubts began to assail her, how much and for how long she had been wanting Celia to say yes to Louis Vinutti.

There was something about him, his size, his uncomplicated good looks, his obvious decency, and his even more obvious solvency, that made Julie feel he would quiet the vague, mysterious, troubling unrest she sensed in Celia, an unrest that Julie hated to admit even to herself was in her mind somehow connected with the seething inner turbulence that had driven Biaggio Sarno to his grave. That this might some day happen to Celia was a horrifying notion.

She shoved open the street door, and hurried down Daly Avenue. At the corner she became aware of an automobile horn honking insistently behind her.

"Hey, Julie!"

She stopped and turned. Louis Vinutti's black Packard had pulled up to the curb beside her.

"Oh, hi," Julie said. "Where's Celia?"

"That's just what I was going to ask you," Louis said, leaning across to open the front door. "Hop in. I'll give you a lift to the station."

"I thought you were driving Celia downtown to work this morning," Julie said as she got into the car.

"Wish I was," Louis said, starting the Packard with a roar. It caused Chin Ying, the proprietor of the hand laundry, to leap nervously and peer out through his plate-glass window. "Look at him," Louis said with a laugh. "I love to fire this bus off with a bang when I'm anywhere near Chin. He thinks it's the Chinese New Year or something. Speaking of thinking, where did you pick up the thought that I was driving Celia to work this morning?"

"I don't know," Julie said, aware that the lie came so easily only because it was in defense of Celia. "Just she left the house a little earlier than usual this morning, so I assumed it was because she had a date with you to drive downtown."

"I haven't had a date with Celia for nine days," Louis Vinutti said.

He said it quietly, which was or should have been of no particular significance, since Louis Vinutti always spoke quietly. It was one of the nicest things about him, one of the things that always made Julie feel relaxed in his presence. She did not feel relaxed now. Turning to look at Louis, trying to assess the significance of what should have been an insignificant remark, Julie realized it was his use of the number nine. If Louis had said he hadn't seen Celia for some time, or for a week, or even a month, it would have been different. Or rather, it would *not* have been. What made the difference was the specific nature of his remark. It was as though Louis was trying to nail down the facts with absolute precision before embarking on the phrasing of an indictment.

"She's been pretty busy," Julie said.

"That's what Celia told me," Louis said. Even though there was plenty of room to pass, he pulled the Packard in behind an ice wagon, which reduced the speed of the big car to the same pace as the plodding horse, and Julie knew there was nothing accidental about this. Louis Vinutti had something on his mind. He was going to make the short lift last until he got that something off his mind. Louis said, "What's she busy with, Julie?"

"Oh, gosh, I don't know, Louis."

"Is that the truth?" he said, and then, before Julie could reply, in the same quiet, unhurried voice, he added, "Don't get sore. I'm not calling you a liar. It's just I know how you feel about Celia, and what you'd do to protect her."

"Protect her from what?" Julie said. "You sound as though she's just busted into Tiffany's, a crook or something."

"I wish she were," Louis said. "I could handle that."

"Louis, I wish I knew what you're talking about."

"I wish something much better for you," he said. "I wish you never do know." Julie gave him a quick, shocked glance. Louis Vinutti was staring straight ahead, at the back of the ice wagon. There was nothing in the side of his face that Julie could see to indicate the depths of pain out of which the quietly spoken words had come. Even more quietly, Louis said, "Julie, what's Celia busy with?"

"I just told you," Julie said. "I don't know. I mean I don't know what she's busy with that's anything special. It's just, oh, I don't know, you know how girls are."

"I don't," Louis said. "That's why I'm asking one of them to tell me. I know it's not fair, Julie, but I don't feel very fair. Julie, is there another guy?"

For a long moment, watching the horse's tail come twitching out from both sides of the ice wagon up front, right, left, right,

206

left, like a pendulum seen in one of those crazy mirrors at Coney Island, Julie didn't see how she could duck the question. Louis had dropped it right in her lap, where she had to look at it. But she didn't want to look at it. For most of the past eight months, ever since she had gone to work at Ellentuch, Prohst & Wadsworth, she had not wanted to look at it. She had been so successful in not looking at it that she was suddenly furious at finding herself forced at last to do so, and the anger saved her. If you made enough noise you could drown out anything, especially a nagging inner voice you didn't want to hear.

"Celia?" she said angrily. "Louis, are you *crazy?*"

"Not quite," he said to the windshield. "But pretty damn near." Then he turned, and he smiled, and Julie had the weird feeling that she had given him a great big present. "Anyway, I was, until this moment," Louis said. He took one hand from the wheel, reached across and touched the top of her head, gently, as though he were reassuring a puppy. "I feel better," he said. "Not much, but some. As long as it's not another man I'm up against, I've still got a chance."

"Now, look," Julie said, feeling very grown-up and, at the same time, utterly preposterous. Louis Vinutti, at thirty-five, was almost twice her age. "I *don't* know what goes on in Celia's head, and I *don't* know what she's busy with, if she's busy with anything, but I *do* know my sister Celia, and I *do* know this: there is absolutely no other man she's interested in. I mean that, Louis. If there *was* another man, I wouldn't lie to you about it." The baldness of this lie was in itself so outrageous that Julie, preferring to believe she had not uttered it, hurried right on with a repetition of the fact about which she could still make herself believe she was telling the complete truth. "There just is no other man, Louis," she said. "I give you my word of honor. You're the only guy Celia ever goes *out* with, for heaven's sake. Honest, Louis, I mean it, *there is no other man.*" She paused, heard the echoes of her own shrill insistence, didn't like them, and said with a shrug, "Of course, what there *is,* that I don't know."

"But there's something," Louis said. "You feel it, too."

Julie hesitated, decided the hesitation was no service to Celia, and to counteract it she said with more firmness than she intended, "Yes, I do feel it."

"Got any ideas?" Louis said.

"Yes and no," Julie said. "Yes, because Celia is sort of, oh, I hate the word, but it's the best I can think of, she's moody. No, because I don't think she's moody about you, Louis."

"What's she moody about?" he said.

"I think maybe just any kind of change, and God knows marriage is a big change in a girl's life," Julie said. "So far as you're concerned, I actually think it's a good sign."

"How do you mean?"

"Well, I never thought of it before, but now that you've brought it up, and I *am* thinking about it, I remember it's been like that every time Celia was about to do something big in her life. When we lived down on the East Side and she was getting close to graduation from high school and Celia wanted to go to college, but we had no money at home and she had to go to work, I remember Celia was like that for weeks. Moody. The same after Pa died and she was working up to our moving here to the Bronx. It went on for weeks. Other times, too. Whenever it's something big that she knows she's coming close to, some big change in her life, Celia gets like that. Moody."

Louis swung the car out from behind the ice wagon, turned left under the elevated tracks, and pulled up at the curb beside the iron stairs that led up to the station. He was silent for several moments, staring out over the steering wheel.

"In other words,'" Louis said slowly, "if what you're saying is true—"

"Louis," Julie said, "I *know* it's true."

"In that case," Louis Vinutti said even more slowly, "I've been worrying about something that doesn't—" He stopped and shook his head, as though reprimanding himself for a bit of inept phrasing, and he started again. "What I mean," he said, "I'm beginning to think that maybe I'm much better off than—" Louis paused again, looked around as though hunting something, then laughed as he rapped his knuckles sharply on the steering wheel and said, "Let's pretend this is wood."

"Okay, I'll knock with you," Julie said, and she did, rapping the steering wheel with a conviction she wished she felt. "If there *was* some other man, or if she was getting ready to give you the gate for any other reason, then Celia wouldn't be moody. She'd be, well, I don't know *what* she'd be, but not like this. Like this, all I've got to say, Louis, I'd better get down to work because if I'm going to get you and Celia the wedding present I have in mind, I can't afford to lose my job."

He laughed happily and, again, as he opened the door, Louis Vinutti gently touched the top of Julie's head.

"If I had any brains," he said, "you'd be the member of the family I'd have fallen in love with."

"Then you'd *really* be in trouble," Julie said. "My mother thinks I'm too young for you."

Louis laughed again. "She's given it some thought, I see."

"Listen," Julie said, standing on the sidewalk, "I've learned that anything my mother hasn't given any thought isn't worth thinking about. Louis?"

"What?"

Julie leaned in through the window, gave him a swift kiss, and said quietly, "Don't worry about it. It's all going to be all right. Just the way you want it."

At the top of the stairs, turning for a last look, Julie saw his dark, handsome profile framed in the window of the Packard. A moment later she was sorry she had turned. There was a look on Louis Vinutti's face that moved her heart in a sudden lurch of guilt, the guilt she had earned by trying to make either him or herself—she didn't know which one—feel better. Julie ran across the station, dropped her nickel into the slot, clunked her way through the turnstile, and sprinted for the train.

It was not crowded, the 180th Street station being the end of the line from which all trains started, but Julie could tell from the fact that the train was almost half full that it was about to get under way. She started down the platform toward the last car, in which on most mornings she and Celia usually managed to get seats side by side, but the warning bell rang, so Julie darted through the nearest door. It closed behind her as she began to work her way back through the train to the last car. When she got there and found a seat, Julie found also that, as a result of riding to the station with Louis Vinutti, instead of walking as she usually did, she had neglected to buy a morning paper. This meant that, between the beginning of her ride downtown and the Intervale Avenue stop, where she was to meet Katie Halloran, Julie's efforts at entertainment were limited to her own thoughts.

These, she found before long, were not very entertaining. The speed and skill with which she had invented Celia's moodiness to reassure Louis Vinutti now proved a good deal less than reassuring to Julie herself. There had been no time on the front seat of the Packard, as there now was in the rear car of the subway train, to examine a suddenly startling fact: if what Louis had said was true, namely, that he had not been out on a date with Celia for nine days, what had Celia been doing with her evenings? Most of Julie's evenings were spent with Katie Halloran at C.C.N.Y. Just the same, Julie usually knew, from their casual conversations on the way to work, what Celia planned to do each night while Julie was at school. And while Julie didn't think she could say it even to herself with complete certainty, she suddenly realized that for the past nine days she had got the impression—and from whom could she have got it if not from Celia herself?—that her sister had been out with Louis Vinutti almost every night. Why would Celia want to create this impression in Julie's mind, or, for that matter, in anybody else's? Especially since, according to Louis, it was not true.

Julie got up at the Intervale Avenue station and fought her way through the now crowded car toward the door. She reached it just as the train stopped. The door slid open and Julie stepped out, but she didn't get very far. Katie Halloran, holding up a large blue suitcase in front of her with both hands, as though it was a tray, stepped forward and bore down on Julie.

"Get back in," Katie rapped out. "I'm here."

So were a couple of dozen other people, all just as determined as Katie to get into the jampacked train. None, however, possessed either Katie's equipment or her personality. The former was, of course, on this particular morning, an accident. Katie did not always carry a suitcase which she could use as a battering ram when she wanted to get into a crowded subway train. Her personality, on the other hand, was of course always with her.

It was enough, suitcase or no suitcase, to get Katie Halloran into any place she wanted to enter. No matter how crowded or, as Celia Sarno had once remarked in a moment of exasperation, "no matter how many locks there are on the door or how many guards happen to be posted around it. That friend of yours," Celia had continued, warming to her subject, who, the day before, had outraged Julie's older sister by opening Celia's purse in the alleged belief that Katie was hunting for a cigarette in her own and did not discover her error until she had read through an entire letter Louis Vinutti had sent Celia with a box of birthday roses, "that friend of yours makes Jimmy Valentine look like an amateur with four thumbs. At least when Mr. Valentine got into the wrong safe, he apologized. But your friend Katie would no more think of apologizing than those boys who stole Teapot Dome would think of using it for brewing orange pekoe. Why she wants to spend her time earning nickels and dimes working for a resident buyer is beyond me, since she could make a fortune by renting out a mere fraction of her crust to a pie bakery, and I wish some day, when I'm in the mood to listen, you'd tell me what you see in her."

Julie never did tell Celia. Not because she didn't know, but because Julie was secretly ashamed of the knowledge: what she saw in Katie was the thing Julie felt she herself lacked: courage.

The ugly little eleven-year-old girl with the steel-framed eyeglasses that on East Ninth Street had sat crookedly on the inflamed bridge of her nose had, at seventeen and in the Bronx, thumbed that very same nose at fate or nature, whichever was responsible for the distribution of pulchritude at birth. You wouldn't do it for me, Katie Halloran had in effect said, so I'll do it myself.

She had, too. In Julie's eyes, superbly. The steel-rimmed glasses had been replaced by a pair of heavy, bright green, horn-rimmed spectacles that rose in two impish points at the corners of Katie's eyes, giving to her already lean, bony, sardonic features a Mephistophelian touch that was startling in a face so young. The tangled mop of greasy brownish hair had been cut into a neat, boyish cap and audaciously dyed an improbable yellow. The long, gawky, flat-chested body, once a mass of joints in a middy blouse, now came sheathed in sleek, high-necked, form-fitting woolens that flowed without a wrinkle even over that area where the slenderest of girls inevitably does a certain amount of spreading. The result was not exactly beauty. But even Celia admitted that you couldn't help looking at Katie.

The trouble, Celia added sourly, was that you couldn't help hearing her, either. The razor-sharp tongue, which on East Ninth Street had been the implement with which an ugly little girl had slashed away indiscriminately at the adult world she held responsible for her ugliness, had become a more controlled instrument. Katie Halloran could still slash. She now preferred, however, to stab. Julie didn't doubt that the wounds, though less colorful, gave Katie more satisfaction, because they went deeper. Neither did Julie doubt that the voice with which Katie delivered her thrusts had been remade as deliberately as the body in which it was encased.

The nasal, uninflected little-girl's whine had become a hoarse, throaty bellow that cracked with astonishing charm at unexpected moments, so that those who didn't turn for a second look because they had not seen Katie in the first place, usually turned for a first look at the source of the unusual sounds.

Every one of the dozen or more people waiting on the Intervale Avenue platform did precisely that as Katie swept her way into the crowded train, sweeping her best friend along with her.

"Hey, hold it!" Julie said, clutching her purse. "Take it easy!"

"Last guy who did that on this station is still waiting for a train," Katie said. "How are you, kid?"

"Out of breath and slightly dented," Julie said. "That thing has sharp edges."

"Most suitcases do. Ain't it a beaut? Sixteen ninety-five, and you won't know what a buy Celia's getting until comes May and June, everybody suddenly wakes up it's vacation time, and you'll see this number in Macy's or even uptown, Bonwit's, those places, then try and get one for less than twenty, twenty-five bucks. Here, you take it, kid. It's all yours, or I mean Celia's."

The act of taking was reduced to no more than a token gesture, since the suitcase was wedged between the two girls as tightly as a slice of ham in a sandwich and the girls themselves were as immovably imbedded in the mass of human beings that filled the car as a couple of tent pegs in a campsite. Just the same, Julie made the gesture. She inched her hand up over the top of the suitcase and got her fingers around the handle.

"Thanks," she said. "It's a beauty. It really is. Listen, Katie, did you say on the phone when you called this morning that—?"

"Excuse me a moment," Katie said in a loud, clear voice that brought every head not already turned in her direction craning for a glimpse of the speaker. "Just one simple moment, please," Katie said. She sounded like an orator at a political rally trying to quiet a spontaneous ovation as, turning her bright-yellow head with the movement of the swaying train, she fixed the green-framed glasses directly on a man with a gray hat standing behind and slightly to the left of her. "You better get a leash for those hands," Katie said coldly. "They're wandering, buster."

The man looked startled, as though he had been punched, and then his face grew bright red. "Who, me?" he said. "You talking to me?"

"If I'm not," Katie growled hoarsely, "that guy next to you is growing hands in some damn funny places."

A wave of laughter swept through the car. Julie could tell, even though there was no change in the expression of contemptuous indignation on Katie's bony face, that her friend was pleased by the effect she had created.

"Listen, miss," the man with the red face said desperately, sending terrified glances at the people around him. "You're making a mistake. I'm not—"

"Not any more, you mean," Katie said. "Unless you want to get out of this train minus those wandering hands." Julie was convinced as, in the wake of the second wave of laughter, Katie turned her head back, that her friend had invented the whole incident to attract attention. "Now what were you about to ask me, kid?"

"I can't remember," Julie said, which was not true. In the diversion created by Katie, Julie had lost her courage. She couldn't ask her friend to clear up the troubling discrepancy between Katie's version and Celia's version of who had initiated the suitcase purchase. It would have been an act of disloyalty to Celia. Julie said, "If I think of it, I'll ask you later."

"While you're thinking," Katie said, "think about registration. Speaking of which, listen."

Julie did, along with the flustered man in the gray hat and almost every other passenger in the car, while Katie outlined her plan of attack for the following night. The details escaped Julie, and they could have had meaning only for those passengers who attended the evening session of C.C.N.Y. and were aware of how difficult it was to get registered for desirable classes, but so compelling were Katie's voice and personality that Julie and the other passengers listened as though the skinny girl with the yellow boyish bob and the green harlequin-shaped glasses was Jenny Lind and they had stumbled on the Swedish Nightingale while she was trying out a new number that had just been whipped up for her by Richard Wagner.

"Well, that's it, and this is where I get off," Katie said when the train pulled into Times Square. "See you tomorrow night. If you remember what I said, and do it the way I said it, you'll be another leg up on the old B.A. If you forget, I'll remind you. Meantime, I'm off to shop for bonnets that will knock them dead in Toledo. Have fun with the torts."

Julie always did. Not that she actually knew what a tort was or, if she had, would have had anything to do with them in the course of her day's work. Ellentuch, Prohst & Wadsworth was not that sort of law firm. Just what sort of firm it was had been explained to Julie by Celia when, shortly before Julie graduated from Fenimore Cooper High, her older sister came home one evening and reported that she had talked to Mr. Prohst, the youngest of the senior partners who also happened to be Celia's boss, and he had said he was pretty sure when Julie graduated they could find a place for her in the steno pool.

"It doesn't sound like much," Celia had said, "and in most law firms, the big downtown ones, Wall Street, Lower Broadway, those, I guess it *isn't* much. But *any* kind of a job with Ellentuch, Prohst & Wadsworth is a *good* job, not only because they pay a little more than anybody else, and not even because they believe in promotion for merit—after all, the steno pool is where *I* started, too, and I'm private secretary to one of the three senior partners—but the thing that makes any kind of a job with Ellentuch, Prohst & Wadsworth a good job is the *kind* of firm it is. It's like, oh, say you have a checking account, and it's in the First Delancey Street Bank & Trust Company, or some such cheesy little outfit like that, that's *one* thing, it gives people *one* idea about you. But you have a checking account in, say, the Fifth Avenue Bank or the Bank of New York, that's something else again. Or somebody is looking up your credit rating, let's say, and they find out you shop in like say Hearn's. All right, you pay your bills on time and all that, fine, but if they find you have a charge account not in Hearn's but in, oh, I don't know, Bergdorf maybe, that's *again* something else again. It gives you sort of like status. You know? You're not just another person in the crowd. You're *somebody*. You're sort of up there on a little platform, something just a little special, and that's the thing about Ellentuch, Prohst & Wadsworth: everybody in the firm, everybody who works there, even if you're only in the steno pool, everybody at Ellentuch, Prohst & Wadsworth is *somebody*."

Julie felt this, of course, even before she set foot in the offices, because of Katie Halloran's reaction when she learned that Julie had landed the job. Even without her best friend's understandable jealousy, however, Julie was certain she would have sensed at once, just from the look and feel of the place, what Celia meant. After eight months, during which a good deal of first-hand knowledge had been added to that first day's look and initial feel, Julie knew that Celia had not exaggerated.

There was something about Ellentuch, Prohst & Wadsworth

that reminded Julie of the small gilt lettering she saw now and then on the wrapper of a piece of English soap or under the name of the manufacturer in an advertisement for British raincoats: "By Appointment To." While the firm stood solidly in the market place, so to speak, and obviously earned by its skill in that market place the large sums of money necessary to keep its extensive staff functioning, the word money was never mentioned in the Ellentuch, Prohst & Wadsworth offices.

Even when, for example, sums involved in a client's affairs had to be spoken aloud by a staff member while dictating a letter concerning those affairs, Julie had the feeling that the man thought he should apologize for the necessity that drove him to the use of words he really would have preferred not to utter in the presence of a member of the opposite sex. It was part of this feeling toward money, to take another example, that had brought into existence one of the firm's many unwritten but inflexible housekeeping rules: the cashing of the week's payroll check in the bank on the street floor of the Garner Building, in which the Ellentuch, Prohst & Wadsworth offices were located, was always the duty of the firm's newest employee.

It was as though the cashing of a check was a slightly dirty chore, like refilling inkwells, which it was only fair to relegate to the youngest staff member. To Julie, who had been performing this weekly chore since she came to work for the firm, it had soon stopped seeming odd, in fact, that in the age of the fountain pen every desk in the Ellentuch, Prohst & Wadsworth offices was actually equipped with an inkwell. She didn't know, of course, how the other firms in the Garner Building were equipped, but Julie somehow felt that they, too, had inkwells.

It was that kind of building, massive rather than tall, built in the days when twenty stories made a skyscraper, and the corner of Fourth Avenue and Twenty-third Street, which the Garner Building dominated, had probably been an appropriate location for a law firm specializing in corporate trusts. The fact that the neighborhood had changed, and the building as well as the surrounding streets were now full of textile houses, did absolutely nothing to detract from—and, in fact, added to—the appropriateness of the location of Ellentuch, Prohst & Wadsworth.

After passing through the monstrous marble-and-guilt lobby downstairs, which always reminded Julie of a cathedral built by a sect that had long ago died out and been forgotten; and ascending in one of the eight cage elevators, which still made Julie feel now and then that if she peered closely at her fellow passengers she was bound to recognize Stanford White or Harry K. Thaw; entering the mahogany reception room of the Ellentuch, Prohst & Wadsworth offices on the eleventh floor gave the visitor the same feeling that the men who guided the destinies of the Prudential Life Insurance Company must have wanted to instill in their investors when they decided to place on their policies a picture of the Rock of Gibraltar. It would no more occur to anybody to ask how long Ellentuch, Prohst & Wadsworth had been in the Garner Building than it would occur to anybody to ask how long the firm had been in existence. The answer, like the monument to Sir Christopher Wren for those who stepped into St. Paul's, was all around those who stepped into the Ellentuch, Prohst & Wadsworth offices: in a word, always.

Stepping into those offices now, Julie felt the small, solid, pleasurable inner nudge that she experienced every morning, a sort of unspoken reminder of belonging to something solid and substantial and enduring. Miss Lilly, the white-haired switchboard operator who presided over the reception room, spoke to Julie.

"Mr. Prohst wants to see you," she said.

"Me?" Julie said.

"Well, he said Miss Sarno, and your sister was in with him when he said it, so it must be you, Julie. He said for me to tell you as soon as you arrived."

"Okay, thanks, Miss Lilly. Everybody's in so *early* this morning."

"Not everybody. You're in same as usual, and I got here eight forty-five sharp, same as always. It's just Mr. Prohst and your sister."

Julie, on her way past the switchboard, faltered. It was as

though something in the tone of Miss Lilly's voice had tripped her. This, of course, was preposterous. Miss Lilly's voice, like her face, was sweet and colorless and completely devoid of anything that could trip anybody. She looked like the conventional figure drawn by greeting-card artists on the less expensive Mother's Day numbers.

"Going some place?" she said.

"What?" Julie said, and then she saw that Miss Lilly was looking at the suitcase. "Oh, no. A friend of mine bought this for— She works for a resident buyer and she gets things at big discounts once in a while. When she sees a bargain, she sort of tips me off. She got this as a bargain."

"It's lovely," Miss Lilly said.

Her switchboard buzzed. While Miss Lilly busied herself with keys and plugs, Julie escaped into the corridor behind the library that led to the girls' rest room. She wondered uneasily as she moved up the corridor why she had caught herself up before revealing the perfectly innocent fact that the suitcase had been bought for Celia. In the rest room each of the twenty-six female Ellentuch, Prohst & Wadsworth employees who ranged in age from Miss Lilly's sixty-odd down to Julie's just-short-of-eighteen, had a green steel locker. Four of these employees were gathered around the table in the middle of the room. They had started brewing in the jointly owned electric percolator the first of the morning's many pots of coffee.

"Good morning," Julie said.

On her first morning, eight months ago, when Celia introduced her to the other girls in the rest room, Julie had said, "Hi." She had never made that particular mistake again. Ellentuch, Prohst & Wadsworth was not a "Hi" office.

"Good morning," said Miss Grienwalt, secretary to Mr. Ellentuch. "Coffee will be ready in a moment."

"Thanks," Julie said, "but first I'd better go see what Mr. Prohst wants." She went to her locker and hung up her coat. "Miss Lilly told me he said I should come right in as soon as I arrived."

"I guess one Sarno isn't enough for him," said Mrs. Tiergarden, who ran the file room. The others joined in her amiable chuckle.

Julie started to laugh with them, but at the moment she was dipped down, setting the suitcase on the floor of her locker, and from that angle it seemed to her the four women around the table had exchanged a swift glance. The laugh stopped in Julie's throat. Mrs. Tiergarden said, "What's the suitcase for?"

"Nothing," Julie said. "I mean I just picked it up from a friend who bought it for me. She works for a resident buyer and gets things at big discounts now and then. There's nothing in it. I mean it's empty. She comes down on the subway with me. My friend. And so she brought it along and gave it to me this—" It occurred to Julie that she was saying too much about something that needed very little, if anything, said about it. "Well," she said, "I guess I'd better get in there."

"We'll save a cup for you," said Miss Cooley, who worked for Mr. Trench, the chief clerk.

"Thanks," Julie said, making her escape. As she hurried back up the corridor toward the senior partners' corridor, which was known to the staff as Mahogany Row, she wondered what she was escaping from.

"Julie!"

She stopped outside Mr. Trench's door. The chief clerk, who looked like the picture on the left-hand side of the Smith Brothers cough-drop box, was waving a slip of paper at her from the far side of his office.

"Good morning, Mr. Trench," Julie said in the doorway. "I was just going in to see what Mr. Prohst wants."

"And I was just trying to find Miss Cooley so she could trot this down to you," Mr. Trench said. "But I guess it's still coffee time, and I certainly wouldn't want to interfere with that. A law office, like Napoleon's armies, travels on its stomach, a fact of which very few clients are aware."

Mr. Trench, who was not a lawyer, knew more law than anybody on the Ellentuch, Prohst & Wadsworth staff. Like most chief clerks, he had learned it not in a law school, which as a young man he had been too poor to attend, but in the day-to-day management of a busy organization owned and staffed by men who had not been too poor to obtain the education that had been denied Mr. Trench. It was remarkable that the discrepancy between his capacities and his achievements had not made him bitter. Or so it was said in the women's rest room. What was not said around the communal coffee pot, and what Julie had figured out for herself, was that Mr. Trench's neatly trimmed but full beard, and his affection for dropping elaborate historical or literary allusions into the most commonplace conversations, were his way of narrowing the unjustified gap that existed between himself and his employers. People usually looked twice at a man with a beard, especially if when passing the salt he told you how it used to be done in the days of Pliny the Younger.

"I think about Miss Cooley and her endless stream of coffee," Mr. Trench said to Julie, "the way the British think about the ravens at the Tower of London. They believe that if those ravens ever flew away, the Tower would fall to an invader, which is why they keep the wings of those ravens clipped. If Miss Cooley and her colleagues ever stopped making all that coffee, I think this office would fall apart, and if you don't think I haven't often thought of getting Miss Cooley's wings clipped, you're quite wrong. I've marked the denominations on the back," Mr. Trench said, stroking his beard as he handed Julie the payroll check. "You'd think after all these years they'd know the denominations, but they got the tens and the twenties mixed up last week, as you recall."

"I certainly do," Julie said. "Would you want me to check the count myself downstairs in the bank before I bring the payroll up?"

"That's very thoughtful of you, but I don't see why you should be saddled with that additional task. The least one can expect of a bank clerk, as Carlyle pointed out in *Sartor Resartus*, is that he should know how to count. You'd better trot along and give Mr. Prohst a chance to tighten his monopoly on the Sarno family."

The fact that Julie did not trot, but completed the rest of her journey up Mahogany Row at a pace closer to a crawl, was due to her uncomfortable wondering about the connection between Mr. Trench's final remark and the look Julie thought she had seen exchanged a few minutes earlier by the four women in the rest room.

"Snap out of it, kid. Mr. Prohst is waiting."

Julie came up out of her uncomfortable wondering and found herself face to face with Celia. Her older sister, carrying a batch of blue-backed documents, was coming out of her boss's room.

"Waiting for what?" Julie said.

"He'll tell you," Celia said. "Did you get the suitcase?"

"It's in my locker," Julie said. "Listen, Celia, on my way to the train I ran into Louis Vinutti."

"Oh, God."

"What do you mean, oh, God? You told me you were riding downtown with him," Julie said. "But *he* said—"

"I'm sure he did," Celia said. "I'm also sure he didn't tell you he promised to pick me up in front of the house at seven-thirty sharp. By ten to eight I was tired of waiting, so I thought nuts to Mr. Vinutti, and I walked myself over to the subway."

"Now don't get sore at Louis just because he was a little late," Julie said.

"Twenty minutes is not a little, and besides—"

The door opened and Mr. Prohst poked his head out. "I thought I heard voices," he said. "Good morning, Julie."

"I'll just take these down to the file room," Celia said, lifting the batch of documents a few inches higher. "Be right back, Mr. Prohst."

"Okay, Celia." He held the door wide. "Come in, Julie."

Coming in, Julie felt as she always did in the presence of Frank Prohst: as though she had stepped out of real life into the middle of a movie set.

It didn't seem possible that in a firm with, on its letterhead, nine names above the short black line that separated the list of senior partners from the names of the twelve junior partners below the line, one of the three names by which this organization of twenty-one partners chose to have itself identified to the world at large should belong to Frank Prohst. Not that he didn't deserve the honor. On the contrary. Even in the relentless judgments passed over the coffee cups in the women's rest room, there was no doubt about Frank Prohst's considerable talents as a lawyer or his impressive skill as a bringer-in of new business. It was simply that, at least in Julie's eyes, he did not look like an El-lentuch, Prohst & Wadsworth partner.

Mr. Ellentuch, who had once served briefly as a committing magistrate under Mayor Gaynor and was therefore known as "Judge," looked the part: frail, bald, stooped, and ancient, his sparrow's body encased in the kind of high-buttoned jackets that Julie associated with school history-book pictures of Grover Cleveland. Mr. Wadsworth, who was supposed to have written for Theodore Roosevelt the first draft of the Sherman Anti-Trust Law, looked his part, too: tall, heavy-set, white-haired, with the kind of face Julie imagined you would find on the King of England if he shaved off that beard. Seeing either Mr. Ellentuch or Mr. Wadsworth, and certainly seeing them together, Julie felt you could not help also seeing the marble or bronze statues that one day, inevitably, would be unveiled in their honor in some public place like Central Park. Seeing Mr. Prohst, however, Julie felt you could not help wondering about the name of the silent movie in which, years and years ago, you had seen him play the villain.

Everything about him—the gleaming patent-leather hair parted in the middle; the thin black mustache which streaked across his upper lip like a line drawn with an eyebrow pencil; the pearl-button spats he wore in the winter; the black and white shoes with complicated perforations he wore in the summer; the pearl stickpin in the tie that always arched out dashingly from the dickey-bosom shirt—everything about Frank Prohst made you think of the traditional scene in which the villain, tugging his mustache, leered at the sobbing golden-haired heroine as he asked her to make the choice between foreclosure of the mortgage on her father's farm or You Know What.

Everything about Frank Prohst made you think of that, except two things: his voice, which was low and hesitant, and his manner, which was shy and awkward. It was, Julie always thought, like meeting Jack Dempsey wearing not only his boxing gloves and ring trunks but his famous fighting scowl, and then discovering, as you start to duck, that you are facing, not Jack Dempsey, but a kindly old minister of the gospel who has raised his hand in benediction.

Raising it now, Mr. Prohst produced from the inner pocket of his jacket a green check. "I wonder if you'd do me a favor?" He spoke haltingly, through a small, worried scowl, as though he expected an angry refusal.

"Of course," Julie said.

"When you go down to the bank to cash the payroll check," Mr. Prohst said, "could you cash this personal check for me at the same time?"

"Certainly," Julie said.

"Thanks a lot. I've indorsed it and written the denominations I'd like on the back. There's no rush, Julie. Any time this morning after Mr. Trench gives you the payroll check."

"He gave it to me just a minute ago," Julie said. "So I'll go right down now."

"Good," Mr. Prohst said. "And Julie?"

"Yes, sir?"

"Don't say anything about it, will you?"

"Say anything about—?" Julie's puzzled voice ground to a halt.

"I mean it's something personal," Mr. Prohst said. "It's for a surprise I'm getting for my wife."

He sounded and looked, Julie thought as in response to his blush she could feel her own face grown hot, as though the surprise Mr. Prohst was asking Julie to help him get for his wife was some item involving what the advertisements called "feminine hygiene."

"Oh," Julie said, and she pushed a smile up through her own blush. "Don't worry. I won't say anything."

She started toward the door but Mr. Prohst, unexpectedly, put his hand on her elbow. It was as though they actually were on a movie set and the unseen director had suddenly signaled to Mr. Prohst that his performance was too wooden.

"Tuck it into your pocket," he said, blushing harder as he touched the check in Julie's hand.

"Oh," she said again, and she did so, wondering what was the

223

matter with Celia's boss this morning. To conceal her own puzzled embarrassment, Julie said, "Not much point in keeping my mouth shut if I go waving it all over the office, is there?"

Mr. Prohst laughed and opened the door for her. It was not until she was in the elevator on her way down to the bank that Julie realized the most awkward part of Mr. Prohst's entire awkward performance was that final, nervous little laugh. Walking across the Garner Building's cathedral-like lobby toward the street door, Julie glanced at Mr. Prohst's green check, and she stopped short: it was drawn to "Cash" for five hundred dollars.

The Ellentuch, Prohst & Wadsworth payroll check, which always came to at least ten times that sum, had never had quite this effect on Julie. The size of the payroll check was impressive, but in a remote way, like budget figures published in the newspapers when President Hoover or some other public figure made a speech or sent a message to Congress. Julie knew, even as her eye skimmed across those enormous figures, that they were not really enormous when divided up by the hundred and twenty or thirty million people in the country on whom the money was going to be spent, just as she knew that the big fat figure on the weekly payroll check was not so big and fat to the several dozen Ellentuch, Prohst & Wadsworth employees among whom, minutes after Julie brought the cash up from the bank, it would be distributed.

But this five hundred dollars, this sum scrawled in Mr. Prohst's handwriting, this figure which came to almost one half the amount Julie earned in a whole year, this small fortune was going to be spent by one man on a surprise present for one woman!

"Wow!" Julie murmured and, as she resumed her progress toward the street, there was a sudden spring in her step. The notion that any man would care enough about any woman to spend that much money on her, a notion that had never crossed Julie's mind before, went trampling across it in a wild rush of discovery, filling her with an unexpected sense of exaltation and pride in the fact that she, too, was a woman. It was almost as though she had discovered that Mr. Prohst's surprise for his wife was actually

224

intended for Julie. Shoving through the revolving door into the street, she said to herself happily, "Holy smoke!"

A few seconds later, on the sidewalk in front of the bank that occupied half the Garner Building's street-floor space, Julie repeated those two words, but in an entirely different way. She stood there for several stunned moments, aware that she was being jostled by fragments of the small crowd that kept gathering and dispersing around her as newcomers paused to look and then moved on to be replaced by other newcomers, and she was aware that she had walked head-on into something shattering, but Julie's strongest emotion was a feeling of regret for Mrs. Prohst, whom she had never met. That unknown woman, that fortunate member of the proud sisterhood to which moments before Julie had realized she too belonged, would not get the wonderful surprise her husband had planned for her. It did not occur to Julie until she was back upstairs in Mr. Trench's office that what *she* would not get was infinitely more important: her salary.

"Are you kidding?" Mr. Trench said, and even in her confusion and excitement Julie knew, from the fact that the chief clerk's startled statement had emerged through his beard unadorned by historical or literary reference, that she had not underestimated the shattering nature of the event.

"No, honest, it's true," Julie said.

"You mean the doors are really *locked?*" Mr. Trench said, snatching up his phone. Before Julie could reply, he said into it, "Connect me with Mr. Prohst. What? No, cut in on him! Yes, please. I don't care who he's talking to. I said cut in on—" He looked up at Julie and said, "What?"

"I said I didn't test them myself," Julie said. "The doors. But other people, there was a small crowd in front, some kept going up and trying the door, shaking it. The door was locked, Mr. Trench, and on the glass there's this paper, pasted on, it's a proclamation. I read it, Mr. Trench. It says Governor Lehman issued the proclamation in Albany—"

"Excuse me, Julie," Mr. Trench said, and the fingers of his free hand went nervously to his beard as he said into the phone,

"Frank?" Julie had a small stab of surprise. She had never before realized that the chief clerk was on a first-name basis with any of the senior partners. "Frank, look, something really terrible has happened. Maybe terrible is the wrong word. I don't know, but the banks are closed, Frank. Closed. Yes. That's what I said. *Closed*, Frank. Apparently by proclamation of the governor. No, I don't know any of the details. I just learned it from Julie. I sent her down with the payroll check, and when she got there, she says she saw—Well, I mean, there are going to be some immediate problems. We won't be able to pay the staff today. We won't be able to—No, there's not enough in the petty-cash box for any sort of—What? I always replenish the petty cash out of the payroll check. Which means—What I mean, Frank, we'd better have a staff conference at once, and maybe get some more dope on this, how long it's for, what it means, and so on, so we can— What?" Mr. Trench's rush of words stopped. He turned slowly and looked at Julie as though he had never seen her before. "Sure, yes, of course, Frank," the chief clerk said. "But don't you want me to—? All right. Yes." Mr. Trench hung up slowly, scowled at the phone as though annoyed with the inanimate object for withholding from him some piece of vital information, and then he said to Julie, "Mr. Prohst wants to see you right away."

"I guess I'd better give you this, Mr. Trench." Julie put the payroll check on the desk in front of him.

"Yes, I guess you better had," the chief clerk said. He picked up the check and, as Julie left the room, Mr. Trench was staring at the piece of paper with a worried frown and saying softly, "My God, my good sweet God."

Hurrying down the corridor toward Mr. Prohst's office, Julie could see a group of girls gathered around Miss Lilly's switchboard in the reception room. Julie couldn't hear what they were saying, but there was a curious tone in the mixed voices. Julie caught scraps of the same tone from every open door as she moved down through the office toward Mahogany Row. Even as she was puzzling about it, Julie was struck by the speed with which the news had traveled. She couldn't have been in Mr. Trench's office more than a minute. Probably less. The chief clerk's telephone talk with Mr. Prohst had just ended. Twenty seconds ago. Ten seconds. And already everybody in the large office seemed to know—

Outside Mr. Prohst's office, Julie stopped. She had suddenly understood the curious tone in the voices with which the whole office seemed all at once to be humming: it was the blend of shock and disbelief and fear crossed by an involuntary excitement at being caught in the middle of a totally new experience that the participants knew, even in the moment of danger, was making them all unique, an experience about which they would be able to talk for years. Julie supposed, as she pushed in the door of Mr. Prohst's office, that this was the way the people on board the *Titanic* reacted in the first moment of discovery that the vessel had struck an iceberg.

In the open door, Julie stopped short, the way she had stopped short downstairs in the lobby when she read the figure on Mr. Prohst's check. This time, however, the reason for stopping was not so clear. Or rather, this time what had stopped her was the realization, even in *this* moment of shock, that the perfectly obvious reasons were not the real ones. Julie knew, as her heart seemed to turn over with a lurch of panic, that she had not stopped short because her sister Celia, seated at Mr. Prohst's desk, was sobbing. Julie knew, as the breath seemed to leave her body, that neither was it because of the way Mr. Prohst was patting Celia's shoulder reassuringly. Nor was it their words, which Julie absorbed without thought as she tried desperately to force her suddenly frozen legs to carry her backward, out of the room.

"You didn't have to leave it for the last minute," Celia was saying through her sobs. "You could have cashed it yesterday, or the day before, or *any* time."

"Celia, please, please be reasonable," Mr. Prohst said awkwardly. "I had no way of knowing the banks were going to close."

"You knew you'd need the money! You knew it! You've known it for weeks! Now, at the last minute—!"

"But, Celia, please. I couldn't carry a sum like that around with me for weeks. I mean, in my pocket. I had everything else prepared. Even this. It seemed sensible not to do it, *you* know, like I was making preparations. At the last moment, the bank being downstairs—"

"Locked!" Celia sobbed. "Closed! Oh, why did I ever listen to—?"

"It's not the end of the world, Celia. There are other places where checks can be cashed. It's inconvenient, sure, that the banks had to close. But there are other places—"

"What other places?" Celia cried helplessly. "Who carries that much cash around and is willing to—?"

The rest of Celia's words were lost as Julie suddenly realized what had stopped her in the doorway. It was Mr. Prohst's hand on Celia's shoulder. Out of the past, like a lantern slide dropping into place on the screen of her memory, came the evening when Julie had carried her dyed parasol through the rain to the Tenth Street trolley stop to meet Celia coming home from work.

Julie could see herself at the age of eleven, standing there stunned because Celia had not come out of the trolley car as she always did. Julie could feel again the surge of relief inside her as moments later the Luxor cab pulled up to the curb and Celia stepped out, lifting the folded newspaper to shield her lovely red hair from the rain. Julie could hear again the unknown man's voice saying quietly from inside the taxi, "You're sure?" and Julie could hear again Celia's hasty, "Yes, positive," and then she could see again the large tanned hand, with the thick gold ring on the small finger, appear in the open taxi window and touch Celia's small white hand in two short, reassuring pats. And now, six years later, from the open doorway of Frank Prohst's office, Julie could see what she had never before noticed during her eight months as an Ellentuch, Prohst & Wadsworth employee: Mr. Prohst's hands were deeply tanned. At least the right one was, the hand with which he was now patting Celia's shoulder. On the small finger of that hand Mr. Prohst wore a thick gold ring.

Then he looked up, and Frank Prohst saw Julie in the doorway and, as he came hurriedly toward her, the lantern slide flickered out inside Julie's head, and she was holding out the green check drawn to "Cash" for five hundred dollars, holding it out as though it were a shield or a lance with which she was trying desperately to fend off the meaning of what she had just seen and heard and remembered, and wished desperately she hadn't.

"I'm sorry, Mr. Prohst," she said hastily. "I couldn't cash this for you. The payroll check, either. The banks are closed. I guess you know, though. I mean I was in his room when Mr. Trench called you and—"

"Yes, thanks, Julie," Mr. Prohst took the check, and a shy, hesitant smile crossed his movie villain's face. "This is sort of embarrassing," he said. "I'm afraid we won't be able to pay anybody's salary today. I do hope you have a little cash, Julie? If not—?"

Mr. Prohst started to put his hand in his pocket.

"No, no," Julie said quickly. "Thanks, Mr. Prohst. But I'm all right. If this doesn't last too long, I mean."

"I can't imagine that it will," Mr. Prohst said, scowling down at the check in his hand, as though he found it much easier to do that than face Julie. "Probably no more than a political stunt on the part of this new administration. To impress the public with the fact that they're *doing* something. But the country, *no* country can function without a banking system, so you can be pretty sure they'll be opening the banks again in a day or so. Right after the inauguration, it wouldn't surprise me."

"Oh, well, in *that* case," said Julie, also addressing the check in Mr. Prohst's hand, staring at it hard to avoid seeing anything else in the room behind him.

"You're sure you'll be all right, now?" Mr. Prohst said. "I don't want you going around penniless just because a bunch of foolish Democrats, drunk with sudden power, are throwing their weight around down in—"

"No, no, I'm really fine," said Julie, who had, she thought, approximately two dollars in coins in her change purse. "Well," she said, starting to back out of the room, "I guess I'll—"

"Wait!"

Julie stopped. Celia was coming across the room, wiping away the tears with the back of her hand.

"Celia," Mr. Prohst said worriedly, "I wish you wouldn't—"

Celia took the check from Mr. Prohst's hand, led Julie out into the hall, and pulled the mahogany door shut.

"Julie, listen," Celia said, speaking rapidly, in a low voice. "I know one place where you can get this cashed. Louis Vinutti. His drivers, the ones that come in late at night, they turn in their cash first thing in the morning, and Mrs. Cooper doesn't make the deposit until she goes out to lunch. Louis told me that himself once. Well, nobody is going to be making any deposits today, so Louis has all that cash. The money that came in last night and this morning. What I want you to do, Julie, I'd like you to go right up to the Bronx, will you? I'll call him in the meantime, so he'll know you're coming, and then you bring the money back here to the office."

"Sure, Celia, if that's what you want, but what—?"

"Don't ask any questions, sweetie, please, or I'll go jumping out of my skin. I've had all I can take for one day. Just *go*, sweetie, *go* and *do* it."

"Sure," Julie said, taking the check. "Of course. But I'd better ask Mr. Trench if it's okay to leave the office. You know how he is about—"

"No, that's all right," Celia said. "I'll get Mr. Prohst to tell Trench he sent you out on an errand. Don't worry about that. Just go and get back fast."

"Okay," Julie said.

"Good, thanks, swell," Celia said, and unexpectedly, with a small sob that turned into an odd little laugh, she brushed Julie's cheek in a swift kiss. "You're the nicest sister anybody ever had. Go on, now. I'll call Louis you're coming. Hurry."

Julie did. At least until she had to leave the hurrying process to the train, so that she was left free to examine her own thoughts. It proved, before the train had carried her as far as Ninety-sixth Street, to be a freedom she would have preferred doing without. The puzzling events of the morning, beginning with the phone call from Cockeye Katie that had blasted Julie awake, were refusing to remain puzzling. All at once, like eager children in a classroom competing with each other to attract their teacher's attention, the events of the morning were signaling wildly, waving their hands, calling out: *Look at me! Look at me!*

Julie didn't want to look. The suitcase that Celia had not wanted her mother to know about; Louis Vinutti's revelation that the nine evenings Julie thought had been spent by Celia in his company had been spent elsewhere; the look exchanged by Miss Cooley and Mrs. Tiergarden across the coffee percolator in the rest room; Mr. Trench's remark about Mr. Prohst's monopoly on the Sarno family; the six-year-old recollection about the heavy gold ring on the tanned hand that had come back to Julie in the doorway of Frank Prohst's office; Celia's sobbing words directed at the man who to Julie had never been anything but her sister's boss; the check-cashing errand on which Celia had sent her—each of these events was clamoring to take its place in a pattern that could be read as plainly as the face of the clock on the Paramount Building.

But Julie didn't want to read it, just as she had not wanted to answer the question Louis Vinutti had dropped in her lap. She didn't want to see the pattern. Seeing, the kids on East Ninth Street used to say, was believing. Julie didn't want to believe. She wanted things to go on the way they were, the way they had always been. Sitting there in the almost empty subway car, shaking with the roaring movement of the train, staring up stupidly at the gaily printed words "Coming Events Cast Their Shadows Before" in the Lucky Strike ad, Julie fought back the vision in which the fires that had consumed Biaggio Sarno were creeping up on his lovely, red-headed daughter. By an effort of will, Julie held off the tears as well as the vision, but inside her head, which refused to co-operate, and inside her heart, where the refusal was unbearable, Julie wept.

She wept for Celia, whom she loved, and she wept for herself, who didn't want her love put to this test. Cockeye Katie wouldn't have minded the test. Cockeye Katie wouldn't have wept. Cockeye Katie had courage. Cockeye Katie would have known what to do. It was always easier for people who had nobody to love.

Julie was still weeping, although nobody who saw her would have known it, when the train pulled into the 180th Street station, and she pushed her way out through the turnstile into which not quite three hours ago she had dropped her nickel, and she climbed down the iron steps, and she started up the street toward Louis Vinutti's building.

Dotted along the street, in front of Metzger's bakery and Coteletti's grocery and even Chin Ying's laundry, Julie saw without looking the small knots of people from which, as she passed, she caught the same curious tone she had first heard in front of the bank, but Julie did not stop. By the time she reached the wide plate-glass window on which, in gold letters, was printed "Louis Vinutti, Inc. Cigars Cigarettes Tobacco," Julie had herself under control. Not because she had found Cockeye Katie's courage, but because she had worked her way back to the innocent-looking truthful-sounding lie behind which she had been hiding all her life: if you loved someone, you didn't ask any questions.

"Hi," Julie said to Mrs. Cooper. "Is Mr. Vinutti in?"

"No," the bookkeeper said. "Isn't it terrible about the banks?"

"Awful," Julie said. "Nobody seems to know what it means. Where is Mr. Vinutti?"

"I'll tell you what it means," Mrs. Cooper said. "It means a lot of people, until they open them up again, if they haven't got some credit with the grocer, they're going to starve, that's what it means. I don't know. He went out about an hour ago, and he didn't say. Could I help you?"

"An hour ago?" Julie said, glancing at her watch. "Did he talk to my sister? Miss Sarno?"

"Julie," Mrs. Cooper said, "I know who your sister is. No, she called, but it was just after Mr. Vinutti went out."

"Did she leave a message?" Julie said. "Celia?"

"No, just you'd be in to see Mr. Vinutti, and you'd give him the message. You want to wait?"

Mrs. Cooper gestured toward the single chair near the desk in the small cleared space among the packing cases that served as her office.

"I don't know," Julie said, and she didn't. The concept of waiting didn't seem to go with the urgency in Celia's voice when she had sent Julie off on her mission. "You have any idea when he'll be back, Mrs. Cooper?"

"He didn't tell me where he's going," the bookkeeper said, "so how can I tell you when he'll be back? Ordinarily a normal day, he's always back here around twelve, he checks the messages and orders before he goes for lunch. But today, who knows?"

Julie glanced again at her watch. It showed twenty minutes after eleven. "In other words, there's a good chance he'll be back in a half hour or so?"

"If he's still running a business, and he's still interested in eating," Mrs. Cooper said, "why not?"

"Would you do me a favor?" Julie said. "When he comes in, would you tell Mr. Vinutti I'd like to see him? I'll be back in a minute."

"If it's only a minute, why don't you wait?" Mrs. Cooper said.

"There's something I want to get," Julie said. "I really won't be more than a minute."

"I'll tell him," Mrs. Cooper said.

Out on 180th Street, just before she went into the drug store to make the call, it occurred to Julie that perhaps she'd better count her money. She did, found she had $1.65, and decided it might be wiser not to waste any of it. Calling Celia from the drug store would cost a nickel. If she made the call from home, the nickel would not have to be paid until the phone bill arrived, by which time the banks would probably be open again, and nickels would not be so precious.

Julie hurried up 180th Street and turned into Daly Avenue with the muttered promise that if anybody tried to stop her she would punch him in the nose. This proved to be unnecessary because, even though Julie did get stopped, it was done by a beat-up old Pierce-Arrow convertible with an Oregon license plate. It was covered with dust and parked directly in front of the apartment house, which was one reason why Julie stopped, although even if it had been further down the street she probably would have done the same, since she had never seen anything like it. Neither had a number of other people, who were gathered around the car.

None of these, however, had to call Celia and advise her that there might be a slight delay in cashing Mr. Prohst's check because Louis Vinutti was out but Julie would keep after him, so she hurried into the house, ran up the steps, and opened the apartment door with her key. Before she could close it, Mrs. Sarno came out of the living room.

"Hi, Ma," Julie said. "Did you hear about the banks? Some surprise, huh? Mr. Prohst says it's only for a day or two. I had to come home to get something. I'll explain in a minute. I have to make a call first."

She was moving toward the telephone table when the tall, slender figure appeared in the living room doorway beside her mother. The sun was behind them, so Julie couldn't make out the stranger's face, but there was something familiar about the way he brushed the yellow hair back from his forehead with a short, nervous thrust.

"The banks are only a small surprise," Mrs. Sarno said dryly. "I have here a bigger one. Julie, you remember Mr. Ivey from the Clock House?"

11

What she remembered first, what came flooding into Julie's mind with all the overwhelming totality of an unexpectedly released torrent, was the moment when she had last seen him: standing on the Avenue B sidewalk, slowly rubbing the back of his hand across his lips as he stared worriedly off into the distance, across Cockeye Katie's head, struggling with the meaning of Katie's report on the questions Mr. Crispin and his Board of Governors had just been asking her in the director's office about Mr. Ivey's relations with the girl members of the Nature Club, and in that suddenly re-created moment Julie relived once more the crazy feeling that Mr. Ivey had gone away from them, that what was standing there on the sidewalk in front of her and Cockeye Katie was only Mr. Ivey's hollow skin. Then—*now*—standing in front of her in the Sarno living room in the Bronx, Mr. Ivey smiled, and the moment vanished together with the crazy feeling that was part of it.

"*What fond and wayward thoughts will slide into a lover's head,*" he said quietly. In spite of the six-year separation, Julie could tell from the way Mr. Ivey's slightly resonant voice grew more resonant that he was quoting poetry. " '*Oh, mercy!' to myself I cried, 'If Lucy should be dead!'* "

"Hello, Mr. Ivey," Julie said. "I guess that's your car out in front of the house."

The smile vanished from the thin, handsome face. "Is that all you have to say to me?" he said. "And what's this *mister?*"

"You were mister when I last saw you," Julie said. "Head of the Nature Club, associate director of the Horace Judson Clarke House, and I was a member of both, eleven years old. Mr. Benjamin Franklin Ivey is the way I remember it." She wondered if she dared risk a smile. It was a bad time to encourage anybody to stay. She had to call Celia at the office. Deciding that any risks she took would be for Celia and nobody else, Julie said, "I suppose I ought to ask a lot of questions about where you've been and what you're doing here—"

"So far, all he's doing is standing," Mrs. Sarno said. "He came just before you did. The bell rings, I go, it's Mr. Ivey from the Clock House six years ago, and before I can ask like you said where he's been and what he's doing here, the door opens with a key, and it's you."

"I'm sorry," Julie said. "I really would like to ask a lot of questions, but I'm in a hurry—"

"Julie," Mr. Ivey said. "I thought we were friends."

"I'm sorry," Julie said again, wondering what had made her forget that. The six-year gap of time? Her preoccupation with the errand on which Celia had sent her? "I really am," she said. "It's just this terrible thing, the banks closing—"

"It's terrible only to short-sighted boobs, among whom I never numbered my friends the Sarnos," Ben Ivey said. "To people with sense and vision, it's the most wonderful thing that's happened to this country since the Armistice."

Julie and her mother exchanged a glance. Mrs. Sarno clearly felt the way Julie did.

"Mr. Ivey," she said, "I don't—"

"Ben," he said.

"What?" Julie said.

"Ben," Mr. Ivey said.

"Oh," Julie said. "Well, what I started to say—"

"No," he said. "Say it."

"What?" Julie said again.

"Ben," he said. "Say it."

"Ben," Julie said.

He smiled. "Now I feel at home," he said. "Thank you, Julie. You've given me the keys to the city, and even though I won't have time to use them, I appreciate the gesture. Now, what's *your* hurry?"

"Well, I wanted to make a phone call—"

"Go ahead." Mr. Ivey gestured toward the telephone table out in the hall. "Make the call. Put it behind you, so we can relax and have a visit."

Julie thought fast, then shook her head. "No, that's all right," she said. All she could accomplish for Celia by making the call would be to reassure Celia that she was doing what Celia had asked her to do. Celia knew that already. The important thing was not to let anybody else know what she was doing for Celia. Julie said, "The call isn't all that important."

Mr. Ivey turned with a slight bow to Mrs. Sarno. "I am glad to learn that your daughter's talent for inconsistency, which was one of her more charming traits on East Ninth Street, is still with her here in the Bronx. *Both* your daughters, Mrs. Sarno. How is Celia?"

"She's fine," Mrs. Sarno said.

"Good," Ben Ivey said. "You?"

"I'm fine," Mrs. Sarno said.

"I can see for myself that Julie is, which leaves only Mr. Sarno. How is he?"

"Dead," Mrs. Sarno said.

The smile dropped from Ben Ivey's face. "Oh, I'm sorry," he said. "I really am. I was very fond of Mr. Sarno. I liked him."

"He liked you," Mrs. Sarno said.

There was no change in her flat, uninflected voice, but Ben Ivey gave Mrs. Sarno a sharp glance. So did Julie. She had suddenly remembered something else that was six years old: the night Ben Ivey came to dinner over the barber shop, the night he ran out after Celia before her *Saturday Evening Post* buffet was even touched, the night Biaggio Sarno's wife came out of the bedroom with the tortoise-shell combs in her hair and said, "That young man with the smile that comes so quick, and the yellow hair that makes him look so innocent, I don't trust him. He wants something from us." Julie turned back to Ben Ivey.

"I'm proud of that," he said to Julie's mother. "There are those who say a man is known by his enemies. I'm old-fashioned enough to prefer to be known by my friends. I'm pleased that Mr. Sarno thought of me as his friend. When did he die?"

"Six years ago," Mrs. Sarno said. "Soon after you went away."

"Oh," Ben Ivey said, and he thrust the cowlick back from his forehead. "Well, then." He turned to Julie. "Now that the telephone call you had to make doesn't have to be made after all, aren't you going to ask me to sit down? Tell me how an eleven-year-old girl can become so beautiful in six years? Insist on my giving you an account of my activities during the long—?"

"I'm afraid I don't have the time," Julie said. "I came home only for a minute to make this call— Not that it's important or anything, but with the banks closed, like everybody else in the office I've got only a little cash on me, and not knowing when the banks will open again, I didn't want to waste even a nickel of it on a phone booth—"

"You were always the most practical and level-headed member of the family," Ben Ivey said. "As an old friend, I'd appreciate your applying both those qualities to what is beginning to sound like an awfully fishy explanation."

"Mr. Ivey!"

"Ben," he said.

"There's nothing fishy about—"

"You came home to make a phone call. That's out of the way. Now what?"

"I have to go—"

He stepped forward, took Julie's arm, and said, "I'll go with you."

"But you don't even know where I'm going!"

"How can I, if you refuse to tell me? But by sticking to the root of the matter, which seems to be the closing of the banks, I am able to figure out that you probably are just as reluctant to waste your small hoard of coins on carfare as on phone calls, which means I can be of service to you. I have a car downstairs. The tank is full. I will drive you wherever you want to go." Ben Ivey turned back to Mrs. Sarno. "I'm sorry this visit has to be so short. And don't worry about the banks. If during the past six years Celia has improved in appearance as much as your younger daughter, you are going to own a bank of your own before long, because these girls can't help marrying millionaires." The light tone vanished abruptly, along with the easy, relaxed smile. "And thanks again for what you said about Mr. Sarno's feelings for me," Ben Ivey said quietly. "He was a wonderful man."

The tortoise-shell combs quivered as their owner's already ramrod-straight back achieved the impossible and grew straighter. "Nobody will ever know how wonderful," Mrs. Sarno said. "Nobody."

In the street, as Ben dipped down to open the door of the convertible, Julie said irritably, "How can you say things like that with a straight face? Wonderful! My God! You know what he was like. A drunken, irresponsible, savage—"

"Who cares about *him?*" Ben Ivey said, handing her into the car and slamming the door. "He's dead. Why don't you learn to stick to the root of the matter?" Ben came around the front of the car and slipped in beside Julie. "Your mother's the one who counts," he said. "She's alive. All she's got left is a memory. Who

238

says it has to be a memory she can't take to bed with her? Why shouldn't she have something to warm her? Not the way it was. The way she *wanted* it to be. The way she now *thinks* it was. Especially since it doesn't cost anything. Just a few words, something we can all afford, especially on a day when the banks are closed. Grow up, beautiful. It's more fun to give pleasure than pain." Ben Ivey turned a key and stepped on a button. The big car came to life with a roar. "Where to?"

"Just around the corner," Julie said. "Exactly one block."

"Hell," Ben said. "It hardly seems worthwhile firing up this Baldwin locomotive for a journey as short as that."

"It was your idea," Julie said. "I didn't ask you."

"No, of course not," Ben Ivey said, making the turn. "You never ask for anything. You're always giving."

Julie gave him a sharp glance. "I have no objection to your helping my mother polish up a completely false image of my father," she said. "But don't go to work on me. You don't know any more about me than I know about you. We met six years ago, when I was a kid of eleven, and after a few months you disappeared. The past six years are an absolute blank. You know nothing about what I've been doing—"

"True, but my memory is unimpaired," Ben Ivey said. "If you doubt it, I'll make you a little bet. I'll bet you that whatever it is you're all worked up about right now, whatever it is you're in such a swivet to be doing, I'll bet you're doing it for Celia."

"Oh, *you*," Julie said.

"Too bad I didn't get a chance to mention the stakes before I won that little bet," Ben said. "Which corner?"

"That one," Julie said. "On the left. And I'm *not* in a swivet, and I'm *not* doing anything for—"

"Easy, beautiful," Ben said as he pulled the car up to the curb and turned off the ignition. "You lost the bet. Now don't lose your temper as well. I'm not asking questions. I'm not prying. I don't give a damn what it is you're doing for Celia. I'm just giving you a lift. Want me to go in with you?"

"No, thanks," Julie said.

239

She got out of the car and tried to slam the door hard but Ben, leaning over with a low chuckle, caught it with his outstretched hand and pulled the door shut gently.

"Don't stay long," he said. "I've got to be down in Washington some time tonight, and it could be a five-, six-hour drive. I don't know the roads. Step on it."

Julie did, but not because of Ben Ivey's urging. The image of her sister Celia, sobbing in the chair beside Mr. Prohst's desk, was suddenly almost unbearable.

"No, he hasn't showed or called up," said Mrs. Cooper when Julie came into the office, and she turned to look at the clock on the wall. "But it's getting around to his eating time, so whatever it is that's changed his plans for today—"

"Would he maybe go to eat before coming back here?" Julie said.

"It happens once in a while, something unusual comes up, but today—" Mrs. Cooper paused, and then, "Where's my head?" she said, tapping it sharply with her pencil. "Of course today. The banks closing and all, what could be more unusual? Look, Julie, I don't know what he's been doing. Some customers he had to see maybe, I don't know. But his *stomach*, *that* I do know. Twelve o'clock, no matter what, Mr. Vinutti eats." Mrs. Cooper picked up the phone. "I'll call Marletta's and—"

"Don't bother," Julie said quickly. She didn't want to get involved in telephone explanations to Louis while Mrs. Cooper was listening. "I'll just go over and catch him there."

"When you do, do me a favor," Mrs. Cooper said. "Tell him he's got an office with a bookkeeper in it that likes to know once in a while where the boss is, and am I going home to my family tonight with my week's salary in money or cigar-store coupons?"

"All right," Julie said, "I'll tell him." Out on the sidewalk, leaning down to the open window of the Pierce-Arrow, she said, "I have to go over to Marletta's."

"What's that?" Ben Ivey said.

"A restaurant," Julie said. "It's—"

"Good, hop in," Ben said, leaning across to open the front door. "I'm hungry, too."

"No, I'm not going there to eat," Julie said. "It's just—"

"I see where we're going to have to put our backs into it down in Washington to do anything as interesting as what you're doing up here in the Bronx. You come home to make a phone call, but then you don't make it. Now you're going to a restaurant, but not to eat."

"I have to meet somebody."

"Somebody you're ashamed of?"

"Of course not."

"Well, then, hop in and introduce me to him," Ben Ivey said. "I'll look him over and see if he's worthy of you."

"No, no, it's nothing like that. He's actually a friend of Celia's."

"Then why isn't Celia lunching with him instead of you?"

"I'm *not* lunching with him."

"Then lunch with me and stop arguing," Ben Ivey said. "My arm is beginning to ache as badly as my stomach. Hop in."

Julie hopped in and wondered, as she directed Ben toward the restaurant just off Southern Boulevard, whether the purpose of her meeting with Louis Vinutti would in any way be affected by the fact that she was not alone. The problem became academic soon after Ben parked the car and they came into the restaurant. It was empty.

"Aren't you baking today?" Julie said.

"We're baking," Mrs. Marletta said. "But nobody's eating."

"*We* are," Ben said.

"What's wrong?" Julie said.

"The banks," Mrs. Marletta said. "Everybody's got a few cents in their pockets, they want to keep them there. Who knows when they'll open again?"

"I do," Ben said.

"Who you got with you today?" Mrs. Marletta said to Julie as she led them to a booth. "This new Vice-President Garfield?"

"The new Vice-President is Garner," Ben said. He waited for Julie to sit down and then slid onto the bench facing her. "John Nance Garner. A perhaps unfortunate middle name for a member of a new and virile administration, but what's in a name? Look at Hoover. He's had everything named after him from a vacuum cleaner to a dam, and the best he could come up with was vote for me or the grass will grow in a thousand cities. Well, you can take it from me, Mrs. Marletta, what's going to grow, indeed what will have started growing before this day is done, is not grass but hope. When this young lady who led me here asked if you were baking today, she meant pizzas, I assume?"

"What else?" said Mrs. Marletta.

"Good," said Ben. "And what kind do you bake?"

"What kind do you want?"

"Back where I come from, in Oregon, there's a place where they make the world's greatest pizza, and—"

"Where the world's greatest pizza is made," Mrs. Marletta said, "you're sitting now."

"They use sausage and anchovies and mushrooms and cheese and tomatoes and capers and—"

"We use the same but less words," Mrs. Marletta said. "What you get in this Oregon we call here The Works. One or two?"

Ben looked at Julie.

"Two," she said.

"Two," Ben said.

"Two The Works!" Mrs. Marletta shouted to her husband out in back, and then, "When they'll open the banks?"

"When the moment is propitious," Ben said.

"You sound like Hoover," Mrs. Marletta said.

"If your knives were sharper," Ben said, "I would cut my throat."

"Order a steak and I'll show you the kind of sharp knives we have," Mrs. Marletta said. "When is propitious?"

"I will know better by tomorrow," Ben said.

"A conference with this Mr. Garner?" Mrs. Marletta said. "Correct?"

"Not quite, but almost," Ben said.

Mrs. Marletta winked at Julie as she said to Ben, "Bring him up here after the conference for a pizza on the house. We got customers two state assemblymen and once in a while the borough president drops in, but so far no vice-presidents."

"Everything is going to be different from now on," Ben said.

"A steady flow of vice-presidents through your establishment will be arranged."

"It's sure starting different," Mrs. Marletta said. "With closed banks."

"Louis Vinutti been in yet?" Julie said.

"No, but any minute," Mrs. Marletta said. She turned to look at the clock on the wall and added, "He's already a couple minutes late. I'll go propitious the pizzas."

She walked out into the back.

"Nice woman," Ben said. "Good sense of humor."

"Were you really in Oregon?" Julie said.

"Do you think I would lie to an old friend like Mrs. Marletta?"

"No kidding," Julie said. "I mean it, Ben."

"Sorry," he said. "I didn't hear the gears shift. Yes, really in Oregon. Why are you pursuing this tobacco tycoon?"

"What are you talking about?"

"Louis Vinutti, Incorporated. Cigars. Cigarettes. Tobacco. Where I drove you from your home, and whence or whom we've just driven here in pursuit of, if you will pardon the syntax. Don't look so flabbergasted. It's not the FBI I'm going down to Washington to meet with. It's just I learned to read at an early age, and while I was waiting for you to emerge from that place, I managed to spell out the not very complicated gold lettering on the window. Louis Vinutti, Eye En See. What's Celia doing with a tobacco corporation for a friend and why are you chasing after it?"

"She's not *doing* anything with him," Julie said. "He's just a friend, and I'm not chasing him. Louis has something for Celia and I'm supposed to pick it up. What were you doing in Oregon?"

"Settlement-house work. Same as down on Avenue B. Don't paint them."

"What?"

Ben picked up a fork, reached across the table, and touched one of Julie's blood-red fingernails with the tines. "Wrong color," he said. "Or if you must be in the cosmetic swim at your advanced age of what—seventeen? almost eighteen?—try something less vulgar. Your hands are too pretty for that slop."

243

Julie put her hands in her lap. "Ben," she said. "Why did you run away?"

He nodded, a slow movement of the head that was almost a deferential bow, as though he wanted to acknowledge the fact that she had displayed the greater courage in being first to bring up the subject they had both been avoiding.

"Is that how they described it on East Ninth Street?" he said. "I ran away?"

"What other way was there to describe it?" Julie said.

"*The good die first, and they whose hearts are dry as summer dust burn to the socket.*"

"Nobody down on East Ninth Street uses words like that."

"What kind of words did they use?"

"They said Mr. Crispin had something on you," Julie said, talking to the small yellow-crusted craters in the open sugar bowl. "They said he called a meeting of the Board of Governors so you could hear the charges and answer them, but at the last moment you got scared and ran away."

"Meaning I was guilty," Ben said.

"Well," Julie said.

"What else did they say?"

"That's all."

"That's *all?*"

"That's all," Julie said.

"What about the charges?" Ben said. "What kind of words did they use on East Ninth Street for them?"

"Nobody said anything about the charges."

Ben's eyes crinkled at the corners. "I don't understand," he said.

"Nobody said anything about the charges," Julie repeated.

"You mean *you* didn't?"

"I mean nobody did," Julie said.

"Not even Cockeye Katie?"

"Not even Cockeye Katie."

"Why not?" Ben said. "I mean, I can understand *your* not saying anything. You were my friend. But *that* girl?"

"I said I'd kill her," Julie said.

The crinkles vanished as Ben's eyes spread wide. "You told Katie—?"

"If she said anything to anybody about the questions Mr. Crispin and those other people had asked her," Julie said, "I said I'd kill her."

"And she believed you?"

"She never said a word," Julie said.

"Then the only people who *could* have said a word," Ben Ivey said slowly, as though he were running down the names on an invisible list, "were Mr. Crispin and the members of his Board of Governors and Steve Shupka and possibly—"

"No," Julie said. "Nobody."

"Why would *they* shut up? You didn't threaten to kill Mr. Crispin, did you?"

"I didn't have to. All he wanted was to get you out of the Clarke House. You got out. He had nothing to gain by making a scandal out of it."

"If I understand you correctly, then," Ben Ivey said, even more slowly, "while it was generally felt on the pavements of East Ninth Street that I had quit under fire, nobody knew what the fire was about?"

"Nobody but me and Katie and those others," Julie said.

Ben made an impatient gesture with the fork. "I mean *aside* from you and Katie and those others?"

"Aside from us, nobody."

Ben started to laugh.

"What's funny?" Julie said.

"*Those obstinate questionings of sense and outward things, fallings from us, vanishings.*"

"Say it in English, Ben."

"For six years, all the time I've been in Oregon, there's been this nagging thought in the back of my mind that Crispin, out of sheer malice, would spread his filthy charges to the four winds, that by leaving as I did, I had also left behind me in his hands a weapon with which—" Ben paused to look down at his hand. The

245

fork was bent double. He laughed again, brushed the yellow hair back from his forehead, straightened the piece of metal, and said, "Julie, do you know what you've just done for me?"

"It's what you wanted, isn't it?"

Ben's eyes crinkled again. "What I wanted?" he said.

"That's what you came for, isn't it?"

"Julie," Ben said. "What are you saying to me?"

"I can't quote Wordsworth," she said. "I have to say it in my own words. You ran away. You were gone for six years. You never wrote or anything to say where you are or what you were doing or *why* you ran away. Then, all of a sudden, six years later, you're on your way from Oregon to Washington for I don't know what, you stop off in the Bronx. It's not exactly on the way. And you must have done at least *some* detective work to trace us and find us up here on Daly Avenue. Why would you do all that? Why would you go out of your way?"

"I can answer that," Ben said quietly. "You heard what I said to your mother a little while ago about your father. It's true of all the Sarnos. They're part of that first extraordinary year I spent in New York. Inseparably, inextricably, and wonderfully a part of it. The Sarnos were my friends. I've never stopped thinking of them as my friends. This is the first time I've come east since I left New York six years ago. It didn't require much work to find you. All I had to do was look in a phone book and ask a cop how to get to Daly Avenue. I'd have done a lot more work than that, cheerfully—I'd have gone a lot further out of my way than the Bronx, with pleasure—to see my friends again. Have I answered your questions?"

"Not the first one I asked," Julie said. "Why did you run away, Ben?"

"You just told me," he said. "To avoid the scandal that Crispin would have started if I had stayed, the scandal that could have ruined me."

Mrs. Marletta arrived with the steaming pizzas. "The Works," she said, setting down the two big round tins. "And to drink?"

"Coffee, please," Julie said. "American."

246

"Espresso for me," Ben said.

Mrs. Marletta went away. Ben picked up his knife, started to cut across the middle of the pie, and looked up.

"Better eat it while it's hot," he said.

"I'm not hungry," Julie said.

Ben put down his knife. "Julie, do you believe those charges?"

"You never told me they were not true."

"I'm telling you now," Ben said.

"All right," she said.

He picked up his knife. Julie did not move.

"You don't believe me," Ben said.

"I believe you."

"Then eat."

Julie shook her head. "You go ahead," she said.

"Julie, what's wrong?"

Julie shook her head again. "I don't know," she said. "Something is missing."

"In what I've told you?" Ben said. "You think I lied?"

Julie shook her head once more. "No," she said.

"Then what do you mean?"

"I don't know," Julie said.

"Then for God's sake eat," Ben said. "Until you find out, anyway."

He cut into his pizza. So did Julie. Mrs. Marletta arrived with the coffee.

"One American, one espresso," she said. "How do we stack up against Oregon?"

"You've got them backed off the map," Ben said around a huge mouthful. "I'm going to see this new administration puts a star on the flag for you."

"First open the banks," Mrs. Marletta said.

She went away. Ben swallowed his mouthful of pizza, cut himself another piece, started to lift it to his mouth, and stopped with the fork in the air.

"Is that all you want?" he said.

"I told you I'm not hungry," Julie said.

247

"Tell me something else," Ben said. "Your mother said your father died soon after I left the Clarke House six years ago. How soon after?"

"Nine days," Julie said.

Ben nodded, as though she had uttered the answer he had expected to hear. "And how did he die?"

"He went off on one of his regular bats," Julie said. "The coroner or whatever they call him, he said the deceased had been drinking steadily for three or four days before he fell in the river and was drowned."

Ben nodded again. "And do you know, or can you guess, what set him off on this particular drinking bout?"

"The same thing that usually set him off," Julie said. "One of his wild get-rich-quick schemes blew up in his face."

"Which one?"

"Don't you remember?"

"I'm asking you, Julie."

"He'd bought a carload of shovels without handles," she said. "He expected to sell them at a huge profit to farmers out west."

"You mean, don't you, Julie, that he expected *me* to sell them for him?"

"I didn't say that," she said.

"No, I said it," Ben said. "I promised him I'd sell those shovels for him. But I broke my promise, so he took to the witch-hazel bottle and died. In effect, then, it was I who killed him."

"I didn't say that," Julie repeated.

"You don't have to," Ben said. "It's written all over your face."

"Why are you doing this?" Julie said.

"You just said something is missing," Ben said. "You said you didn't know what it is. All right, I've just showed you the missing piece."

Julie shook her head. "I don't think that's it."

"I do," Ben said. "You think I'm guilty of your father's death. That's why you can't eat your pizza." He raised the piece he had just cut and put it in his mouth.

"You can, I notice," Julie said. "From which I assume you don't agree with what you think I think."

"If you mean do I feel guilty of Biaggio Sarno's death," Ben said, "I can say only that whatever my feelings might be on that point, they are, like the point itself, completely irrelevant."

"Irrelevant to what?" Julie said.

"My reason for leaving the Clarke House as I did."

"Ben, I'm not following you."

"You've fallen into slovenly thinking habits," he said. "We'll have to do something about that. You've got too good a brain to allow it to grow lazy or rusty. Julie, the difference between the great mass of human beings and the few who emerge at the top of the heap as their leaders is not talent, which helps but is not essential, or personal magnetism, which is absolutely essential but is not in itself enough. The main and crucial and deciding difference, Julie, the only one that really counts, is the capacity to choose the right ball and then keep your eye on it, regardless, irregardless, come hell, come high water, come the end of the world. Most people's lives consist of a series of flounderings after what they think or hope or pray is that right ball.

"To your father, for example, it was one day a couple of hundred bundles of white kid gloves, all right-handed, and the next day a carload of shovels, minus handles. Most people's flounderings are just as ludicrous, only they don't know it. The born leader doesn't flounder. He knows. By instinct. My instinct, when I learned from Steve Shupka that Mr. Crispin had called a Board of Governors meeting to bring charges against me, my instinct was to fight back. That's why I asked Celia to meet me at the Clarke House that night. She was my best weapon. A few minutes later, out in the street, when I learned from you and Cockeye Katie the *nature* of Mr. Crispin's charges, my instinct told me that the only sensible course was not to face them. The charges were lies. But they were one of those peculiar kind of lies from which, no matter how totally a man refutes them, he never completely recovers. There's always that little stain in the picture when, years later, people look back. The important thing was not to prove Tyler Crispin a liar, which I could have done with ease. The important thing was to keep my record clear, so that years later, today for instance, anybody looking back to see what sort of young man Benjamin Franklin Ivey was, that anybody who is looking will not see any stains that would have to be explained away.

"The fact that my reasoning was correct, the proof that I was right in doing what others would label a cowardly act and point to as sure proof of my guilt, is the fact that now, today, there is absolutely no stain on the record of Benjamin Franklin Ivey. I am on my way down to Washington to see some people in this new administration. I know they did some checking before they sent for me. I was pretty sure before I left Oregon that they had found nothing. Now, from what you've just told me, I'm certain of it. If my talks in Washington turn out the way I think they will, these people will do some more checking. They will still find nothing. Not merely because in actual fact I have *done* nothing I wouldn't want them to find. But because six years ago my instincts told me to act not quixotically but sensibly. In short, Julie, if you always stick to the root of the matter, the matter, as well as its roots, will stick to you. Why are you scowling?"

"Couldn't you have stuck to the root of the matter and still sold my father's shovels?" Julie said. "Or told me and Celia you were leaving? Or let us know after you left where you were?"

"The important thing was to leave Tyler Crispin with the impression that I had fled in panic and would never return," Ben said. "Any one or all of the things you just mentioned would have diluted that impression in Tyler Crispin's mind. The dilution might have been fatal to my plan. There's no point in reasoning your way up to a plan and then cutting the ground from under its feet by vacillating. If you have the brains to make a plan, you should also have the guts to stick to it. No matter what the cost."

"Would you have stuck to this one," Julie said, "if you had known it would mean the death of Biaggio Sarno?"

"I'm not going to answer that question."

"Why not?"

"I don't think you're ready for it," Ben Ivey said.

Mrs. Marletta shouted something from her seat behind the cash register.

"What?" Julie said, turning.

250

"The telephone," Mrs. Marletta called, holding it out. "It's for you."

Julie had a moment of confusion. Then she saw the fresh-cut lump of pizza on its way to Ben's mouth, and she remembered where she was, and how she had got there, and the confusion turned to panic. How could she have forgotten all about Celia and the errand on which her sister had sent her back to the Bronx?

"Excuse me," Julie said, slipping out of the booth.

"Of course." Ben placed both palms on the table and pushed himself up as far as the narrow space would allow him to get toward the position he clearly felt a gentleman should assume when a lady leaves his table. "My regards to the tobacco tycoon."

Julie didn't realize what he meant until, moments later, having taken the phone from Mrs. Marletta, she realized she was talking not to Louis Vinutti but to his bookkeeper.

"Julie," Mrs. Cooper said. "He there?"

"No," Julie said.

"You mean he hasn't come in yet for lunch? Julie, it's a quarter after one!"

Julie looked up at the clock on the wall. Troubled, she saw that it *was* a quarter after one.

"No, I'm still waiting," she said.

"How do you like that?" Mrs. Cooper said.

Julie, who didn't like it at all, said nervously, "You called because—?"

"Because I'm getting good and worried about whether I'm going to get *paid* today," Mrs. Cooper said. "I got exactly eighty cents in my pocket, and if I come home with my week's pay check, what am I going to do with it a day like this? *Frame* it till the banks open? Honest to God, that boss of mine—"

Julie, who knew Mrs. Cooper adored Louis Vinutti, understood the bookkeeper's annoyance. Julie felt it herself. On this of all days why couldn't the man of regular habits be what he always was: regular?

"Where could he be?" Julie said.

"I'll tell you where in about one half minute I'm going to *want* him to be," Mrs. Cooper said. "Wait a minute." Julie waited,

251

wondering worriedly what she should do next. Mrs. Cooper came back on the line. "You know Bud Birnbaum?"

"Who?" Julie said.

"Bud Birnbaum. One of our drivers. Well, it doesn't matter you know him or not. He just came in, and I asked him, and he says he saw Mr. Vinutti's car a little while ago, it was heading for the park, so you know what I think? I mean it's just possible?"

"What?" Julie said.

"Sometimes, small deliveries, he doesn't want one of the trucks to go all the way out of the way, Mr. Vinutti takes the stuff himself. I could be crazy, but I think, the way I remember it, I think he loaded some cartons of cigarettes and stuff in the car before he left, and if Bud saw him heading for the park, it could be Mr. Vinutti is making a delivery to the Zoo Café. You know that sort of restaurant they got? All the tables outside? By the Small Mammals House, where the—?"

"Oh, yes, sure," Julie said.

"Well, I'll give them a call and ask—"

"No, I'll go right over," Julie said. "Thanks, Mrs. Cooper."

"Wait! If you find him—!"

"I'll tell him," Julie said. She hung up, said, "Thanks, Mrs. Marletta," hurried back to the table, and said, "I better go, Ben. I've got to—"

"I'll go with you," Ben said, slipping out of the booth.

"No, that's all right. You don't have to."

"Of course I don't have to," he said, pulling out his wallet as they walked across toward Mrs. Marletta. "But I want to. Besides, I'm getting curiouser and curiouser about this tobacco tycoon. How much, Mrs. Marletta? It was marvelous."

"Thirty-five, seventy, and two coffees, ninety cents," Mrs. Marletta said. "I'm glad you liked it. You get back to this Oregon, you want a good pizza, just let us know, and I'll put a stamp on one and take it to the post office myself."

"Airmail, please," Ben said. "They lose a lot of flavor if you eat them cold." He put a dollar bill on the glass counter. "Do you mind if I let it go at that, Mrs. Marletta? I don't want to leave behind the impression that your first customer today is a cheap-

252

skate, but I, too, think I'd better preserve my small hoard of ready cash until—you know."

"Of course I know," Mrs. Marletta said. "Propitious."

Out in the street, Ben said, "Where to?"

"The park," Julie said. "But if it's out of the way, I can walk."

"The entire borough of the Bronx hasn't been out of my way, so this fragment of it is hardly likely to be. Hop in." Julie hopped in, and directed him to the zoo entrance gate, where Ben stopped the car and said, "What do we do now?"

"Walk," Julie said.

Walking along the winding path through the fenced areas, Julie was again aware of knots of people huddled around little invisible bonfires of words, and she caught again without listening that same curious tone by which she had been struck first in front of the bank, but she really heard nothing except the inner voice that alternated between accusing her of helping Celia down the road to destruction and screaming at her to hurry and get Mr. Prohst's five-hundred-dollar check cashed because everything Celia wanted out of life depended on it. Julie felt Ben's hand tighten on her arm and she shook her head, as though to clear it.

"I'm sorry," she said. "I wasn't listening."

"The same thing was true of a lot of people in the little town of Bethlehem almost two thousand years ago," Ben Ivey said. "Nobody listens when a world changes course. Not many, anyway. They're always all wrapped up in their own far more monumental concerns. Such as locating a Bronx tobacco tycoon for some damn-fool reason."

"You don't even know why I'm trying to find Mr. Vinutti," Julie said irritably. "So how can you say it's a damn-fool reason?"

"If it wasn't a damn-fool reason, you wouldn't be ashamed to tell me what it is."

"I'm *not* ashamed!" Julie snapped. "You have no *right* to say—!"

"I've known you since you were a kid of eleven. You think you're all grown up now, a woman of the world, or whatever phrase you prefer out of your favorite comic strip. Well, maybe. But you're still Julie Sarno, and I've always known what goes on under that crown of beautiful blue-black hair, and what's going on there right this minute is something you're ashamed of."

"I am not!"

"Then worried by," Ben said. "If you weren't, you'd have been listening to me."

"What makes you think everything you say is so fascinating?"

"The way you *used* to listen to me," Ben said. "Six years ago, when all I had to talk about was a foolish little nature club in a slum-area settlement house. Agog, was the way you used to do it, beautiful. All agog, honeybunch. Mouth agape. Hanging breathlessly on my every word. Now, today, when what I've got to talk about is a turning point in history, you walk along sitting on your hands."

"You know," Julie said, "I think you're crazy."

"Because I accuse you of walking along while sitting on your hands? Nonsense. It's done all the time. By all sorts of people. Take President Hoover. Or, happily, ex-President Hoover. For four solid years— Is this it?"

"Yes," Julie said.

Ben dropped her arm as they threaded their way through the green metal tables, not one of which was occupied, toward the small brick structure at the far side of the cement terrace. When they came in, the man behind the soda fountain was leaning down, his ear close to the brown silk covering over the speaker of a small radio tucked between the malted machine and an electric orange juicer. The man looked up and took the cigarette from his mouth.

"The inauguration," he said. "Down in Washington. It's about to start."

"Have you seen Mr. Vinutti?" Julie said. "Louis Vinutti?"

"Who?"

"Louis Vinutti? Cigarettes and things? His bookkeeper said he was coming here with a delivery? He *might* be coming here, she said?"

There was a low roar of static from the radio. The man behind the fountain dipped down and put his ear to the brown silk.

"It's the introduction," he said. "The guy introducing him.

254

The Chief Justice of the Supreme Court, I think. Anyway, he finished, and they're clapping."

"What about Mr. Vinutti?" Ben said.

The man straightened up. "What?" he said.

"Mr. Vinutti," Julie said. "He was supposed to come here with a delivery?"

"Oh," the man said. "No, I ain't seen him."

"But is he expected?" Julie said.

"I don't know," the man said. "Maybe the boss knows."

"*Your* boss?" Ben said.

The man, whose head was moving back down toward the radio, nodded and hung the cigarette back in the corner of his mouth.

"Where is he?" Julie said. "Your boss?"

"I don't know," the man said. "Trying to round up some cash some place. On account of the banks. He ought to be back soon." The radio emitted another roar of static. "I guess he's getting up now," the man said. "The President." He listened hard while the cigarette smoke curled up past his narrowed eye. "Yeah, that's it. The announcer says he's coming to the mikes. His son is helping him. The oldest one."

"James," Ben said.

For the first time the man behind the fountain seemed to look at his visitors.

"Yeah, that's the one," he said and then, unhooking the cigarette from the corner of his mouth, he gestured with it toward the terrace. "Whyn't you sit down and wait? He ought to be back here any minute."

His ear was back at the radio before Julie could say anything, and Ben must have known that what she was trying to say would contribute nothing to the situation, because he took her arm and led Julie away from the fountain.

"That man is performing a religious rite," Ben said. "Let's not interrupt him. Besides, since the trail seems to have gone cold, his advice is sound. Let's just sit down for a few minutes and wait for his boss or your tobacco tycoon, whichever shows up first."

He led Julie to a table at the far end of the terrace, near the cement steps that led down to the circular walk in front of the Small Mammals House.

"What religious rite?" Julie said.

Ben looked at her either with puzzlement or with his face deliberately arranged to simulate puzzlement.

"Julie, baby," he said finally. "Is it possible that you're so wrapped up in this pursuit of Mister L. Vinutti that you don't know what's happening today?"

"Ben, if you start quoting Wordsworth at me again, I'm going to—"

"Even *he* never wrote anything that can measure up to this day," Ben said. "Julie, I know you weren't listening a few minutes ago when I said a world was changing course, but it's true, so I want you to listen now, while I say it to you again. I won't beat you over the head with facts you surely must already know. That nearly thirteen million people in this country have been for nearly three years desperately hunting work. Work that doesn't exist. That the richest nation in God's green world is slowly dying of malnutrition. That the whole fabric of our western civilization as we've known it for centuries has broken down, ground to a halt, fallen apart at the seams. That for months now we have been rolling downhill, faster and faster, toward certain destruction. What I *want* to beat you over the head with, what I *want* you to hear, is that a miracle has happened. It's happening right now. At this very moment."

Ben stopped and looked up. So did Julie. A uniformed zoo attendant had appeared at the table. He seemed terribly excited, as though he had just won a sweepstakes.

"I got a radio going in there," he said, nodding toward the Small Mammals House. "He's speaking now. Just started. You haven't missed much yet. I saw you sitting out here, and I thought maybe you'd like to hear him. The speech. What he's saying. Come on in. You're welcome."

Julie started to get up, but Ben took her arm. She sank back into the chair beside him.

"Will you please get out of here and stop interrupting me?" Ben said irritably.

The man in uniform looked startled, then his face grew red, and he backed away.

"Why did you have to do that?" Julie said. "He was just trying to be nice. He wanted us to hear—"

"Will you stop interrupting, too?" Ben said, and Julie could see that his irritation with the zoo attendant had turned to anger with her. "I'm trying to *tell* you something. You're living in a moment of history. There's never been anything like this. What's happening now, this instant, will change the course of the world as surely as—"

Julie didn't know when his voice stopped, or indeed if it did stop, any more than she knew how the space between their chairs had suddenly vanished. She knew only that all at once Ben was holding her close, and she could hear his heart and feel his lips, and she was crying quietly, not only with her eyes but with her whole being, in a completely new way.

All at once, with a sadness that was sweeter than anything she had ever known, Julie was crying for the stranger who had been her father and had died before he knew what she knew now; and she cried for the blows that had sent her reeling across the East Ninth Street barber shop when she was a little girl who had not yet learned to cry; and she cried for Celia who was pursuing so desperately and so hopelessly what Julie had just without asking been given as a present; and she cried for Cockeye Katie who had to dye her hair yellow and pretend to be insulted in the subway to get people to look at her; and Julie cried for Mr. Trench who had to wear a beard and quote Gibbon to stand almost level with people on whom he felt he should have been looking down; and she cried for Mrs. Cooper who would not be paid today.

When she ran out of people in her known world, Julie cried for all the people in all the world she did not know who did not have what she had, and she cried for all those who thought they had it but didn't, and then she cried for herself, because while she knew that all of her life would now be different, she knew also that none of it would ever again be like this moment.

So she cried harder, because she knew, in a way that neither time nor experience would ever make more clear, that by falling in love she had committed herself to something as terrible as it was wonderful, something from which she would never again be free, and she enjoyed every tear so much that Julie wished she could go on crying forever.

12

"Julie."

She came up out of her happiness slowly, like a diver surfacing. "Hmmm?"

Ben pulled a handkerchief from his pocket. "Better towel yourself dry, beautiful," he said. "I think here comes your tobacco tycoon."

Julie turned. Louis Vinutti was striding toward them, across the circular walk, a long square tube of lashed cigarette cartons swinging from one hand. Julie dried her eyes hastily, thrust the handkerchief back at Ben, and ran down the stone steps. She met Louis in front of the Small Mammals House.

"Where have you been?"

"Me?" he said.

"I've been looking all over for you," Julie said. "First the office, then Marletta's, and here. Mrs. Cooper said—"

"Julie, what are you doing in the zoo this time of day?" Louis said. "This morning, when I dropped you at the subway—"

"I didn't know the banks were closed. I mean *nobody* knew. In our office, I mean. Until I went down to cash the payroll check, the way I do every week. Everybody's caught short, and we thought, I mean Mr. *Prohst* thought, we were trying to figure where we could get some cash to sort of tide us over, just a token payment for each employee, until the banks open again, and Celia remembered about you and the drivers who come in with their collections at night, so she thought—" Julie paused, not only to fish in her purse for Mr. Prohst's check but, she noted, to congratulate herself on the plausible explanation she had invented without thought. "We were wondering, Celia and I, Louis, could you cash this check for us? The office? Out of your drivers' collections?"

He set down the bundle of lashed cigarette cartons and took the check.

"If you weren't looking at the biggest sap in four states, I could cash it," Louis said. "You know what *I* did? Listen. When I left you at the subway this morning, I went on to the bank, and I saw they had this piece of paper pasted on the door, so first I carefully dropped the deposit down the night depository slot, because it was only a few minutes after eight and the bank wasn't open yet, then I walked over to the door and I read the piece of paper, and then I started kicking myself around the block, which I've been doing ever since. Including driving all over the Bronx trying to cash a check of my own so I could at least pay Mrs. Cooper. But it looks like everybody in the Bronx is fresh out of cash, so I don't know what I'm going to do about that bookkeeper of mine. She's got three kids and a husband out of work and she's always one jump ahead of the sheriff."

"Louis," Julie said. "You mean you *can't* cash this check?"

"Julie, I've got exactly eight dollars and some change on me, which I was going to give to Mrs. Cooper when I get back to the office, but if it will help you and Celia, you're welcome to half of it and I'll tell Mrs. Cooper—"

"Aren't you going to introduce me?"

Julie turned. Ben had come down from the terrace.

"Louis," she said, "this is an old friend of mine, Ben Ivey. Please talk to each other while I make a phone call."

Julie left the two men shaking hands in front of the Small Mammals House, hurried back up the steps, across the terrace, and into the brick structure, where the man behind the fountain still had his ear close to the small radio. Julie went into the phone booth, dropped one of her few coins into the slot, and asked the operator for the Ellentuch, Prohst & Wadsworth number.

"Miss Lilly," she said when the switchboard operator answered. "Julie Sarno. Could I talk to my sister Celia, please?"

"She left about an hour ago, Julie."

"The *office?*"

"Yes, about an hour ago."

Julie glanced at her watch. "She went out to lunch?"

"I don't know," Miss Lilly said. "I imagine so, but most of the girls are eating in. I mean, we chipped in and sent down for some bread and cheese and salami, things like that, to make sandwiches, and luckily we have plenty of coffee. Mr. Trench says there's no telling how long the banks will be closed, so the little cash we have, we're all trying to make it last until—"

"Miss Lilly, how about Mr. Prohst? Could I talk to him, please?"

"He's out, too, Julie."

"Oh," Julie said, and she turned to look through the glass door of the booth. She could see Louis Vinutti and Ben Ivey talking, and even in her perplexity she was struck by how handsome Ben looked in profile. It made her heart beat a little faster. She turned back to the phone and said, "Well, Miss Lilly, I guess—"

"You want to leave a message, Julie? Or are you coming back? Or what?"

"I don't know," Julie said.

"What?" Miss Lilly said.

Julie pulled herself together. "When Celia comes back, or Mr. Prohst, either one, tell them I'm still trying, will you?"

"You're still trying," Miss Lilly said. "Anything else?"

"No, that's all, just I'm still trying."

"Julie?"

"What?"

"Would you like us to save you a sandwich? I mean, it'll save you using up money on lunch. I don't know how much you've got, but if you're like the rest of us—"

"No, that's all right, thanks, Miss Lilly. I've had my lunch."

Julie hung up and came out of the booth just as Louis Vinutti came in to the café with Ben Ivey. Louis heaved the lashed cigarette cartons up on the marble counter. The man behind the fountain nodded but did not move his ear from the radio until Louis pushed his receipt book across the counter. Then the man moved just long enough to scrawl his name at the bottom of the receipt. By the time Louis had the book back in his pocket, the man behind the fountain had his ear back against the radio.

"I guess I'd better get back on the trail of some cash for Mrs. Cooper," Louis Vinutti said. He put out his hand to Ben. "Nice to have met you, Mr. Ivey."

"Same here," Ben said as they shook hands. "I wish I could help you out, or your bookkeeper, I mean, but I've got to get down to Washington by tonight, and I think with the cash I've got I can just about make it."

"No, that's all right," Louis said. "I've got a few spots in mind I think I can cash a check. Not a big one, but big enough to carry Mrs. Cooper for a few days. You sure you don't want part of my eight dollars, Julie?"

"Thanks, no, I've got enough for today," she said. "If this goes on *very* long—"

"It won't," Ben said.

"In that case," Julie said, not daring to look at him because all at once she felt like crying again.

"Anybody want a lift?" Louis said. "My car's parked in the lot back there."

"Thanks, but I've got my own car parked somewhere out over there," Ben said, nodding across the terrace. "I don't know what it—"

"The 180th Street entrance," Julie said, still looking at Louis.

"Okay, then," Louis said and, after a moment of hesitation, "Best to Celia."

He walked away, and Julie kept her eyes fixed on the tall, striding figure. She didn't dare turn and look at Ben. Then Julie felt his hand fumbling for hers, and she took it, and they started to walk. They walked across the terrace and down the steps and back along the paved path that wound through the fenced areas, and Julie was vaguely aware that two giraffes stared down without much interest at her and Ben, and she thought she heard the water buffalo—the smaller one with the ugly naked patches in the hair on his rump—snort as she and Ben floated by, but Julie was unaware of any forward movement, so that when they came through the gate, and they reached Ben's beat-up old Pierce-Arrow, she stared at the car in surprise, wondering how she had managed to get there.

"Hop in," Ben said.

She didn't hop. Julie seemed to glide into the car, and when Ben came in from the other side and started the motor and her hand slid across the few inches of front seat that separated them, it was no surprise at all to find his hand waiting for hers. He held it all the way, and only released it for the Daly Avenue turn, which required two hands, but before they reached the apartment house, and before he had stopped the car and turned off the motor, Ben had recaptured her hand. Julie sat in silence for several moments, staring straight ahead, through the windshield, steeped in the calm turbulence of love.

"Well, if I'm going to get to Washington in time for my date tonight," Ben said finally, "I guess I'd better roll."

Julie said nothing. There were no words in her mind. She just sat there, holding Ben's hand, vaguely pleased by the fact that the world was standing still, but not feeling that she owed it any expressions of gratitude for being so thoughtful. It seemed right that the world should have come to a halt for her and Ben.

"What are you doing tomorrow?" he said.

Julie drew a deep sighing breath and said, "What?"

Ben laughed and bumped her hand up and down on the piece of dirty gray seat upholstery between them, as though he were rapping a gavel to call a meeting to order.

"Come on, beautiful, snap out of it," he said. "I really must get going. What are you doing tomorrow?"

Julie sighed again, and made an effort, and tomorrow—an astonishing and improbable and totally strange landscape—came sliding into view.

"Well, I guess I'll go to work in the morning," she said. "And then after work, six o'clock, I'm meeting Katie Halloran and we'll get something to eat and then go down to C.C.N.Y. to register."

"How long will that take?" Ben said.

"I don't know," Julie said. "Last time, our first term we registered, we were finished around nine o'clock, I think, a little after."

"Good," Ben said. "I'm pretty sure I can polish off my appointments in Washington by midafternoon, say three or four o'clock, so if I leave by then, I should be back up here in New York by nine o'clock. Where can I meet you?"

"Well—" Julie said.

"That's no help, beautiful. Where's this C.C.N.Y.?"

"Twenty-third Street. Why?"

"Because I don't want to drive all the way up here to the Bronx. It's another hour or more. Can I meet you in the college building, or outside, or any place near?"

"Sure, why not?"

"I'll come direct to Twenty-third and look for you in the lobby of the building," Ben said. "You wait for me there, will you?" Julie nodded happily. Ben said, "And don't bring Katie Halloran. The way I remember her—"

"She's changed," Julie said.

"Who hasn't?" Ben said. "Just the same, leave her behind somewhere."

Julie giggled once more and turned toward him and stopped. A taxi, whooshing by, suddenly slammed on its brakes, cut in ahead of them, and parked against the curb, a few yards up from the Pierce-Arrow. Blinking through the curtain of dust the cab had raised, Julie saw the rear door open and Celia step out. Then, as though she were watching a movie she had seen before, Julie saw Celia close the taxi door and lean down to say something through the open window to somebody inside. Julie couldn't see who it was, but she knew, and she was not surprised—it was, after all, a film she had seen before, wasn't it?—to see a man's tanned hand, with a heavy gold ring on the small finger, emerge through the taxi window and give Celia's slender white hand two gentle, reassuring pats. Then the cab started with a roar, and pulled

263

away from the curb, and Celia turned, and the frown on her lovely face changed to a look of astonishment.

"It's Celia," said Ben.

He got out of the Pierce-Arrow and went toward her. By the time Julie had got out on the other side, come around the car, and reached her sister and Ben as they were shaking hands, Julie had made her decision: she was not going to dilute her happiness by thinking about Celia's problem. She would think about Celia later. Now she wanted to think only about herself. Or rather, about herself and Ben. Having made the decision, Julie had room in the midst of her happiness for a stab of astonishment at her being able to make the decision without a feeling of guilt.

For the first time in her life, she understood the secret pleasures of selfishness.

"I'll run along upstairs," Julie said. "I want to see Mom, and besides, I've heard everything Ben has to say."

Ben laughed and said, "So long, beautiful. See you tomorrow."

13

He might just as well have said, "See you at the turn of the century."

It was Julie's first contact with one of the lover's basic laws: any unit of time, however short, spent away from the side of the loved one is unendurable eternity. Her intelligence told Julie that a single day was nothing even remotely unendurable. She had, after all, lived without strain through almost eighteen years of them. Julie's intelligence, unfortunately, could scarcely make itself heard in the soundless shriek of impatience by which she was surrounded from the moment she went into the apartment house, leaving Ben and Celia making polite conversation out on the sidewalk.

Julie supposed she should have stayed, if only for a few minutes, to make things easier for Celia. In view of what Julie now knew about her sister and Frank Prohst, it could not have been easy for Celia to find herself caught in a "Where have you been" and "What have you been doing" talk with a man she had known briefly six years ago, at a time when, Julie now realized, the relationship between Celia and her boss had already started. Easy or not, Julie left her sister in the middle of it.

She was certain, if she had remained behind, she would have given herself away. Not that Julie would have minded giving herself away to Celia. When the moment of revelation arrived, Celia would of course be the first one to know. The trouble was that Julie did not know if Ben would have minded. It had not occurred to her to ask him and, by the time Celia stepped out of that taxi, it was too late to ask. Like all lovers, however, Julie knew, or thought she knew, a great many answers to questions that did not have to be asked. One of these told her that Ben wanted her to say nothing about their future life together until the next day when he got back from Washington. Julie was certain, from the hints Ben had dropped about a job with the new administration, that the details of their future life were going to be settled in the nation's capital within the next twenty-four hours.

This certainty did not prevent her, however, from submerging herself in the delicious game of inventing details of her own. These proved so intoxicating that Julie scarcely heard her mother's questions or her own answers about how she had spent the afternoon; she was only dimly aware, when Celia finally came upstairs and Julie tried to explain why she had been unable to cash Mr. Prohst's check, that Celia seemed totally uninterested in the explanation; and Julie had absolutely no recollection of the evening meal she shared with her mother and sister or the radio broadcasts about the bank crisis and the inauguration of the new President to which they listened after supper.

By morning, her happiness had entered a new or *This Wonderful Thing Should Happen to Everybody* phase.

Knowing the reason for her own happiness, namely, Ben, she was certain she knew the reason for everybody else's lack of happiness, namely, lack of Ben. Knowing, however, that everybody else could not possibly achieve happiness the way she had—*anybody* else, let alone *everybody* else, who would have been dumb enough to try it would have got her eyes scratched out—Julie kept herself pleasantly busy all day inventing substitutes for the unfortunate. Surely there was somebody, somewhere, for Cockeye Katie? For poor old dried-up but sweet Miss Lilly? Did Mr. Trench have a wife, and if not why not?

The peak of this phase was achieved in the evening, when Julie met Katie after work for the C.C.N.Y. registration session. They met in Madison Square Park, which was half a block from Julie's office and two short blocks from the school, and settled down on a bench with the sandwich suppers they had brought from home that morning along with their sandwich lunches. Mr. Trench had divided up the contents of his petty-cash box among the members of the Ellentuch, Prohst & Wadsworth staff, and Katie's boss had been able to give her almost half her salary in cash, so neither girl was exactly strapped. Until the bank crisis ended, however, Katie and Julie, like most girls they knew, were drawing on their small hoards of cash only for absolute necessities. Among these, at their age, hot lunches and suppers were not included, but subway fares definitely were. Besides, in the magic world to which Julie had been introduced the day before in front of the Small Mammals House and in which she had been living ever since, the temperature of food had about as much importance as a Bronx streetcar transfer in Outer Mongolia.

"Wait a minute," Katie said, pausing in her fastidious plucking of strings from a segment of tangerine. "I must have like wax in my ears. I'm all of a sudden not hearing right. Say that again, please?"

"I said I think I'll skip registration tonight," Julie said. "You want my apple?"

"I want your head examined," Katie said. "You skip registration tonight, it means you got no classes for a whole term. Don't you know that?"

"Sure I know it," said Julie. "What's so terrible about having no classes for a whole term?"

She held out the apple. Katie, taking it, dipped down and peered, as though Julie's face were hidden under a bonnet and Katie was trying to get a better look at her friend beneath the brim.

"Funny," Katie said. "You *look* perfectly normal, and yet—" She popped the tangerine segment into her mouth, chewed hard, worked her lips violently back and forth until a seed came popping out, and then said, "Must be like they call amnesia."

"Who?" Julie said.

"You," Katie said. "Somewhere between the time I left you yesterday morning and a little while ago, when we met tonight, you've been hit by this loss of memory thing. Amnesia."

"I have *not* been hit by any amnesia," Julie said.

"Then what?" Katie said. "Because you've sure as hell been hit by something. You got a secret, why don't you tell your old friend Katie? One of those jerk kids you've been dating, all of a sudden it's serious?"

For a moment or two, overwhelmed with greediness for the suddenly glimpsed pleasures of confession, Julie almost did. Then she remembered Ben's words: "Don't bring Katie Halloran." And Julie remembered also that to tell Katie would be an act of disloyalty to Celia, who was entitled to learn the wonderful news first.

"There's nothing to tell," Julie said.

"Then maybe you'd better listen," Katie said. "Because it looks like you've forgotten an awful lot. A B.A. in these crummy city colleges takes ninety-six points. Day session, you got a rich old man can send you to college, you carry twelve points a semester, two semesters a year, twenty-four points a year, four times twenty-four comes to ninety-six, so day session you take home a B.A. under your arm in four years. Right?"

"Katie, what's the matter with you? All I said—"

"With *me?* What's the matter with me is all of a sudden my

best friend is making like a boob. Last semester, first time we registered in this dump, what did we get? Eco. One, three points, and French One, three points. A great big fat total of six points, and everybody says we were yet *lucky* to land *that* many. At that rate, six a semester, twelve a year, twelve into ninety-six, it'll be eight years before a couple of old buddies from East Ninth Street tuck any B.A.'s under their arms. Eight solid years, and you, all of a sudden, you come out with I think I'll skip registration tonight. Don't you understand that means automatically eight and a *half* years to that lousy degree?"

"Sure I understand," Julie said. "It's just that—"

"Just that what?" Katie said.

Julie hesitated. She couldn't explain to Katie what she had only this moment articulated for herself: the Bachelor of Arts degree which, until yesterday, had been the outer limit of her worldly ambitions had become, since yesterday, a pointless irrelevance. Why did she need a B.A., or for that matter anything else, now that she had Ben?

"I don't know," Julie said. "They make it so tough, eight long years minimum, maybe even longer, I'm just beginning to wonder if it's worth all the fuss."

Katie bit into the apple and chewed in silence for a while. She did it with every muscle in her face, so that the green harlequin-shaped glasses bounced up and down on her nose. It was as though the skinny tube of a body was a gun barrel, and Katie was loading it with shot, ramming home the charge for a huge explosion.

"Listen," she said finally. "I agree with you one thing: they make it tough. Which is just exactly the reason I'm not quitting and neither are you. Those bastards, the day session, just because their old man can afford it, they get an education? And me, just because I got to work for a living, for me an education is out? In the pig's eye, and I don't mean eye!"

Julie, whose mind was on Ben and what he might at this moment be doing, was shocked by Katie's vehemence into the first clear look she had taken at her friend since they had met a half hour ago. Julie had never seen Katie look like this.

"I'm sorry," Julie said uneasily. "I didn't mean to—I mean, I never knew you cared this much about an education."

"Education?" Katie said. "What's education got to do with it? Frig the education." She hurled the apple core at a tree and stood up. "I'm sick and tired of being an ex-cop's daughter on Kelly Street working for a lousy resident buyer. It's great for you, up there on Daly Avenue, facing the park, working in a fancy law office. But what have *I* got? What chance have I got to *get* anything without something to show? Everybody's got to have a badge. Okay, God damn it, it's not much of a badge, but it's **the** best I can get, and I'm getting it. I don't care if I don't do *anything* with the God-damn B.A. I don't care I spend my life shopping dollar-ninety-eight hats for jerks in Idaho I never saw or ever *will* see. What I *do* care, nobody is stopping me getting the same thing those stuck-up day-session bastards are getting. It takes *eighty* years, *not* eight, *eighty*, I'm getting it. Come on."

Coming on beside Katie down Twenty-third Street to the C.C.N.Y. building at the Lexington Avenue corner, Julie kept shooting glances at her friend. It had never occurred to her that Katie felt so strongly about something that had ceased to have any significance for Julie. She wondered, as they approached the school building, if it had *ever* had any significance for her. It must have, or she wouldn't have spent an entire semester struggling with Eco. One and French One after her long days in the Ellentuch, Prohst & Wadsworth office, but Julie was not sure. She could no longer be sure of anything that had happened to her before yesterday's extraordinary moment. It was as though at that moment her nearly eighteen-year-old life had actually begun.

"Okay," Katie said. "Now remember the plan."

The C.C.N.Y. registration procedure was not unlike a cross between an auction sale Julie had once seen on Fourteenth Street and newsreel shots of the New York Stock Exchange in action, which, it seemed to Julie, it was impossible to avoid seeing whenever she entered a movie theatre. All the students who wanted to register for courses were crowded into the auditorium on the ground floor, and crowded, Julie felt, was about as accurate a word under these conditions as it would have been in an eyewitness account of the Black Hole of Calcutta: the C.C.N.Y. auditorium on Twenty-third Street had twenty-four hundred seats; at her first registration six months ago, Julie had been told what she could have guessed from the number of standees: thirty-three hundred boys and girls tried to register for evening courses; and Julie could see, as she followed Katie into the auditorium now, that this figure had already almost been equaled, even though the registration session had not yet begun.

"On the aisle," Katie said out of the corner of her mouth as she and Julie shoved their way forward into the mass of moving students. "The closer up front the better, but the main thing is on the aisle."

The essence of Katie's plan, like that of Antony's at Actium, was movement.

"Look at them," Katie muttered as she and Julie, in a sudden, lurching dash, managed to fling themselves into a couple of aisle seats about halfway up from the platform. "Just look at the bastids."

Looking at the platform, Julie saw what she had seen at her last registration session: twenty or more small tables, behind each one a man or woman seated under a hand-lettered placard that announced the subjects available for study during the next semester: Eco., French, Comm. Law, English Comp., Psych., Accountancy, German, Chem., Trig., etc. Examining their faces, Julie was surprised to discover that none of them looked like what at her last registration session she had believed they all were, and what Katie had just called them: bastids.

"Attention, please," Mr. Clementino suddenly called from the platform. He was the assistant director of the Twenty-third Street branch and it was clear to Julie that his role tonight, as it had been six months ago, was similar to that of a basketball referee: Mr. Clementino was going to toss up the ball and then duck. The voices in the auditorium died down. Mr. Clementino said, "I assume you are all familiar with our procedure—?"

The rest of his words were drowned in a roar of groaning laughter but Mr. Clementino, his face impassive, continued to talk. At any rate, his mouth continued to open and close, and

Julie, moved by a new compassion which had been awakened in her the day before in front of the Small Mammals House, suddenly felt sorry for the skinny figure in the unpressed blue suit. All at once she could feel the effort it was costing that small man, who looked undernourished and Julie was willing to bet earned barely enough to feed his family any better than he fed himself, to stand up there and play for a faceless giant conveniently called The City the role Julie's mother used to play down on East Ninth Street for the drunken lout who had been her husband: the buffer in the screaming fights between Biaggio Sarno and his daughter Celia.

"Darn it," Julie said worriedly, "it's not *his* fault."

"What?" Katie said, leaning close.

"I said what are they yelling at *him* for?" Julie said in Katie's ear. "The poor guy, look at him. *He* can't help it if—"

"What do *I* care who can help it?" Katie snapped. "You're getting nutzier every minute. Now shut up and remember what—"

The groaning laughter began to simmer down, and out of the comparative silence, like a ship emerging from a dense fog, came Mr. Clementino's expressionless voice, saying, "—if you will begin filling in your applications, then, which we will now pass out to you—"

As though the fog had reappeared, Mr. Clementino's voice vanished again, drowning in the new sounds that filled the auditorium: voices hissing, calling, imploring, all addressed to the officials who started moving up and down the aisles, distributing the application cards.

"Now get set," Katie muttered into Julie's ear. "As soon as these guys are finished with the—"

Katie's voice beside her, like Mr. Clementino's on the platform, sank into the mass noise by which Julie was now engulfed. But that didn't matter. Katie had explained the plan the day before, when she and Julie were riding down to work in the subway, and she had explained it again a little while ago while they were eating their sandwich suppers on the bench in Madison Square Park. The C.C.N.Y. evening session registration system was based on the apparently democratic principle known as first come first served. The fact that, in actual practice, this principle was as remote from democracy as the court of Louis XIV, became obvious to anybody who, like Julie and Katie six months ago, actually tried to put it into practice. Not before the application blank was filled in, could any student make the dash up to the tables on the platform where the available credits were handed out. And since all students received their application blanks at the same time, the ones who reached the tables first were, of course, those who wrote fastest and ran fastest. By the time the slower writers and runners arrived at the tables on the platform, most classes were full.

Katie, after studying this inequitable situation, had solved it in a characteristic manner: a week ago she had managed to steal two application blanks from the bursar's office, and an hour ago in Madison Square Park she and Julie had filled them in. Therefore, all they had to do now was wait until all the blanks were distributed and, after a reasonable interval, during which everybody else in the auditorium would be scribbling desperately, Katie would give the signal and she and Julie—

"Okay," Katie whispered tensely. "*Now!*"

She jumped up. So did Julie, who was aware, as she started following Katie down the aisle to the platform, that students all around were wasting precious moments by staring. How, their stunned faces were asking dumbly, could anybody have filled in all those complicated answers so rapidly?

Avoiding their eyes as she ran, Julie suddenly realized she was avoiding something else: a feeling of revulsion for herself.

It had all sounded so reasonable and clever and even fair when Katie had explained it in the subway yesterday. But that explanation had preceded the moment when Julie's life had changed, and now what she was doing seemed far from clever or fair. It was exactly what Julie knew Ben would have called it: cheating. And the thought of being in any way diminished in Ben's eyes was suddenly so unbearable that Julie did not stop when she reached the platform.

Refusing to look at the backs of Katie's legs as her friend went scrambling up toward the men and women waiting at the small tables, Julie veered left and kept right on running, toward the red EXIT sign, through the double doors under the sign, out into the side corridor, around the auditorium, and into the front lobby.

Here she stopped and, with a gasp of relief, saw that the clock on the wall over the elevators showed five to nine. Ben would be here in a few minutes. She ran out into the street and there he was, getting out of the Pierce-Arrow. Her heart was pounding as she moved toward him, and then Julie saw who was behind him and her heart seemed to stop.

She couldn't understand why. It was true that Julie had not expected to see her sister, but the sight of Celia should not have done that to her heart.

Then the lantern of memory played its old trick on her, dropping a slide into place, and Julie forgot that she was almost eighteen years old. She was a kid of eleven again, and she was sitting with Katie Halloran on a scrap of pebbly Hudson River shore, eating a shoebox lunch, or trying to, because the flint-hunting expedition on which Mr. Ivey had brought the Nature Club had suddenly changed into something upsetting as Julie watched the associate director of the Horace Judson Clarke House approach, smiling and holding Celia's hand.

Then the lantern flickered out, and Julie was back on Twenty-third Street, but the sense of impending disaster remained.

"I'm sorry to be late, beautiful," Ben said, smiling down at Julie. "We came as fast as we could, because we wanted you to be the first to know, but there were so many things to straighten out before we could—"

"No, please," Celia said. "Let me tell her." She didn't exactly push Ben aside, but he was no longer in front of Julie when Celia took her hands and smiled down into Julie's face and said quietly, her voice shaking just a little, "Darling, Julie darling, Ben and I are going to get married."

14

Whenever Julie thought of the Great Depression, and for reasons that had nothing to do with economics her thoughts returned to that time more often than she liked, she thought of the morning after the C.C.N.Y. registration.

Julie was coming down the Ellentuch, Prohst & Wadsworth corridor toward the reception room, on her way out to lunch, when the reception room door in front of her was thrust open and a girl came running into the corridor. The girl was carrying the bottom half of a large, square cardboard box, holding it out in front of her with both hands, and she leaned forward as she ran, as though somebody was chasing her. Julie stopped dead. The girl, who reached her with a few long strides, did the same.

"Please," the girl said, holding out the open box. "Buy something? Razor blades? An apple? Tangerines? I got needles, thread, all colors? Candy bars? Anything? *Please* buy?"

Julie, whose mind had been far away, stared for a moment or two without comprehension, absorbing only externals: the girl was thin, with brownish-blond hair and a pinched little face, and she wore what Julie later learned to call a cardigan but on East Ninth Street had been known as a coat sweater. The buttonholes were frayed, and two buttons were missing. It was a man's sweater, thick and not very clean and much too large for the thin blond girl, on whom it sagged. Julie had the uncomfortable feeling that the torn, bulging pockets were filled with some sort of metal or stone, and what was making the girl look so desperate, and causing her to crouch like that as she held out her cardboard tray, was the weight of the garment. It was clearly too much for her frail frame. Then the door at the foot of the corridor burst open again, and Julie saw that the girl was indeed being chased. Miss Lilly, her white hair disheveled, her withered old cheeks flustered, her detached switchboard mouthpiece bouncing up and down on her sparrow chest, came running in.

"Here, now, please," she said, clutching at the girl's arm. "You mustn't do this. You *can't* do this. I'm sorry, but it's forbidden."

The desperation with which the girl was offering the cardboard tray to Julie, the fierce tension that held her body out in a hunched-over you-*must*-buy thrust, the terror in her watery blue eyes that the answer which had to be—it *had* to be!—yes might nonetheless be no, all that seemed to collapse under the touch of Miss Lilly's hand. The girl pulled the box back against her body and dipped her head over it. She might have doubled up with a sudden pain. She might have been praying. Julie, seeing the girl's thin shoulders inside the thick sweater shiver as though with a chill, was sure she heard a sob. But a moment later Julie was sure of nothing. The thin body straightened up and Julie, still numb with the abruptness of the incomprehensible incident, was shocked by something else: the girl's eyes. No longer watery, no longer terrified, they blazed with a searing hatred that could almost be touched.

"All of yiz," the girl snarled. "You got no feeling for a fellow human being, I ain't ate nothing since yesterday except three my own candy bars, I hope yizzawl drop dead!"

She turned and ran, back down the corridor, hunched over, as though she were an animal trying to make herself smaller as she fled a pursuing enemy. The door to the reception room banged shut behind her. Julie, still dazed, was beginning to make some effort to understand what she had seen, when she saw something else: Miss Lilly was crying.

"It's not my fault," the little old lady was saying through her sobs. "I can't help it. They come all day long, trying to get in, but Mr. Trench says I'm not to allow them. He says nobody would

275

get any work done if we allowed peddlers to walk in and out of the office all day long, and I suppose he's right, but it's nothing I can do anything about. It's my *job,* can't she see that? If I don't do what Mr. Trench says, I'll be fired, and then I'll be in *her* shoes, trying to peddle razor blades and candy bars. It's not *my* fault. What can I *do?* I have to obey my orders. I can't afford to lose my job just because—"

Julie, to whose lips empty words of reassurance rose like bubbles in a glass of seltzer, did not release them. She had the feeling that, if she heard another word, everything inside her, which since the night before had been held together by the fragile tissue of will power, would fall apart right there in the office, like a suitcase full of dirty clothes bursting open on a train platform.

She circled the sobbing Miss Lilly and hurried down the corridor. Out in the hall, afraid that she might meet the girl in the sweater, Julie avoided the elevator area, ducked into the fire-escape staircase, and ran down several flights of stairs before she dared come out and ring for an elevator.

Even in the lobby downstairs, crossing to the revolving doors, she kept her eyes fixed on the marble floor. By the time she walked into the Child's on Eighteenth Street, where Katie was waiting near the coat rack, Julie had herself back under an approximation of control.

"Before you start answering questions about last night, and you better make them good answers," Katie said, "let's get a table."

This, even though it was the height of the lunch hour, was no problem. The restaurant was more than half empty.

"You think we ought to do this?" Julie said. "I brought my lunch from home."

"Take it back home," Katie said. "This is my treat."

"No, you don't have to do that," Julie said. "I called you—"

"Who said anything about I have to?" Katie said. "You called me, but I *invited* you, and I invited you because I *want* to. I'm celebrating."

In her present frame of mind the word sounded so outlandish to Julie that she looked at Katie in surprise. "Celebrating what?"

"My system," Katie said. "It worked. Guess what I got last night? All right, don't waste time guessing. I'll tell you. Eco. Two, three. French Two, another three, makes six. Commercial Law One, three more, makes nine. And Elocution One, one, makes ten. Ten credits, kid. At this rate I'll be a B.A. before I'm a Daughter of the American Revolution. It's really like these boys are saying down there in Washington, a New Deal for Katie Halloran. Anyway, when you called and you said how's about lunch, I figured you bet, and I said to myself this is my treat. So order anything you want, kid, and as much as you want."

"That's fine, Katie. I mean about the credits. I'm really glad, but I'm not going to let you waste your money on—"

"Waste nothing," Katie said. "Look at this."

She pushed a menu across the table. Under the word Child's, a small red slip of paper had been pasted. Printed on the slip were the words: "60¢ All You Can Eat 60¢."

"What does it mean?" Julie said.

"Look around you," Katie said. "That chariot race from *Ben Hur*? They could run it in this joint and Ramon Novarro wouldn't even get his axle scratched. And this is the *lunch* hour, yet, the busiest part of the day. Believe me, if this eat-all-you-want-for-sixty-cents doesn't bring them in, they'd have to start giving away wrist watches with every plate of soup. What'll you start with, and I suggest as an appetizer an explanation for why you ran out on the registration last night."

"I don't know," Julie said. "About why I did it, I mean. I guess I was just fed up with, oh, you know. Listen, Katie, I'm not really hungry."

"This is a time not to be hungry? When they've got an all-you-can-eat deal going? Come on, kid, read and order."

Julie read, or tried to read and, when the waitress came, she ordered the first thing on the list: fish cakes and spaghetti. She didn't hear Katie's order, nor did she hear what Katie said after the waitress went away, because all at once Julie was doing what she had been doing at regular intervals since the night before: she was trying to keep back the tears, and the effort caused a roaring inside her head that blotted out all other sounds.

"Katie," she said, hearing the tightness in her own voice, "Katie, something terrible has happened, and if I don't tell somebody I'm going to bust, but you've got to promise you won't tell."

Katie stopped smearing butter on a roll. Her eyes, behind the green harlequin-shaped glasses, were suddenly as motionless as the Central Park lake on a hot summer morning before the rowboat concession opens for business.

"What?" she said.

"You've got to promise first."

"Of course I promise."

"No," Julie said. "You've got to *promise*."

"I promise," Katie said impatiently. "What?"

"You remember Mr. Ivey from the Clarke House?"

"The Nature Club? He ran away that day they were going to—?"

"He did *not* run away!" Julie said angrily, and then the pointlessness of her anger caught up with her and she said, "Yes, him."

"What about him?" Katie said.

"He and Celia are going to get married."

Katie put down the roll and the butter knife. "Where?" she said.

In Julie's total absorption with her own misery there had been no room for wondering what Katie's reaction would be. Now that Katie had registered her reaction, Julie felt a stab of annoyance for its irrelevance.

"What difference does it make where?" she said. "I don't *know* where. They just told me last night. They probably don't know where themselves yet. What I wanted to see you about, the reason I called you this morning—"

"You mean he showed *up*?" Katie said. "Here in New York?"

"In the Bronx," Julie said. "Day before yesterday. He came to our house and he—"

"From where?"

"Oregon."

"*Where?*"

"Oregon," Julie said. "It's a state. It's—"

"I know it's a state, for God's sake," Katie said. "It's just so *that's* where he's been hiding all these years!"

"Hiding?" Julie said. "Who said anything about hiding?"

"You mean you *knew*? All this time, since he beat it that night down in the Clarke House? It must be five, six, seven, no *six*, it's six years? All this time, those six years, you *knew* he was in Oregon?"

"Of course not," Julie said irritably. "I just told you he showed up without warning, out of the blue, day before yesterday—"

"Then *Celia* knew?"

"Katie, for God's sake, *please*, what are you *talking* about?"

"Celia and Mr. Ivey. You say he showed up unexpected? Without warning?"

"That's right, yes. He—"

"And they right away told you they're getting married?"

"Not *right* away. He showed up day before yesterday. Just for a few hours because he had to go down to Washington, which he did, and then last night, when he got back from Washington, they told me."

"That's right away enough," Katie said. "A guy doesn't disappear for six years and then the day he shows up, or the day after, a dame doesn't announce she's going to marry him, just like that, unless she's been seeing the guy all those six years or—"

"*Seeing* him? Katie, he's been in *Oregon!*"

"I know, I know, I know, but what I'm getting at is *Celia* must have known. Letters. Post cards. Carrier pigeons, for God's sake. *Something.* Unless she did, unless Celia's known all these six years where he was, unless they've been like you could say carrying on this love affair by mail, what kind of a dope you think your sister is? She sees this guy the first time in six years and right away, boom, they're getting married? This isn't the movies, kid. This is real, and I'm telling you, that's how it was. They been corresponding all these six years, which doesn't surprise me."

Julie was glad the waitress arrived at this moment with their food. Watching the girl set down the plates, Julie was actually examining the mental picture Katie's words had evoked: six years of letters traveling back and forth across the continent, between

Oregon and the Bronx, and not even the slightest hint of this traffic registering on the consciousness of either Julie, who knew or until this moment thought she had known everything there was to know about her sister Celia, or on the consciousness of Mrs. Sarno, whose life work it was to learn everything that could be learned about her daughters. It didn't seem possible. Not even if Ben had been sending the letters to some prearranged address away from the Sarno apartment or Celia's office. It was too long a masquerade. In six years there would have been a slip somewhere. The fact that there hadn't been proved the masquerade couldn't have taken place, and yet, as Katie had pointed out, it was the only explanation for what had happened the night before.

"You want to order your dessert now?" the waitress said.

"No," Katie said. "They must be modeling the size of these fish cakes after the buffalo nickel. You might as well bring me another order."

"I'm sorry," the waitress said. "The rule is you can't order another order of anything until you finish what's on your plate first."

"Okay," Katie said. "You want to stick around and watch, or come back in like eight seconds? This won't take long."

The waitress did a funny thing with her lips, as though she had false teeth and she was trying to keep them from popping out of her mouth, and she went away.

"They advertise all you can eat for sixty cents," Katie said, "and then before you can open your mouth to start eating, they're plugging you up with the dessert. What are you staring at? It's just fish cakes, like yours."

"What did you mean you're not surprised?" Julie said.

"About Celia and Mr. Ivey getting married," Katie said. "I always thought they were stuck on each other." She cut a fish cake in half with her fork. "Way back there on East Ninth Street. Remember that time we went to the Palisades for flint? When they were building the George Washington Bridge? The way Celia and Mr. Ivey they were canoodling around together—?"

"I thought," Julie said carefully, "it came out later that was only because he wanted Celia to take over the Nature Club?"

"Boy, kid," Katie said pityingly as she attacked the second fish cake. "You are but real slow. You're stuck on a dame. Your job is running a settlement house full of clubs. What's a better way to spend more time near the tomato you're stuck on than getting her to run one of the clubs it's your job to supervise? Aren't you eating?"

"I'm not hungry," Julie said.

"Eat anyway," Katie said. "It'll be sixty cents on the check no matter what, and furthermore to show you I'm right, I can *prove* it."

"How?"

"The suitcase," Katie said. "Day before yesterday? The suitcase Celia asked me to shop for her? I turned it over to you on the subway?"

"I know," Julie said impatiently. "But how does that prove what?"

"They been corres*pond*ing," Katie said. "Celia and Mr. Ivey. She knew he was coming. She knew he was about to show up. And she knew they were about to get married. It was all arranged between them by mail. That's why Celia asked me to shop her the suitcase. Isn't that like two and two? Pure, simple ay, bee, see? You're not going on sitting there looking *dumb*, are you? What *else* would Celia want the suitcase for?"

Julie, who two days ago had thought Celia wanted the suitcase for the same reason Frank Prohst had wanted his five-hundred-dollar check cashed, now did not know what to think.

The waitress came back to the table. "Ready for your dessert now?" she said.

"I never eat dessert till I've had a meal," Katie said, picking up the menu and tipping back her head as though the harlequin-shaped glasses were a lorgnette. "There's chipped beef, I see. My favorite fruit. I'll have an order of that, please, with mashed potatoes and string beans."

The waitress again did that funny thing with her lips, made a note on her pad, and turned to Julie. "You, miss?"

"Nothing," Julie said. "Thanks."

The waitress went away. To her departing back Katie made a gesture with her middle finger that on East Ninth Street used to mean: "Put up your fists or beat it; the talking phase is over."

"They advertise sixty cents all you can eat, I'm going to eat all I can eat for sixty cents. When's the wedding?"

"I don't know," Julie said. "He had to go back to Oregon—"

"When?"

"Last night. It's something about a government job out there. I didn't understand it too well. I guess maybe I wasn't listening, but he came east just to see these people in Washington—"

"Just my eye."

"What?" Julie said.

"He came east to nail himself his bride," Katie said. "In addition to this job, I mean, whatever it is."

"So nobody's supposed to know yet they're going to get married," Julie said. "Except me. They wanted me to know. And now you know, but remember you promised."

"In other words," Katie said thoughtfully, "he gets back out there in Oregon, he settles whatever he has to settle about this job thing, then they'll get married and she'll *live* out there? Celia? I mean if the job is in Oregon, and they get married, then it's out *there* she'll be living?" Julie nodded. Katie poked the glasses up on her nose, the way she used to do on East Ninth Street, and she said, in a voice Julie had never heard her friend use, on East Ninth Street or anywhere else: "The lucky stiff."

Julie said, "Who?"

"*Who?*" Katie said. "Celia, stupid." Then, as though she had suddenly remembered something, Katie said in her normal voice, "Didn't you say you called me to have lunch because something *terrible* happened?" Before Julie could answer, or perhaps the expression on Julie's face was answer enough, Katie said, "I thought you liked that sister of yours." The word was so hopelessly inadequate for the way Julie felt, that she didn't even attempt to reply, but apparently a reply was not necessary, because Katie said quietly, "Don't you see what a wonderful thing this is for Celia? To go live in Oregon? With a guy she loves? To get the hell out of this rotten garbage can where everything she does, every place she goes, every minute of the day she's reminded she's a lousy nothing from East Ninth Street? Don't you see what this means to Celia? A whole new world? A place she's never been? Nobody out there with any idea where she came from? Central Park West or the Bronx? East Ninth Street or Park Avenue? Just she's from New York? That great big fourteen-carat nothing that out in Oregon they probably think it's Mecca or something, but you and me and Celia we know it the way it really is, a rat race for nickels and dimes, it stinks on ice and for my money you take it off the ice, the ice stinks? For God's sake, don't sit there looking so dumb, like it's the end of the world. For Celia it's the beginning. This puts her out of it. From now on Celia doesn't have to fight for no badges. She doesn't have to break her neck to get credits for a lousy B.A. From now on she doesn't need *nothing*. She's starting all over again, clean. She's getting something nobody ever gets. A second chance. It's like being *born* again, for Christ's sake. Can't you *see* that?"

Julie, who suddenly could, thanks to Katie, saw something else: the answer to the sickening turmoil into which she had been thrust the night before: Love, which to those who talked and wrote about it was an accident, was in the final analysis to those who lived it a matter of choice. What Julie had felt for Celia ever since she could remember was as overwhelming as what Julie had felt for Ben ever since the moment in front of the Small Mammals House two days ago. But what Julie saw now was that she couldn't have both. It was either Celia or Ben, and even as the pain of denial began to take hold, Julie knew that between the two, so far as she was concerned, it was no contest. Her feelings for Ben were nothing by comparison with the feelings that were part of what she now knew: the disaster that had overtaken and destroyed Biaggio Sarno would never catch up with his lovely red-headed daughter. Celia Sarno had at last found what had been denied her father: a way out of the prison imposed by the accident of birth. Rather than thrust Celia back into that prison which meant certain death, even assuming Julie could do it by taking Ben away from her, Julie preferred not to go on living herself.

"Chipped beef," the waitress said, setting a plate down in front of Katie with a thump. "Anything else?"

The note in her voice brought Julie up out of her thoughts.

She had heard the same note half an hour ago, in the voice of the girl who had hoped Miss Lilly and Julie and everybody else in the Ellentuch, Prohst & Wadsworth offices would drop dead.

"No, that's all," Julie said quietly, before Katie could say anything herself. "And please may I have the check?"

The waitress gave Julie a startled glance in which disappointment and then resentment began to appear. She had not counted on this interloper. Her quarrel was with the little bitch in the green glasses. The waitress had earned the luxury of her rage. It was infuriating to be cheated of her imminent outburst by a third party who had done nothing to create it.

"But I thought—?" the waitress said.

"You thought right," Katie said, and to Julie, "I invited you. It's my treat. I'm celebrating."

Even though Julie knew her heart was breaking—she could see the tiny cracks widening into fissures; she could feel the pieces falling away like petals—she managed to smile on her old friend, and she was aware that in the smile there was more than a touch of condescension. Poor Katie. Would she ever know what Julie had just learned? That in the act of renunciation there was just as much pleasure as pain?

"No, it's my treat," Julie said. "I'm celebrating, too."

15

The celebration did not last long.

A couple of weeks later, when Julie had grown so accustomed

to the burden of her secret that she rarely thought of the time before she started to carry it, Katie called her at the office one
morning and asked her to come to supper at the Halloran
apartment the following Sunday.

"Why?" Julie said.

"That's what I call real gracious," Katie said. "Right out of
Emily Post. You invite someone to supper, so instead of saying
ooh, gee, wow, or even a simple thanks, I get a why?"

"Okay, okay," Julie said. "Mr. Trench just rang for me. I don't
have time for the window dressing. Why the invitation?"

"Why not?" Katie said.

"You want me to tell you?" Julie said.

There was a pause at the other end. It was true that, in moving from Ninth Street on the Lower East Side to Kelly Street in
the Bronx, the Hallorans had taken a step upward on the social
ladder. Their income, however, had taken a step downward after
Mr. Halloran's death. Feeding anybody but themselves, therefore,
involved at the very least a minor strain on their very strict food
budget. As a result, an invitation to the Halloran table was so unusual an event that Julie, as a friend, felt it required an explanation before it called for an acceptance.

"Look," Katie said finally. "Can't we just let it go my mother
says she hasn't seen you a long time, so come have supper Sunday and she *will* see you?"

"We can let it go," Julie said, "but I won't believe that's the
reason."

"Who cares what you believe," Katie said, "so long as you show
up."

"When it comes to graciousness," Julie said, "that's not bad,
either."

"Just say you'll come," Katie said. "We'll discuss graciousness
after you get here."

They didn't get a chance. A few minutes after Julie arrived in
the Halloran apartment, the phone rang. Katie answered it and
then held the instrument out to Julie.

"For you, kid."

Julie, who had forgotten to tell even her mother that she was coming here, assumed Katie was joking. "Take a message," she said. "It's probably my broker calling for more margin."

"Come on, quit it," Katie said. "It's long distance."

Julie, who was helping Mrs. Halloran set the table, looked up in surprise. "You mean it?"

"Look, kid, you don't have to travel very far to verify this. It's for you. Long distance."

Julie put down the batch of paper napkins, stepped across the kitchen, and took the phone from Katie.

"Hello?"

"Julie?"

"Yes, who is this?"

"One in whom persuasion and belief had ripened into faith, and faith become a passionate intuition."

"Ben!"

"Hi, beautiful."

"Ben, where are you?"

"Apartment 2B, 2146 Mercerville Drive, Portland, Oregon."

"Ben, is something wrong?"

"Good Lord, no. Everything is wonderful. Listen."

Julie tried to. For a while, however, she could hear nothing but the beating of her own heart, and then she could hear only the contemptuous inner voice telling her to stop being a dope, reminding her where her loyalty lay, calling her names for being stupid enough to hope. Worse than stupid. Whatever hopes she had for herself could only be realized at the expense of Celia's. Didn't she know that? Couldn't she remember it? What a sturdy thing was her love for Celia if a voice on the phone could make her forget it.

"I'm sorry, Ben. We must have a bad connection. I can't hear you."

"That's funny," he said. "I can hear you clear as a bell. What haven't you heard?"

"I don't know," Julie said. "Start from the beginning."

"At these rates, beautiful, let's get it right the first time. I asked how's Celia?"

"Fine, Ben. You?"

"Never mind me. I'm great. Have you kept your cute little kisser shut?"

"I haven't said a word, Ben. To anybody." Since this was not true, Katie having been told about it during their lunch in Child's, Julie pretended she had not used the word anybody, and hurried on. "Ma doesn't know yet. Celia and I have just pretended nothing's happened. We've been waiting to hear from you about when you're coming east."

"That's why I'm calling, beautiful. I can't come east."

"You can't come east?"

"Remember what I said about getting it right the first time?"

"Sorry," Julie said. "You can't come east. What does Celia say?"

Ben laughed. "I see you're learning to get to the root of the matter, beautiful. I haven't told Celia yet."

"Ben, maybe you'd better tell me more."

"Before I left New York, as you know, Celia and I arranged that as soon as I got myself squared away out here on this new job, I'd come east and we'd get married. I now find that I *can't* come east for at least two months."

"Why not?"

"That's *not* the root of the matter. The why part of it is peripheral to the immediate problem, and when that problem is solved, I'll be glad to explain *why* I can't come east. Right now, however, I'm working on the problem of what happens to the wedding as a result of my not being able to come east, and the only solution that will work within the framework of my present setup is for Celia to come *west* for the wedding, which is why I'm calling you. Do you follow me?"

"No, Ben."

"I don't believe you, beautiful."

"Ben, please."

"No, I'm serious. I've got your education to think of. I can't believe you don't know why I'm calling you rather than Celia, so I want you to tell me."

"I can't, Ben."

"Why not?"

"Ben, I can't."

"Oh, wait, I know. Somebody is there with you?"

"That's right."

"Katie?"

"And—"

"Her mother?"

"That's right, Ben."

"Well, in that case I'll excuse you this time, but in the future you will be expected to turn in your exercises before I will go on to the next lesson. The reason I'm calling you instead of Celia, as I'm sure you know, is that I want you to help me persuade Celia that coming west for the wedding does not mean she's going to be scalped by wild Indians or anything else. As I'm sure you know, Celia's got her heart set on being married in New York, and I promised her she would be, but when I made the promise I didn't know what I was heading into out here. Now that I've found out, I also find it's impossible for me to come east. After I hang up on you, I'm going to call Celia and tell her, and since I know the news is going to be a disappointment to her, I don't want to call her until I have your promise that you'll help ease the disappointment for her, as only you can, beautiful. Do I get the promise?"

"Of course."

There was a pause at the other end.

"What did you say?" Ben said.

"I said of course."

"Just like that?"

"I could say it some other way if you like."

Ben laughed and then, as though for some reason he suddenly found the sound offensive, he stopped abruptly. "You make me feel like the Pied Piper of Hamelin," he said. "I don't want you doing anything you don't *want* to do."

Julie wondered why, all at once, she was thinking of the day, six years ago, when Ben disappeared. Then she remembered the discussion with Celia, in the barber shop, before Ben collapsed, the discussion in which Ben had maintained that all he wanted Celia to do at the hearing Mr. Crispin had called for that night was tell the truth. Not *his* version of the truth, Ben had insisted. *Her* version. That was what he wanted.

"It's not a question of whether I want to, or don't want to," Julie said. "It's what *you* want, Ben."

"I want *you* to want it also."

"How can I, Ben, if I don't know why?"

There was another pause at the other end.

"Julie?"

"Yes, I'm on."

"You remember that day a few weeks ago? The day the banks closed? In front of the Small Mammals House?"

Julie's heart lurched with the shock of disbelief and horror. Could he be mocking her?

"Yes," she said carefully. "I remember."

"Do you remember what I said? That we were living in a moment of history? That there's never been anything like this? That what's happening now will change the course of the world?"

"I remember," Julie said again.

"Well, I was excited that day, but it's true," Ben said. "Every word of it. I never realized *how* true until I got back out here and took over this assignment. We're remaking a world, Julie. We're refashioning man's environment from the ground up. It's Genesis all over again, Julie, but this time done right. It's the biggest job man has ever undertaken since God finished His. It's the chance this sorry old world has been waiting and praying for since Golgotha. We can't miss it. We won't. If everybody pitches in and helps. This is your chance to help, Julie. It may not seem like much, convincing Celia that she should come west for the wedding instead of my coming east, but some day you'll understand how big your contribution was. Now do I get the promise?"

"You've had it all along, Ben."

"I want it without reservations."

"You've got it any way you want it, Ben."

"Without reservations?"

"Without reservations."

"Thanks, Julie. Now I'll call Celia. It's wonderful to have someone like you to rely on, beautiful."

"Me and Katie."

"What?" Ben said.

"I said me and Katie."

"What's Katie got to do with this?"

"She's made her contribution, too, hasn't she? She invited me here to supper tonight. So you could talk to me in a place where Celia wouldn't hear us."

"Of course," Ben said, and the touch of irritation in his voice came through so clearly across the width of a continent that Julie could almost see him tossing the yellow cowlick back from his forehead as he spoke. "What's wrong with that?"

"Nothing," Julie said. If you knew how to stick to the root of the matter. She didn't. Not as well as he did, anyway. Julie couldn't tell him that she was suddenly wondering how he had managed to persuade Katie, whom he had not seen for six years and who had never been one of his greatest admirers, to perform this particular service for him. "I didn't say it was wrong," Julie said. "I merely wanted to make sure that everybody gets his, or rather her, share of the credit."

"I'm going to disregard the sarcasm, beautiful, because the words themselves sound exactly like the sensible girl I put this call in for," Ben said. "Yes, everybody should get his or her share of the credit, just as everybody should do his or her part in this great enterprise, so you be a good girl and thank Katie for me, will you?"

"All right," Julie said.

But she didn't. She couldn't be jealous of Celia. That was denied her. Whatever solace she could get from that particular emotion, therefore, would have to come from other sources.

"What was that all about?" Katie said as Julie hung up.

"Don't you know?" Julie said.

"Look, if you want to start a fight, okay," Katie said. "But before you punch me in the nose, remember who I did it for."

"I'm sorry," Julie said.

There was very little solace in being jealous of third parties.

"He called a couple of days ago and said he had to talk to you about something important," Katie said. "He didn't want to

290

call you at home or at the office, because it was personal, and neither did he want you to know in advance he was going to call, because you might get scared or something, so he asked could I invite you here for like Sunday and he'd make the call around supper time. What did you want me to do, I'm a friend of yours, say no?"

If she had, Julie thought, it would probably have been a brand-new experience for Benjamin Franklin Ivey.

"Of course not," Julie said. "I don't know what I'm getting all worked up about."

"I do," Katie said. "Every time you Sarnos make contact with that guy, you do something crazy, like try to take over a nature club, or run out on your college registration, or decide to marry him. God knows *what* you'll be doing now after *this* phone call. Come on, let's eat."

"No, thanks," Julie said. "I think I'd better get home."

"See?" Katie said. "You came for supper, kid. Remember?"

"I know," Julie said. "But I'm afraid I can't stay."

"Why not?" Katie said. "What's the rush?"

"I can't explain now," Julie said, which was true enough. She had never been able to explain the sense of urgency Ben Ivey managed to convey when he handed you an assignment.

16

A half hour later, when Julie let herself into the Sarno apartment, she discovered that Ben had handed her the wrong assignment.

"Julie?"

"Yes, Ma," she called down the hall toward the kitchen. "Just let me get rid of my coat."

A few moments after that, in the kitchen doorway, Julie wished she had remained at the Hallorans for supper. The trip from Kelly Street had given her time to prepare herself for carrying out Ben's orders. She had not had time to prepare herself for the step beyond those orders.

"Hello," Celia said. "You're just in time."

She was sitting at the kitchen table, smoking a cigarette. Even if she had not been doing it with the almost ludicrous exaggeration of a challenger slapping somebody's face with a pair of gloves to meet the traditional comic-opera prerequisites for a duel, Julie would have known her sister was engaged in a major act of defiance. On the subject of smoking Mrs. Sarno had long ago made her position clear: she could not control what her daughters did when they were out of her sight, but in her own house, under her own eyes, they were not going to kill themselves by inches.

"Hello," Julie said, trying to sound casual. "In time for what?"

"To see a girl kill herself," Mrs. Sarno said from the other side of the room before Celia could reply. The tall, handsome woman stood with her back to the sink, her arms folded, and Julie's heart jumped with a mixture of fear and pride. Fear because she sensed at once she had walked into a moment of crisis from which there was no retreat. Pride because her mother looked so much like pictures in Julie's P.S. 64 history book of a pioneer woman standing in front of the bedroom door behind which her children are asleep, trying with nothing but the fierceness of her courage to hold off the marauding Indians who have burst into her frontier cabin in the middle of the night. "Not by inches, with cigarette poison," Mrs. Sarno said. "But quick, like with a knife or a gun."

"Typical peasant exaggeration," Celia said, hissing out a huge stream of smoke as she turned to Julie. "I just had a long-distance call from Ben. He can't come east for the wedding. So I'm going west."

Julie had the weird feeling that she had been running to catch the shuttle at Times Square and, after the doors had closed behind her and the train started, she found she was on the Queens

Express. For weeks she had been steeling herself for the awful moment when Celia would break the news to her mother that she was going to marry Ben Ivey. For perhaps half an hour, as a result of her telephone conversation with Ben in the Halloran apartment, Julie had been thinking hopefully that perhaps this awful moment would never come. After all, Celia had said yes, she would marry Ben, but she had said she would marry him in New York. If Ben now said he couldn't come to New York, Celia might very well say in that case I won't marry you at all. That this possibility had crossed Ben's mind, indeed that he considered it a probability, was proved by the fact that he had called on Julie for help even before he called Celia. Julie had come home, therefore, full of arguments designed to convince Celia that she should go to Oregon to marry Ben but which Julie felt would do no more than convince Celia she should not marry Ben anywhere. Staring at her sister and her mother, Julie felt she'd better get out of that Queens Express and back onto the shuttle. The task Ben had assigned her on the phone, the job of helping convince Celia to go west for the wedding, that task had been accomplished. Julie didn't know how or by whom. She knew only that the moment she had for weeks been dreading, the moment she had for half an hour been hoping would never come, that moment had arrived.

"Did Ben say why he can't come east?" Julie said.

Celia gave her an irritated look. Julie had apparently asked the wrong question.

"What difference does that make?" Celia said. "He's involved in something very important. If you read the papers you'd know that anybody connected with the New Deal is too busy to waste time on long unnecessary transcontinental trips."

It had never occurred to Julie that Celia would describe Ben's journey to their wedding as an unnecessary trip.

"When are you going?" Julie said.

"That's all you have to ask?" her mother said. "When?"

All at once Julie felt the small sick feeling in her stomach. Her mother was counting on her. She was being asked to take sides.

"As soon as I can tell them at the office I'm quitting," Celia said, "and I can get myself packed, and buy a ticket to Portland."

"Why waste the money?" Mrs. Sarno said. "Take the gas pipe. Or here, the bread knife. It's quicker, and it doesn't cost anything."

Please don't, Julie thought, knowing the plea was wasted, wishing she were a little girl again, and she had just seen a Luxor cab, and she had earned the right by punching home a blob of spit in her palm to make a wish that would come true, so that she could make the wish now, and stop what these two people she loved were doing to each other.

"That's all you think about," Celia Sarno said to her mother. "Money."

"No, it's not all I think about," Mrs. Sarno said, and Julie suddenly understood from the way her mother's voice shook why she had her hands folded like that, and why she was leaning against the sink: she was holding herself together, forcing the separate pieces of her dismay and confusion and terror into a single manageable lump, a platform on which she could stand to give the marauders who had come to destroy her world the impression that she was unafraid. Mrs. Sarno said, "I think about how did this happen? I have a daughter who is never satisfied with what she is. All her life she hates what she is and where she comes from. A man comes who can change everything for her. A rich man. With a business. An office, a warehouse, a bookkeeper, trucks, a payroll, everything. Louis Vinutti says come, marry me, it's all yours, the whole thing. So what does my daughter do? She decides to marry a great big nothing."

"That's your opinion," Celia said, and Julie's frightened glance turned to her sister. Celia's voice was also shaking. The defiantly held cigarette, the calm words, the contemptuous glance, all were pieces of another platform, the platform on which Celia had to stand in order to deliver her blows. Why does she have to deliver them? Julie thought hopelessly. Why does she have to do this? You mean, the mocking inner voice retorted, why can't she marry Louis Vinutti and leave Ben Ivey to you?

"What is he?" Mrs. Sarno said. "*Who* is he?"

"The man I'm going to marry," Celia said. "That's enough for me."

"For fools that's enough," Mrs. Sarno said. "Not for a daughter of mine. Not for a daughter who screamed her father into his grave because he couldn't afford to build her a shower. Not for a daughter who made us spend every penny of her father's insurance to move here and furnish on Daly Avenue. Not for a daughter who is marrying somebody she'll never get what she wants from."

"Does it ever occur to you that you might be wrong?" Celia said, and Julie could see the platform shake. Her sister's pale face had suddenly flushed red.

"No," Mrs. Sarno said.

"Even the saints had their moments of doubt," Celia said.

"I'm not a saint," Mrs. Sarno said. "I'm a mother. I have my corns. Every time I think of that young man, they hurt. They hurt when he first stuck his nose in our kitchen on Ninth Street. They hurt a few weeks ago when he stuck his nose here on Daly Avenue. They hurt me now."

"I'm sorry if you're in pain," Celia said, and for a hopeful moment Julie thought her sister *was* sorry. Celia was scowling at the end of her cigarette. "But that's not going to change my decision."

Mrs. Sarno drew a deep breath. It was as though the marauders had driven her a step backward, against the bedroom door. "I don't think you're sorry," she said. "To be sorry a person must have feelings for another person. You don't have feelings for anybody except yourself. If you did, you wouldn't do this thing to me."

There was a moment of silence. Mother and daughter stared into each other's eyes. If they would only get up, Julie thought, and move toward each other. Do it, she prayed fiercely inside her head. One of you, please, one of you give way. Don't sit like that, she screamed without words at Celia. Ma, don't stand like that. Both of you, please. Please don't.

"I'm glad you're admitting the truth at last," Celia said finally. "It's not me you're worrying about. It's you."

Mrs. Sarno shook her head, quickly, as though the marauders, recovering from their momentary hesitation brought on by her audacity in daring to face them, had moved forward to seize her.

"You're my daughter," Mrs. Sarno said. "You're doing something crazy. You're running away from a big, handsome, rich man who loves you, and you're grabbing a skinny little shrimp without a nickel who you knew for a little bit six years ago and after six years you saw only once or twice a few weeks ago. A mother who doesn't see this is crazy. A mother who doesn't try to stop it, such a mother is not a mother."

Her words ended on a rising note, as though the self-imposed calm had faltered. It was Celia's turn to draw a deep breath. Julie, who could only guess at what was coming, hoped desperately Celia would not say it. There was a look of finality in the lovely face as the blood drained out of it slowly.

"I suppose you know what you're saying," Celia said quietly.

Julie blinked stupidly. Was this all?

"I'm saying you're killing yourself," Mrs. Sarno said. "That young man with the yellow hair and the smile that comes so quick and easy, he always wanted something from us. I felt it the first time I saw him. I feel it now. What I feel worst is I don't believe what he wants is you. If it was just you, all right. So long as he loves you, and you love him, all right. I'd say never mind he's nothing. I'd say never mind he'll never be more than nothing. At least they love each other. But he doesn't love you. I know that. And you don't love him. I know that, too."

The silence in the small kitchen was for Julie suddenly unbearable. She was holding her breath. There was no pretending she could not hear the mocking inner voice that said: You, too, want to know it; you, too, want to believe Ben doesn't love Celia and Celia doesn't love him.

"You're lying," Celia said.

Julie's breath escaped in a small hiss of dismay. A door had been closed.

"God will forgive you for what you just said to your own mother," Mrs. Sarno said.

Who, Julie thought dully, will forgive me?

"I hope He's as generous with you for what you've just said to your own daughter," Celia said.

"I spoke the truth," Mrs. Sarno said.

"Then it's high time I did the same," Celia said, and the soundless voice inside Julie's head screamed: Don't! The door had closed, not only between mother and daughter, but between Julie and the last lingering hope for entertaining which she knew she would never be forgiven. Let it stay closed, the soundless voice screamed at Celia. Don't say any more. But Celia didn't hear the soundless scream. Celia said to her mother, "You keep calling me a duchess. All my life you've thrown in my teeth the fact that I hate living in a garbage pail. You know why? Because *you're* the duchess. *You're* the one who hated living on Ninth Street. *You're* the one who hates living here in the Bronx now. You're exactly what Pa used to say: a rice eater from Milan with fancy ideas. You made a mistake when you married a spaghetti eater from Naples, but you couldn't admit your mistake. So you spent all the years of your married life with your eyes closed, and the next six years pretending that what happened didn't happen. That's why since he died Pa isn't any more the drunken bum we all knew. No. Now he's what you want to *believe* he was: a saint who was killed before he could put you where a rice eater from Milan believes in this country she ought to be: on Park Avenue. The saint is dead, but I'm alive, so you figure you have another chance. You don't care about me as a person. To you I'm just a sweepstakes ticket. All I have to do is say yes to Louis Vinutti, and you're where you always wanted to be: on Park Avenue. Well, I'm sorry, Ma." Celia crushed out her cigarette and stood up. "You'll have to get there without me."

For a long time after her sister's footsteps died away at the end of the hall and the bedroom door had slammed, Julie was afraid to look at her mother. When she finally did, Julie had a moment of shock. Her mother, Julie thought, had gone blind. The strong, handsome face had the sightless look of beggars Julie had seen inching their way along sidewalks with rattling tin cups. Then Mrs. Sarno shivered, as though she were shaking herself out of a trance, and her eyes once again began to reflect light.

"Julie," she said in a low voice. "You'll do me a favor?"

"Of course."

"Not only for me," Mrs. Sarno said. "For your dead father also."

"Anything, Ma."

"You will go with your sister to this place Oregon," Mrs. Sarno said. "You will see she is married by a priest."

A priest, Julie thought incredulously.

"Ma," she said. "A priest?"

"Maybe you forgot your religion," Mrs. Sarno said. "Maybe we all did. But there comes a time to remember."

"Ma, I can't go," Julie said. "I've got a job. It's a long way to Oregon, and then back. I couldn't get away from the office to—"

"There are other jobs."

"Not today, Ma. It's bad times, Ma. With Celia getting married and going away, all we'll have is what I make. If I lose my job—"

"It doesn't matter," Mrs. Sarno said. "The only thing that matters is what your father would have wanted. She should be married right. By a priest."

"But she could do that even if I don't go along," Julie said. "I'm sure Celia will promise—"

"Her promises mean nothing," Mrs. Sarno said. "Even if she makes them, she won't keep them. She's not the girl I gave birth to, and nursed. She's now somebody different. Something this young man with the yellow hair and the quick smile changed into her. He's like a magician. He makes people do things they don't know or want. He's done it to Celia. I want you to go with her. To see she's married right. To represent the family."

The inner voice didn't bother with words. It didn't have to. Its mocking laughter was infinitely more eloquent.

"All right," Julie said.

Mrs. Sarno reached up and, with two slow movements, removed the tortoise-shell combs from her hair.

"Take these with you," she said. "I wore them at my own wedding. I want my daughter to wear them at hers."

"All right," Julie said again.

"Promise," Mrs. Sarno said.

"I promise," Julie said.

She took the combs and looked at them. It was as though she were standing in a stonemason's yard, examining the marker that had been selected for the grave of her hopes.

"Be careful not to lose them," Mrs. Sarno said, and the sudden change in her voice caused Julie to look up in surprise. "All these, on the edges," Mrs. Sarno said, pointing to the complicated design in rhinestones on the combs, "these stones are glass. But these, these two in the middle," she said, pointing to twin dots of twinkling light, "your father gave them to me. These," Julie's mother said proudly, "these two are real."

17

There were times, during the days that followed, when Julie wished she could say as much for herself. The feeling that nothing was real, that she was trapped in a dream, that the events by which she was surrounded and in which she was herself engaged could not possibly be happening, would at unexpected moments of the day or night become suddenly unbearable. Celia is not going to marry Ben, she would say to herself. Celia is not going to Oregon. I'm not going with her. Then the moment would pass. The struggle to break out of the dream would end. The world of reality, toward which she had been so desperately clawing her way, would flow in, and again recede.

And, with the reluctant efficiency of the trapped, Julie would again be doing the things she could not believe she was doing: thanking Cockeye Katie for getting her a suitcase wholesale; explaining to Mr. Trench that since she would be back on the job in two weeks, she hoped he would not fire her and merely treat her absence as her vacation time; packing and repacking the clothes she thought she would need in a place she knew nothing about; ducking down 180th Street to avoid Louis Vinutti, wondering how it had all happened.

There was one moment, just before she stepped into the taxi that was to take her and Celia down to Penn Station, when Julie suddenly stopped wondering and wanted to tell Celia the truth about her feelings for Ben. But she knew she could never do that, and so that moment vanished, too.

It was followed by a whole series of other moments, all equally tinged with unreality even though they were charged with the excitement of new experience: her first night in a sleeper; her first meal in a dining car; her first glimpse of a continent that had until then been only a schoolbook statement, like the fact that the earth revolves around the sun even though the evidence of her own eyes indicated clearly to Julie that it was as motionless as a sidewalk, a statement taken on faith by a child to please a teacher who had the power to flunk those who displeased her.

Then, abruptly, without warning, in Pocatello, Idaho, the dream ended.

It was late afternoon. Julie was sitting beside Celia, staring out the train window as she had been staring for almost three days, ever since they had left New York, aware of changing shapes and colors flowing by, yet not really seeing any of it, trying not to look as uneasy as she felt about the silence in which Celia had wrapped herself the night she announced her decision to Mrs. Sarno, a silence behind which the sister Julie had known and loved all her life had receded so far that she sometimes felt Celia was more of a stranger than the conductor or the other passengers in the train. Then, suddenly, Julie leaned forward.

"Look!" she said. "Celia, look!"

Far off, like a wedge cut out of a birthday cake, a gap had appeared between the mountain peaks through which the train had been snaking all day. Beyond the gap, shimmering in the sun, stretching away in gently rippling waves to the end of the world, lay a golden blanket of wheat. Julie had never seen a wheat field. She remembered only dimly from her days in the Nature Club what, in some of the pictures on the Clarke House wall, a wheat field looked like. And this one was too far away to be identified even by someone who did know. Just the same, Julie was certain it was wheat she was looking at. Just as she was certain she knew why the sight had torn that cry of excitement from her own throat. Moses, when he was granted a glimpse of the Promised Land, must have sounded like that. Or almost like that, Julie thought, because Moses had known that for him the promise would not be fulfilled.

"Oh, God," Julie breathed. "Isn't it beautiful?"

It was more than that. It was a revelation. For the first time in her life, Julie grasped what it was that had driven Biaggio Sarno from the slums of Naples to the slums of New York. He had not meant to exchange one form of degradation for another. He had set out on a journey upward, from the prison of his birth to the golden freedom of his dream. This world of plenty glimpsed by his daughters through the gap in the mountain peaks was what he had sought. This was the vision he had been struggling to achieve. He had been unable to describe it in words. But every man, no matter how inarticulate, or illiterate, is Shakespeare inside his own head. If Biaggio Sarno had been able to tell the world where he wanted to go as clearly as he could tell himself, if he had been able to ask for the proper directions, if he had not bogged down on East Ninth Street, if he had known where to look, if he had only kept going—

The train lurched into a curve, and the gap in the mountain peaks was sealed, but the warmth of the bright vision remained. Julie turned to her sister. Celia was smiling.

"I don't know why," Celia said, her voice a little shaky and breathless. "But all of a sudden I have this feeling that, that, that everything is going to work. You know?"

Julie nodded. She did know, but she was suddenly so happy that she didn't quite trust herself to speak. All at once the confused dream in which she had been living had come into sharp focus. The bits and pieces of the tortured puzzle to which her life had been reduced had fallen abruptly into place. Ben's reappearance in the Bronx on the day the banks closed; the moment in front of the Small Mammals House when her life began; the moment outside C.C.N.Y. the following night when her life ended; these and the apparently unrelated events that had followed suddenly assumed a pattern in which Julie could read an exciting truth: Biaggio Sarno, who had been lured by a vision, had died en route. Destruction had overtaken the restless immigrant from Naples before he had even caught a glimpse of what he sought. But he had not died in vain. His tortured life, which had seemed a pointless waste, Julie now saw as the bridge on which his tortured daughter was being allowed to cross to the safe harbor that had been denied her father. If Biaggio Sarno had not left Naples, Celia Sarno would not now be entering the promised land.

The next morning, when the train pulled into Portland and Julie saw Ben hurrying up the platform toward them, even his clothes seemed a part of the pattern in which the truth had been revealed to her. Ben was wearing yellow corduroy pants tucked into heavy knee-length boots laced with thick leather thongs, and a gaudy black and red checked lumberjack shirt open at the throat. He looked, Julie thought, like the young engineer hero who against overwhelming odds, ranging from pestilence to hostile Indians, cuts the railroad bed through the trackless wilderness in one of those movies in which the sneering, pencil-mustached villain always reminded her of Frank Prohst.

"Ben," Celia said, "what are you doing in that get-up?"

"If Wordsworth's Lucy had been away on an electioneering trip to get him the Poet Laureateship," Ben Ivey said, "I don't think when she finally got back he could have come up with a more touching greeting."

Celia laughed and said, "I'm sorry, but you do look, well, different."

"*You* don't," Ben said quietly as he took her by the shoulders, and Julie developed a sudden and concentrated interest in the conductor who had helped them out of the train with their bags,

302

so she didn't actually see Ben kiss Celia. A moment later, however, Julie did feel his hand on her shoulder, and as she turned, Ben said, "Neither do you." Julie saw his face coming closer, but she also saw Celia watching with a sisterly smile, so Julie was able to get through the brotherly kiss without difficulty. Especially since Ben talked all the time he was doing it. As he drew his face away from Julie's and dipped down to seize her large suitcase, she heard him say, "—to the apartment, where you can drop your luggage and wash up, or whatever girls call what men do when they say they're going to wash up, and then we'll have some breakfast."

"We had breakfast on the train," Celia said as he snatched up her large bag with another stabbing nervous motion, as though he were spearing fish. "Ben, hadn't we better get a porter? Those two big ones weigh a ton. You'll—"

"Porters are one of those effete eastern refinements with which we have managed thus far not to soil the invigorating simplicity of life out here in God's country," Ben said as he started staggering up the platform. "My God, what are you girls carrying in these bags? Ore samples? Grab those two little ones and let's go. We have a lot to do."

What they did first was stow the luggage in the Pierce-Arrow convertible, which, against a background of small frame houses and tree-shaded streets, did not look quite so shabby and beat-up as it had looked in front of the yellow-brick apartment houses of Daly Avenue and Bronx Park South. Then they were riding along those tree-shaded streets, and while Celia answered Ben's questions about the trip, what Julie found herself doing was not unlike what she used to do when she sat down to a written examination in P.S. 64 or Fenimore Cooper High: to avoid panic, to give the apprehensive racing of her heart a chance to calm down, Julie would pretend she was not actually sitting in the examination room. She would pretend it was the day before, so that there was still time to study, and somebody had slipped her an advance copy of the questions. She would read the paper very slowly, from beginning to end, as though hunting only those questions for which she was inadequately prepared, so that she could go back to her textbooks and fill in these gaps in her knowledge before she had to go into the examination room the next day. It was just a trick, of course, but it always worked. By the time she reached the end of the paper, Julie's panic had vanished, her heart was beating normally, and the terrifying ordeal had been cut down to its proper proportions: just another examination, one of hundreds she had taken in the past and hundreds of others she would take in the future.

Sitting between Ben and Celia on the front seat of the Pierce-Arrow, Julie pretended it was the day before when, near Pocatello, she had at last understood where Celia was going and why she had to go there, and once again the old trick worked. The fear that the bright vision she had glimpsed on the train might vanish or even be dimmed by the reality of their arrival, that fear disappeared after a few minutes. The sound of Ben's voice on her left, the way Celia leaned forward to peer at everything on her right, these helped make it disappear, but the main reason, Julie knew, was the look and feel and smell of her surroundings: the small frame houses, the tree-lined streets were bathed in a special fragrance. Julie had never encountered it before, not on East Ninth Street and not in the Bronx, but she needed no help to identify it. She knew what it was. It was the smell of peace.

"Here we are," Ben said, and Julie realized he had stopped the car. "*An ampler ether, a diviner air*, or home sweet home."

He got out, came around the front, and opened the door for Celia. She slid out, and Julie slid after her and then, on the sidewalk, Julie stopped and stared. Looming up over the small frame house in front of which the car was parked, climbing up into the ice-blue cloudless sky at an improbable angle, the way the Empire State Building did if you tried to see it all while standing too close, was a great mountain peak topped by a gigantic inverted ice cream cone of snow. Julie felt as though she had walked into a picture post card from Switzerland. Then she heard Ben's voice and Julie turned and she saw that Celia had also been looking up in wonder.

"Mount Hood," Ben said. "I remember the first time I saw it. You get used to it after a while. You have to. You can see it from every part of town. No matter where you are, there it is, staring down on you like some reassuring snow-clad Buddha without a face. But that first time—" Ben shook his head as he opened the luggage compartment and started pulling out the bags. "That first glimpse really rocks you. *No fear to beat away—no strife to heal, The past unsighed for, and the future sure.* If you girls will once again grab the small ones—"

As Julie and Celia followed Ben, Julie realized that the snow-capped peak made her feel somewhat the way she had felt as a little girl when, preoccupied with some Nature Club problem as she hurried down a corridor in the Clarke House, she stumbled unexpectedly into the white-haired Uptown presence of Mr. Tyler Crispin: something larger than life, something not quite of this world, something awesome had cut across her consciousness.

Perhaps that was why she had no reaction to what her eyes recorded about the house into which she and Celia were following Ben: the white paint was not quite as white as the paint of the houses on either side, the cement walk was a network of spidery cracks that looked like a spreading case of varicose veins, the lawn needed cutting, and there was something about the place that brought to Julie's mind the word naked. Then Ben set the bags down, and opened the front door, and he held it wide for Celia and Julie to precede him, and on the threshold she knew why the word had come to mind: there were no curtains.

"It's all a little untidy and unfinished," Ben said. "I've been sort of camping out in the place, waiting for you to get here and take over, if you know what I mean."

Julie, who did know, didn't dare look at her sister. Celia had told her nothing about Ben's job or how much he earned. Julie, who had assumed this was because Celia felt it was nobody's business but hers and Ben's, had also assumed that Ben's salary was large enough to enable him to support a wife. Looking around what she supposed was a living room, Julie wondered if this assumption was correct.

The only visible piece of furniture was an army cot with tumbled bedclothes in one corner. In the other corners stood piles of dusty newspapers, magazines, and pamphlets that looked like U. S. Government publications. A telephone, with a long tangled wire that corkscrewed across the room, sat on the bare floor near the cot. The room reminded Julie so much of N.Y.U. and C.C.N.Y. fraternity houses in which she had attended parties that she expected to find the bathroom exactly where it was located, at the far end of the apartment, and just as untidy. So were the two rooms in between, one of which was empty and presumably served, or was intended to serve, as a bedroom. The other room, which was the kitchen, had a cheap enamel-topped table and two chairs against one wall, a brand-new broom in one corner, and an open garbage pail full of tin cans. It was not until she saw the size of the pile of dirty dishes in the sink that Julie realized what the sight of the place must be doing to Celia.

She hurried back to the living room, her heels banging hollowly on the uncarpeted floors, and found Ben talking to Celia, who had apparently not budged since she stepped into the house, while he dragged the bags away from the door and lined them up neatly near the cot.

"I didn't want to buy any furniture or curtains or carpets on my own," he said. "I figured you know more about that sort of thing than I do, and you'd probably prefer to do it yourself. Besides, I took it on a month-to-month basis, no lease or anything like that, so it seemed silly to put down a lot of expensive carpets and hang a lot of expensive curtains if it turns out you don't like the place and you'd rather we look around for some other—" The phone rang. Ben scooped it up and said, "Yes? Oh. Just a moment, please." He looked surprised as he held the instrument out to Celia and said, "What a sense of timing. It's for you. Long distance."

Celia's face brightened, and she took an eager step forward, her hand outstretched toward the instrument, but then she seemed to think better of it. She stopped and dropped her hand and shook her head. "No," she said. "It can't be for me. Who'd be calling me long distance out here in Oregon? It's some mistake."

Ben put the phone back to his ear and said, "Who'd you say you want?" There was a pause and he asked, "Who's calling, please? Just a moment." Again he held the phone out toward Celia. "No mistake, honeybunch. Your ex-boss calling from New York. Mr. Frank Prohst."

"But that's ridiculous," Celia said sharply. "What does he want?"

"Want me to ask him?" Ben said.

"No," Celia said, and the sharper edge in her voice must have sounded as odd to her as it obviously did to Ben, because, as he looked at her curiously, Celia said with a gesture of exaggerated boredom, "It's probably about the Leventhal case."

"The what?" Ben said.

"The last thing I was working on before I quit," Celia said, taking the phone. "It's a will, a huge real-estate thing, downtown, and Mrs. Leventhal, she's the widow, she's contesting her husband's will, and Mr. Prohst has been trying—" Celia's voice trailed away as she put the receiver to her ear and then, with elaborate casualness, said into the phone, "Hello? Yes, this is— No, I'm not."

Julie wondered if it was the way Celia's eyes flicked guiltily toward her and Ben, or if it was a matter of simple politeness that caused Ben to say, "If you'd like to speak in private—?"

"No, no, of course not," Celia said hastily, and then, into the phone, "No, I was just—" She paused, and again her eyes moved in the same way, and again, very distinctly, she said into the instrument, "No, I'm not." She paused and then said, "Wait." Celia covered the mouthpiece and smiled apologetically at Ben and said, "Maybe I'd better. There's a million details, stuff I've got in my head from all the dictation I took before Mr. Leventhal died, when the will was being prepared, I mean, and Mr. Prohst wants me to try and remember if he said—"

"Of course," Ben said, and again Julie wondered if she was hearing and seeing more than mere politeness as Ben opened the door and pointed into the bedroom. "You can take it in there."

Celia nodded gratefully, and carried the phone into the other room, and Ben pulled the door shut as far as it would go with the wire lying in the corner of the threshold, and Julie wished she was

307

somewhere else. Apparently so did Ben. He walked to the window and stared out into the street and Julie tried to think of something to say, anything that would drown out the low hum of Celia's voice in the other room, but all Julie could think of was the day before, in Chicago, when they had changed trains and she saw Celia, who had said she was going to the ladies' room, come out of a phone booth beyond the newsstand.

When Julie asked her about it, Celia had said she'd stepped into the booth to fasten one of her stockings, which had come loose from her garter belt on the way from the washroom. It had not occurred to Julie to doubt the simple explanation. What occurred to her now was that she was insane to think Celia had lied to her and had actually been talking to Frank Prohst in New York. Certainly such thoughts were nothing out of which to fashion small talk now with Ben Ivey. Neither were they anything with which to fortify the sudden desperate hope that Frank Prohst's call was indeed about the Leventhal case.

Ben Ivey had commented, before he knew who was calling Celia, on the caller's sense of timing. Now that he did know who was calling, Ben's failure to make further comment indicated clearly to the uneasy Julie that he must have reached the same conclusion she had reached: Frank Prohst's timing could only have been due to help from Celia.

Who else could have given him Ben Ivey's home number in Oregon?

The bedroom door opened. Ben turned from the window as Celia came in with the telephone.

"Everything okay?" he said.

"Yes, fine," Celia said, but she neither looked nor sounded fine. She looked and sounded angry. She must have realized this because, as she set the phone back on the floor, Celia said, "These darn lawyers. They're such big shots, and they charge such enormous fees, but when they really want to know something they have to call their secretaries to tell them what—"

There was a knock on the front door.

Ben said, "Yes?"

The door opened and a tall, dark-haired young man poked his head in. "Ben" he said, "Brahmin's office called about twenty minutes ago. Want you to call back."

"Brahmin?" Ben said. "Or the office?"

"I don't know," the young man said. "Some girl said you there, and I said no but any minute, and she said have him call Mr. Brahmin's office as soon as he gets back, and I said okay."

"Thanks," Ben said. He stepped to the cot, took the phone from the floor and, as he started with it toward the bedroom, he said to Julie and across his shoulder to Celia, "Excuse me a minute, will you girls? I'll just make that call in here and then—" Ben paused and said, "Oh, by the way, meet my neighbor and yours. Vic DeGenero. He's got the other half of this house. Vic, my fiancée Miss Sarno and her sister, also Miss Sarno. Will you girls sort yourselves out for Vic while I attend to a fragment of the U. S. Government's business?"

Carrying the phone, Ben stepped through the bedroom door and pulled it shut behind him.

The young man in the open front door smiled. "I guess you're Celia," he said. "Because of the red hair. So you must be Julie. Welcome to Oregon."

The innocent statement, uttered in a pleasant voice, gave Julie another troubled moment. She wished Ben had said that.

"Thanks," she said.

"I don't doubt you're about to marry a great man," Mr. De-Genero said with a grin as he came further into the room toward Celia. "But he sure ain't neat. I've been telling him for days that he's got to do something about this place. You can't welcome a bride from New York into an unemptied wastebasket, I said, but great men are above that sort of thing, as I'm sure you're aware, so I better close my trap before I put my foot into it, but I think you should know that these apartments can be made quite attractive. I've got the one next door, the other half of the house really, and if you'd care to step in and take a look and see what can be done with a few chairs and a couple of curtains and a little soap and hot water and a broom and—"

The pleasant voice and its half-kidding monologue ground to a halt. Julie, who knew what was wrong, wanted to tell Mr. De-Genero that her sister's silence was in no way a reflection on him. Luckily, the door from the bedroom, opening at this moment as Ben came back with the phone, seemed to shake Celia out of her trance.

"Ben," she said sharply. "We can't stay here!"

He stared at her through a small scowl and then, as though the cutting edge in her voice had finally got past whatever it was he had heard on the phone to distress him, Ben blinked.

"What?" he said.

"Julie and I," Celia said. "Until the wedding, until this place is—is—is—" She shook her head, took a deep breath, and said, "Until it's cleaned *up*, Ben, until this place is, is, is— It's not fit for *animals*, Ben. We've got to have a place to *stay!*"

"Oh," Ben said. The scowl grew deeper. He set the phone down slowly on the floor, shoved the yellow hair back from his forehead, and even more slowly looked around the room as though he had never really seen it before. Apparently he hadn't, because what he now saw seemed to come to him with as much of a surprise as Celia's outburst. "My God," he said irritably. "How can *anybody* live in a place like this?"

"It's a question I've been asking you for some time," Mr. De-Genero said dryly.

Ben snapped his fingers. "Vic."

The dark-haired young man saluted. "Sir?"

"Cut it out," Ben said. "This is serious. Brahmin's dropped another ball. A big one. I've got to get over to the office right away and field it before the Secretary of the Interior writes us all off as a bunch of incompetent dolts. Could you get the girls settled while I—?"

"Where?" Vic DeGenero said. "In a hastily staked-out land grant in the Columbia Basin? A pup tent on the lawn, perhaps? Or maybe we could hijack a houseboat from—?"

"Save the jokes for the girls," Ben said. "They've been well brought up, and are terribly polite, and they'll laugh as though they think you're genuinely funny. Right now I want you to prove

310

your years as a newspaperman in this town have served some useful purpose. Name a good hotel that I can also afford?"

"There's only one I'd want a girl I intended to marry to stay in," Vic DeGenero said, and then nodded to Julie. "A girl I intended to marry and her *sister*. The Mercerville House."

"Okay," Ben said. "Be a good scout and drive them over and see that they get settled while I pull Mr. Brahmin's bacon out of the fire."

"Chestnuts," Vic DeGenero said. "Bacon is what one brings home. Let me just call the Mercerville House and warn them we're on our way."

He went toward the phone on the floor, but Ben stopped him.

"Use your own, Vic, will you?" he said. "I want to keep this wire free. Washington will be calling any minute and I want to take the call before I go see Brahmin."

"Okay," Vic DeGenero said and, to Celia and Julie, "I'll be right back."

He went out the front door and, a moment later, Julie heard another door open and shut.

"I'm sorry," Ben said. "I really am, Celia." He smiled, the quick, wide, infectious smile that was like the opening of a stove door on a bitterly cold day, and Julie could feel the uneasiness melt away inside her. With it went the upsetting suspicions about Celia and Frank Prohst as well as the gap between the bright vision near Pocatello and the dreary reality of this shabby apartment. Ben Ivey had done again what he had never yet failed to do for her: he had re-established her belief in the future. "You too, Julie," he said. "Bringing you here without any preparation was damned stupid of me. Stupid and rude. I've been so damned busy—"

"Doing what?"

Even Julie was surprised at the tone of Celia's voice.

"I beg your pardon?" Ben said.

Celia took a step forward. It was as though a sluice gate had been opened. "You've known for two weeks, almost three, that I was coming," she said, pouring the words out in a desperate rush. "I don't know what I expected. Not a palace or a mansion or a— a—" She shook her head, as though reprimanding herself for using the wrong words. "Oh, I don't care what the place looks like, except that this—this—" She gestured toward the room. "That man, whatever his name is, he's right. It's a *waste*basket!"

"Celia," Ben said quietly, "I told you I'm sorry. I told you I've been so damn busy that I forgot—"

"Why don't you tell me why you couldn't come east for the wedding?" Celia said. "Why don't you tell me why you insisted I come west? Why don't you tell me when we're going to be married? Why don't you tell me that?"

The muscles in Ben's thin face moved. So did Julie's. It had never occurred to her until this moment that Celia did not know the answer to this question.

"All right," Ben said even more quietly as the phone started to ring. "Right after Vic gets you settled at the hotel and I've fixed up this thing at the office, I'll take you for a ride."

"I don't want a ride," Celia said, and her voice shook, so that Julie thought she was going to burst into tears. "I want an answer to my question."

"I'll show you the answer when we get there," Ben said gently as he took the receiver from the hook and, closing the door in Celia's face with his elbow as he backed into the bedroom, he said crisply into the phone, "Yes, this is he. Put the Under-Secretary on, please."

18

The car slowed down. Ben swung it off the paved road into a narrow dirt track that cut through the sagebrush on the right.

"It'll be pretty bumpy for a few minutes," he said. "If you'd rather walk, it's not very far?"

"What?" said Celia, who had been staring worriedly at the catch on the purse in her lap, clicking the two bits of metal open and shut, open and shut, as though she were hunting a defect in the simple mechanism, and then Ben's words seemed to get through to her, and she made an effort to come back out of wherever it was her troubled thoughts were wandering and take part in the conversation on the front seat of the Pierce-Arrow. "I don't think I'd better," she said without much conviction. "I mean not in these shoes I don't think."

"You're right," Ben said. "I'm sorry. That's another thing I forgot to warn you about. Heavy walking shoes. We'll have to get you a couple of pairs." He turned to Julie. "Too bumpy for you?"

"No," she said, "I'm fine."

This was at least an exaggeration and possibly a lie. Julie wasn't quite sure. The busy flow of movement involved in checking into the Mercerville House, unpacking bags, lunching at the hotel with Vic DeGenero, and then, after Ben came back from the office, the long drive out from Portland had dulled some of the shock of discovering from Celia's outburst in the shabby apartment that she had agreed to come west for the wedding without learning from Ben, or possibly without even asking, why he couldn't come east. Julie had assumed that, before they left New York, Ben had given Celia, either on the phone or by mail, a better reason than the one he had given Julie, namely, that he was too busy to come east. She certainly had assumed that he had given Celia the details of what it was he was busy with. Would *I* have come three thousand miles to marry Ben without asking for details, Julie asked herself as she bumped up and down on the front seat of the Pierce-Arrow. The answer, which came slapping back at her like a torn rubber band, was so sharp and clear that Julie hastily shoved the subject out of her mind.

"Where are we?" she said.

"Mercerville," Ben said.

Julie looked around. On the road they had traveled, which ran straight as a line drawn with a ruler from one horizon to the

313

other, there was no sign of movement. Ben's Pierce-Arrow might have been the only car in the state. The sagebrush, which flowed from both edges of the road to Mount Hood on one side and a range of distant hills on the other, looked like a brownish sea. Julie had the feeling that she and Ben and Celia were the only people in the world.

"But I don't see anything anybody would give a name to," Julie said. "I thought when you said Mercerville it sounded like a town or a, I don't know, a *place*."

Ben grinned across the steering wheel into the sunlight as he stopped the car. "How about this?" he said.

The Pierce-Arrow stood on a slight rise in the dirt track. Celia and Julie leaned forward. The car was poised on the western rim of a rocky canyon. At the bottom, moving swiftly enough to crest the water with patches of foam, ran a river.

"The Columbia?" Julie said. Ben nodded. She said, "What's that?"

From the foot of the dirt track, near a weather-beaten shack on the river bank, two cables stretched across the foam-flecked water to the opposite bank.

"Let's go down and see," Ben said.

He started the car. It bumped slowly down the track, kicking up clouds of reddish dust. As the track began to level off, Julie saw a small flatboat just beyond the shack. It was moored to the cables overhead as well as to a tree stump on the shore.

"It's a ferry," she said.

"Smart girl," Ben said. He pulled the car up beside the shack as a white-haired man came out. He was dressed almost exactly like Ben, except that the old man's lumberjack shirt was frayed and faded, his corduroy pants were dirty and patched, and his knee-high boots were scuffed and scratched. Ben said, "Howdy, Jim."

The man smiled. "Howdy, Mr. Ivey."

"I've brought a couple of visitors from New York. They wanted to take a look at Mercerville."

"Afraid there ain't much to look at," the old man said. "But you're more than welcome. I could show—"

He paused and turned to squint across the river. From the far side, where Julie could suddenly see a great deal of indistinct swarming movement, near the other end of the cables, came what sounded like a series of whistle blasts. The old man pulled a whistle from his pocket, blew three long answering blasts, and turned back to the Pierce-Arrow.

"Afraid I'll have to go across and get that load of sheep first," he said. "But you make yourself at home, Mr. Ivey." He bobbed his head at the girls on the front seat. "Excuse me, ladies."

He bobbed his head again, went down to the boat, climbed in, cast off the mooring line around the tree stump and, hand over hand, began hauling the boat across the river on the overhead cables.

"Look carefully," Ben said. "Imprint the sight on your mind. You'll probably never see anything like it again. That's the last ferry of its kind in these United States."

"Is that why you couldn't come east for the wedding?" Celia said.

Again, as in the apartment, the tone of her voice shocked Julie into a quick glance at her sister, and she saw that Ben had also turned to look at Celia. His thin lips grew a trifle thinner.

"*Though inland far we be*," he said, "*Our souls have sight of that immortal sea, Which brought us hither.*" He took Celia's hand. "Come on, honeybunch," Ben Ivey said quietly. "I'll show you why I couldn't come east."

He led her down to the river bank. Julie followed. Near the tree stump Ben stopped and pointed upstream.

"That's Canada," he said. "Up there, about three hundred miles away. You can't see any of it, but you can take my word for it that from this point here, where we're standing now, up to that Canadian border there are approximately two and a half million acres of the most potentially fertile land in these United States. Note the word potentially, because right now it isn't really land. It's desert. Dead. Worthless. Except for a few sheep herds on those upland pastures"—Ben pointed to the other side of the rocky canyon—"this gift from God is slowly burning away in the sun, completely unused, while across this great land some thirteen million human beings can't find or beg or borrow or steal a crust of bread to put into the mouths of their children. A nation is on its knees, its stomach empty, its head light with hunger, a world is slowly dying of starvation, and here, right where we are now standing, within our grasp, here in front of us is the soil from which could spring the bounty that would make of this great nation a paradise on earth. You and I, we three, we're standing at this moment like Moses, on the threshold of the future, staring into our promised land."

Feeling her heart leap, remembering the moment on the train the day before at Pocatello when the same vision, practically the same words, had crossed her mind, Julie turned to look at Ben. The wind was blowing his yellow hair down over his narrowed eyes as he peered up the rocky gorge into the sunlight. The slender figure in the lumberjack shirt and the knee-high boots no longer looked like a character in a movie. He was real, completely believable, and because he had uttered the words, what he had said was for Julie real and believable, too.

"How?" she said, hearing the excitement in her own voice. "What has to be done?"

Ben gave her a short glance. It made Julie blush. Turning away to conceal her embarrassment, she saw Celia leaning forward, to look around her and up at Ben, as though she had forgotten what he looked like and she wanted to refresh her recollection. The troubled look, the tense little creases around the beautiful eyes, had come back into Celia's face. Without knowing what it meant, Julie suddenly understood what it was that had been puzzling her about Celia's conduct: she wasn't acting the way Julie would have thought an imminent bride should be acting under these circumstances. There was nothing shy or tremulous or even embarrassed about her. Celia was acting like a banquet guest at the speaker's table, who has been forced for political or business reasons to put in an appearance even though a member of her family is critically ill: scarcely able to conceal her impatience for the guest of honor to finish his speech so she can hurry back to the bedside of her loved one. Julie supposed all imminent brides were impatient. They were certainly portrayed that way in books and movies. It struck her, however, that Celia's impatience had in it a touch of desperation.

"First you must understand," Ben said. "You and the rest of the country."

"Understand what?" Celia said.

Ben's glance shifted to her.

"*Our birth is but a sleep and a forgetting,*" he said. "*The soul that rises from us, our life's star, Hath had elsewhere its setting, And cometh from afar.* Millions and millions of years ago, honey-bunch, before there were such things as men and women, in what we now call the Pleistocene Epoch, this whole continent was covered with sheets of ice. Right here, right on this spot called Mercerville after that ferry-owner's great-grandfather who put those cables across the river and built that shack, right where we're standing now, a great, enormous ice cake blocked off this deep canyon. The dammed-up river backed up and became an enormous lake which began cutting a new channel for itself up there" —Ben gestured again toward the far side of the canyon—"at right angles to the river's previous course. For thousands of years the Columbia ran happily along its new course, and then the Pleistocene Epoch ended, and the ice melted, and the river came back to its old course, this one, the one we're looking at now, leaving that second course empty, high and dry, a great big enormous channel like a gigantic valley out of which every sign of life had been torn."

Ben paused, and he flung the hair back from his eyes with a short, sharp twist of his head, and he said, "We're going to refill that valley. We're going to put this great river back where it once was, before men were men"—Ben's finger stabbed up into the sky—"up there. We're going to do with our hands and our minds and our hearts what nature in the Pleistocene Epoch did without thought. Here"—Ben's stabbing finger pointed at the river— "where the great enormous ice cake once blocked off the Columbia, we will build the Mercerville Dam. The great lake will form again. The course once carved by the river out of the solid rock will be refilled by life-giving water. And two and a half million acres of desert, the largest compact body of undeveloped land remaining in these United States, will bloom with crops to feed a nation, to give work and a new chance at life to people who never even had a first chance, to slum dwellers from the east, immigrants now living where you and I used to live, in places like East Ninth Street and Avenue B, impoverished sharecroppers from the south, bankrupt victims of the middlewestern dustbowl, any and all who need help and want it, this is where they will get it. Here."

For several moments after Ben's voice stopped, Julie had the eerie feeling that she was back in P.S. 64, in the morning, during assembly, when the pledge of allegiance was followed by a short reading from the Bible: for several moments after Mrs. Koenig used to finish the Twenty-third Psalm or a section from Proverbs, it always seemed to Julie that she could hear music.

"Ben," she said, feeling the excitement churning inside her. "Ben, when are you going to start?"

He shrugged wearily and ran his bony fingers through his yellow hair. "There's always a serpent in Eden," he said. "Even an Eden that's still in blueprint. When you build a dam, whether you like it or not you generate electricity. We're not interested in generating electricity. We're interested in fashioning a world in which no child need go hungry. In the process of doing it, however, by building the Mercerville Dam to reclaim all this land, we will be generating the world's largest single supply of electric energy, six times as many kilowatts, for example, as the great Dnieper Dam in Russia. You do that, you produce electricity on a government project, and you have the private utility companies up in arms. They're screaming right now, and we haven't even started. They're fighting on every front from Washington to Seattle. They're trying to prevent the construction of the Mercerville Dam.

"As director of publicity for the project, I've got to hold them off by keeping the people informed, so this great enterprise will not die a-borning, so this great people will not perish, so no future minstrel, musing over the dust and ruins of what was once the mightiest nation on earth, will not say as Wordsworth said: *Where is it now, the glory and the dream?*" Ben paused, and he looked at Celia, and he said quietly, "That's why I couldn't come east for the wedding, honeybunch."

Celia, who was again looking at Ben with that tense, impatient frown, as though she could not wait to go home, opened her mouth to say something, but Julie spoke first.

"You mean they're going to *stop* you?" she said indignantly. "A bunch of *electric* companies?"

"Not a bunch," Ben said. "Just one, really. The only one that matters in this part of the country. Pacific Northwest Power & Light. And at the moment they're merely *trying* to stop us."

"Will they succeed?"

Ben smiled at the indignation in Julie's voice.

"Not as long as Arnold Brahmin remains alive," he said.

"Who is Arnold Brahmin?" Julie said.

"Our rod and our staff," Ben said. "You're having dinner with him at Lotus Lodge tonight."

"Lotus Lodge?" Julie said.

"Let's get back to the car," Ben said. "I'll explain while we're driving back to Portland."

19

Until she came to Oregon, Julie's knowledge of China and things Chinese had been limited to a few vaguely recalled details from schoolbook accounts of Marco Polo's journeys; the clean warmish sweet smell of Chin Ying's hand laundry around the corner from

Mrs. Pyser's apartment house; and the occasional chop suey lunches she had with Cockeye Katie Halloran when the latter, spurred by one of her frequent impulses for the exotic, would call up and say, "How's about we go have some chinks?"

No explanation, therefore, not even Ben's admirably thorough one during the drive back from Mercerville to Portland, could have been an adequate preparation for the reality of Lotus Lodge.

"It's a great big rambling place on the lower slopes of Mount Hood," Ben had said. "Sort of on the rustic side, and facing the Pacific, of course, because of the Brahmin family's oriental background."

It was not unlike describing Grand Central as a large railroad station with a few shops scattered about on the street level. The description gave no hint of the feel or complexity of a structure that always made Julie think of the Parthenon, and in which it was possible, while waiting for the Scarsdale local, to purchase anything from a hot shower to a controlling interest in AT & T.

"The Brahmin family, generations of it, is as inextricably intertwined with China as the Vanderbilts are with the New York Central and the Adamses with Boston," Ben had said. "So don't be surprised too much by the oriental touch."

He might just as well have told his innocent companions, on the way to their first Papal audience, not to be too surprised at the rather obvious touch of Catholicism in the atmosphere.

"Good Lord!" Celia said as the Pierce-Arrow came around a bend in the beautifully raked winding driveway and the strangely shaped white structure exploded into full view. "The Taj Mahal!"

Ben laughed. So did Julie. It was the first relaxed remark Celia had made all day.

"No, that's in India," Ben said. "But I know what you mean. The first time I saw this place my mind went scrambling wildly for the biggest thing I could think of on the Asian continent. What did you say, Julie?"

"I said it looks like Loew's Avenue B," she said.

Ben gave her one of those sharp glances in which Julie never knew what she was seeing more clearly: appreciation for providing him inadvertently with some unexpected fragment of revelation, or annoyance with what Ben seemed to feel was misplaced irreverence on her part.

"Loew's Avenue B, as I recall it," he said, "was an architecturally pathetic mixed grill of Grand Concourse Modern, Shanghai Gothic, and Coney Island Colonial. What you're looking at may strike you as a trifle ludicrous, but you might bear in mind that it's not ludicrous to people like Arnold Brahmin, who understand what it means. In actual fact, Lotus Lodge is modeled on the great White Dagoba at Peking, which was built a trifle earlier than Loew's Avenue B. In 1652, to be precise. You will note, if your vision is not being impaired by your fit of girlish giggles, that the structure is shaped exactly like a Buddhist reliquary. The base, body, spire, crown, and that gilded ball at the top are symbols of the five elements: earth, water, fire, air and ether. Good evening, Yang."

"Good evening, sir," said the thin, gaunt-faced, slant-eyed man in the ankle-length blue kimono. "The music has started, so you are asked please, Mr. Ivey, to go softly."

Following Ben and Celia across the gravel turnaround, Julie tried to go softly, but it was like trying to cross a blanket of walnut shells in hobnailed boots. Luckily, neither Yang, who was parking the car, nor Ben, who was helping Celia up the stone steps, seemed to hear what Julie heard. This gave her a chance to note with surprise that the line of cars at the far side of the turnaround, into which Yang was backing Ben's jalopy, all seemed to be in even worse condition than the Pierce-Arrow. It was, Julie felt, as though she had been given a glimpse of the façade of the Metropolitan Opera house on an opening night and, turning from the dazzlingly lighted spectacle to the street for a look at the top-hatted and ermine-wrapped patrons, she saw to her amazement that the men and women all a-glitter in boiled shirts and diamond tiaras were arriving on bicycles and being handed out of ice wagons.

"The Mercerville group is almost completely made up of government employees like me," Ben said quietly. "People living on civil-service salaries rarely can afford new cars."

321

Turning back, before she even saw his amused smile, Julie was aware of the small stab of curiously mixed pleasure and embarrassment that she experienced whenever Ben, out of a perception that Julie found troubling as well as remarkable, answered one of her questions before she had a chance to ask it. Mind reading, she was beginning to understand, is entertainment only when it is somebody else's mind that is being read.

"What about Mr. Brahmin?" Celia said. "If he's as rich as you say, can't he afford something in better shape than those things?"

Julie wished her sister hadn't said that. Celia sounded tense and impatient again.

"These cars all belong to guests," Ben said. "Mr. Brahmin travels by rickshaw."

It was not until they stepped through the huge gold-latticed doors, and Julie saw Ben grinning at her, that she realized he had made a joke. It made her feel better about the way he had sounded outside when she had said Lotus Lodge reminded her of Loew's Avenue B. Even so, when she turned from Ben to look into the huge room that stretched away in front of her like an unfilled swimming pool, Julie thought it best not to mention the fact that what she was looking at reminded her of a C.C.N.Y. party in which the endless talk about Marxism that swirled around the guests like fog in a British movie had been replaced by a downpour of thin, reedy music that set Julie's teeth on edge.

"For a while," a low voice said, "I thought you'd decided to stay on at Mercerville and run the cable ferry."

Julie turned toward the voice and saw Vic DeGenero smiling down at her.

"Oh, hello," she said. "You didn't say at lunch you'd be here tonight."

"I didn't know what kind of impression I'd made," he said. "If I'd announced I'd be here, you might have developed a headache or decided you'd rather drive back to Mercerville and watch those sheep being ferried back and forth. I wasn't taking any chances."

Julie, who had not even thought about Vic DeGenero since he had helped her and Celia get settled in the Mercerville House that morning, decided she liked him.

322

"I don't know about those sheep," Julie said. "We didn't really see any. Just the ferry starting out across the river to pick some up. But they'd have to go some, I think, to beat this as an attraction."

"Miss Sarno," Vic DeGenero said, and stopped. "I don't much like the sound of that, do you?"

"Sound of what?" she said.

"Miss Sarno," he said. "Nor is Miss Julie much of an improvement. Sounds like a play by Strindberg. How would it be if I called you just plain Julie?"

"Why," Julie said, "I think that would be very nice."

"So do I," he said. "And if you could get started on calling me Vic, I'd be very grateful, because with a name like DeGenero, you're bound to stumble sooner or later into the joke my college chums thought was so great, and I would find it painful, I really would, if a girl as pretty as you thought it funny to call me Rio."

"Rio?" Julie said, and then she got it. "Oh, no," she said, laughing. "I promise not to do that."

"Prove it," he said.

"How?"

"By *not* calling me Rio."

"I think those sheep would have to go some to beat this as an attraction," Julie said, and added, "Vic."

He laughed. "Niagara Falls reversing itself and squirting not water but pink champagne would have to go some to beat this as an attraction," Vic said, and added, "Julie."

They both laughed and, turning to see if Ben and Celia appreciated the joke, Julie saw that they were gone.

"Don't worry about it," Vic said. "You're in good hands." Julie turned back. He said, "I told Ben before he went over to pick you up I'd take charge of you when you arrived. Do you mind?"

"Of course not," Julie said. "I was just wondering—"

"So was I," Vic said. "I took a look at your recent movements, and I suddenly realized ever since you arrived this morning, all three of you have been together practically every minute. It occurred to me that maybe Ben and your sister would like to be alone for a while, which is a fairly simple thing to do in this fantan game Arnold Brahmin calls his weekly At Homes, so I arranged it."

"I'm glad you did," Julie said, pretending to be unaware of the small twinge of jealousy as she looked around the large room. "But how did they manage to disappear like that?"

"People have been known to vanish at a Brahmin party for weeks," Vic said. "Did Ben explain the background of this circus?"

"He told me and Celia that Mr. Brahmin's grandfather or great-grandfather, somebody way back, was an original Oregon settler who made a huge fortune in the Japanese and China trade after Commodore Perry opened up Japan to the West."

Vic DeGenero nodded. "And like all rich men who spend the early years of their lives raking in their billion, he spent the last years of his life feeling guilty about it and trying to figure out a way to rake some of it out in Good Works. The Orient America Institute is no Rockefeller Foundation, speaking purely in terms of financial size, but it's pretty much cut from the same Do Gooding Loaf. The Rockefeller descendants devote most of their time and a lot of the old man's money to philanthropic enterprises of all sorts, and the Brahmin descendants, especially the current Arnold, devote *all* of their time to the Orient America Institute or, as we happy beneficiaries of its largesse affectionately call it, the OAI. Speaking of which, here comes some largesse."

A man in a blue kimono, who looked exactly like the man Ben had called Yang out on the turnaround, approached with a copper tray as big as an automobile tire. On it, arranged in concentric circles around a copper sauce bowl, were several dozen of what to Julie's startled glance looked like huge jet-black cockroaches, each with a toothpick stuck into its back. The man in the blue kimono bowed low before her, as though offering Salome the head of John the Baptist, and Julie thought she was going to be sick.

"Don't look like that," Vic DeGenero said. "They're not what you're thinking."

"Then what are they?" Julie said.

"Only God and the Shanghai exporter who keeps Arnold

Brahmin supplied with his exotic and expensive hors d'oeuvres can possibly know," Vic said. "All I can tell you, since I've been here before, is that they're delicious."

He took one of the toothpicks from the tray, and Julie closed her eyes tight.

"Tell me when," she said.

"When," Vic said.

She opened her eyes. He was grinning as he munched.

"You really ought to try one," he said. "They're like nothing you've ever eaten before."

"I'm sure of it," Julie said. "Can't we sit down some place? I'm feeling a little faint."

Vic dropped the toothpick into another copper bowl on the tray and waved the man in the kimono away.

"Sitting is frowned upon, as you can see," Vic said, gesturing toward the men in tweed jackets and women in dirndls who were sprawled around the room on mats, munching things from trays as they listened to the music. "But we can find—" Vic paused and looked anxiously at Julie. "Are you *really* feeling faint? I'm awfully sorry. I shouldn't have eaten that—"

Julie laughed. "No, of course not," she said. "But please, if you're going to eat any more of those—"

"I'll turn my back," Vic said. "Before we find a mat and a drink, I think maybe we'd better say hello to our host, don't you?"

"All right," Julie said.

He took her arm and they began to work their way in and out and around the clusters of music listeners on the mats. When they were passing the musicians, a girl on the mat at Julie's feet hissed into the ear of the man lying on his elbow beside her, "Chester, I've got to go to the john, I've got to!"

"Not now," the man hissed back. "Mr. Brahmin has his eyes closed."

Julie looked inquiringly at Vic.

"When Mr. Brahmin closes his eyes," he said quietly, "it means the music is approaching its climax, and all movement must cease. Do you mind? It won't be long."

Julie shook her head and looked at the musicians. All except one were sitting cross-legged on a vermilion mat under what looked like a complicated altar made of thick shafts of dull bronze and very shiny black wood. The player who was not squatting cross-legged sat on a low gold-colored bench. He held between his knees the bottom of a two-stringed fiddle on which he sawed gently back and forth with a bow.

"That's called an *erh hu*," Vic DeGenero whispered. "The guy who's playing the thing that looks like a guitar? That's a *pi-pa*. And that hand organ thing, sort of, that's a *sheng*."

"You're an expert," Julie said.

"Not really," Vic said. "It's just that if you're a practicing journalist in and around Portland, you keep in touch with the OAI, because the institute is the source of a good deal of news here in the Pacific Northwest, and the best way to keep in touch with the OAI is to come to these weekly At Homes given by the institute's great white father, because Brahmin always springs something new at every one of these things, imbedding the piece of news in all this oriental tissue paper sort of like the little slip that tells your fortune in the middle of a Chinese cookie, and if you come to enough of these things, and you have any sort of curiosity, pretty soon you get to know the names of the things that make the noise. Personally, I rather like the sound of that one the boy on the end is playing, the sort of slender-necked lute?"

"Yes," Julie said. "I see it."

"The strings are made of twisted silk," Vic said, "and if you listen carefully you can pick out the sound from all the others. Sort of mournful and sad and lonely and, and, I don't know, *nice*."

Julie gave him a quick glance. "You like that?" she said.

"Very much," he said. "Don't you?"

Julie listened and, after a few moments, when she found she was able to separate the mournful sound of the lute from the sounds made by the other instruments, she became aware of an odd little feeling in her heart, as though from somewhere she had received a secret message that said her jealousy of Celia, while sad and upsetting, was not shameful, because others before her had suffered in the same way, and even though it was right for her to be troubled, soon her troubles would vanish, as they had vanished for others, and she would once again know the innocent peace that had been hers before the moment when Ben took her in his arms in front of the Small Mammals House.

"You're right," Julie said. "It *is* nice." Vic DeGenero smiled at her and, because she was suddenly embarrassed, Julie said, "News about what?" He looked blank for a moment, and she added, "You said Mr. Brahmin always reveals some big piece of news at these weekly parties, and I was wondering what sort of news?"

"It used to be mainly international," Vic DeGenero said. "Because the OAI has hundreds of students on scholarships in China and Japan, and the institute's field workers from almost every American college are doing something or other in the way of research in almost every corner of the Far East, Brahmin gets a good deal of information that even our State Department and military intelligence services don't get. Two years ago, for example, in 1931, it was right here in this room, immediately following a dose of this music you're hearing now, that Brahmin broke the news of the Japanese decision to invade Manchuria. It was denied, of course, and the State Department made some nasty cracks about self-styled policy makers whose wealth gives them an arrogance and claim to the public ear that their achievements don't justify, but by God, thirty-six hours later the Japs crossed the border.

"This new administration that's just moved into Washington is much more friendly to Brahmin and the OAI. I'm not too sure why, but I think it's because all of a sudden Washington is full of college professors and settlement-house workers and economic planners who want to remake the world, and people like that naturally incline toward college professors and settlement-house workers and economic planners in all parts of the country who have a similar itch. That's the only possible explanation for what on the face of it seems a little incongruous. I mean Brahmin being chosen by the Secretary of the Interior as director of the Mercerville Project. All the years the Brahmin family has lived in this area, I don't think any one of them, including the current Arnold, ever had a thought in his head for anything but China and the Far East and how to make this country more China and Far East conscious. Now, all of a sudden, look."

Vic gestured to the young men in tweed jackets and the girls in dirndls sprawled on the mats in the large room like lily pads on a pond.

"All of a sudden Brahmin is the head of a whole bunch of double-domed young thinkers, engineers, planners, and what have you, all gathered on government salary from all parts of the country, and all dedicated to building a dam that will cause two or three million acres of worthless desert to come alive with pork-chop trees, bread-and-butter bushes, and gushing rivulets of milk and honey. It was at one of these At Homes that Brahmin announced his appointment as head of the Mercerville Project, and it's been at these weekly At Homes that he's given the world the latest bulletins in his running fight with Pacific Northwest Power & Light, which is determined to kill the Mercerville Project before it gets going. Unless I'm dead wrong, which I don't think I am, what we're going to get tonight is some decision he's reached about the next phase of the PNP&L battle. Okay, we can move now."

They moved around the musicians' mat and stopped in front of an old man in a red kimono covered with embroidered golden dragons who was sitting cross-legged on a low bench which, like the altar looming over the musicians, was made of dull bronze and shiny black wood.

"Mr. Brahmin," Vic DeGenero said, "I'd like to present Miss Julie Sarno."

The old man smiled and, with his palm, cupped the lobe of one ear into a trumpet. "You resent what?" he said.

"Present," Vic said in a louder voice. "I want to present Miss Julie Sarno."

"Present," the old man said. "Of course. How do you do, my dear?"

"How do you do?" Julie said.

Mr. Brahmin's white hair, which was as fine as silk and parted

328

in the middle, seemed completely lifeless. It hung down and forward, on both sides of his liver-spotted face, like an oval frame, and the strands billowed gently, not only with each movement of his head, but also with every word he uttered, so that Julie had the feeling she was talking to him through a shifting curtain of gauze.

"Miss Sarno has just arrived in Portland," Vic said. "Her sister is going to marry Ben Ivey."

"But I thought Ben said he was marrying that pretty redheaded girl he just introduced me to?" Mr. Brahmin said.

"He is," Vic DeGenero said. "This is her sister."

"You're getting a wonderful husband, young lady," Mr. Brahmin said. "Ben Ivey is one of the finest men I've ever known."

"Miss Sarno is not marrying him," Vic said. "It's her sister."

"But I thought," Mr. Brahmin said, "Ben told me she had just come all the way from New York for the wedding?"

"She did," Vic said. "But that's the *other* girl."

The curtain of white gauze billowed more vigorously. "I don't like to mix into people's private affairs," Arnold Brahmin said. "But in this case, young woman, I can't help saying I think you're making a grave mistake. You'll look far and wide before you'll find another man as decent and able as Ben Ivey."

"She knows that," Vic DeGenero said. "That's why she's marrying him."

"Good," Arnold Brahmin said. "I'm glad you changed your mind, young lady. Ben Ivey will make you a wonderful husband."

The curtain of gauze billowed toward the left and, turning to see what had caused the shift in Mr. Brahmin's attention, Julie saw that Ben and Celia had arrived at the bronze and black bench.

"What do you think, Ben?" Arnold Brahmin said. "Is it time?"

"I think so, sir," Ben said, glancing at his wrist watch. "Yes, just about."

"Then sound the gong," Arnold Brahmin said. "I want everybody to hear this announcement."

329

20

"Ma, you don't have to yell," Julie said into the phone. "Just speak normally."

"You're three thousand miles away," Mrs. Sarno said. "How can I speak normally?"

"The distance doesn't matter. What carries your voice is the electricity. If you yell, it does something to the current and all I hear is a lot of booming. Now say it again, just as though I were sitting in the room with you."

"If you were sitting in the room with me, I wouldn't have to make phone calls," Mrs. Sarno said. "Can you hear me now?"

"Perfectly," Julie said. "Now what did you say?"

"I said are they married yet?"

"Ma, I told you before we left New York the minute they get married I'll send you a telegram. Have you received a telegram from me?"

"If I received the telegram, would I waste money calling you?"

"Well, don't waste any more of it on pointless arguments. They're not married yet, Ma, but we—"

"Why not?" Mrs. Sarno said. "It'll be a week tomorrow since you left. You've been there in Portland more than three days."

"Well, Ben is awfully busy and he—"

"If he's too busy to get married, why did she have to go running all the way out there three thousand miles in such a hurry?"

"That's not the point, Ma."

"Tell me the point short and sweet. Long distance is expensive."

"They were *going* to get married as soon as we arrived," Julie said. "Anyway, that was Ben's plan. But then this thing broke on Ben's job—"

"Something broke? What broke?"

"The referendum thing."

"You're full of advice to your mother about I don't have to yell because what carries my voice is electricity, but your *own* voice I don't understand what *you're* saying. What broke?"

"Not broke like in break a glass or something. I meant broke it *happened*, like *news* breaks."

"What news?"

"I'm trying to tell you, Ma. If you'd only listen instead of—"

"Julie, I'm listening."

"Good. This government job Ben's got, he's the director of publicity for the whole thing."

"What thing?"

"The dam. The government is building a dam. The Mercerville Project, it's called, because the place where the dam will be built is called Mercerville, and the electric light company is against it."

"Julie, all I asked was why Celia isn't married yet."

"I'm trying to tell you, Ma."

"You're telling me about the electric light company."

"Because it's holding up Celia's marriage. Not directly, of course. The company doesn't even know Celia is alive. It's just they're against the dam, and so Mr. Brahmin—"

"Julie—"

"He's Ben's boss. Mr. Brahmin. He's the head of the whole Mercerville Project. He had the idea, instead of fighting the electric company, why not put it up to the people?"

"What people?"

"The people who live in the area. Farmers, sheep raisers, like that. Mr. Brahmin said let's have a referendum. Let's ask the people if they want this dam."

"Couldn't they ask the people after Celia gets married?"

"I suppose so, but Mr. Brahmin wanted the thing done fast, and so Ben's had to work night and day, traveling all over the area, setting the thing up."

"How long does it take to get married?" Mrs. Sarno said. "Couldn't he stop working night and day for a few minutes?"

"First you screamed bloody murder when Celia said she was going to marry Ben, and now you're in just as much of a hurry as *she* is."

"Because now she's three thousand miles away, and I don't know what's happening."

"I'm telling you what's happening, Ma."

"You're telling me about electric light companies and dams and asking farmers do they want it. I'm not interested in all that. I want to know what's happening to my daughters."

"Nothing you have to worry about, Ma."

"What do you do with yourself all day?"

"Well, I'm helping Celia furnish the apartment—"

"What apartment?"

"Where Celia and Ben are going to live after they get married."

"When will that be?"

"I don't know, Ma, but maybe after tonight's meeting—"

"What meeting?"

"The grange meeting. It's like, oh, a union, you might say. A union of farmers. They're having this meeting tonight, and Mr. Brahmin is going to make a speech to them, and Ben thinks maybe after the speech, from the way things go, the reactions of the farmers and all, if it goes well and they react favorably, then maybe he'll be able to get away for a while and—"

"*Maybe?*"

"Ma, Ben can't *help* himself," Julie said patiently. "It's his *job*, Ma."

"Other people have jobs and they manage to get married. Everything that young man with the quick smile and the yellow hair does comes out different from the way it comes out for other people. What about your job? They gave you a two-week vacation from the office to go to your sister's wedding. You keep telling me it's bad times, jobs are hard to get, and you, you've got

332

a good one, what are you doing? Sitting in Oregon waiting for—"

"I wrote Mr. Trench this morning. I told him there was a delay. I asked him to give me another week without pay."

"That's a week's pay you can blame on your brother-in-law. When he gets to *be* your brother-in-law. Where's Celia now?"

"With Ben," Julie said. "On their way to this grange meeting."

"And you? They left you alone in the hotel?"

"I'll be joining them later," Julie said. "I have a date for dinner first."

"With who?"

"A young man."

"What young man?"

"Ma, will you stop playing public prosecutor? He works on a newspaper, and he's Ben's friend, and he lives in the apartment next door to where Ben and Celia will be living after they're married, and he's as nice as Louis Vinutti."

"Poor Louis. I saw him today on 180th Street. He looked so terrible, I don't know how to tell you *how* he looked. If Celia had any brains—"

"Let's not rehash all that, Ma, and I'm going to have to hang up or it'll be too late for my dinner date as well. Vic said he'd come by for me at six-thirty."

"Vic?"

"The young man I was telling you about."

"Vic what?"

"Vic DeGenero."

"An Italian boy?"

"I suppose so. I didn't ask him."

"DeGenero is an Italian name. There was a DeGenero family near us in Milan when I was a girl. They were very rich. Is this young man rich?"

"He works on a newspaper, I said."

"Since when do only poor boys work on newspapers?"

"I didn't say he was poor. I've known him for only ten days. I haven't checked his bank account, Ma."

"Julie."

"I know, Ma, I know. Stop worrying. I'm not a baby."

"Not that, Julie."

"What?"

"The thing you promised?"

"I'll keep my promise, Ma."

"You're sure?"

"Positive."

"You're a good girl, Julie."

"Okay, Ma, okay."

"And the telegram?"

"The minute they're married I'll send it."

"All right, Julie. God bless you."

"You too, Ma."

"Julie."

"What?"

"You'll tell Celia I called?"

"Do you want me to?"

There was a pause at the other end.

"No," Mrs. Sarno said finally. "Don't tell her. She'll think I'm— She'll say I'm— *You* know."

"All right," Julie said. "I won't tell her."

"Good-bye, Julie."

"Good-bye, Ma."

The phone rang again before Julie took her hand from the receiver she had just put down.

"If that was a long-distance call," Vic DeGenero said, "I'd hate to foot the bill."

"As a matter of fact—" Julie said, and then abandoned the notion of an explanation. She said, "Where are you?"

"Where I've been for what seems like a long week end," Vic said. "Down in the lobby, trying to get through to you on the house phone."

"Oh, I'm sorry," Julie said. She looked at her watch and added, "Ouch! I didn't realize it's so late."

"Well, don't make it any later, or we'll have to go to that grange meeting on empty stomachs."

"Not me," Julie said. "I'm starved."

"Then I'll give you exactly thirty seconds."

Julie didn't take very much more than thirty to join him downstairs and, shortly after that, in the shiny little Ford coupe, Vic said, "Any special preference about dinner?"

"Only one," Julie said.

"What's that?"

"If we have a drink before we eat, could you make it something other than that Uncle Ben's whatever it is that everybody seems to be so crazy about out here?"

"Uncle Ben's Blended," Vic DeGenero said. "Don't you like it?"

"There's something about the smell that reminds me—" Julie paused, and she gave Vic a quick glance. On the verge of telling him that the Mercerville group's favorite tipple reminded her of the odor of the oil Biaggio Sarno used to use for lubricating the base pivots of his barber chairs, it had suddenly occurred to Julie that, after three days of a pleasant friendship during which she had learned very little about him and he had asked even less about her, she did not want the first fact Vic DeGenero discovered about her past to be that her father had been a barber on East Ninth Street. Julie said, "The smell bothers me. I don't know why. I'm sure it's a perfectly good drink, but—"

"It isn't," Vic said. "It's dreadful stuff but, on government salaries, it's the best the Mercerville crowd can afford."

"Oh, I'm not *criticizing*," Julie said quickly. "It's just that—"

"For a New Yorker it's pretty inelegant stuff," Vic said. "Is that what you mean?"

Julie, who had meant nothing of the sort, suddenly remembered what Cockeye Katie had said during the lunch in Child's when Julie had told her friend about Celia's decision to go west and marry Ben Ivey: "Don't you see what this means to Celia? A whole new world? A place she's never been? Nobody out there with any idea where she came from? Central Park West or the Bronx? East Ninth Street or Park Avenue? Just she's from New York? That great big fourteen-carat nothing that out in Oregon they probably think is Mecca or something?" It had not occurred to Julie until this moment that Cockeye Katie's words applied not only to Celia but to Celia's kid sister as well.

335

"No, it's *not* what I mean," Julie said. "What I mean is very simple, and I'll try to explain it again as simply as I can. The smell of Uncle Ben's Blended makes me feel just a little sick. Since I don't like to feel sick, just a little or otherwise, I thought it would be nice if you ordered something else. I didn't realize, when I made the suggestion, that it's a matter of expense—"

"It's not," Vic said. "A newspaperman's salary isn't much of an improvement over a civil-service salary, but I think I can probably afford the difference in price between a martini and a shot of Uncle Ben's Blended. That is," he added with exaggerated sarcasm, "if there's nothing about a martini that you find offensive?"

"Nothing except the olive," said Julie, who in her entire life had drunk exactly one martini, which she had loathed. "Back home we now use small pickled onions instead, and call them Gibsons."

It was Vic's turn to give her a sharp glance. He took it, and Julie, staring loftily ahead through the windshield, felt only the slightest twinge of guilt, so slight that it did not even stain the totally new and unexpected pleasure of being lifted by the accident of a foreigner's ignorance to a station in life far above the rank to which at home one in fact belongs.

"I'll see what we can do with the backward innkeepers in this primitive country," Vic said as he stopped the car. "This all right?"

Julie looked out the window at a chromium and maple roadside diner above which a crescent-shaped neon sign blinked on and off, exploding into the gathering dusk, in alternate splashes of red and green, the words: "DeGenero's Steaks Chops Spaghetti Pizza."

"I see it all," Julie said. "The job on the paper is just a front for your large network of financial interests."

"No," Vic said. "I'm exactly what I've been representing myself to be, an ink-stained wretch scrabbling for a living on Portland's New Grub Street. This place belongs to a member of the family."

Inside the diner, after Vic had helped her into a booth, Julie had the startled feeling that the place was run by members of *her* family. A plump, handsome woman with gray hair, whose face kept appearing and reappearing at the window through which hot dishes were passed from the kitchen to the waitresses, reminded Julie of her own mother. None of the waitresses was as beautiful as Celia, and none had red hair, but they were all pretty enough—with a dark, brooding intensity that vanished abruptly in a white-toothed flashing smile—to be Celia's cousins. Then, a few moments after Julie and Vic sat down, from somewhere out in the back came a tall, handsome, powerful-looking man in a white apron who looked so much like Biaggio Sarno that Julie's heart jumped.

"Hi, Pop," Vic DeGenero said. "This is Miss Sarno. Julie, I'd like you to meet my father."

Mr. DeGenero smiled as he examined her with calm, unhurried care while he rubbed his big hand up and down the front of his apron. When it was dry enough, or perhaps when he had seen enough, Vic's father put the hand out to Julie and the smile grew wider.

"Here in America it's different from where I come from," Mr. DeGenero said as Julie took his hand. "Here in America the father doesn't give orders to the son. But me, when I opened this place, I gave Victor one order. I said don't ever bring in here anything but a pretty girl. He's a good boy, my Victor. He obeyed my order."

"Thank you," Julie said. "Does he do it often?"

Mr. DeGenero tipped his head back and his laughter poured out so thunderously that every eye in the diner turned toward him. "A question like that," he said when he finally got his vocal cords back under control, "only a Jewish girl could ask a question like that."

Julie looked at him in surprise, and then she turned the look on Vic. He laughed and shook his head.

"Sorry, Pop," Vic said. "Wrong again."

Mr. DeGenero looked more surprised than Julie. "She's not a Jewish girl?"

"Nope," Vic said.

"Then she must be from New York," his father said. "Right?"

"Right," Vic said.

Mr. DeGenero laughed again and Julie said to Vic, "What's the connection?"

"Before he came out here to Oregon, when he arrived in America, Pop spent some time in New York. He didn't speak any English then, but naturally he heard a lot of it, or what passes for English in New York, and since he lived down on the East Side, in what I gather was an almost completely Jewish neighborhood, he's never got over the notion that all New Yorkers are Jews."

"It's not true," Julie said. "I don't have any population figures, but I know there are—"

"No, of course it's not true," Vic said. "But Pop's misconception is based on a sound phonetic principle. I've got to know quite a few New Yorkers since the Mercerville Project came into existence, a lot of the staff members having been born, they tell me, in Brooklyn and the Bronx and so on, and I don't think there's any doubt that New York has evolved a language all its own. If you watch the cadence, the word arrangement, the predicate structure and, oh, I don't want to be technical, but the fact is that in almost every area of phonetics there is something distinctly Jewish about New York speech." Vic turned to his father and said, "Miss Sarno would like it if you make her a drink that I gather is the latest fashion in her native city. Do you think you can make something called a Gibson?"

"You tell me what goes in," Mr. DeGenero said. "I'll make it come out."

"It's a martini with a pickled onion instead of an olive."

"This is what makes New York so wonderful?" Mr. DeGenero said.

"There are other attractions," Vic said.

"This I can see," Mr. DeGenero said, winking at Julie. "Two Gibsons are coming up in a hurry."

"Make it only one," Julie said. "For Vic. I don't really want a drink."

338

The smile fled Mr. DeGenero's face as though, in the midst of a celebration, he had received news of a personal tragedy. "You're afraid we can't make them here in Portland like in New York," he said sadly.

"No, no. I'm sure you can make them better," Julie said. "But Vic and I are going on to a grange meeting, and I want to hear what's said, which I won't be able to do if I have a drink, because when I have a drink I usually get sleepy and doze off."

"On one drink?" Mr. DeGenero said.

"Sometimes on one sip," Julie said.

"Maybe I'd better skip the drink, too," Vic said, glancing at his watch. "We've got a long drive ahead of us, and Julie said she was hungry."

"Then I'll make her a pizza," Mr. DeGenero said.

"Well, now, wait, Pop. Maybe she doesn't want pizza."

Mr. DeGenero's handsome features arranged themselves in an expression of outrage. "Not want pizza?" he said. "Here? Where we make the world's greatest?"

The combination of words struck a cord. Once again, as though a button had been pressed, a picture appeared on the lantern slide of Julie's memory, a picture in which she was sitting in Marletta's on the day the banks closed, listening to Ben tell the woman who owned the restaurant just off Southern Boulevard how they made pizza back where he came from.

"Of course I want pizza," Julie said, and with a smile she added, "The works, please."

Mr. DeGenero's face lighted up like the crystal chandelier in Loew's Avenue B after the last show. "New York!" he said disdainfully to his son. "Jokes on the old man you're still trying." He gestured toward Julie and said with a happy roar, "She comes from *my* city—Milan!"

Julie laughed as the big man whirled and hurried off down the diner and then, all at once, the laughter stopped in her throat.

"What's wrong?" Vic said.

"I just thought of something," Julie said.

"Something bad?"

339

"No," she said. "I just thought what a wonderful thing that your father should have come all the way out here to a place like Portland."

"Wonderful?" Vic said. "Why wonderful?"

"He seems so happy and prosperous and, well, proud of you."

"What's Portland got to do with all that?" Vic said.

"Suppose when he left Milan he hadn't got any further than New York?" Julie said. "Suppose he'd done what so many immigrants do, settled down permanently among other Italian immigrants, in some slum on the Lower East Side—" She paused and then said, "Now what have I said wrong?"

"Nothing," Vic said.

"You're looking at me awful funny."

"Because I feel awful funny," Vic said. "What you just said. Six years ago, when I was still in college and I first met Ben Ivey, and I brought him to Pop's old place for a pie, this one's pretty new, Pop opened it last year, when Ben came in, he said the same thing, in almost those exact words. He said the thing about Pop, the wonderful thing was that he hadn't got bogged down in some Eastern Seaboard Little Italy breeding ground for unhappiness and discontent and—" Vic's voice stopped, and he looked curiously at Julie, and he said, "You mind telling me something?"

"If I can."

"How come a girl like your sister Celia, beautiful, a New Yorker, how come a girl like that will travel all the way out to a place like this to marry a guy like Ben Ivey?"

"You mind telling *me* something?" Julie said.

"If *I* can," Vic said.

"How come a man like you, a man who is Ben Ivey's friend, or claims to be, how come you ask a question like that?"

Vic's dark face flushed a shade darker. "I wasn't asking an unfriendly question," he said. "I'm honestly curious."

"So am I," Julie said.

Vic turned to look out the window of the diner. He seemed troubled. The neon sign, blinking on and off somewhere above, blinked the shadows on and off in the creases of his scowl, so that he seemed to be twitching.

340

"Look," he said finally. "About six years ago, in my senior year, I started dropping in at the Zacharias House on Grove Street every now and then for a game of pool. If you want to know the reason, I was stuck or thought I was stuck on a girl in my class who was doing a paper on settlement-house work, and it was an easy way to get to take her home every night. By the time I discovered what I'd discovered on a number of earlier and subsequent occasions, namely, that she wasn't the girl, I'd come to know and like the associate director of the place."

"Ben Ivey."

"That's right," Vic said.

"What did you like about him?" Julie said.

"A number of things, although I didn't bother to analyze them at the time," Vic said. "First and foremost, he seemed to like me, and I'm simple-minded enough in my personal relations to like people who like me and dislike people who dislike me. Also, Ben Ivey shot a good game of pool, and even though he was associate director of Zacharias, and he had a lot of work to do, he always had time to spend with a callow college boy who was mooning around over a callow college girl."

"I have a hunch you're not being very fair about your description of either one of those college students," Julie said.

"Maybe not," Vic DeGenero said. "But it doesn't matter because neither one belongs in this answer to your question, the main point of which is that what I liked about Ben Ivey, the big thing I liked about him, the thing that would have kept me interested in him even if he hadn't liked me or shot pool with me, was that from the moment I met him, the moment I ran into him, I knew, don't ask me how I knew, I just *knew*—" Vic DeGenero paused and said, "How's your Latin?"

"I'm afraid it's limited to the words they print around the edges of coins," Julie said.

Vic laughed and shook his head. "No, that won't help. At any rate, the phrase I'm thinking of doesn't get printed on coins."

"What phrase?"

"*Sui generis.*"

"What does it mean?"

"Special," Vic DeGenero said. "Unique. Peculiar. One of a kind. There ain't no other like."

"When they turned out this one," Julie said, "they destroyed the mold?"

Vic nodded. "Precisely," he said. "The minute I met Ben Ivey six years ago I knew I'd run into something I'd never run into before, which may not seem very startling, since at twenty-one, the law of averages being what it is, most things you run into are new to you, but I also knew, and this is the point, I knew immediately I wasn't going to run into anyone like this boy ever again. In six years, I still haven't."

"What made you feel that?" Julie said.

Vic shook his head. "I didn't know."

"But in six years—?"

"Yes, in six years I've had time to think it over," Vic said. "And now I do know."

"For God's sake," Julie said, "tell me."

"A patient impatience," Vic said.

"A what?"

"A patient impatience."

Mr. DeGenero, arriving with the pizza, started to say something and then, apparently as a result of the quick glances Julie felt rather than saw the big man direct at her and Vic, the owner of the diner changed his mind. He set the big pie on the table and went away.

"You said," Julie said, "I *think* you said, what you sensed in Ben Ivey, what made you feel when you met him that he was so unique, was a patient impatience?"

"That's right," Vic said as he cut the pie in half and, with a deft lifting and sliding movement, transferred one half to Julie's plate. "Eat that while it's hot," he said. "Do you know much about General Grant?"

"Of Grant and Lee?" Julie said. "Appomattox? That Grant?"

"Civil War, yes," Vic said. "Do you know anything about him?"

"Only that he won."

"Well, I don't know very much more, but I once had to read a

342

biography of him for some course or other, and when I met Ben Ivey, when I felt this thing that made him unique in my eyes, I remembered some of what I'd read about Grant. He'd been a flop most of his life. He was just a little storekeeper in this town called Galena, a little general store, I think it was, and not a very good one, either, when the Civil War came along and he got the nod from Lincoln. What I remembered from this biography was not just those simple facts, but the feel of them, the feel *around* the facts. You got the feeling that Grant was marking time, that he was waiting, that all those years in Galena he was even seething, burning up inside with impatience for his big chance to come along, and yet, because he had complete faith in his destiny, because he never doubted for a minute that his big chance *would* come, he was completely calm and patient all through the waiting period. In short, patient impatience."

"But General Grant must have had military training," Julie said. "You don't get picked from behind the counter of a small store to run an army and a war and—"

"Oh, yes," Vic said. "He'd had that."

"Then what do you mean?"

"Ben gave me the feeling six years ago that he was waiting with patient impatience. That's all. Just waiting."

"For what?"

"That," Vic DeGenero said, "is what I want *you* to tell *me*."

Julie looked at him for several moments, just long enough to convince herself that Vic was not joking, and then she shook her head. "I don't *think* I'm stupid," she said. "Certainly not as stupid as I feel right now. You really believe I know the answer to that?"

"If you don't," Vic said, "who does?"

"Wait a minute," Julie said. "Go back a little. I think maybe what's wrong here is you've left out a step or two in the chain. After all, six years—"

Vic shook his head again. "No, I don't think the six years make any difference. For pretty near all six of them, while I finished college and got this job on the paper I still have, Ben Ivey remained down at the Zacharias House, plugging along at being associate director, just like Grant at Galena. Then, this last election, back in November, when Hoover got thrown out on his ear, Ben said once or twice when we'd be playing pool that he was thinking of going east for a trip. I didn't pay too much attention. People in a place like Portland are always talking about going east for a trip, the way I suppose empire builders in the jungle talk about going to England for a holiday.

"One day though, back in February, near the end of the month, Ben suddenly disappeared, and a couple of weeks later, in March, very soon after this new administration took over in Washington, at one of those At Homes in Lotus Lodge, Brahmin announced he'd accepted the Secretary of the Interior's appointment as director of the Mercerville Project. And there was Ben Ivey, back from the east, and I discovered he'd resigned his job at Zacharias House. He was now a government employee. Publicity director for the Mercerville Project, and he wanted me to help him find an apartment. When I told him the other half of my house was for rent, and Ben came over the next day to look at it, he told me he was going to get married. I thought he was kidding, especially when he said his bride was coming out from New York, and then, well, three days ago—"

Vic DeGenero paused. He looked at Julie for a while with so much unblinking concentration that she felt her face flush and she dropped her glance to the last piece of pizza on her plate.

"I now repeat my question," Vic said quietly. "How come a girl like your sister Celia, beautiful, a New Yorker, how come a girl like that will travel all the way out to a place like this to marry a guy like Ben Ivey?"

"Would you ask that question if we were not in Portland but in Galena and I had arrived with my sister who was going to marry a storekeeper named Grant?"

"I would," Vic DeGenero said.

"You mean my sister Celia is too good for General Grant?"

"Ben Ivey is not yet General Grant," Vic said. "He's just a poor storekeeper."

"Maybe my sister sensed in him what you sensed. That he's that Latin thing."

344

"*Sui generis?*"

"Yes," Julie said. "And that some day, as you put it, he'll get the nod from Lincoln—"

"As publicity director of a screwball thing like this Mercerville Project?"

"Is it screwball?"

Vic opened his mouth, closed it, chewed on his lower lip for a while as he stared across the empty pizza tin at Julie, and then started to slide out of the booth.

"Let's go over to this grange meeting," he said, "and see."

What Julie saw, when after a forty-minute drive Vic stopped the Ford, was that they were late.

The grange hall, a large unpainted weather-beaten wooden building set in what looked to Julie like a vast, deserted expanse of sage brush, was surrounded by what she calculated hastily were several hundred pick-up trucks, flivvers, hay wagons, buggies, and tethered horses, all, including the animals, long past the prime of their different ways of life.

Vic parked the coupe and, after several minutes of complicated zigging, zagging, backing, and filling in and out of the haphazardly scattered vehicles and animals, he and Julie emerged in a small, bright cleared space around the entrance to the building. A couple of dozen men in flannel shirts and denim pants, all looking as though they had been fashioned from the desiccated materials that had gone into the construction of the building, were clustered around the door, peering in. Every seat in the place was filled and the walls along both sides, as well as at the rear, were hidden to shoulder height by men who were dressed and looked very much like those clustered around the door.

On the platform up front stood Arnold Brahmin, addressing the audience in a rolling, sonorous voice that was curiously musical and oddly compelling and took Julie by surprise. In Lotus Lodge, wearing a gold-embroidered kimono, squatting cross-legged on a bronze and teakwood bench, and making because of his defective hearing a garbled hash of Vic DeGenero's attempt to introduce her, Julie had thought Brahmin a ludicrous figure. Now, to her considerable astonishment, she found him impressive. Part

345

of the reason, of course, was that the preposterous kimono had been replaced by a black broadcloth suit of old-fashioned cut, and standing up straight, with shoulders squared, instead of squatting like the bronze mandarin on Mr. Tyler Crispin's complicated inkwell, with his silky white hair and his crinkled old skin and his turkey-wattled throat, Brahmin looked larger than life, a figure who might have stepped out of a scene from the Old Testament.

A few moments later, when the deep, hypnotically cadenced voice began to shake down into words Julie could understand, she realized that much of the stature Brahmin seemed to have achieved so abruptly, and all of the totally absorbed attention he was getting from his audience, were due to what he was saying. Julie was not surprised. She, too, had been moved and held enthralled when, ten days ago, she had first heard the same words.

"—give you now my solemn promise," Arnold Brahmin was saying, "that whatever energies and resources I still at my age possess, whatever time God in His infinite wisdom has still allotted to me, all will be devoted to this tremendous struggle, so this enormous enterprise will not die a-borning, so this great people will not perish, so no future minstrel, musing over the dust and ruins of what was once the mightiest nation on earth, will not say with the immortal Wordsworth: *Where is it now, the glory and the dream?*"

The explosion of applause was so sudden and so loud that Julie, in the doorway, winced and took a step backward. Vic DeGenero moved back with her.

"That noise you hear," he said dryly, "is Pacific Northwest Power & Light common dropping three to five points."

Julie looked from Vic to the audience inside the grange hall. The men in flannel shirts and overalls were pouring out of the seats, stamping their feet, whistling and cheering as they surged forward toward the tall, white-haired figure in black on the platform. Julie turned back to Vic.

"I guess you're driving at something that I don't understand," she said.

"You're not the only one," Vic said. "The Brahmin family fortune, which is probably the largest in this neck of the woods and certainly one of the biggest in the country, is mostly in PNP&L stock. Brahmin's father was one of the founders of Pacific Northwest Power & Light. Brahmin personally is the largest single stockholder. If this Mercerville Project becomes a reality, if that dam really gets built and cheap government-produced electric power comes to this area, the value of PNP&L stock will fall to just about the same price as peanuts. Even now, when the Mercerville Dam is still no more than a plan that may or may not become a reality, PNP&L stock has already taken a beating. And yet Brahmin is so convinced of his mission, he's so dedicated to the Mercerville Project, that even though turning it into a reality means inevitably wiping out a large part and maybe all of his personal fortune, the old boy is determined to go through with it."

"He must be a great man," Julie said.

"Either that," Vic said, "or the man behind him is a great man."

"Ben?"

"You heard the end of Brahmin's speech," Vic said. "You don't think he thought up those words himself, do you?"

"But isn't that part of the job of almost any publicity director?" Julie said. "Writing the speeches for his boss seems a perfectly natural thing for Ben to do."

"It's not just the speeches," Vic DeGenero said. "You've seen Brahmin off parade. You've heard him talk when he's using his own words. He's about as close as a man can get to being an idiot without having the boys with the nets stalking his footsteps. I don't think he's ever had a thought in his head that wasn't in some way connected with China and the whole foolish rigmarole he and his China hands have whipped up to make the world think they're involved in something more serious than an international vaudeville act subsidized by sentiment and unearned increment. And yet now, all of a sudden, practically overnight, this foolish old man whose long and even more foolish life has been circumscribed by Ming vases and wan-tun soup is dedicated to reclaiming a vast part of the American wilderness, reshaping this country's shattered economy, refashioning our capitalist civiliza-

347

tion so that every member of it shares and shares alike in its golden goodies. Somebody, it seems fairly obvious to me, has done a miraculous job of persuasion or conversion or hypnotism, call it what you like, in an amazingly short time, and I would not be inaccurate enough to apply the words miraculous and amazing to anything less than the performance of a great man."

"Maybe you're not being inaccurate," Julie said. "Maybe Ben Ivey *is* a great man."

Vic DeGenero turned to look into the grange hall, where the cheering crowd was heaving and splitting and re-forming itself around the platform like a heavy sea breaking against a rock.

"If Ben Ivey is a great man," he said, "what's he doing hiding behind a foolish puppet like Arnold Brahmin?" Vic nodded toward the open door. "Why aren't these people cheering the man who deserves their cheers and has earned them?" Vic DeGenero said through a puzzled scowl. "Why aren't they yelling themselves hoarse for Ben Ivey?"

21

The next morning, while Julie was brushing her teeth and puzzling over the meaning of Vic's question, Celia hammered on the bathroom door.

"You finished?"

"Almost," Julie shouted.

"Well, step on it."

"What's the rush?"

"Ben just called. He said can we be ready to leave for Seattle in twenty minutes and I said yes."

Julie opened the door, and her heart jumped. Celia looked radiant.

"Seattle?" Julie said. "What for?"

"What did we come all the way out here from New York for?" Celia said with a happy laugh.

"Hey!" Julie said. "You mean—?"

"I do, and will you stop spraying toothpaste all over me? Go in and rinse. Ben said twenty minutes, which means the way he figures time he won't be here for at least three-quarters of an hour, but even so we'd better shake a leg."

They did, scurrying back and forth across the hotel room, packing their small bags while Celia excitedly explained that, according to Ben, Mr. Brahmin had been so impressed with the favorable response at the grange meeting the night before that he had decided the PNP&L opposition to the Mercerville Project was temporarily on the ropes, and as a result he felt he could spare his publicity director for a couple of days, and so Ben planned to dash up to Seattle, get married, and be back on the job in Portland the next day.

"But why Seattle?" Julie said.

"Something about the marriage license," Celia said, and the happy laugh lighted up her face again. "Up in Washington you can get them without any waiting, Ben said, just walk in and pay your two dollars, but here in Oregon it seems you have to wait a week before you can get—"

"A week?" Julie said. "But we've been here four days already. Do you mean to say in all that time you and Ben haven't done anything about—?"

The phone rang and, as Julie snatched it up, Celia giggled and said, "It never occurred to me. How would I know anything about marriage licenses? I've never been married before. But what difference does it make? Ben says up in Seattle you don't need— Who is it?"

"Ben," Julie said and, into the phone, "I'm sorry, Ben, I didn't hear you. Celia and I were talking and—"

"Stop talking and let's get going," he said. "I'm in a hurry."

"We'll be ready when you get here."

"I *am* here."

"We're just—" Julie stopped and then, sharply, she said, "Where?"

"Downstairs," Ben said. "In the lobby. Will you two girls please—?"

"But, Ben—" Julie stopped again, glanced at her watch, and then said, "You told us twenty minutes. It's only—"

"Never mind what I told, beautiful. Let's go by what I'm telling. I'm down here in the lobby, and I'm anxious to get going, so won't everybody please get the lead out?"

"Here we come," Julie said. She hung up and said, "Well, I never really believed all those stories about how matrimony changes a man, but in the face of this display of highly uncharacteristic and quite startling promptness on the part of your husband-to-be—"

"You mean *Ben* is *downstairs?*" Celia said.

The laughter had disappeared from her face. She looked frightened.

"And pawing the carpet," Julie said. "From the sound of his voice—" Julie paused, studied her sister's face, and then said, "Celia, for heaven's sake, what—?"

"Something is wrong."

"Wrong? What's wrong?"

"I don't know," Celia said slowly. "But all this rush, all of a sudden, after four days of not—"

"Celia, you're not making very much sense. You know as well as I do that Ben hasn't been able to get away because Mr. Brahmin's been on his neck. You just told me yourself it's only because of the response at the grange meeting last night that Brahmin's finally decided he can spare Ben for a couple of days. And since it *is* just a couple of days, in fact less if he's going to be back on the job tomorrow, what do you expect Ben to be if not in a great big tearing hurry?"

Celia looked at her for several moments in troubled silence.

Julie was reminded of the way Celia had looked at her years ago, in their bedroom on East Ninth Street, when Julie had asked her sister why Celia was coming along on the Nature Club's flint-hunting expedition to the Palisades.

"I guess you're right," Celia said finally.

The phone rang. Julie picked it up.

"If you girls are not down in this lobby by the time I count ten," Ben Ivey said, "I will—"

"No, you won't," Julie said. "I want this to be a pleasant trip."

It wasn't. At least not for Julie. Ben was in high spirits, talking a blue streak about the success at the grange meeting the night before, quoting Wordsworth, pointing out arid stretches of land that would be bearing bumper crops as soon as the Mercerville Dam was built, racing the Pierce-Arrow to eighty and ninety miles an hour in sudden spurts of excitement, making jokes about the management of Pacific Northwest Power & Light, inventing cute jingles about the color of Celia's hair and slightly embarrassing ones about the size of the family they were about to start raising. At any rate they were embarrassing to Julie, who, since she did not have to dig very deep into her tangled emotions to come up with the answer to why she found the jingles embarrassing, did not have to work any harder to find an explanation for why she found the trip unpleasant.

"I'll register myself for a single room," Ben said when, early in the afternoon, they pulled up in front of the hotel in Seattle. "And you girls register for a double. That'll give us all a chance to wash up in privacy without embarrassment and then, tonight, Julie can take my single and Celia and I can take the double. That okay?"

He spoke with the pleasant, impersonal efficiency Julie had first encountered when, as director of the Nature Club, Benjamin Franklin Ivey used to hand out the week's assignments to the members. There was nothing in his voice or manner to indicate that he was making arrangements for his wedding night.

"Yes, fine," said Julie, speaking more crisply than she intended in her effort to conceal the fact that, all at once, she was too embarrassed even to look at Ben or her sister. "While you two go off to City Hall or wherever it is you get marriage licenses in this town, I'll go find that priest."

"What priest?" Ben said.

It was as though a warning shot had been fired across the bows of a merchant ship by a man o' war.

"The priest who is going to marry you," Julie said carefully.

Ben shifted on the front seat to look at her directly. "You mean you've arranged for a priest to marry Celia and me here in Seattle?" he said and, without pause, on the same note of incredulity, Ben answered his own question with another: "How could you have done that when you didn't even know until a few minutes before I picked you up at the hotel in Portland that we were *coming* to Seattle?"

"I didn't know, and I didn't arrange anything," Julie said. "I plan to go off and arrange it now, while you and Celia go off to get the marriage license."

Ben leaned around to look at Celia. "Do you know anything about this?" he said.

"Not until this moment," Celia said sharply and, to Julie, even more sharply, "What's this all about?"

"A promise I made to Ma before we left New York," Julie said, telling herself to speak slowly, enunciate clearly, and get the words spoken without paying any attention to how she felt. "Ma felt badly about the fact that she couldn't be at the wedding herself, which is why she asked me to come along as sort of representative of the family, and she made me promise I'd see to it you got married by a priest."

"Why?" Celia said.

"Ma said it's the way Pa would have wanted you to get married."

"God damn it," Celia said angrily. "That disgusting, sadistic drunk has been dead six years, and he's still—"

"Just a moment," Ben said. "There's no point in that sort of thing, Celia. Let's just stick to the root of the matter. Julie, why did you keep this a secret from Celia and me?"

"I was afraid you'd object," Julie said.

352

"Me?" Ben said, and he sounded genuinely amazed. "On what ground?"

"Well, you once said your father was a Methodist minister and I thought—"

"I see," Ben said. "Well, Julie, if I were going to have any objections on that particular ground, I would have raised them with myself at the time I proposed to a Catholic girl. If you had thought the thing through, instead of acting in a childish panic of concealment, I'm sure you would have realized that."

"Then you don't have any objections?" Julie said.

"Not on religious grounds," Ben said. "No."

"What other grounds are there?"

"Time," Celia broke in impatiently. "We're in a hurry."

"It's *purely* a matter of time," Ben said. "I've got to be back in Portland tomorrow."

"Why should it take any longer than getting married by a judge or a clerk or whoever does it down in City Hall or the place where you'll be getting the marriage license?"

"That's precisely my point, Julie. Do *you* know?"

"I don't see any reason why it should take any longer—"

"Look, beautiful, what one sees and what one knows are often two entirely different messes of pottage. If it doesn't take any longer to be married by a priest than by a civil servant in the marriage bureau, then fine, okay, good, count me in. On the other hand, if it's a long drawn-out process—"

"Oh, no," Julie said. "I know it isn't."

"Julie Sarno, how can you sit here and lie like that?" Celia said, and she leaned around her sister to address Ben at the steering wheel. "She doesn't know anything about it, Ben. She's never been inside a church in her life, and neither have I, so how—?"

"Isn't that rather unusual for a couple of Catholic girls?" Ben said.

"Not in the family of which that crazy drunk was the head," Celia said. "He was so sore at God for not making him a millionaire the moment he got off the ship from Naples, he refused to let my mother ever set foot in a church again."

"Celia," Julie said. "That—"

"You pipe down," Celia said and, to Ben, "He wouldn't even let us be baptized when Julie and I were born. Not that I care, or ever worried about it, but it burns me up that now, after all these years, my idiot mother should say that's how my *father* would have wanted it. I'm sorry, I'm just not going to let *that* kind of lying nonsense control what—"

"I suggest we abandon the name-calling and stick to the root of the matter," Ben said. "Julie has made a promise to your mother. If it is at all possible to help her keep it, I have no objections to doing the necessary. Do you have any objections, Celia?"

"I certainly do."

"What are they?"

"I've just told you. I'm not going to start my new life out here as a hypocrite. That disgusting drunk kept us out of the church while he was alive, and I'm not going to be pushed into it now by his dead hand working through my stupid mother's reconstruction of what she thinks or believes or wants to think and believe he was like. *It's the way Pa would have wanted you to get married!* My good God, what a laugh!"

"Celia, sweetie, your merriment is completely irrelevant," Ben said patiently. "I repeat that the point here is Julie's promise. Are you willing to join me in helping her keep it?"

Celia hesitated, scowling as she twisted the catch of the purse on her lap, and then she looked at her sister. "Julie," she said. "Does it make any difference to you?" Julie nodded. Celia said, her voice rising in surprise, "Just because it's a promise to Ma?" Julie shook her head. Celia said, "Then what?"

It was Julie's turn to hesitate. How could she put into words what keeping the promise meant to her? "Not only that," she said finally.

"I don't understand," Celia said.

Julie didn't blame her. She wasn't sure that she understood it herself. "You're beginning a new life out here," she said. "Tomorrow, or the day after, whenever I can get on the train to go back, it will be a new life for me, too."

"Why?" Celia said.

"From tomorrow on," Julie said, "all I'll have left is Ma."

There was a moment of silence on the front seat of the Pierce-Arrow. Then Celia Sarno leaned over and kissed her kid sister's cheek. "You go on and find that priest," she said in a voice even lower than Julie's. "Ben and I will get the license and then meet you back here at the hotel."

They did, but before the meeting took place, Julie met somebody else. She didn't know this was going to happen when she got out of the Pierce-Arrow and walked down the street of this strange city. She knew only that, with less difficulty than she had for weeks been anticipating, she had got over a hurdle that had been a secret worry ever since her mother had set it in Julie's path. Now that it was behind her, Julie was free to enjoy in retrospect the moment when Celia had put it behind her. Julie was touching her cheek, the way years ago in the rain on Avenue B she had touched the place where Celia had unexpectedly kissed her kid sister, when she heard the scrape of tires against the curb on her left. Julie stopped walking and turned. A taxi driver was grinning at her.

"You look lost," he said. "Anything I can do to help?"

"No, thanks," Julie said and then, because he was bald and tanned and his crinkly smile reminded her of Steve Shupka, she said, "As a matter of fact, I think maybe you could. I'm looking for a Catholic church."

The smile changed quickly to the look of uneasy gravity with which Julie had noticed long ago so many people feel it is proper to greet any mention of religion.

"You in trouble, miss?"

"No, but I'm a stranger in town and I don't know where to look for things."

"Well, you get in and I'll take you to my own church," the taxi driver said. "It ain't far."

It was, in fact, practically around the corner, which Julie felt she was probably ungracious but nonetheless correct to consider the explanation for the driver's refusal to turn on his meter.

"Thanks," Julie said, looking up at the tan sandstone structure. "He'll probably be in the rectory?"

"This time of day," the taxi driver said, "I think so."

He was right. In fact, Father Wiereck seemed to be alone in the rectory. At any rate, he answered the door himself, which pleased Julie, who was thus relieved of the necessity for explaining the purpose of her visit first to a servant or assistant.

"I hope you'll excuse my dropping in on you like this," she said. "I'm a visitor in Seattle, I just arrived, and I need some advice."

"Come in, Miss— It *is* miss?"

"Yes," Julie said. "Sarno."

"Come in, Miss Sarno," Father Wiereck said.

He led Julie into a study to the left of the hall and said, "Do sit down," pointing to a black leather chair beside a desk. Julie sat down. The priest walked around the desk, took the chair behind it, put his long white fingertips together, smiled pleasantly, and said, "Yes?"

"My sister is about to get married," Julie said. "She's getting the marriage license right now with Ben. He—"

"The groom?" Father Wiereck said.

"Yes," Julie said. "He lives in Portland and—"

"And your sister, Miss Sarno? Where does she live?"

"Celia and I are from New York. That's where she and Ben met, and then he got this job with the government out here. Down in Portland, I mean, and he couldn't get the time off to come back to New York to get married, so I came out here with Celia and, well, they want to be married by a Catholic priest, and while they're getting the license, as I said, they sent me to find out what the requirements are."

"Very simple," Father Wiereck said. "Both parties to the wedding must obtain from the priest of their home parish, in this case your sister must get it from your parish priest in New York and the groom from his parish priest in Portland, a record of their sacraments, including baptism, confirmation, and first holy communion, plus a note from the pastor permitting the marriage to take place outside his parish. Since this is standard, I'm sure they've done all that before they came to—" Father Wiereck's

356

flow of words stopped again. He looked surprised, as though he had been hurrying down what he believed was a familiar street toward a familiar destination and, all at once, perhaps from the strange cut of a passer-by's clothes, he had made the astonishing discovery that he was in a foreign country. "By the way," the priest said, "why did they come to Seattle to get married?"

Julie, who thought she knew the answer to that question, suddenly realized in trying to frame it that all she could think of was her sister's face in their Portland hotel room that morning when Celia had said through a worried frown that Ben's haste indicated to her that something was wrong.

"There isn't any, ah, difficulty, is there?" Father Wiereck asked gently.

"Difficulty?" Julie asked, puzzled.

"Let me put it this way," Father Wiereck said. "Is there any reason why they couldn't get married in Portland?"

"None that I know of," Julie said. "It just seemed more fun to, oh, I don't know, Ben gets sort of excited, and I think he felt it made it more of a sort of party, an occasion, if we drove up here to Seattle instead of—"

"Good," Father Wiereck said with obvious relief. "Then if they have these records with them, after they get their marriage license, I will be glad to perform the ceremony."

The priest paused, but Julie's mind refused to rise above the new dilemma into which Father Wiereck's information had thrust her. She knew that the records the priest had mentioned did not exist: in Celia's case, because like Julie she had never been baptized, and in Ben's case, because he had been born a Methodist. Even with the co-operation of the bride and groom, to which both Ben and Celia had agreed, it was impossible, therefore, for Julie on this day to fulfill the promise she had made to her mother. Did this mean that she was under obligation to make every possible effort to fulfill it on some other day? Was it her duty now, in view of what she had just learned from Father Wiereck, to probe further? To find out what steps had to be taken before a Methodist and an unbaptized Catholic could be married

357

by a Catholic priest? And, if such a marriage was possible, to insist that Ben and Celia go through those steps, whatever they might be, or however long going through them might take?

"Thank you very much," Julie said as she stood up. "I'll go back to the hotel and tell my sister and Ben what you said. Could we call you, then, and find out what time you'd like to perform the ceremony?"

"Certainly," Father Wiereck said. "I'll be here all day." He wrote something on a pad, tore off the page, and handed it to Julie. "This is the phone number here."

"Thanks," Julie said.

It was not until she was back in the lobby of the hotel, that Julie realized she was still carrying the worthless slip of paper. She crumpled it, dropped the pellet into an ash tray full of sand, and went up to the desk.

"Could you tell me if my sister and my brother-in-law are in the hotel?" she said to the clerk, a chinless old man whose shirt sleeves were held in large billowing mutton-chop puffs above the elbows by the sort of flowered silk arm garters Julie had never before seen anywhere except in movies about the Yukon. "Ivey? Benjamin Ivey?"

"No, they're not," somebody said behind Julie, and she turned to see a tall man in a dark blue suit with a black and white polka-dot bow tie smiling down on her. "I'm waiting for Mr. Ivey to come back," he said. "Did you say he's your brother-in-law?"

Julie hesitated, decided the explanation necessary to straighten out her relationship to Ben would not interest and probably confuse this stranger, and so she said, "Yes."

"Then perhaps you might be willing to do me a favor," the man said. "My name is Klamath, Harold Klamath, and I'm with the Department of the Interior."

"Oh," Julie said. "Then you're—?"

The man smiled and nodded. "Yes, I'm your brother-in-law's opposite number, so to speak, at the Washington end." The fact that this was not what Julie had been about to say must have been clear from her face because Mr. Klamath, losing his smile, said: "I do for the Secretary of the Interior what Ben Ivey does for Arnold Brahmin. I handle press matters."

"Yes, of course," Julie said, trying to sound intelligent even though she had no idea what Mr. Klamath meant. "What can I do for you?"

"Well, the Secretary won't be in Seattle more than the one day. We're flying back to Washington right after breakfast tomorrow, and we've all got quite a lot to do before we take off, so whatever time I can switch from sitting around in hotel lobbies to getting my chores done, why, I'd be pleased and grateful. I'm also a little tired, to be perfectly honest. This Alaskan trip was rougher than any of us anticipated."

"Oh," Julie said, still trying to sound intelligent. "Were you in Alaska?"

Mr. Klamath looked puzzled. "Why, yes," he said. "I thought perhaps you knew. Not because it's been publicized in the papers. As a matter of fact, we've tried to keep it *out* of the press as much as possible, because the Secretary feels these inspection trips are sometimes construed by people at the other end as grandstand plays on the part of the new administration, a sort of criticism of the old regime, which of course they're not, since there were and are a great many able people doing the actual day-to-day work out in the field, but I thought since you're Ben Ivey's sister-in-law, and you came up here to Seattle with him, you might have known that the Secretary's just come down from this trip to Alaska. In any case, it doesn't matter, so long as you'd be good enough to give your brother-in-law the Secretary's message?"

"Of course," Julie said.

"Would you tell Ben Ivey that the Secretary has seen the Brahmin story in this afternoon's paper and the Secretary would like Ivey to join him for breakfast tomorrow at eight in his suite at the Vancouver."

"The Secretary of the Interior has seen the Brahmin story in the afternoon paper," Julie repeated, "and he'd like Ben to have breakfast with him tomorrow morning at eight in his suite at the Hotel Vancouver. Is that right?"

359

"Yes," Mr. Klamath said. He smiled and nodded and said, "Thank you very much."

Ten minutes later, when Celia and Ben came into the larger of the two hotel rooms, Mr. Klamath's message was driven from Julie's mind by her sister's first question.

"Did you find a priest?" Celia asked.

"Yes," Julie said. "But we might as well forget him."

"Why?"

Julie explained. "What it adds up to," she said when she had repeated everything Father Wiereck had told her, "is that you can't put your hands on all these papers during the next few hours because the papers don't exist, so I think we'd all better forget the priest business."

"When you say we," Ben said, "does that include you, Julie?"

"What difference does that make?"

"Quite a lot," Ben said. "You were the one who wanted the ceremony to be performed by a priest in the first place."

"No," Julie said. "Ma did."

"Yes, I know," Ben said. "But you're acting as her emissary or agent or representative, call it, or yourself rather, what you will, and so the major forgetting must be done not by me or Celia, but by you."

"I've just explained," Julie said. "What Ma asked me to do, what she made me promise I'd see is done, it's impossible. It can't be done."

"Through no fault of mine," Ben said.

Julie looked at him curiously. "I didn't say it was any fault of yours, Ben."

"No, but your mother might. In fact, your mother will. It's important that when she does say it, you should correct her."

"It's *not* important," Celia said impatiently. "I don't give a damn what Ma thinks. I agreed to let Julie go find a priest because—" She paused and glanced at Julie. "Because Julie gave her promise," Celia said. "I didn't want Julie to go home and look like—"

"Julie won't look like," Ben said. "Her skirts are clear. She made the effort to keep her promise. It turned out to be impossible to

360

keep it. I'm sure your mother, when presented with the facts, will understand that and absolve Julie from responsibility."

"Then what are you getting so worked up about?" Julie said.

"*My* skirts," Ben said. "I want to make sure that in your mother's eyes they will be just as clear as yours. Because unlike Celia, I happen to give quite a large damn about what your mother thinks about her son-in-law. That's why I let you go off on this wild-goose chase after a priest."

"Wild-goose chase?" Julie said.

"Of course," Ben said. "I knew before you went to hunt for a priest that you'd never find one."

"But how could you?" Julie said. "There are priests in every city in—"

Ben shook his head. "No, no, no, no," he said impatiently. "Of course there are priests in Seattle. What I knew was what you would be told when you found one."

"You did?" Celia said suddenly, and even though she was standing beside Ben in the middle of the room, she seemed to lean forward, the way she did so often on the front seat of the Pierce-Arrow, to get a better look at him.

"Of course I did," Ben said. "Surely you haven't forgotten that I've been working in settlement houses ever since I got out of college. The problems of marriage and intermarriage come up in the life of a settlement-house worker about as often as the red or the black comes up in the life of a roulette player. I can tell you the prerequisites for marriage in pretty nearly every religious faith you ever heard of, or at any rate those practiced by the citizens surrounding places like the Clarke House and Zacharias House, and that certainly includes quite a few Catholics."

"Then why did you let me go out and try to find a priest?" Julie said. "I mean, if you knew what he'd tell me—"

"I wanted you also to know that it was a priest who had told you," Ben said. "There is no substitute for first-hand knowledge. Certainly not in moments of crisis, and for all practical purposes your surprise revelation a couple of hours ago about the promise you'd made to your mother was a moment of crisis. Any explanation I made out of superior knowledge at that moment would have sounded inevitably like an attempt to get you to break your promise. I had no desire to do that. I wanted you to learn something. I let you go off on your own, and you learned it."

"Learned what?"

"Don't give your promises rashly," Ben said. "Always find out what you're getting into before you commit yourself. Even if the commitment is to someone you're as close to as your own mother. Now that you've learned that, we can consider school out for the day, and go on to the serious business of getting married. Celia and I have the marriage license. Let's drive down to City Hall and—" The phone rang. Ben picked it up and said, "Hello? Who? Yes. Yes, she is." Ben held the phone out to Julie. "For you, beautiful."

Julie took the phone and said, "Hello?" A moment later, when the voice at the other end replied, she uttered a startled, "Who?"

"Me," Vic DeGenero's voice said. "What's going on up there?"

"Where are you?" Julie said.

"Portland. Why?"

"Oh, I thought you were here in Seattle."

"Why would I be up there?"

"I don't know," Julie said. "Everybody else seems to be. How did you know where we were?"

"I see your association with Ben Ivey has taught you how to get to the root of the matter."

"Well, I mean, we left Portland early this morning with about ten minutes' notice, I didn't even know where Seattle *is*, much less what hotel we'd be staying at, and here you are, in the afternoon, on the phone—"

"I have a fairly clear idea of Ben's salary," Vic DeGenero said. "I know if he went to New York he probably would not be able to afford the Waldorf, indicating that up there in Seattle he wouldn't be staying in the Vancouver, so all I had to do was call a few of the moderately priced—"

"Oh, my God!"

"What?"

"Nothing," Julie said. "I mean, Vic, please hold it a moment."

"Julie, for the love of Pete, what are you—?"

"No, please, one moment," Julie said and, to Ben and Celia, who were staring at her in puzzlement, "It's Vic."

"What does he want?" Ben said.

"I don't know, but he just happened to mention the Vancouver, and I remembered what Mr. Klamath told me to tell you when you returned to—"

"Mr. *who?*" Ben said.

Julie explained about the man who had given her the message downstairs in the lobby and then she repeated it. She had assumed the words would mean more to Ben than they had meant to her, just as the letters Frank Prohst or Mr. Trench dictated to her in the Ellentuch, Prohst & Wadsworth offices obviously made more sense to them than they did to Julie, but she was completely unprepared for their effect on the man who, she realized with a small stab of astonishment, was now almost her brother-in-law.

"Wow!" Ben said, releasing the single syllable as a yelp of delight. "Wow-*wee!*" He seized Celia by the shoulders and waist and, while she blinked and gasped and stumbled in her effort to keep up with him, Ben whirled her across the hotel room in an awkward, improvised dance which took them circling around the two beds, and came to a halt beside the startled Julie, to whom Ben said, "Repeat it, please, beautiful, repeat it again."

"Mr. Klamath said the Secretary of the Interior has seen the Brahmin story in the afternoon paper," Julie repeated, "and he'd like you to have breakfast with him tomorrow morning at eight in his suite at the Hotel Vancouver. Where are you going?"

"For a copy of the afternoon paper, of course!" Ben shouted at the door and, reaching back into the room to grab Celia's hand, he said with a laugh, "Come on, you almost wife, on their wedding days it is customary for the principals to do everything together."

"What was that all about?" Vic DeGenero said at the other end of the phone after the door had slammed.

"I don't know," Julie said. "Your mentioning that hotel, the Vancouver, reminded me that I had a message for Ben, and when I gave it to him, he seemed to go a little nuts."

"What was the message?"

Julie repeated it once more.

"I think," Vic DeGenero said, "I'm beginning to see something."

"I wish you'd show it to me," Julie said.

"Well, it struck me as funny right from the start that the story should break up there in the Seattle papers rather than down here in Portland, where Brahmin is based."

"What story, Vic?"

There was a pause at the other end.

"You mean to say," Vic DeGenero said slowly, "you don't know what—?"

"I do mean to say exactly that," Julia said. "I've been up to my ears all day in a wedding, being rushed by car to Seattle, hunting for priests, repeating messages, and—"

"And you haven't seen the Seattle papers?"

"No," Julia said. "What's in them?"

"A front-page story that says during the past two months, or almost exactly from the moment he took over as director of the Mercerville Project, Arnold Brahmin, through several different brokers, with each one of whom he has used a different assumed name, has sold short almost two hundred thousand shares of Pacific Northwest Power & Light common."

There was another pause at the other end. Julie knew it was designed to give her a chance to absorb the full meaning of what Vic clearly considered an astounding piece of news. Unfortunately, Julie did not understand it.

"What does it mean?" she said.

"You really don't know?"

"I'm a stenographer," Julie said. "My idea of high finance is coming out with enough lunch money for Fridays at the end of the week. Brokers, common stock, selling short, all that stuff is just confusion to me, and when I'm confused—"

"I'll try to unconfuse you," Vic said. "Remember a little talk we had last night over one of my old man's pizzas before the grange meeting, and then at the meeting itself after we heard Brahmin knock his audience in the aisles?"

"Which part of our talk?"

"The part that dealt with Brahmin's dedication to this great vision of reclaiming our northwestern desert by means of the Mercerville Dam? The fact that his family's fortune is largely tied up in Pacific Northwest Power & Light? The fact that if the Mercerville Dam actually gets built, and government-manufactured cheap electric power becomes available in this area, PNP&L will take a licking? The fact that the mere announcement of the project, the mere threat that the dam *might* be built, has already sent PNP&L stock tumbling? Remember all that?"

"Of course," Julie said. "What about it?"

"According to the story that broke in the Seattle papers this afternoon, plenty. They seem to indicate clearly that all of Brahmin's dedication is just so much hot air. Or rather, his dedication is to Arnold Brahmin's private interests. All the time he's been sounding off with his brave talk about making the desert bloom, brave talk which has kicked the bottom out of PNP&L stock, Mr. Brahmin has been secretly selling millions of dollars of that stock, pledging to deliver the stock later, when his government service will have driven the price far enough down to give him a handsome profit."

"In other words—?"

"In *plain* words," Vic said, "Mr. Arnold Brahmin looks to be about the shrewdest little financial conniver since a boy named Ponzi showed up on the American scene. His only intention, according to the stories in the Seattle papers, is to line his already handsomely lined pockets."

"You mean Mr. Brahmin has admitted all this?"

"Admitted it? Of course not. Don't you know the rules of this kind of game? You deny everything in a tone of deep outrage, preferably leaning on a quotation or two from the Bible. You announce yourself as the victim of a shocking and disgusting calumny. And you demand at once a hearing before your superiors so that your side of the story, meaning the truth, can be laid before them. Which is exactly what Brahmin has done, and which is why I'm calling you."

"What have I got to do with it?"

"I want you to give a message to Ben."

"Oh, no! Not another one!"

"This one is really the second part of the first one."

"You mean you know Mr. Klamath, too?"

"No, I don't," Vic DeGenero said. "But I know, or I *think* I know, Benjamin Franklin Ivey, Esquire."

"Then why don't you call him and give him the message direct? Why do you call me and—?

"You're more fun to talk to, for one thing. For another, before he took off this morning, Ben told me the wild dash to Seattle was for the purpose of getting married, and I thought he might be so involved in *that* that he might not appreciate the significance of my information— Was that a laugh I heard?"

"It was," Julie said.

"Why?"

"You don't know my brother-in-law as well as you think you do."

"*Is* he your brother-in-law?"

"He will be in less than an hour. They've got the license."

"Congratulations."

"I'll tell him."

"I wasn't congratulating him," Vic said. "I was congratulating you."

"On what?"

"Being that close to being legally related to an honest-to-God genuine no-kidding for-real genius. You ready for my message?"

"Do I have to write anything down?"

"Not any more. Being related to Ben Ivey ought to put a high gloss on even the dullest of brains, and you've got a pretty shiny one to begin with. Tell Ben I called Arnold Brahmin for a statement as soon as I saw the Seattle story on the office ticker. Brahmin told me it was all a dirty lie, planted by his enemies. He said he'd already been in touch with Washington by phone, as a result of which he has an appointment tomorrow morning with the Secretary at the Vaucouver at eight o'clock—"

The door burst open. Ben came dancing in, waving a newspaper in one hand and leading a bewildered Celia with the other.

"*Than strength of nerve and sinew, or the sway of magic potent over sun and star,*" he chanted happily as he danced around the room, "*Is Love, though oft to agony distrest, And though his favorite seat be feeble woman's breast.*"

Vic DeGenero's voice said dryly in Julie's ear, "I take it from the murmurings of the ubiquitous Mr. Wordsworth that the happy groom has returned?"

"Yes," Julie said. "Would you like to talk to him yourself?"

"Not while he's in *that* mood. Besides, you've got my message, and besides besides that, I prefer the last thing I hear on this wire to be your affirmative reply to my invitation that you have dinner with me when you get back to Portland tomorrow."

"I'll be glad to," Julie said.

"Do you *mean* glad, or are you just giving it the New York touch and saying yes in four syllables instead of one?"

Julie thought for a moment. "I *mean* glad," she said.

"This call has paid for itself," Vic DeGenero said. "See you tomorrow."

"See you tomorrow," Julie said, and hung up.

"All this time?" Ben said. "You've been on the phone with Vic since Celia and I left this room to buy—?"

"He had quite a lot to tell me," Julie said.

Ben winked at Celia and said in a gleeful whisper, "Was it interesting?"

"Very," Julie said. "Especially the message for you."

The impish grin on Ben's face disappeared in a look of surprise. "For me?" he said.

"Yes," Julie said. "Vic wanted me to tell you he talked with Arnold Brahmin as soon as he saw that story on the ticker in his office." She pointed to the newspaper in Ben's hand. "Brahmin denied the whole thing, said it was an effort by his enemies to unseat him, and he has been in touch with the Secretary's office in Washington, where he learned the Secretary of the Interior is here in Seattle, and Brahmin is flying up tonight to have breakfast with the Secretary in his suite at the Vancouver at eight o'clock tomorrow morning."

"But, Julie," Celia said through a small frown. "Isn't that the same time you said that man in the lobby told you the Secretary wants *Ben* to have breakfast with him?"

"Yes," Julie said. "Probably the Secretary arranged it that way, so Ben and Mr. Brahmin could—"

Her voice stopped, and she started forward, but Celia reached him first.

"Ben," she said. "What's the matter?"

"I—I don't know," he said, running a hand across his forehead. "I—I think I'd better sit down."

It seemed to Julie such a funny thing to say, because Ben *had* sat down, with a gentle thump, on the bed nearest the window. It was the way he had done it, abruptly, as though something had struck sharply at the back of his knees, that had drawn Julie forward and caused her voice to stop. Then, all at once, what Ben had said didn't seem to Julie to be funny at all. Because all at once she could remember another time, when Ben had said the same thing, in almost exactly the same words. Julie remembered that time so clearly that she was not surprised to hear Celia also use almost exactly the same words she had used then.

"Ben," she said. "You're sick."

She leaned over him, the way six years ago she had leaned over him in the barber chair a couple of hours before Ben disappeared from East Ninth Street on the night of the showdown with Tyler Crispin, and Celia put her hand to his forehead. This time, however, it was not exactly the same. This time, as she eased Ben down on the bed, Celia did not tell her kid sister to go get Dr. Zuckerberg. And this time it was not Biaggio Sarno, but his daughter Celia, who made the first move.

"Julie," she said. "In my bag, over there in the corner."

Even as she moved toward it, what seemed odd to Julie was not that she was certain she knew what she would find inside Celia's bag, but that she should be wondering how it had got there. Pulling out the old black leather box that Biaggio Sarno had brought with him from Naples to the New World, Julie wondered where it had been during the years since her father's death. Had her mother kept it hidden and turned it over to Celia before she left New York two weeks ago? Had Celia been the one who had secreted it all these years, ever since the little glass cups had first put Ben Ivey back on his feet? Did Ben know that Celia was carrying the black leather box?

"Light the buttonhook," Celia said. She had already removed Ben's tie and opened his shirt and rolled the undershirt up to his neck. "And give them to me one at a time."

When the last cup had been attached, and once again Ben Ivey's chest looked the way Julie remembered it six years ago, as though twenty or thirty unlighted electric bulbs had been screwed into the skin, Celia straightened up with a small tired grunt and blew out the dancing blue flame at the end of the buttonhook.

"I guess maybe you better bring Ben's bag in here. I'll stay with him here."

For a moment or two, Julie did not understand. Then she remembered the arrangements for checking into the hotel as Ben had explained them on the front seat of the Pierce-Arrow—could it have been only an hour or two ago?—and Julie remembered something else: this was supposed to have been her sister's wedding day.

"Sure," she said and, a few minutes later, after she had made the transfer, and Celia had taken off the cups, and Ben was sleeping quietly, Julie said in a whisper, "Maybe he'll be all right in a little while and then we can go downtown—?"

Celia, who was gnawing her lower lip as she stared at Ben, shook her head. "It's too late for today," she said. "They told us when we got the marriage license they close at four-thirty." Celia looked at her watch. "It's almost that now." Again she caught her lower lip in her teeth and, after a moment, she said, "I only hope—" Her voice stopped.

"Hope what?" Julie said.

"Oh, I'm just being silly," Celia said, but she didn't look silly. She looked worried. "What difference does one day make?" Celia said. "He'll certainly be all right in the morning and we can get married then."

"He's got this date with the Secretary of the Interior at eight," Julie said.

"That shouldn't take long," Celia said. "Besides, the marriage bureau doesn't open until ten. We'll get married right after his meeting with the Secretary. Yes," Celia said, as though trying to win an argument with herself, "that's how we'll do it. Right after the meeting with the Secretary. One more day won't make any difference," she repeated and then, apparently becoming aware of the repetition, Celia seemed to become embarrassed. "I'll stay with him in here until he wakes up," she said. "Why don't you go down and get something to eat?"

"All right," Julie said, although she wasn't hungry. "Can I bring you something?"

"No, I'm fine," Celia said. She pulled open the door, then stopped, held it a moment, and pushed the door shut again. "Julie," she said with a frown, "Vic DeGenero, when you were talking to him? Did he say anything to make you think Ben knew, when he said this morning in such a rush let's go up to Seattle, you think Ben knew the Secretary of the Interior was up here?"

Julie thought hard for several moments. "No, Vic didn't *say* anything," she said finally. "Nothing specific or direct, but—"

"But what?"

"Well, when I told him you had the license and the wedding was about to take place in less than an hour, Vic congratulated me on being related to what he called a real authentic genuine genius."

The worried scowl on Celia's face eased into a small smile. "You mind if I ask for my wedding present now?" she said.

"I haven't got it now," Julie said. "What I was thinking, I thought in a few days, when I get back to New York—"

"I don't want to wait that long."

"Well, gee, I don't know how—" Julie paused and then said, "You see, Cockeye Katie helped me pick it out, and I arranged with her to order it shipped when I came back, but I *could* send Katie a letter in the morning, or a telegram, so we'll save a few days, and you could have it by, oh, I guess—"

Celia shook her head. "I want it now."

Julie tooked helplessly at her sister. "But I just told you. I can't give it to you now."

"Yes, you can."

The tone of her voice made it clear that what Celia wanted could not be obtained at wholesale rates through the intervention of Cockeye Katie Halloran.

"What do you want, Celia?"

"I want you to promise you won't hate me."

"That's pretty silly," Julie said. "You know I—"

"Of course I know," Celia said. "It's like promising somebody you won't ever catch a cold or get older, but I'd like the promise just the same. For a wedding present, Julie. It's all I want."

Julie shook her head, feeling stupid. "Why would I *ever* hate you?" she said.

"For taking Ben away from you," Celia said, and they were both suddenly immobilized in the silence.

"This is crazy," Julie said.

"Probably," Celia said. "But I'd still like your promise."

"No, I don't mean that. I mean what you said. About taking Ben away from me. He's, he's—Celia, for God's sake, *please*, he's going to be your husband tomorrow morning."

"I know, but he might have been yours, and that's why I want—"

"He couldn't. He wouldn't. I didn't. I never—"

Celia's lips moved in a small smile. "Words, no," she said. "But this afternoon, right here"—Celia nodded to the room behind her —"when Ben said we'd got the license, I happened to be looking at your face, and all of a sudden I saw—"

Julie shook her head desperately. "No, no," she said. "Celia, please. It's not true. I don't know about my face, how I looked, whatever you saw, but it wasn't *that*, Celia. Honest to God, it wasn't."

"Then what was it?"

The lie came so readily and smoothly that for a moment or two, certainly as the words were uttered, Julie believed them herself.

"The promise I made to Ma," she said. "The second one. I couldn't keep the promise about the priest. But this one—" Julie opened her purse and clawed about for the small flat package she had been carrying for weeks. "I promised Ma I'd see you wore these at your wedding," Julie said, tearing away the tissue paper.

"She wore them at her wedding, and Ma wanted you to wear them at yours, and I realized I'd almost forgotten this promise, too, so whatever you saw in my face—"

Her words stopped as Celia reached out and took the rhinestone-studded combs.

"All right," she said as, with two slow, graceful movements, she set the combs in her lovely red hair, "I'll wear them tomorrow, and when you get back to the Bronx, you can tell Ma what she wants to hear. All right?"

Julie nodded. "Sure," she said. "Thanks, Celia."

"Now you can give me my wedding present," Celia said.

During the new pause, Julie hastily invented and weighed several other lies, but Celia was watching her carefully, and Julie could tell from her sister's face that, even if the inventions had been good, which they weren't, they would not have worked. Celia knew.

"I don't hate you," Julie said slowly. "I never will."

"Thanks," Celia said. "I remember once telling you I don't deserve a kid sister as nice as you are. It's still true. But I'm glad I've got one."

"So am I," Julie said.

"It's funny, but I believe you," Celia said. "I always have. Even when things were—" She shook her head, as though to fling away the recollections of the specific things, whatever they were. "I always knew I could count on little Julie. It's a wonderful thing. Like a small warm secret little reservoir inside you, so no matter what happens or doesn't happen, no matter what they take away from you, you've always got that to draw on."

"You always will," Julie said.

Celia nodded. "I know I will," she said. "That's why I'm going to give you a little present in exchange. It's not much. It can't do for you what yours has done for me, but it's true just the same." Celia paused and then said quietly, "Julie, that day when the banks closed, the day Ben came back, that night when he asked me to marry him, I didn't know how you felt. I didn't, Julie. It never came into my head. You were just what you'd always been. My kid sister. I didn't know what I found out this afternoon.

I didn't, Julie. I didn't know. You've got to believe me. I didn't know."

"I believe you," Julie said.

Celia smiled and reached out and touched her sister's cheek. "Of course you do," she said. "You believe anything your big sister says. Want me to say more?"

"Well," Julie said, and she hesitated, but she knew the hesitation would accomplish nothing. She had to ask the question. "That night when Ben came back and he asked you to marry him, would it have made any difference, your answer, I mean, if you *had* known?"

Celia shook her head. "It was too late then," she said.

"Too late for what?"

"What do you think for what?" Celia said with a small shake of her head in which hopelessness and impatience were equally mixed. "Don't you understand? It was too late, Julie. It was too late. I had to marry him."

It seemed odd to Julie, as the moment of comprehension exploded inside her, that what she should suddenly be remembering was the way Cockeye Katie had sounded at the luncheon table in Child's on the day after Celia had broken the news about marrying Ben. Cockeye Katie had grasped at once what Julie had grasped only now: she and her mother were the only members of the Sarno family for whom Ben Ivey's disappearance had lasted a full six years.

"That's why you said no to Louis Vinutti," Julie said slowly. "That's why, just before Ben came back, Louis said he hadn't seen you for nine nights. You were seeing somebody else. Somebody I never even thought of, until nine days later he showed up as though he—"

Celia shook her head slowly. "I couldn't marry Louis," she said in a low voice. "He was too—too—" Celia shook her head again. "I couldn't do it to him."

Julie nodded. She understood that. She couldn't have done it, either. Not to anybody as nice as Louis Vinutti.

"Some day, maybe, when it's all over," Celia said, "I'll tell you the whole thing."

"No, that's all right," Julie said.

There wasn't any more to tell.

"It isn't," Celia said. "Not yet." She sent a quick glance at the slender figure asleep on the bed. "But it will be in the morning. And then—" Celia paused, and she shrugged and with an effort that moved Julie's heart, she managed a smile. "Thanks for my wedding present, sweetie," Celia Sarno said to her sister. "It's made things easier for me. God knows I don't deserve them made easier for me, but I'm glad you did. Some day, maybe—" She paused again. "Some day I hope—" But whatever it was Celia hoped, she couldn't seem to get into words. "Go on down and get something to eat," she said, pulling open the door. "I'll rest awhile."

Julie went down to the coffee shop, ordered a sandwich and a glass of milk, tried to eat, couldn't, and went back up to her room. It was very small, the bed and the chair and the dresser filling the narrow space almost completely. Julie lay down on the bed and stared up at the ceiling and tried not to think. She wasn't very successful, but she persisted, pretending her mind was a blackboard covered with messages scrawled in chalk and she was wiping them away with a wet cloth, and soon she was doing it so rapidly that some of the terrible words began to lose their meaning, but then the phone rang and all the effort was wasted. She picked it up.

"Hello?"

"New York calling Miss Celia Sarno."

"She's not here, but I can—"

"Julie?"

The man's voice, cutting across the voice of the operator, made Julie sit up.

"Hello?" she said.

"Julie, is that you?"

"Yes, Mr. Prohst."

"Where's Celia?"

"She's in the next room," Julie said automatically, without thought. "I'll have the call switched to—"

Her voice stopped, because she had started to think, and her

374

thoughts took the form of a single question: How had Frank Prohst known they were staying at this hotel?

"Julie?"

"Yes, Mr. Prohst?"

How had he known they were in Seattle?

"Julie, I'd like to talk with Celia. It's important. I've got to—"

"Yes, Mr. Prohst," Julie said quickly, hiding behind the fact that he was her boss, acting as though she was in the office and he had asked her to do something in connection with her job and she was doing it because she was paid to do it. In that way she didn't have to think about Celia and Mr. Prohst and what she had learned the day the banks closed. "I'll just switch the call," Julie said hastily. "Hold on, Mr. Prohst." She jiggled the hook and the voice of the hotel operator came on, saying something Julie did not catch. "Operator," Julie said, "will you please switch this to eleven-oh-four? It's not for me. The call is for my sister. She's in eleven-oh-four, next door. Would you please switch this to—?"

"I'm sorry," the operator said. "There is no answer in eleven-oh-four. I tried to ring there first, and then the New York operator asked for you, miss."

Julie had hung up, and crossed the room, and pulled open the door before she was aware of a twinge of uneasiness, some instinct warning her that what she was going toward would wait, but she couldn't. For several long moments, standing in the open door of 1104, where she had last seen Celia, Julie stared stupidly at the bed on which she had last seen Ben. Then she came into the empty room and picked up the phone between the beds.

"Yes?" the operator said.

"Mr. Ivey," Julie said. "Where's Mr. Ivey?"

"Who?"

"This is his room. He and my sister were—"

"Just a moment, please."

There was a click, and a low roaring sound, and then a man's voice was on the wire.

"Desk, here."

"Mr. Ivey?" Julie said. "Benjamin Franklin Ivey? Where is he?"

"Who is this?"

375

"Miss Sarno. His—" Julie paused. It sounded silly even before she said it, but there was no time to think of anything else. She said, "His sister-in-law. Where is he?"

"Mr. Ivey?"

"Yes, I want—"

"Why, Mr. Ivey checked out two hours ago."

"He—he's *gone?*"

"Yes, ma'am. Checked out at five-thirty. Said he was called to Washington. Is there anything—?"

Julie didn't hear the rest of the question because she had moved the receiver from her ear to look at her watch. It showed a quarter to eight. For at least part of the time that she had thought she was staring up at the ceiling, wiping the frightening thoughts from the blackboard of her mind, she had obviously been asleep. Slowly Julie put the receiver back to her ear.

"My sister," she said. "Could you tell me where—?"

Julie never finished that question, any more than the chinless old man in the doorway, his face gray with shock, his faltering fingers plucking at the mutton-chop puffs the arm garters made of his shirt sleeves, ever got a chance to finish the sentence that bubbled in erratic spurts through his liver-spotted lips: "The other girl, your sister, she's, they, the police, on the sidewalk, she fell otta the window, she's asking for—"

By the time the stunned night clerk and the faulty elevator got them down the eleven floors to the sidewalk, it was too late to do anything about the question that would always remain in doubt: What had Celia with her last breath been asking for?

There was never any doubt, after the police finished presenting their evidence at the inquest, that the night clerk's initial statement was wrong. Celia Sarno, who was three months pregnant, had not fallen from the window of the hotel room in which she had planned to spend her wedding night.

She had jumped.

22

Ten years later, in another hotel room six thousand miles away, Julie Sarno's mind was flooded again by the helpless thought that had momentarily held off the numbed hysteria into which soon enough the shock of Celia's death had plunged her: the attempt to evade fate had failed; the journey to the promised land had been a waste of time; in the long run, what difference did it make whether destruction came, as it had to Biaggio Sarno, on an East River dock or, as it had come to his daughter, on a Seattle sidewalk?

"None whatsoever."

Turning quickly, Julie saw that the quietly spoken words had been addressed not to her but to Colonel Uxbridge.

"Is he still unconscious?" the colonel said.

"Yes, sir," Harry said, and he repeated: "No change whatsoever."

The man in the sweatshirt gave Julie a short glance, then leaned close to Colonel Uxbridge and whispered something in the ear of the white-haired man from Washington. As he listened, Colonel Uxbridge turned to look at Julie.

"All right," he said finally to the man who, from the moment two hours ago when Julie had entered this suite in Claridge's, had reminded her of Steve Shupka. "I'm just going into my room for some papers," Colonel Uxbridge said to her. "I won't be long."

He walked out through the arch at the far end of the room, and Julie was not surprised to see Harry come down toward the arch at the other end. He had obviously asked Colonel Uxbridge to be left alone with her.

"Miss Sarno," he said. "You mind I talk to you a few minutes?"

"Of course not," Julie said. "Only please don't repeat anything Colonel Uxbridge has said. His eloquence failed to persuade me, and I doubt that his arguments will work second time around. Besides, it's getting late, and I'm tired."

"Me, too," Harry said. "No, I won't say nothing the colonel said. One reason, I don't talk his type talk. Another, I don't know what he said."

"Why not?" Julie said. "Tired of listening at keyholes, or are you losing your knack for eavesdropping?"

The round tanned face flushed all the way up and across the bald tanned head.

"I didn't do it when you was in there with Mr. Ivey because I'm nosy or a snooper or anything like that. I did it because—"

"It was your duty," Julie said. "I know. Colonel Uxbridge told me that, too. What part of your duty are you about to perform now, and to whom?"

"You, ma'am," Harry said.

"The only duty you can perform for me in which I'd be interested, is to unlock that front door and let me out of here."

"I think you're wrong, Miss Sarno."

"About what?"

"That ain't the only thing I can do for you."

"I'll consider myself the best judge of that," Julie said. "If you don't mind."

"I don't mind," Harry said. "I just wanna tell you something I think you'll wanna know."

"What's that?"

"Tell me something first, ma'am. You know anybody named Celia?"

"*Know* anybody?"

"Yeah," Harry said. "A friend? A relative? A maybe neighbor? Someone you went to school with? Or worked with on a job somewhere? *Anything.* The way you get to know somebody. Somebody named Celia?"

378

"Why do you ask?"

"I don't know how much the colonel told you about me and Mr. Ivey," Harry said. "But I been with him some time now. Not the early days, when he first became, you know, a big shot. The depression times, when he was something with the NRA, I forget exactly, except you saw his name in the papers all the time. Then the ATVAA, when he ran that. And the Supreme Court, the time there was that big fight, and everybody said the Boss was trying to pack the court, and he sent Mr. Ivey to see—"

"I know all that," Julie said.

"Well, I wasn't with him in those days," Harry said. "When I got with him, the time they assigned me to Mr. Ivey, it was just after the fall of France, when things started to get hot over here in Europe. I mean when they woke up this was no game of pisha-paysha and they realized all of a sudden they got a *war* on their hands, and Mr. Ivey, he moved his office into the White House. To be right there, near the Boss all the time. That's when I got assigned to him, which means like, say, forty to forty-three is three, and the few extra months from the time of year France folded up, the early summer, to now, the fall, say another half, so all together, I been with Mr. Ivey three and a half years."

"Not long enough, apparently, to teach you how to get to the root of the matter," Julie said.

Harry's eyeballs rolled in a quick, sharp, stabbing glance. "I guess maybe I'm on the right track all right," he said, and waited. Julie let him wait. His references to Celia, coming on top of Julie's unwelcome recollections about Oregon, had shaken her. She felt like one of those puzzles in which a number of small steel balls under glass have to be dropped into a number of matching holes by tipping the box back and forth. The balls had all dropped into the proper holes. The picture of her past, from which Julie Sarno had been fleeing for ten years, had been completed. She was free, or she would be free as soon as she got out of this hotel suite, to start running again. And then this bald man in the sweatshirt had come into the room and, by mentioning Celia, had given the box a violent shove, so that all the steel balls had leaped from their holes and were again rolling about wildly under the glass of her

379

memory. Harry said, "Him with his root of the matter, only somebody who knew Mr. Ivey quite a while would know how he is about that, but what I'm getting at by telling you I been with him three and a half years, I been taking care of him."

"Colonel Uxbridge told me about that," Julie said.

"He tell you how Mr. Ivey, he gets these sort of attacks like? They happen pretty often?"

Julie nodded. "And how he usually reacts, but this time it's different, because this time, for the first time since you've been taking care of him, this is the first time Mr. Ivey has lost consciousness," she said. "Yes, Colonel Ivey told me that, too."

Harry nodded. "Because *I* told *him*," he said. "What I didn't tell the colonel, what I'm telling *you*, Miss Sarno, lots of times when Mr. Ivey has one of these attacks, he like, well, yes, he *talks* to himself. Nothing much, or anything you can understand. Mumbling like more, I'd say."

"Mumbling about what?"

"Something that happened to somebody name of Celia," Harry said, and he waited again. Julie did the same. Harry yielded first. He said, "I never paid much attention. People, *everybody*, they got people they knew, or they know, or something happened, that kind of stuff, so I figured a long time ago this person Celia, whoever she was, she was someone Mr. *Ivey* knew a long time ago, and something happened. That's all. I mean it didn't do anything to me special. I didn't figure it meant anything. It was just a name, and just a thing, and that's all. None of my business, until now."

This time, when Harry paused, it was Julie who yielded. "Why now?" she said.

"A little while ago, after you came out from being in there with him"—Harry nodded to the arch at the far end of the room— "and Colonel Uxbridge sent me in to handle it, Mr. Ivey was mumbling the way he usually does, which was okay. I expected that. Even when he mentioned Celia, again okay. Situation normal. But then he said something that was different. Completely new. Something I never heard before, and your name was in it.

I mean your first name. It's Julie, right?" Julie nodded. Harry said, "Mr. Ivey said this thing that I been thinking over all the time I been in there with him, and finally I figured I better tell you. Even if I don't know what it means, maybe you do, I figured. Maybe it means something to you. At least hearing it, that much, I figured, even if it's only a favor to a stranger, that much any guy ought to—"

"What did Mr. Ivey say?" Julie said.

"Just before he conked out," Harry said, "I heard him say: *Julie, if you knew the truth of what happened to Celia, you wouldn't walk out on me like this.*"

In the silence that followed, while she looked directly into Harry's eyes, Julie wasn't quite sure why she was doing it. What did she hope to discover by her anxious scrutiny? Whether or not the man in the sweatshirt had made it all up? Whether, in the hope of getting her to do something for his beloved boss that Julie had already refused to do, Harry had taken a shot in the dark? By taking hitherto unrelated fragments gleaned by his eavesdropping and putting them together into what sounded like a plausible whole?

Then Harry's glance shifted, toward the arch through which Colonel Uxbridge had suddenly re-entered the room, and in the release from the scrutiny that had held her, Julie was able to see what was happening to her. It was as though the scattered steel balls inside the jolted puzzle had settled down, all the bits of round shiny metal dropping back neatly into the appropriate holes, and all at once she had discovered that one hole was empty. A ball had disappeared. The puzzle, which the agonized grinding of memory's wheels had seemed to leave complete, was not complete at all. Was there a missing piece? Was it locked in the brain of the unconscious man in the bedroom?

Julie made her decision. She said, "Come on."

She led the way through the arch at the far end, but by the time Julie reached the bedroom door at the left, Harry had caught up with and passed her. It was he who opened the door and held it wide for her. Julie went directly to the dresser. From among the expensive toilet articles she picked up the battered black leather box that, an hour ago, had reminded her of a tramp at an embassy ball.

"Anything I can do to help?" Harry said.

"Yes," Julie said. She nodded to the motionless figure on the bed. "Take off the top of his pajamas, please."

By the time Harry had stripped his boss to the waist, Julie had ignited the alcohol-soaked wad of cotton at the end of the buttonhook.

"Anything else?" Harry said.

"Hold this," Julie said. She came to the bed and handed him the black leather box. As she dipped down over Ben Ivey and slid the dancing blue flame under the first little glass cup, Julie said, "Hand them to me one at a time."

By forcing herself to concentrate on her movements rather than their meaning, the way at her BEW typewriter she got through much of her meaningless work by concentrating on the shorthand outlines rather than on the words for which they stood, Julie was able to get through the next dozen minutes. Finally, when she had finished what she had first seen her father do to Ben Ivey sixteen years before in the barber shop on East Ninth Street, and what six years later she had helped Celia do to her fiancé in the Seattle hotel room on what was to have been their wedding day, Julie straightened up and became aware that her knees were shaking.

"Now what?"

She turned sharply and realized she had forgotten she was not alone in the room with Ben.

"If it still works," Julie started to say, paused, and then started again. "In a few minutes he ought to wake up."

She went to the desk near the bed, tried to pull out the chair, and found she couldn't. Harry, apparently grasping what was happening, took three quick steps, reached the desk, pulled the chair out, eased her into it, and said quietly, "Cigarette?"

Julie shook her head. She was watching the bed. The slender figure in blue pajama pants lay motionless. *If it still works,* Julie had started to say. It had not occurred to her until she heard her own words that she did not know what "it" was. A child of eleven, watching her father apply a remedy for which his neighbors regularly asked and paid, had accepted the remedy's efficacy without question. A girl of seventeen, helping her sister apply the same remedy, had not even thought about whether it would or would not work. The adult of twenty-seven, driven to applying the remedy herself, was suddenly terrified by how much depended on something in which with equal abruptness she realized she found it difficult to believe. If the remedy her sister had once derided as a peasant's preposterous superstition had not worked for Biaggio Sarno, who wanted his shovels sold, or for Celia, who wanted a husband, Julie would have been sorry. If the remedy did not work now, she would be helpless. She could no longer turn and run. The spectator had become participant.

"Holy smoke!"

Julie turned toward Harry, who had uttered the words, then toward the bed, at which Harry's wide-eyed glance was directed. The slender figure in the blue pajama pants was yawning.

"All right," Julie said. "Let's take the cups off."

By the time the glass bulbs were back in the velvet-lined box, Ben Ivey was sitting up against the pillows, buttoning his pajama tops.

"Thanks, Julie," he said, and his voice changed, as it always did when the resonant tones were diverted to the works of William Wordsworth: "*Small service is true service while it lasts. Of humblest friends, bright creature! scorn not one: The daisy, by the shadow that it casts, Protects the lingering dewdrop from the sun.*"

Harry laughed. "I guess you're okay, boss," he said, and turned to Julie. "When he starts making with the poetry, we're in the clear."

"Not quite," Ben said, frowning at his wrist watch. "We may be a bit on the late side. Where's Colonel Uxbridge?"

"Out in the sitting room."

"Get him."

Harry vanished on the heels of his own nod. As Ben swung his legs over the side of the bed, he looked up; his glance crossed

Julie's stare. It seemed to jolt him. His mind, apparently absorbed in some problem far from his present circumstances, came back into the room. Ben forced a smile, clearly almost literally driving it to the front of whatever it was he really was doing inside his head.

"I wish I had time to thank you properly," he said. "I'm not only grateful. I'm also proud. I knew in the long run, no matter what your personal feelings might be, you'd see your duty clearly and do it promptly."

"I didn't do it because I saw it as my duty," Julie said.

Ben, who had kicked his toes into a pair of bright yellow pigskin slippers, rose and turned.

"If you didn't do it because it was your duty," he said, "why the hell did you do it?"

Julie repeated what Harry had told her. Anger invaded the thin, neatly put-together face.

"The stupid son of a bitch," Ben said. He had crossed the room, and his hand was on the doorknob, before he turned and snapped, "He say anything else?"

"About what?" Julie said.

"*Anything* else. For Christ's sake, Julie, you know what *anything* means."

"No, just that thing about Celia."

"You sure?"

"Of course I'm sure. That's why I changed my mind about doing the"—she touched the black leather box on the dresser—"this thing."

The anger on Ben's face rearranged itself to make room for incredulity. "You mean to say the only reason was because of some stupid words that boob muscle builder out there"—Ben's head jerked toward the door behind him—"says I said?"

"They're not stupid words to me."

The door opened. Colonel Uxbridge and Harry, starting across the threshold, stopped short.

"Oh," the colonel said, apparently confused for a moment by finding himself standing so close to the man he had last seen lying flat on the bed at the other side of the room. "Good to see you on your feet, Mr. Ivey. Harry said you wanted me."

"Yes." Ben glanced at his wrist watch, scowling, as his lips moved slightly. He was apparently making a calculation. "Yes," he said again and looked up. "We can do it nicely. Call Sloane four-seven-seven-three and say your brown shoes are ready."

"Sloane four-seven-seven-three," Colonel Uxbridge said. "Your brown shoes are ready."

"Right," Ben said. "Then get that paper I was working on out in the living room."

"In the typewriter, yes," Colonel Uxbridge said.

Ben nodded and said, "You've read it, I'm sure, but if you haven't, read it at once, as I'll want to discuss it with you on the way, then pack your bag if it isn't already packed and stand by. I'll be ready in ten minutes." He ran his hand down one lean cheek and said, "Damn, no, make it fifteen. I have to shave. Come back in here after you've read the paper and we'll discuss it while I'm shaving."

"Very good," Colonel Uxbridge said, and disappeared.

"You," Ben said to Harry. "Get out of that sweatshirt and into some clothes. By the time you've done that, Colonel Uxbridge will be off the phone. You get on it, and call that number the man from the Embassy gave you, and say you want a car here at the hotel in five minutes." Ben turned to Julie. "The car will look like a taxi, but it won't be, and the driver will look like a taxi driver. Harry will take you down and see you get into the car okay. All you have to do then is give the driver your address. He'll get you home safely. Don't pay him or talk to him. Don't talk to anybody else, either. The girl you live with, that drunken general who is her boy friend, nobody. If they or anybody else ask where you spent the evening, you were out dancing with Colonel Uxbridge. So far as you're concerned, you haven't seen me, you've heard nothing, the last few hours did not take place. Good-bye, Julie."

He put out his hand. Julie did not take it.

"I'm not going, Ben."

385

The look of irritation came back. His mind, already on its way to the next step in the mission that had brought him to England, had been stopped in its tracks.

"What?" Ben Ivey said.

"I'm not going," Julie said again.

"Now, look, this is no time for—"

"You're talking about your time," Julie said. "I'm talking about mine. I've got lots of it, and I'm spending as much of it right here as I have to in order to get what belongs to me."

"Belongs to you? What the hell belongs to you? What do you want?"

"My *quid pro quo.*"

"You sound as though you were back in the steno pool of Ellentuch, Prohst & Wadsworth."

"I wish I was."

"Wishing won't get you there. Or anywhere else. There's no going back, Julie. You'd think after all the years the human race has been in business, the stockholders would have grasped that fact."

"I've grasped it," Julie said. "I don't want to go back. All I want is what I've earned."

"You're using some pretty funny words."

"I learned them from you. I'm sticking to the root of the matter, Ben. I want to know what really happened to Celia."

His face, crisscrossed by lines of puzzlement and annoyance, suddenly jerked smooth, as though the skin were loose and somebody seizing a handful of it at the back of his head, had given it a hard twist.

"She jumped out of a hotel window in Seattle ten years ago," Ben Ivey said harshly.

"That's what the police said, Ben."

"Julie, for the love of God, *please*, I don't have time now. You just heard me tell Colonel Uxbridge—"

"You told him you had fifteen minutes. Give me one or two. Is it such a lot to ask after all these years? You once said I was always giving, never taking. Let me take something now, Ben. It belongs to me. I want it. Harry reported that before you passed out you

386

said: *Julie, if you knew the truth of what happened to Celia, you wouldn't walk out on me like this.* I didn't walk out on you, Ben. Don't walk out on me. Please, I'm begging, Ben."

"For *what?*" he said. "For Christ's sweet sake, for *what?* You know what happened to Celia. You were there. You—"

Julie shook her head desperately. "I thought I knew. But now I don't know any more. I have to start at the beginning. My mother used to say you wanted something from us. My father said she was crazy. I thought he was right. Not that she was crazy, but that you could want something from us. What could you want from a family of Italian immigrants? On the Lower East Side? This?" Julie shoved the scuffed leather box on the dresser, pushing it away from her savagely, as though it were a shambling drunk who had wandered into her path as she raced to catch a train. "I don't believe it. You didn't even know it existed when you first came into our lives. Even if you had known, it's not enough. It's just what Celia said it was. A peasant remedy. Anybody can do it for you. Harry. A bellhop. *Anybody.* But you send Colonel Uxbridge, you practically turn out the whole U.S. army to find *me* to do it. Why? Ben, why? Why? Why?"

"I don't know why."

In the sudden silence, which hummed with the echo of his whispered words, they stared at each other in embarrassed consternation, like dancers at a masquerade ball who, at the moment of unmasking, discover that each has been wrong about the suspected identity of the other. Ben Ivey recovered first.

"I mean that I knew you, yes, I knew I wanted *you* to do it, because—" He paused and scowled as he ran a hand down the side of his face, repeating the gesture he had made moments before when he learned he needed a shave, but this time the stubble did not distract him. Ben Ivey said quietly, "Julie, do we have to go through this?"

"Maybe you don't," she said. "You've got what you always wanted. A seat at the top, in the control tower, where you can run things, the way you once wanted to run the Horace Judson Clarke House and later the Mercerville Project, except now you're running the biggest thing there is, a piece of the world. How you got

387

it, what you did to others besides the Sarno family to get it, I don't know and I don't want to know. All I know is you've got it. But what have I got? You came into my life one night sixteen years ago on East Ninth Street, when I was a kid, and a few months later my father was dead. You came back into my life six years after that, the day the banks closed, and four weeks later my sister was dead. A month after that, when I was back in New York, my mother was dead. She never recovered from the shock of Celia's suicide. You know what that means to a Catholic. And where were you after Celia died? Ten thousand miles away? No, in Washington. Couldn't you even write a letter? Did you ever wonder for one single minute what was happening to me? I didn't die like my mother did. But I didn't recover either. Ellentuch, Prohst & Wadsworth wanted me back, but I couldn't face going back, so I got another job, and soon I couldn't face that one, either. It's been like that for ten years, not only with jobs, but people, too. Louis Vinutti, whom you didn't know, and Vic DeGenero, whom you did, and others I can't even remember. The moment anything becomes real for me, a job or a person, I turn and run. I never knew why, until tonight, when Harry told me what you said, and I suddenly understood it was Celia. That's what was missing. Celia was me, what I wanted to be, and when Celia died, a piece of me died, too. I thought I knew why she died—because you ran out on her—"

"But I didn't, Julie. My God, is that what you've been thinking all these years?"

She shook her head impatiently. "Not now, Ben," Julie said. "Don't lie now. It's too late for that."

"I'm not lying," Ben said.

"Yes, you are," Julie said. "Celia died in Oregon, while you were on your way to Washington. The night before your wedding."

Ben Ivey shook his head. "That was the way Celia arranged it," he said.

"No wonder they call you Poison Ivey," Julie said. "Nothing stops you. Nothing. Not even murder."

"I didn't kill Celia," Ben Ivey said.

"If she hadn't known you, she'd be alive now."

"There are hotels in New York," Ben Ivey said. "People who want to jump out of eleventh-story windows can always arrange it without taking transcontinental trips."

"Celia took that trip because you asked her to," Julie said, and then she added: "Because she had to."

Ben turned to the open door, in which Harry had appeared, and said, "Yes?"

"The car will be downstairs for the young lady by the time we get out of the elevator," Harry said.

"Good," Ben said.

Julie crossed the room and shut the door in Harry's face. "No, it isn't," she said to Ben. "It's not good enough. I'm not leaving this room until you make it better."

He gave her a long look. Again she had the feeling he was making a calculation. Finally, and very slowly, Ben Ivey said, "She was pregnant."

Julie made an impatient gesture. "I know that," she said.

He nodded, not to her but to himself, as though correcting the calculation. "Yes, of course you would know that," he said. "That point came out at the inquest."

"What didn't come out was that you ran out on her two hours before she jumped," Julie said. "After we put the cups on you, after we put you back on your feet the way we'd done down on Ninth Street when you were scared to face Tyler Crispin, when you woke up in that Seattle hotel room you knew you couldn't face Arnold Brahmin the next morning in front of the Secretary of the Interior, so you ran again—the day before you were supposed to marry Celia."

A look of surprise crossed the thin, tense, handsome face. "You think that's why she did it?" Ben said. "All these years you've believed Celia killed herself because I refused to make an honest woman of her?"

Something in the tone of his voice warned her: a note Julie remembered from the early days in the Clock House when some bit of verbal dexterity, some forensic trick, his own or somebody else's, elicited Ben Ivey's excited admiration.

"Yes," Julie said slowly. "That's what I've believed. Until to-night, when what your man Harry said to me out in the sitting room made me believe there was more to it."

The line of Ben's thin lips went down at the corners in a sud-den dip that should have produced a sardonic effect but didn't. All at once he looked the way he had looked in the barber chair on East Ninth Street sixteen years ago, on the bed in the Seattle hotel room six years later, and in this room less than an hour ago. Ben Ivey looked vulnerable.

"There sure is," he said with quiet bitterness.

"What?" Julie said.

He looked at her curiously. "You really want to know?" Ben said.

Julie hesitated. Did she really want to know? All at once she grasped the dangers concealed in complete awareness. What was better? Living the way she had lived for the last ten years, nursing a wound and a hatred for the man who had caused it, existing in the half-light of a resentment on which she could blame all? Or moving out of the semi-darkness into the harsh light of total il-lumination? Where what she would see clearly might forever pre-vent her, because there would be nobody left to blame, from re-treating back into the cozy comfort of dim half-knowledge?

"Yes," Julie said in an unsteady voice. "I really want to know."

For a moment the look Ben gave her was disturbing. She did not understand it. Then she remembered the way he used to look at her in Oregon when she said something that surprised and pleased him. It was a look of admiration.

"Okay, beautiful, you asked for it," Ben Ivey said in a low voice. "Celia was pregnant all right. But not by me. Your sister Celia wanted to marry me to get out of New York. Not because she loved me. Not for any reason other than that. Transportation. I was her railroad ticket out of the mess she was in with Mr. Frank Prohst, her boss, a married man with four kids, who had either promised to divorce his wife and marry Celia, or hadn't promised. It doesn't matter. I don't think Celia herself knew that part of it. What she did know, she told me in a letter she wrote and mailed a few minutes before she jumped. She wanted to be sure I could never think she had loved me. Frank Prohst was the only man she loved. They'd been having an affair for years."

"Yes, I know that," Julie said. "I found that out the day the banks closed, when I saw her crying in Mr. Prohst's office."

"Did you also find out," Ben said, "that he wanted the money because they were planning to go off for an abortion that day? When that plan was spiked because Prohst was caught without the necessary cash on hand, Celia panicked. It was the last straw in a long series of disappointments, so when Celia came home that day, and she found me on her doorstep, fresh out of Oregon, she decided to use me as a front to save her honor and a club with which to pay back Mr. Prohst. She didn't mind wielding the club for a couple of weeks, while the preparations for the wedding went on, but at the last moment, in that Seattle hotel room, she finally faced the truth. Or rather, she finally couldn't face it. I told her we had to go to Washington for the wedding. I had her ticket in my pocket. She said, 'Go ahead, Ben, I'll meet you in Washington tomorrow,' and then she said—and I remember the words, Julie—she said, 'I can't go off like this, without explaining to my kid sister.'"

"Oh God," Julie said.

"We all have our moments of honesty, Julie," Ben said quietly. "Not all of us do anything about them. Celia did. I kept my mouth shut all these years because I was trying to spare you this last bitter truth about Celia." He paused, and with a helpless shrug, said, "And you knew it all the time."

"I didn't know everything, Ben," Julie said. "I didn't know about the ticket for Celia."

"Now that you know that," he said, "is there anything else you want to know?"

"Yes," Julie said, and she paused to take a deep breath. "Did you love Celia?"

The lines in the thin, handsome face rearranged themselves in an expression of bitterness. "Look me up after this war is over," Ben Ivey said savagely as he pulled open the door. "If we've won it, I'll have time to answer all the damn-fool questions you can think up."

391

A few minutes later, on the blacked-out sidewalk, as Julie was about to step into the car that looked like a taxi, Harry said, "This is for you, ma'am."

In the faint bluish glow from the dashboard, she could just barely make out his hands and the box he was holding toward her.

"For me?" Julie said stupidly, feeling the scuffed leather before she realized she had reached out for it. She drew her hands back quickly. "I don't want it," she said, and then, feeling the necessity for some explanation, she added, "He may need it again."

"Probably," Harry said, "but it won't do him any good." He paused, and then he, too, seemed to feel the same necessity. "It doesn't work when anybody else uses it," Harry said. "A few times these last three years I been with him, when he got these attacks, he told me how to do it and I tried." The faint bluish glow from the dashboard flickered across Harry's bald head as he shook it from side to side. "No dice," he said. "I guess it only works if you know the combination. That's why he sent for you."

Harry poked the box forward again.

"He's had it with him for years," Julie said. "Why does he want to get rid of it now?"

"He didn't tell me that," Harry said. "But I guess maybe, ma'am, you can figure out the answer for yourself."

By the time the car stopped in Old Quebec Street, Julie had: it was Ben Ivey's way of letting her know that he would never send for her again. Whatever it was he had for sixteen years wanted from the Sarnos, he had either got all he needed or Ben Ivey, who always stuck to the root of the matter, had accepted the fact that there was no more to be had.

Understanding that she was free at last, and puzzled by the fact that she did not know how to feel about her freedom, Julie found herself pawing about in her mind for the proper emotion, and almost at once she found what she was looking for: it was with a sense of relief, a feeling of coming home at last after a long, exhausting, and perilous journey, that Julie put her key in the lock of Mrs. Rangecroft's front door.

23

A major advantage of living in one of Mrs. Rangecroft's key flats —as the landlady made it a point to remind those of her tenants who occasionally let it be known that they thought thirteen pounds a month for a single room with a tuckaway kitchen came perilously close to war profiteering—was that people who by paying their rent earned the right to call Mrs. Rangecroft's house their home, could with strict accuracy also call it their castle.

"There's no prying here," the landlady had said to Julie Sarno and Rita Merlin when they moved in. "I accept as tenants only ladies and gentlemen, and once they have been accepted, I assume they will continue to act like ladies and gentlemen."

Luckily for Mrs. Rangecroft's assumption, by the time one of Rita's dates with General MacNeilson had run its course, the general was never in condition to see the plump companion of his revels to her front door. This task, like many others in the life of a noncom attached to a general officer, fell to Sergeant Danaher, a forty-seven-year-old grocer's clerk and father of four from Julie's old neighborhood, Bronx Park South, whom the fortunes of war had cast in the role of General MacNeilson's chauffeur.

Julie had often wondered how Sergeant Danaher felt about this particular task, since, by the time it became his duty to perform it, Rita Merlin was usually as loaded as her boy friend. When disposing of his chief after a wet night, the noncom's work rarely involved more than helping the general out of his car and across the sidewalk into the Wyndham lobby, where the hotel staff did the rest. More often than not, however, disposing of Rita meant carrying the drunken fat girl up three flights of Mrs. Rangecroft's steep stairs and then waiting until Julie, a sound sleeper, came awake to answer the sergeant's discreet knock, open the door, and take her roommate off his hands.

Julie was not surprised, therefore, on reaching the third landing, to find Sergeant Danaher standing in front of her door, supporting Rita with one arm and tapping gently on the jamb. What did surprise her, since Julie had known the noncom as long as she had known his chief, was what on this occasion the sight of Sergeant Danaher did to her: it shook her loose from the comfortable feeling she had so carefully chosen for herself downstairs on the sidewalk.

"Oh," Sergeant Danaher said as he turned to face her, and that was all he did say. The sight of Julie, who usually opened the door for him, coming up the stairs behind him, was apparently a shock to the noncom. He stared at Julie. She did the same to him, wondering what had happened to the pleasant feeling that, after a long, exhausting, and perilous journey, she had come home at last.

"I thought you were inside, Miss Sarno," the sergeant said.

"I'm sorry," Julie said. "I was detained by—" She allowed the explanation to trail away as she found her key and unlocked the door. "Would you mind—?"

"No, that's okay," Sergeant Danaher said, carrying the heavily breathing Rita across the threshold as Julie held the door wide. "She's okay," he said politely, as he always did when he brought Rita home. "Just a little sleepy, that's all."

He carried Rita to the half of the bisected studio couch from which Julie was taking the brown rep cover. "There," he said, straightening up. "I guess she'll be okay now."

"Yes, thanks," Julie said. "She'll be fine."

"I'll be saying good night, Miss Sarno."

"Good night," Julie said and then, as the sergeant tipped his forefinger to his garrison cap, she understood why the sight of him had shaken her loose from the comfortable feeling of having come home. She wasn't anywhere near home. The long journey that had begun sixteen years ago on East Ninth Street, and which until this moment she had believed had just ended in Ben Ivey's suite at Claridge's, had merely stopped dead at a fork in the road. Julie realized that she had taken the wrong fork. She ran after General MacNeilson's chauffeur, who had started down the stairs, and said sharply, "Sergeant Danaher."

The noncom stopped and turned and looked up at her. "Yes, ma'am?"

"You've got the general's car outside, haven't you?" The puzzled look on the sergeant's face told Julie to try again. "I mean, you'll be driving it back to the garage now, won't you?"

The puzzled look didn't change, but Sergeant Danaher did nod. "Yes, ma'am," he said.

"I wonder if you'd mind giving me a lift?"

"A lift?"

"Yes, I forgot something at—"

"A lift where?"

"To Claridge's," Julie said. "If it's not too far out of your way?"

Sergeant Danaher, who obviously must have had some interesting private opinions about General MacNeilson and the general's friends, even more obviously was aware that, by comparison with other soldiers, he was having himself a pretty good war. His common sense must have told him that, not only was it not his to reason why but, more important, it was not his to *ask* why. Not, that is, if he wanted to continue having himself a pretty good war.

"No, of course it's not too far," Sergeant Danaher said. "Matter of fact, Miss Sarno, I gotta go past Claridge's to get to the garage. Be glad to give you a lift."

"I'm in a hurry," Julie said. "It's very urgent. Do you think you could—?"

"I sure can," Sergeant Danaher said, and he did, so that less than half an hour after Harry had accompanied her across the Claridge lobby from the elevators to the front door, Julie was back in the same lobby, walking swiftly in the opposite direction, from the front door to the elevators. All the way across the blacked-out city in General MacNeilson's speeding car, Julie had been desperately making and remaking a calculation. Ben had told Colonel Uxbridge in her presence that he had fifteen minutes. But that was before Julie had taken some of those minutes away from him, and the discussion about the sheet of paper in the typewriter might easily on this occasion have increased the number of minutes Ben usually devoted to shaving, so Julie figured and prayed she might still be in time.

She was, but only just. As she approached the elevator, the door opened. Ben Ivey, flanked by Harry carrying two bags and Colonel Uxbridge carrying a bag and a suitcase, came out. They stopped short. So did Julie.

"Ben," she said. "I came back because—"

It was the last thing Julie said for several minutes. In a series of deft movements, not unlike hockey players closing in on the puck, Harry transferred one of his bags and Colonel Uxbridge his briefcase to Ben Ivey. The two hands thus freed now appeared, like the armrests of a dentist's chair, under Julie's elbows, and Colonel Uxbridge, in a pleasant, unhurried, but penetrating whisper, said in her ear, "If you utter a single syllable, it will be your last." Astonished by the contrast between what was clearly a threat and even more clearly the gentlemanly manner of its utterance, Julie was incapable of starting to say again the only thing she wanted to say, namely, why she had come back. By the time the power of speech returned to her, she had been whisked by the colonel and Harry out of the lobby, across the sidewalk, and into a car that was gone from the front of the hotel with the speed of a train scooping up mail sacks as it thundered without pause through a railroad station.

"Listen," she said. "I wasn't trying to—"

"My dear girl," Colonel Uxbridge said in a voice from which all the gentlemanly tones had vanished, "what the hell do you think you're doing?"

"I came back to—"

Her voice stopped. Ben Ivey, sitting up front beside the driver, had turned and slid back the glass panel.

"You think we made it?" he said.

396

Julie realized with annoyance that he was neither looking at nor addressing her.

"I'm certain we did," Colonel Uxbridge said.

The light from the dashboard was too faint for her to make out the expression on Ben's face, but Julie knew from the way he jerked his head to fling the cowlick away from his eyes that Ben was angry.

"God damn it," he said, and then, "We'd better take her along."

"I think so, Mr. Ivey," Colonel Uxbridge said.

Ben said something under his breath, slammed the glass panel back into place, and seemed to vanish. Moments later, when her eyes grew more accustomed to the way the shadows shifted as the blacked-out car raced through the night, the tires screaming pleasantly as the driver whipped around curves without bothering to slow down, Julie saw that Ben had dipped down on the front seat.

"You're going on a trip," Colonel Uxbridge said.

"Where?" Julie said.

"If you don't know better than to ask that, you don't know much," Colonel Uxbridge said. "What I want to know is what you thought you were doing a few minutes ago?"

"I came to warn you."

"I thought I had explained clearly in Mr. Ivey's suite that our presence in London is a military secret. If we wouldn't even take the risk of sending for a doctor when he was sick, what in the name of complicated idiocy would lead you to believe we'd stop for pleasant little gossipy chats in the lobby of a hotel while we're trying to get out of it without being recognized by—?" Colonel Uxbridge's voice stopped and then, just as sharply, he said, "Did you say warn?"

"Yes," Julie said.

"Me?"

"Not you personally," Julie said. "Nothing's going to happen to you." She turned toward the lump of shadow that was Harry on her left. "Or you, either."

"Talk English, miss," Harry said.

397

"Yes, do," Colonel Uxbridge said.

"I came back to warn you that something is going to happen to Mr. Ivey."

For a while the shadows on both sides of Julie neither moved nor emitted sounds.

"What's going to happen to Mr. Ivey?" the colonel said finally.

"I don't know," Julie said. "It may not happen to him. It may happen to this mission you're on, whatever it is. I don't know the details. I know only that something is going to happen. Something unexpected and something bad."

"Miss Sarno," Colonel Uxbridge said.

"I'm serious," she said. "I mean it."

"Mean *what* is what I'm asking."

Julie hesitated, listening to the hum of the tires and the beating of her heart, and all at once the hesitation seemed foolish. She had come back to warn Ben, but she had come back to warn a stranger. She and Ben were finished. Communications had been severed. Even if they were re-established, which she knew they were never again going to be, Ben would not listen to her. People were to him what carbon paper was to the girls in the BEW steno pool. He had gotten as many copies, so to speak, out of the Sarno family as they could provide. Only a fool would be sentimental about chucking the worn piece of paper into the wastebasket, and Benjamin Franklin Ivey, no matter what else he might be, was no fool.

"If you won't tell me where we're going," Julie said to the bulked shadow on her right, "could you tell me how long it will take us to get there?"

There was a pause, and then Colonel Uxbridge said, "It will take us long enough for you to tell me—" His voice stopped, the shadow on Julie's right moved slightly, and the voice said, "—to tell both of us, since Harry is on your left, why we shouldn't have you clapped into jail or shot at sunrise, both of which fates I don't mind telling you I think you have earned by what you have just done. Now will you please talk sense? This is not a laughing matter, Miss Sarno. You have jeopardized a mission that—"

"Oh, shut *up!*" Julie said. "I've come back to warn you, and all

398

you can do is talk like a damned old—" It was her turn to pause. "I'm sorry," she said, finally. "Please forgive me and listen, Colonel Uxbridge."

"I will listen," he said.

Slowly and then, as the wheels of memory began to turn, more quickly, Julie told him. Not everything. There were some things, like the moment in front of the Small Mammals House on the day the banks closed, that would never be anybody's business but her own. But she omitted nothing she considered important to the colonel's business. She told him how Ben Ivey had first come into her life and how, on an autumn night on East Ninth Street, he had first gone out of it. She told him about the journey with Celia to Oregon and she told him how it had ended.

"On East Ninth Street he collapsed when he learned he was facing a showdown with Mr. Tyler Crispin over who was going to run the Clarke House," Julie said. "In Seattle he collapsed when he learned he was facing not a pleasant breakfast with the Secretary of the Interior, but a showdown with Arnold Brahmin in front of the Secretary because he had tried to take over the Mercerville Project. Yesterday, here in England, he collapsed again. I don't know what he's facing, and apparently you don't either, but—"

"I know now," Colonel Uxbridge said. "He told me the nature of our mission a few minutes ago, in his bathroom at Claridge's, while he was shaving."

"Is it a dangerous mission?"

"It is an important one. Much more important than I imagined."

"I don't mean that," Julie said.

"If you mean does the mission involve any risk to Mr. Ivey—?"

"That's exactly what I mean."

"The answer is no."

Julie said, "Not even physical risk?"

"The answer is still no."

Julie turned to the bulked shadow on her right. "Is that the truth?" she said.

"Why would I possibly lie to you?"

"For security reasons."

"While you were outside our security pattern, perhaps. I might lie to you to keep you outside. But now you're inside the pattern. You have no business inside it, but you're here and we're going to keep you inside it until the mission is accomplished. Aside from the nature of the mission itself, which is none of your business—"

"It might be."

"No."

"How can you be sure?"

"I just told you I now know the nature of Mr. Ivey's mission," Colonel Uxbridge said. "You can't possibly have anything to do with it."

"Suppose Ben Ivey had told you the nature of the mission two days ago, before you left Washington? Would you have said then that a girl member of the steno pool in the BEW's London office couldn't possibly have anything to do with it?"

"I certainly would."

"You'd have been wrong," Julie said. "Because I've already had a lot to do with it, and you could be wrong again, Colonel Uxbridge."

"Not about the question of personal danger to Mr. Ivey or anybody else involved in the mission. There is absolutely no risk of that."

The sound of a throat being cleared emerged from the shadow on Julie's left.

"You mind I stick my two cents in?" Harry said.

"Of course not," Colonel Uxbridge said.

"I been thinking over what the young lady here, Miss Sarno, what she said. The years she knew Mr. Ivey, two times he had these things, whatever they are, he collapsed. Both times she says he was facing some kind of big deal, that's why now, this third time, here in England, when he collapsed, she figured it was the same thing, some big deal he's facing. The three years I been with Mr. Ivey, the times he's had these things, now I'm thinking back on it, the same thing like Miss Sarno said, it was always just before some big deal. Like the one I remember best, two years

400

ago, right after Pearl Harbor, when the Boss sent those men, that commission, they should find out exactly how bad the Japs hit us, and three nights before the Boss went on the air to give the report to the people, he told Mr. Ivey to fly to Pearl for a personal check, just to make sure the guys on the commission they hadn't fumbled anything.

"I was with Mr. Ivey when he got the call to go, and when this thing hit him, I thought first maybe it was the long plane trip, onna konniv he always hated flying, but it couldn't be that, he flies all the time. I don't know what it was because by the time it came to go to the airport, he was okay, and I'm only mentioning it now because I see how this young lady, Miss Sarno, she could be worried, but if she thinks about it a minute, like I just been doing, those two times she saw it happen, with that settlement-house thing on the East Side, and then out in Oregon, both those times there wasn't any danger up ahead.

"The way I understand that Crispin deal, the worst that could have happened at the showdown, Mr. Ivey might have been canned out of his job in that settlement house, and the other time in Oregon, the worst that could have happened, say he'd faced this Brahmin boy over the Secretary of the Interior's bacon and eggs, what's the worst could have happened? Mr. Ivey'd've been bounced off the project. I mean there was no danger, no *physical* danger, just like Colonel Uxbridge says now."

Harry's voice stopped, and Julie sat there in the swaying car, wondering what was wrong with what Harry had just said. Perhaps Colonel Uxbridge was wondering about the same thing, because he broke the silence with a small exhalation of surprise, as though his thoughts had taken a turn so unexpected that they had startled him.

"Miss Sarno?"

"Yes?"

"A couple of hours ago, when I pleaded with you to help Mr. Ivey, you refused, and I gathered from your refusal that Mr. Ivey had done something in the past to make you feel that his fate is no concern of yours, that whatever happened to him would be a matter of indifference to you. And yet, less than half an hour after you left Mr. Ivey's suite, you came hurrying back to warn him about some danger that you believe is threatening him. What happened to make you change your mind?"

Julie, who had been asking herself the same question, put to the test the only answer that came to her: if she had known on the day of Celia's death what Ben Ivey had just told her tonight, would her feelings toward Ben have been any different during the past ten years? Was the basis of her feelings the fact that during all those years she had believed him responsible for Celia's death? Or was there something more?

"I don't know," Julie said slowly. "Mr. Ivey told me something tonight that I'd never known before. A piece of information about someone we both knew a long time ago. It cleared something up for me, but I don't think that's the reason I came back to warn him. The reason I came back, why I came back to warn him—" Julie paused, shook her head in the dark, then said, "I don't know."

She almost added the larger truth: I don't know what's happening to me.

"I think I know the cause of your difficulty," Colonel Uxbridge said.

Julie turned toward him, realized he could not in the dark see the expression on her face, and said, "I certainly wish you'd tell me."

"You've been thinking of Mr. Ivey as a normal human being."

"Isn't he?"

"I doubt it."

"Hey, now, wait a minute," Harry said.

"Relax," Colonel Uxbridge said. "I don't mean what you think I mean."

"I should hope not," Harry said and, perhaps because even he thought he had sounded too tough, he added, "Sir."

"What *do* you mean?" Julie said.

"Mr. Ivey is not like the average run of humanity any more than Caesar was, or Napoleon, or, if you will, yes, Moses and Jesus. They were all highly successful leaders. That made them dif-

402

ferent from their fellows. Mr. Ivey is a leader. That makes him different from you and me."

"In what way?"

"To be a successful leader of other human beings," Colonel Uxbridge said, "a man must be to some extent inhuman."

The car stopped. The glass panel in front of Julie slid back.

"Colonel," Ben Ivey said.

"Yes, Mr. Ivey?"

"Come out a minute, please."

Ben got out in front, and Colonel Uxbridge opened the rear door and got out behind him, and then both bulked shadows vanished in the deeper darkness of the night. They did not go very far, because Julie could hear their voices in a low, hurried, murmuring conference, Ben's quick resonant syllables cutting across the colonel's lower, slower tones, while Julie's mind worked its way cautiously around the statement the colonel had made just before the car stopped. Suddenly she was reminded of Vic DeGenero in Oregon talking about Ben the night she'd heard Ben's words from Arnold Brahmin's throat. *"Sui generis,"* Vic had said. "Unique. Peculiar. One of a kind." Both Vic and the colonel were good men, Julie thought, and yet what they had said about Ben made her uneasy.

Something in her nature, a touch of prudishness inherited from her mother, perhaps, rebelled against the simple explanation. It was like being told she had no right to think ill of, say, a forger because he was suffering from a terminal disease and, in the few months or weeks of life he had left, surely he should be excused for signing a few checks with names not his own. Julie could sympathize with the forger's plight, but she could not help wishing he had chosen a more useful way to spend his last days on earth. She had been told long ago, by Ben Ivey himself, that the leader of men was someone set apart from other men, but Julie could not help feeling that the argument would carry more conviction if the result of its author's leadership was as tangibly visible and useful to those being led as it was to the self-styled leader.

"Miss Sarno?"

403

Colonel Uxbridge had appeared beside the rear door of the car. "Yes?" Julie said.

"Would you step out here a moment? You, too, Harry."

Julie climbed out of the car and, as Colonel Uxbridge took her arm, Harry came out behind her. Colonel Uxbridge led her a short distance into the darkness and stopped near a high, soaring mound of shadow which, after a moment, Julie identified from the smell as a clump of lilac.

"All right, now, listen," Ben's voice said out of the darkness. "You particularly, Julie. Colonel Uxbridge assures me no damage has been done thus far by your quixotic return to Claridge's—and why you did it doesn't matter now. I am not in danger. None of us is. The only thing that might be in danger as a result of your being with us is the mission I'm on. The people I've come to see were told I'd arrive with a staff of three: a driver, an interpreter, and a valet. I am now arriving with a staff of four. I don't want the people I've come to see to think this in the least suspicious. I don't know that they will, but I can't take any chances. Colonel Uxbridge has, therefore, worked out this deal. Harry will put a small bandage on my right hand. Our story is that in getting out of the car yesterday in London, the rear door slammed on my hand in the blackout. Nothing serious. I'm okay. But I can't handle a pencil to take my own notes, as I usually do at conferences, and as these birds we've come to see know I do. So I've had to bring along a secretary to take notes for me. Understand?"

"Yes," Julie said into the darkness.

"You'll stay with me throughout the whole deal," Ben said. "You'll act as though you're taking notes and you'll keep your mouth shut no matter what you hear or see. If you open your trap—"

"I won't," Julie said. And suddenly she had a hysterical impulse to laugh. Why, he was enjoying this absurd conspiracy. Like a small boy.

"Then we should be finished in an hour, maybe less," Ben said, "and back in London before daybreak. Okay, Harry, let's get back to the car and see how good you are at putting on a bandage in the dark."

He must have been extremely good because, by the phosphorescent dial of Julie's wrist watch, the car was again on the move four minutes after the conference near the lilacs ended. Four minutes after that, two things happened simultaneously: the driver slowed down and there was a sudden break in the overcast. The full moon, emerging abruptly, like the house lights coming on in a darkened theatre, was startling. At least to Julie, who blinked as the driver turned the car from what she now saw was the pebbled road along which they had been running into a narrow driveway. Thirty or forty feet down the driveway the car stopped in front of a wooden gate. Colonel Uxbridge wound down the window beside him.

"Your brown shoes are ready," he said into the clear silvery white night in a clear precise voice. Julie remembered the instructions Ben had given him in the bedroom at Claridge's after she had brought Ben back to consciousness: *Call Sloane four-seven-seven-three and say your brown shoes are ready.*

From somewhere behind the thick shrubbery on the left side of the driveway came a figure in a beret wearing the lumpy, horse-blankets-cut-to-look-like-clothing of British battle dress. Without a word the figure unlocked the wooden gate and held it wide until the car rolled through. It rolled on along the winding driveway to a break in the overhanging tightly packed shrubbery. Up ahead, silhouetted against a background of tall, closely planted trees, black in the bright moonlight, loomed an old stone house.

It was three stories high, with a massive doorway and small, deeply set windows: a square, solid, ugly bulk that Julie guessed must have been built a long time ago: it reminded her of *Wuthering Heights* and *Jane Eyre*. The layer of brown stucco, obviously added to the stone walls by a later owner in whom the Brontë sisters and their problems had apparently stirred no feeling of reverence, was flaking away in ragged splotches. Here and there, like gaps in an old man's grin, tiles were missing from the roof.

The car sped down the driveway, pulling toward Julie and then obliterating from her view completely the outlines of the stone house. The car stopped in front of the huge doorway. As she climbed out behind Colonel Uxbridge, Julie saw that the house

405

stood in an untended but impressive formal garden that sloped gently down to a stream. The front door opened and, in the bright moonlight, Julie saw framed in the doorway two people: a heavy-set man in the uniform of a British army officer and a girl in a gray tweed suit.

"Wait, please," Colonel Uxbridge said across his shoulder to the driver, who, Julie saw for the first time since they had left London, was British.

"Yes, sir," the driver said.

Julie moved along with Ben Ivey, Colonel Uxbridge, and Harry toward the two people in the doorway.

"Good evening," the British officer said, and then, "Oh, there are four of you."

"Yes, I'm sorry," Colonel Uxbridge said. "We had a slight accident in London at the last moment." He pointed to the bandage on Ben Ivey's hand. "There was no time to send word, but fortunately just enough time to round up a secretary." He nodded toward Julie. "In all other respects, no change at all."

The man in the doorway seemed to hesitate, or perhaps it was only Julie's imagination. In any case, it did not last long.

"I'm MacGavin," the man in the doorway said. "This is my adjutant, Miss Peall. Won't you come in?"

He turned and held the door wide. Ben stepped in and Colonel Uxbridge gave Julie a short nod. The polite movement, which did not for a moment disguise the fact that the courtly gesture was an order, indicated that Julie was to go next. She did, and as she followed Ben into the hall, she glanced up at MacGavin, who wore on his shoulders the single crown of a major, and at Miss Peall, who wore on her face the characterless expression of a mannekin. Her gray suit was noticeably frayed, as was most civilian garb in a country where clothes coupons were as scarce as ice cubes, but Julie noticed at once what any girl would have noticed, especially a girl born in poverty and raised with a sister who had taught her early, always in specific terms of quality and price, what was wrong with being poor: Miss Peall's gray suit, when new, must have cost as much as all the furnishings in Biaggio Sarno's barber shop.

"This way, please," Miss Peall said.

"I suppose you'll want your, uh, this chap"—Major MacGavin nodded toward Harry as he addressed Colonel Uxbridge—"to wait out here. Miss Peall will arrange for him to have a cup of tea."

Julie, who had passed the two people in the doorway, turned back and saw what had happened. Major MacGavin had assumed that the white-haired man with the silver eagles on his shoulders was the leader of the group of visitors. The fact that Major Mac-Gavin could make this mistake revealed to Julie that the Englishman probably knew very little more than she did about Ben Ivey's mission. What it revealed about Ben Ivey clearly took his host by surprise.

"I do not carry excess baggage," Ben said. "If any members of my staff were extraneous, Major, I would have left them behind. Where am I going to work?"

Major MacGavin flushed. "The Common Room would be best, I think," he said. The fact that he did not apologize for having assumed Colonel Uxbridge rather than Ben was the leader of the group was, as the major obviously intended it to be, as insulting as an epithet. But it was completely lost on Ben, whose mind had already moved on. Major MacGavin stepped across the hall to a high mahogany door and said, "This way."

Julie followed him and the others into what she guessed, from remembered illustrations in her school copy of *Martin Chuzzlewit*, must once have been a stately Victorian drawing room. However, only the dimensions, the tall French windows hidden by blackout curtains, and the enormous fireplace remained as signatures of former grandeur. A good deal of conversion had taken place.

A large school blackboard hung on one wall. On the others were pinned colored maps, caricatures of Winston Churchill, Franklin Roosevelt, and Charles de Gaulle, and a great many newspaper clippings. The rest of the wall space was lined with cheap golden-oak bookcases and a massive sideboard on which stood several bottles and a couple of dozen cheap glasses. Under the sideboard, a low wooden platform supported a beer keg with a spigot. In spite of the beer keg and the bottles and the glasses, Julie was

407

reminded of the room in the Horace Judson Clarke House in which the Nature Club used to meet. Perhaps Ben Ivey was struck by the same recollection. Julie couldn't be sure, but it seemed to her that, as he crossed the threshold, his quick steps faltered for a moment and Ben looked around in surprise, as though he had expected something entirely different.

"I trust this is all right," Major MacGavin said.

"Yes, yes," Ben said impatiently. "Let's get going."

Major MacGavin flushed again. "I have sent Miss Peall to fetch him," he said.

There was a tap on the door, which opened at once, before anybody in the room could speak. Miss Peall came in with a tall young man. He stopped just inside the door and waited. Miss Peall looked at Major MacGavin. The major looked at Ben.

"Okay, Major," Ben said. "That will be all for the time being."

Major MacGavin's head came down in a nod like the blade of a guillotine dropping. "If there is anything more we can do—?"

"I'll let you know," Ben said.

The major nodded again and went out with Miss Peall. Ben, Colonel Uxbridge, Harry, and Julie stared at the young man standing silently near the door.

There was something familiar and disturbing about him. Julie wondered if it could be his clothes: he was wearing khaki army pants, a khaki army shirt open at the throat, heavy army shoes, and a beautifully cut hound's-tooth sports jacket. It was an odd combination but, Julie decided, hardly disturbing and certainly not familiar.

He stood with his hands clasped behind him, his long, handsome head tipped slightly to one side, a strand of the long black hair fallen forward over the high, white forehead. Julie had just about decided that what was disturbing was the look of shyness on a face that somehow seemed constructed by nature for almost every emotion but shyness, when she realized why the young man looked familiar.

He reminded her of the pictures of Lindbergh that had filled the papers when she lived on East Ninth Street, the pictures taken during the weeks when he was camping out on Long Island, preparing for the flight that was still no more than a kid's crazy dream and he was known to the press as the Flying Fool. Julie remembered the funny windbreaker he always wore in those pictures, and the way he sagged in a slight, embarrassed, leaning crouch as though he didn't want the photographers to feel his height was an insult to their shorter stature, and the way he always stood with his hands clasped behind his back, but what Julie remembered most clearly was the way those pictures used to make her feel, as though the young man in them was helpless and in trouble and it was important for her to drop everything and rush to his assistance. She remembered the feeling now as the tall young man near the door regarded them in passive silence.

Ben Ivey broke it. "Your Majesty," he said.

Even Colonel Uxbridge, Julie noticed, seemed to move in a startled jerk. She looked hastily from the young man to Ben and then back to the young man. He had neither moved nor acknowledged the, to Julie, astonishing two words.

"I bring you greetings from the President of the United States," Ben said. "He trusts you are in good health and hopes your exile will soon end and you will soon be restored to your throne and be living happily again among your own people. We are bending every effort to achieve this result as quickly as possible. That is why the President has sent me here to talk with you."

Ben paused. Colonel Uxbridge began to translate slowly and clearly, speaking a language Julie did not know but assumed, from what the colonel had told her earlier in the evening, was Scandinavian. As the colonel spoke, Julie stared at the tall, slender, appealing young man near the door.

She had been trying for almost an hour to figure out what was happening to her. The last thing she had understood clearly was the emotion that had drawn her back from her home on Old Quebec Street to Claridge's: she had come to save Ben. Julie did not know from what. She did not know why she should be interested in saving Ben. This lack of knowledge had not, however, mattered. Not until Colonel Uxbridge and Harry had assured her in the speeding car that Ben was in no danger. Then the gaps in Julie's knowledge began to matter enormously.

If Ben was in no danger, what had she come to save him from? The conviction that he had to be saved, and that she was the only one who could do it, had been intensified rather than diminished by Colonel Uxbridge's and Harry's assurances. Julie had found this confusing. Now her confusion had been complicated by the young man standing silently near the door.

Kings were a class of people about whom Julie had never done much thinking. Now that she was forced to think about them, Julie realized that her thoughts bogged down on the apple-cheeked, ermine-clad nursery-rhyme figure who, while the queen was in the parlor eating bread and honey, had himself been in the counting house counting out his money. The image was no help. It bore no relation to this attractive, solemn, shy, disturbing young man in dirty army pants and an expensive sports jacket.

Julie did not doubt he was a king. Ben Ivey was never wrong about factual matters. What Julie suddenly doubted was her sanity. How had she, the daughter of a penniless Neapolitan immigrant barber from East Ninth Street, arrived in the drawing room of a Victorian mansion somewhere in the English countryside to share this astonishing moment with an exiled monarch?

Julie turned from the young man near the door to the man whose path, touching and crossing hers again and again for sixteen of the twenty-seven years of her life, had led her here. Ben was scowling slightly as he waited for Colonel Uxbridge to finish the translation.

When he did, Ben said to the colonel, "Shall I suggest he sit down?"

"I don't think so," Colonel Uxbridge said. "Not that he'd mind. There's a war on, and he's in exile, living in another land as the guest of a foreign government, so protocol can be dispensed with."

"I know that," Ben said irritably. "It's just he looks so damned uncomfortable standing there."

"I think he'd be more uncomfortable if you suggested he sit down," Colonel Uxbridge said. "The rest of us would have to remain standing, you see. This way, if we all stand—"

"Okay, okay," Ben said. "Let's get to the root of the matter. Tell him the following." Ben turned back to the young man and said, "The President has instructed me to tell you that the Allies are about to open our second front, to re-invade Europe and drive the Germans out of all the countries they have criminally seized, including yours. The exact date is under discussion at this very moment. The President wants you to know that it will be set as soon as I return to Washington from this conference with you. The exact moment depends on the decision as to where we will make our landings. The decision about where we will land depends largely on the results of this conference I am having with you."

Ben paused and glanced at Colonel Uxbridge, who began at once, in the same clear, precise voice, to translate Ben Ivey's words. As the colonel spoke in the language Julie did not understand, she watched the young man near the door. He remained motionless, his face impassive, his hands clasped behind him, apparently listening intently.

"All right," Ben said when Colonel Uxbridge finished. "Now tell him this." Ben turned back to the tall young man. "The President feels that the greatest advantage of your country as the landing place is that it is probably the last one the Germans think we will try. It means a longer open-water crossing, which increases the risk of loss by air and other attack, but for that very reason the Germans have not bothered to fortify your coastline as thoroughly and heavily as they have fortified the French and Dutch coasts. As of this moment, the President strongly favors landing on your coast. He knows this is what you would want. It would, of course, mean that your people would be the first to be freed from the German oppressor, and you would be the first ruler exiled by the Germans to return to his native land." Ben turned to Colonel Uxbridge and said, "Tell him that."

Colonel Uxbridge did so.

"Now, then," Ben said to the young man when Colonel Uxbridge had finished. "Before the President makes his decision, and before he attempts to urge his decision on Mr. Churchill and the other Allied war leaders, the President must know if the people living in the coastal areas of your country would be receptive to an Allied landing. It is not a question of patriotism. It is a question of simple survival. The President knows that your people want the Germans thrown out. What the President does not know, what he has sent me here to find out, is whether the people who live along the coast of your country, the people who must bear the brunt of the initial attack by us and the brunt of the initial German fury at being attacked by us, whether these people will co-operate with our men or, out of terror or the simple desire to remain alive, will co-operate with the Germans. If we can get this co-operation from your people who live in the coastal areas of your country, the President feels the success of the landings is assured, because he believes the German people are sick of the war and ready to quit, and the news that the Allies are back on European soil via Your Majesty's country will cause the Germans to throw down their arms. The President has asked me to give you his ideas about the German situation, and he felt the best way to do that was for him to personalize it for you in a sort of inner monologue or soliloquy that in the President's opinion is typical of the way the average German is thinking today." Ben turned to Colonel Uxbridge and said, "Tell him all that before I read him the soliloquy."

While Colonel Uxbridge translated Ben's words, Ben pulled from his pocket and studied the sheet of paper that Julie had first seen and read a couple of hours ago while it was rolled into the portable typewriter on the table in the sitting room of Ben's suite at Claridge's.

"Ready?" Ben said when the colonel finished. The latter nodded, and Ben, turning to face the young man, read aloud from the paper: " 'Soliloquy of Reformation. The Ideal German, late 1943. I am suffering now. I do not have enough to eat. The rooms where I live are inadequate. I grieve for members of my family who were killed in the war. I have few opportunities to relax. I suffer because of the Nazis. They drove my country into—' "

As she listened to the resonant voice rise and fall, pause for

Colonel Uxbridge's translation, then begin to rise and fall again, Julie was reminded of the night when Ben Ivey told the members of the Nature Club why it had become necessary for him to abandon his role as their leader and turn the club over to the direction of Celia Sarno. Julie remembered the way her eyes had misted when Mr. Ivey said, *"Come forth into the light of things, let nature be your teacher,"* and she remembered the way she thought her swelling heart would burst and her brimming eyes would overflow and the lump in her throat would explode in a shameful cascade of noisy sobs. Feeling herself moved again by the voice that had never failed to penetrate the most guarded corners of her heart, Julie turned toward the young man near the door, wondering about its effect on a king.

The young man, she saw, had not moved, nor had the expression on his face changed.

"Now that he knows how the President believes the average German feels today," Ben said to Colonel Uxbridge when the latter had finished the last section of the translation, "I want you to tell him this." Ben turned back to the young man. "We know quite a lot about conditions in the coastal areas of Your Majesty's country. But the President does not feel we know enough. Not enough, at any rate, to make him feel completely easy in his mind about urging his plan on Mr. Churchill and the other war leaders. The only man who can find out enough to satisfy him, the President feels, is Your Majesty. He has sent me here, therefore, to ask you to perform a service not only for your own people, but for the entire Allied cause—cross the channel tonight, land on your own soil, make contact with underground leaders who have been alerted to your coming, and bring back the information the President wants. The necessary lift is ready and waiting. We can put you ashore while it is still dark. We have the assurance of your underground that the margin of safety for a brief period is sufficiently high to justify the risk, of which we are all aware. And, of course, speed is the essence of the entire operation. We estimate that in twenty-four hours, at worst forty-eight, we will take you off. I will meet you here and you can give me the information to carry back to the President in Washington." Ben paused and then said, "Will Your Majesty agree to do this for us and for your country?"

Before Colonel Uxbridge could open his mouth to begin the translation, the young man opened his.

"I am afraid there has been some mistake," he said in slightly accented but excellent English. "I am a Polish schoolmaster named Michal Waslewska."

He turned, pulled open the door, and walked out.

24

Ben reached the door as it slammed in his face.

"The stupid bastards," he said. "They've sent me the wrong guy."

"Mr. Ivey!"

Ben turned, his hand on the knob. From the other side of the room Julie could see it happening: the remembered faces from the two barber-shop calendars merging in the living face before her.

"What?" Ben snapped.

Colonel Uxbridge took a step forward. "No, they haven't," he said. He nodded toward the closed door. "That's the king all right."

Ben stabbed his hand up through his yellow hair in a gesture of annoyance. "You heard what he said."

"He's lying," Colonel Uxbridge said.

"Why the hell should he do that?"

"Don't know, Mr. Ivey, but he's the king. I'm sure of it."

"How do you know?"

"He looks exactly like his father. I knew the old king very well in the days when I was a kid there. He rode horseback every morning down the main street from the palace to the Rose Park. We all used to stop and watch. I know the old king's face as well as I know my own. This boy is the son. There couldn't be any mistake about that."

Ben said, "Harry."

"Yes, sir?"

"Get that son of a bitch in here, whatever his name is. The major."

"MacGavin."

"That's right," Ben said, pulling open the door. "Get him in here."

"Yes, sir."

Harry went out and Ben shoved the door shut as though flinging away something distasteful. The bang caused the glasses on the sideboard to tinkle. He paced toward the blackboard, head down, scowling at his toes, running one hand through his hair. Julie, becoming aware of a pain in her chest, realized she had been holding her breath. The feeling that Ben was in danger, that she had to do something to save him, had suddenly become unbearable. The door opened. Harry came in followed by Major MacGavin and Miss Peall. Ben whipped around.

"What are you doing here?" he said.

Major MacGavin made a short rolling backward movement with his head. It reminded Julie of a horse rearing.

"Your man"—the major nodded toward Harry—"this chap said you wanted—"

"Not you," Ben said. "You." He flicked his chin toward Miss Peall. "I asked for Major MacGavin," Ben said. "When I want you, Miss Beal—"

"Peall," she said.

"—I'll send for you," Ben said. "At the moment, I don't."

Miss Peall tossed a glance at Major MacGavin.

"Look here," he said angrily. "There's no need—"

"Let's *drop* this," Ben said. "There's no time for manners."

My God, Julie thought, he's got beyond being scared by the Tyler Crispins and the Arnold Brahmins.

"Okay, young lady," Ben said to Miss Peall. "You go back to studying *Burke's Peerage* until I holler." She stepped out backwards. Harry closed the door on her and leaned against the polished wood. Ben said, "Major, who is that kid we were just talking to in here?"

"One of our students."

"Students?" Ben said. "You mean this is a school?"

"Of course it is."

"What kind of school?"

"Irregular warfare."

"Where do you get your students?"

"From the War Office."

"Where does the War Office get them?"

Major MacGavin hesitated.

"Look," Ben said. "You know who I am. You know what London told you about receiving me here. It now turns out you also happen to know certain things I don't. I can find them out easily enough in London. But that will take a little time and I have absolutely no time to waste. I can also find them out by asking you. If you have any reluctance about telling me, I can overcome that reluctance by using your phone, calling London, and having somebody at the War Office talk to you. Now, do you want me to make that phone call to London, or do you want to start talking?"

Major MacGavin licked his lips for a long time, doing a thorough job, like a little boy who has just finished a particularly gooey lollipop. Julie didn't blame him. She, too, felt overpowered.

"What would you like to know?" the major said finally.

"Where does the War Office get these men they send you here as students?"

"They come from all over Occupied Europe. Nobody really knows how they get out. I mean there are no general rules or avenues. Each man gets out in his own way. All we really know is that they want to go back to fight Nazis. All they know is that we can teach them how. They are funneled into a training program that consists of a chain of secret schools in various parts of the country. They're taught everything from the use of small arms to parachute jumping and, of course, they're put in excellent physical shape, and they're observed carefully to make sure they're capable of going back to the continent on a mission. My shop here is the end of the line. By the time they reach me, they're ready for their missions. They stay with me for approximately two weeks, during which they do some final brushing up on a variety of items that pertain to their particular missions. But most important, it is here that they receive the details of their missions. Until they reach me, they don't really know what they're going to do when they're parachuted back into France or Norway or Belgium or wherever they've come from. Here they find out—and, as I said, for two weeks they study, each with a special instructor—what they are being sent back to do. The missions can be anything from going in for a matter of hours or even less to dynamite, let us say, a bridge or a rail junction, or it may mean going in to establish an underground newspaper and remain for the duration. Whether they come back alive or remain alive for the duration depends largely on what we teach them here. We try to manage things in such a way that they remain alive. All things considered, it's much more satisfactory."

Major MacGavin paused and Julie noticed that Ben's feelings toward the man in khaki had undergone a change. She understood for the first time the importance of Ben's passion for sticking to the root of the matter. On innumerable occasions it must have led him to moments of discovery like this one: it was obviously not because of his connections that Major MacGavin had been placed in charge of this operation.

"Colonel Uxbridge," Ben said.

The colonel came forward. "Yes?"

"Call London." Ben turned to Major MacGavin. "Where's your direct wire?"

"In my office," the major said. "Second door down the hall on your right. The direct wire has the lock across the hand piece." He pulled a key from his pocket. "This key opens the lock." Major MacGavin bowed slightly and, with a short glance at Ben, said dryly to the white-haired man from Washington, "You have my permission to use it, Colonel."

"Thank you," Colonel Uxbridge said, doing the same thing with his eyes as he took the key. Even Julie grasped what was happening: the two men in uniform, though their allegiances were different, shared at least one basic certainty: circumstances might place them temporarily under the orders of a civilian, but nothing could ever change the conviction that theirs was the superior caste. Colonel Uxbridge left the room.

"How does the young man to whom we were just talking fit into your shop?" Ben said to Major MacGavin.

"He doesn't," the major said.

"Could you explain that?"

"Michal Waslewska came to us not two weeks ago, but almost three months ago."

"That's unusual, isn't it?"

"Very."

"Any other unusual aspects?"

"Many," Major MacGavin said. "No mission assignment came with him. My instructions from London were to receive one Polish schoolmaster or ex-schoolmaster named Michal Waslewska and put him up as a student until further instructions."

"Were there any further instructions?"

"Not until three days ago."

"What happened then?"

"I was summoned to London and told in a classified meeting that on Wednesday night, that's tonight, an American gentleman of whom I had undoubtedly heard, that's you, would arrive by car with a staff of three for a conference with our star boarder, as we have come to think of Waslewska, since he has been here, as I said, almost three months. I was told to convey this information to Waslewska, which I did as soon as I got back here three days ago, and I was told to prepare for your arrival, which I also did."

"Do you have any idea about Waslewska's true identity?"

"None whatsoever."

"Is that the truth?"

"I have forced myself during the past three years to make it the truth. If I allowed myself to speculate about the true identity of the students who pass through my shop, I would almost certainly have very little time to get on with my work and quite possibly I might go dotty."

"Is there anything else you want to tell me about Waslewska?"

"No."

"Is there anything else you *can* tell me about him?"

"Yes."

"What?"

"He's a damned unnecessary piece of work to have hanging about, and if the result of your conference with him should be that he left these premises tonight, I would be so pleased that I might even forgive you for your rudeness to me and my adjutant a few minutes ago."

"Was I rude?" Ben said.

"Your words and conduct would be so described by almost any person of breeding on this sceptered isle."

"I wasn't aware of my words or my conduct," Ben said. "I was working." The lean face broke in the smile that so many years ago had melted even that angry man, Biaggio Sarno. Just as suddenly it was gone, and without waiting for a reply, Ben continued: "When you came back from London three days ago and told Waslewska the name of the man who was coming to see him tonight, what was his reaction?"

"He got drunk."

Ben said sharply, "He got *what?*"

"Drunk," Major MacGavin said. He gestured toward the bottles and glasses on the sideboard and the beer keg under it. "It's always available for the men who pass through here. They can have as much as they want whenever they want it. We don't object or even comment, but we do observe. If a man is unable to handle spirits he will probably be unable to handle certain missions. We've canceled a few because the men who seemed otherwise capable proved in this respect to be incapable."

"Would you cancel Waslewska's mission on that ground?" Ben said.

419

"He has no mission. He's just a body lying about, apparently waiting for something or somebody."

The door opened and Colonel Uxbridge came in. Something in the glance he exchanged with Ben had a meaning that Julie missed. She saw nothing that should have caused Ben to say to Major MacGavin, "Would you mind stepping out of this room for a moment?"

"I do mind," Major MacGavin said. "But my instructions were to obey your orders, and if that's an order—"

"It is," Ben said.

Major MacGavin went out, and Colonel Uxbridge closed the door.

"I was right," the colonel said. "Waslewska is the king's cover name and the Polish schoolmaster thing is his cover story. He arrived in England a little short of a year ago. The Germans were not particularly anxious to advertise the fact that he'd got out from under their noses, and British intelligence had a hunch that he might be useful at some later date, so both kept quiet about the escape, and the public's never been told that he's in this country. To keep him under wraps, the War Office has sent him from school to school in their irregular-warfare network, keeping him at each place for a few months and then moving him on. It's possible he would have been completely forgotten if the President hadn't come up with his country as a possible spot for the invasion of the continent and assigned you to contact him."

"Then he is authentic?" Ben said.

"Absolutely," Colonel Uxbridge said.

"Which means the root of the matter is why the hell would the stupid bastard think he can get away with a kid's trick like telling me he's a Polish schoolmaster?"

"That's easy," Julie said.

They all turned toward her, Harry and Colonel Uxbridge and Ben. She had a moment of embarrassment, or rather the recollection of other moments of embarrassment, but it vanished at once. She did not feel embarrassed. Julie felt something so new that she had no name for it. She knew at last the danger that was

420

threatening Ben, and she knew what she had to do to save him.

"You know why that boy out there pretended he's a Polish schoolmaster?" Ben said incredulously.

Julie nodded. "Yes," she said. "He's scared."

"He didn't look scared to me," Ben said.

"It isn't the way a man looks that counts," Julie said. "I learned that a long time ago. In a barber shop on East Ninth Street."

Ben's eyes, fixed on hers, suddenly seemed to dissolve. He dropped his glance, turned, and walked across to the wall on which the newspaper clippings and maps were thumbtacked. For several moments, as his thin shoulders moved up and down, Julie had the terrified feeling that Ben was sobbing. Then he moved slightly, and her angle of vision changed, and she saw what was causing his shoulders to shake: Ben had removed one of the thumbtacks that held the caricature of Franklin Roosevelt to the wall and he was jabbing the tack in and out of the plaster, just below the famous jauntily lifted chin, in short, hard, savage thrusts.

"You're such an expert on what's going on here," Ben said finally, "maybe you can tell me what I do now?"

Several more moments went by before Julie realized he had addressed her. "That's even easier," she said.

Ben turned to face her. "All right," he said. "Tell me."

Julie nodded toward the door through which the young king had disappeared. "You can prove to that boy that 'the margin of safety,' if I am quoting you correctly, Ben, 'for a brief period is sufficiently high to justify the risk, of which we are all aware.' You can take him across the channel yourself."

25

When Julie was ten years old, long before Katie Halloran had thought up the idea of starting the Nature Club and even longer before Julie knew what a bootlegger was, her father sent her one day to Mr. Shiffkarten's house to get his witch-hazel bottle refilled.

Mr. Shiffkarten was a fat German with a smokestack neck who spent his days selling dried fruit from a pushcart on Avenue C, and his nights boiling what to Julie smelled like some of his own inventory in the kitchen of his top-floor flat in the tenement around the corner from Biaggio Sarno's barber shop. Julie was aware that there was something mysterious about Mr. Shiffkarten's evening activities because, even though he was an important figure on the block, nobody ever discussed him. Nobody ever bought much dried fruit from him, either. Or even talked to him in public. It was as though everybody on East Ninth Street had entered into an unspoken agreement to consider Mr. Shiffkarten invisible. His importance was due to the fact that all neighborhood celebrations, such as weddings, graduations, baptisms, engagement parties, and bar mitzvahs, were built around the product Mr. Shiffkarten boiled up at night in his kitchen. Even a little girl of ten could see that.

What Julie could not see was the connection between the gaiety of those occasions and the savagery of her father after Biaggio Sarno had consumed a certain amount of the same liquid that Mr. Shiffkarten supplied to both.

On this particular day Biaggio Sarno had consumed so much that he apparently felt incapable of managing the short trip to Mr. Shiffkarten's house for more supplies. Julie didn't mind doing the errand for him. Whatever time she spent out of her father's presence was time during which he could not wallop her across the barber shop. It was not until she had climbed the six flights of gray stone steps to Mr. Shiffkarten's kitchen, paid over the fifty cents her father had given her, received the refilled witch-hazel bottle from the fat German, and was halfway back to the barber shop, that Julie's mind, which had been tunneling along aimlessly through the hill of apparently unrelated facts she had accumulated in her ten years on East Ninth Street, emerged unexpectedly into an illuminated area.

All at once she saw clearly the connection between her father's savagery and the contents of the witch-hazel bottle she had just had refilled in Mr. Shiffkarten's kitchen. All she had to do, to control that savagery, was cut off the supply of Mr. Shiffkarten's product.

Enchanted by the simplicity of the solution, and pleased with herself for thinking of it, Julie did not hesitate to put it into operation. Half a block from the barber shop she pulled the bottle from the paper bag, went to the curb, gave the bottle a good hard tap against the curbstone, waited till the liquid had run off in the gutter, then put the several pieces of broken glass back into the paper bag. It was not until she came into the barber shop, carefully rehearsing the lie she had invented about dropping the bottle when she tripped on the sidewalk, and she caught a glimpse of Biaggio Sarno's face, that Julie realized she had made a mistake.

Sixteen years later, in the Common Room of Major Mac-Gavin's irregular-warfare school in the British countryside, staring at Ben Ivey's face, Julie found herself wondering if she had made a similar mistake. It had all seemed so simple a few moments ago, when after all those years she had finally grasped the truth about Ben. It seemed far from simple now as Ben's face went white, the way her father's face had gone white when she showed him the broken witch-hazel bottle. For a moment, as she saw Ben stagger toward her, the way her father had staggered toward her from the barber chair, Julie thought Ben was going to do what her father had done. But Ben did not strike her. He did not even reach her. He got as far as the sideboard, which he grasped with both hands to steady himself, and drew a deep breath.

"Boss," Harry said in a low voice. "You all right?"

"Get the car," Ben said. "We're going back to London."

"No, we're not," Julie said, scarcely hearing her own words above the wild hammering of her heart. "You're going across the channel, Ben."

He sent a quick glance at Harry, who had come away from the door, scowling worriedly, and another glance at Colonel Uxbridge, who was slowly stroking his lower lip as he watched the man who had brought him to England and the girl he had located for that man.

"Listen, boss," Harry said. "If this dame is—"

"Get out of here," Ben Ivey said. He jerked his head toward the white-haired man from Washington. "You, too, Colonel."

Colonel Uxbridge went without a word, but Harry had either less pride or more experience. He said gently, "Boss, if there's anything I can do—?"

"There is," Ben said. "Get out." He waited until the door closed before he let himself sag back against the sideboard for support. Then he drew another deep breath and said, "What are you trying to do to me?"

"Save your life," Julie said.

"By sending me ashore on an enemy-occupied coast?"

"You're planning to send a couple of million other men to the same place."

Ben made an impatient gesture. "Aren't you grown-up enough yet to have left that kid's argument behind you? Somebody's got to be up at the top, where they can see the whole picture—"

"Or the small piece of it they want to see." Julie came toward him, wishing her heart would stop making all that distracting noise. She had to get it right. For the first time in her life she couldn't afford to make a mistake. She would never be given another chance. "Ben, I don't know how you straightened out the

Tyler Crispin thing with yourself, or six years later the false story that broke in the Seattle papers about Arnold Brahmin's alleged manipulations of PNP&L stock—"

"I told you," Ben said. "That day in the Bronx, the day the banks closed, I told you—"

"I know what you told me," Julie said. "I'm talking about what you told yourself. If you want to believe you ran away from the Tyler Crispin showdown to keep your record clean, okay. If you want to believe what you did to Arnold Brahmin was justified so you could move another step up to the top, okay. It's all over. It's past tense. I can't do anything about it. This thing, though, this thing tonight, Ben, I can do a lot about that, and I'm warning you, Ben, I'm going to do it."

He shook the yellow hair out of his eyes with a gesture of astonishment. "You're *warning* me?"

Julie nodded. "A few hours ago, when you wanted me to put you back on your feet, you said it was my duty to do it because if you didn't get to where you were scheduled to be, the whole course of this war might be affected and the lives of thousands of men might be lost. That's still true, Ben. That boy out there"— Julie nodded toward the door—"that scared kid who happens to be a king could save those lives if he does what you were sent here to get him to do. Anyway, that's what *you* think. So if he doesn't, it'll be your fault, Ben. And this time I'm not going to shut up about it. This time it's not past tense. This time it's now. You came into my life originally, and over the years you've continued to come into it whenever you wanted to, always on your own terms. You're going out of my life on my terms, Ben. If you don't take that scared kid across the channel, I'm going to do something about it."

"Do what?" Ben said.

"Fix things so you can't cause any more damage," Julie said. "I know a few newspapermen. I know a couple who are on the other side of your political fence. I know what they'll do with the story that only I can tell them about the man they call Poison Ivey. You know it, too, Ben."

He ran a hand down the side of his jaw in the old, hesitant

425

gesture, as though probing for an elusive pain. "What I don't know," Ben Ivey said slowly, "is why you should hate me so much."

"I don't hate you," Julie said, and she paused, as though listening to her own words to make sure they had conveyed what she wanted them to convey. They had. "I once did," she said. "For a long time after Celia died I hated you more than I've ever hated anything or anybody in my life. I knew you had used us for years for something I didn't understand, and I knew that first my father died and then Celia and as a result of Celia's death my mother died, but I didn't know what it was you wanted from us. Now that I do know, now I don't hate you, Ben. Not any more. Because now I understand you. Colonel Uxbridge says all leaders are slightly abnormal, and we mustn't judge them the way we judge other men, and maybe that's true, but you're not a leader, Ben."

"What am I?" he said.

The tone of his voice took her by surprise. Not because he sounded genuinely curious, but because beneath the curiosity, she heard a note of desperation, as though after a long search he had found someone with an answer he needed and all at once it had crossed his mind that, perhaps out of resentment, she might not tell him.

"You're a cripple, Ben. You either don't know it or you won't face it. You go around pretending to be perfectly normal. You even manage to do a normal man's work. Until the clutch comes, the unexpected moment arrives, the moment when the normal man calls up his reserves, the reserves you haven't got to fall back on, and then you simply fall. I saw it happen sixteen years ago, the day when Tyler Crispin unexpectedly called a meeting of his Board of Governors. I saw it happen ten years ago, in Seattle, when Arnold Brahmin unexpectedly arranged to face you across the Secretary of the Interior's breakfast table. I don't know how many times it's happened during the years when I wasn't around to see, but I'm seeing it again tonight.

"The man who pretends he's normal didn't know when he arrived in London last night that something unexpected was going to happen. The cripple did. That's why you collapsed. After you were back on your feet, again looking and acting like a normal man, and I was back in my apartment, I suddenly saw something else: the danger of allowing you to continue to pretend. A cripple pretending to be capable of doing a normal man's job can cause a certain amount of damage in a settlement house on the lower East Side, and in a soil-reclamation project in Oregon. But a cripple pretending to be capable of running a war, or a part of it, can cause more damage than any one man has a right to cause.

"That's what I came back to save you from. I didn't know it was that when I started back to Claridge's. I thought I was coming back to save your life. It wasn't until that scared young man out there did the unexpected thing, the kind of thing I once saw Tyler Crispin and Arnold Brahmin do, not until then, a few minutes ago, right here in this room, did I understand what it was I'd come to save you from. I'm going to do it, Ben."

"Even if it means destroying me?" he said.

There was neither rancor nor sarcasm in his voice. The tone was that of a mathematician ticking off a fact on his unhurried, careful way toward the solution of a problem.

"It's you, one person, or a great many people," Julie said. "If you were a Pasteur, if you were an Einstein, if you were a Churchill or the man you work for, I could see an argument for you. They're leaders. They have a right to sit at the top where they can see what you call the whole picture. You don't have that right. Because you don't have what they have: the whole picture clearly in mind, including their place in it. That's why the best you can achieve is an office in the White House. It sounds grand and important and I'm sure what you do is useful. But it's not irreplaceable, and that's the difference.

"Anybody with above-average shrewdness could invent a plan to unseat a Tyler Crispin. Anybody with enough ruthlessness could set in motion a scheme to discredit an Arnold Brahmin and come out ahead when it backfired. But only a man whose shrewdness and ruthlessness are used to serve more than his vanity or his personal ambition, only such a man has the right to say: You must not question what I do.

427

"When Katie Halloran and I were struggling with Latin in Fenimore Cooper High, I remember reading what Caesar said about some little flyspeck on the map of Iberia where he'd stopped for the night. He said he'd rather be first man among those poor, unsophisticated, isolated villagers than second man in Rome. The trouble with you, Ben, you were born with the abilities of a second man, and the ambitions of a first. You'll never make it, Ben. You've demonstrated that over and over. You're demonstrating it again tonight. Only this time I'm going to stop the demonstration before anybody else gets hurt."

There was a tap on the door. Ben, thrusting at the sideboard with both hands, turned.

"Yes?" he said.

The door opened. Colonel Uxbridge came in. He looked quickly from Ben to Julie and then back to Ben.

"Mr. Ivey," he said. "London is on the phone. They want to know if you'll be using the cross-channel lift that's been laid on. They have to know almost at once because they can count on only four more hours of darkness. What are your orders, sir?"

"Send that young man back in here," Ben said.

"I beg your pardon?" Colonel Uxbridge said.

"The king," Ben said. "Tell London to hold on, and send the boy in here."

"Yes, sir," Colonel Uxbridge said.

He pulled his head out and closed the door. Ben stared down at the floor until the door opened again. Julie noticed, as the young man came in, that he had buttoned the collar of his shirt since he had left the room.

"Your Majesty," Ben said.

"I told you earlier that you've made a mistake," the young man said patiently. "I am a Polish schoolmaster named—"

"Cut it out," Ben said sharply. "There's no time for that nonsense. We have only four hours of darkness left, and if you're going across you'll have to start almost at once."

"I'm not going across," the young man said.

"Why not?" Ben said.

It was as though the simple question had emerged not from a human throat but from a belfry equipped with loud-speakers to attract the attention of a town's most indifferent citizen. For the first time since they had met, Julie saw, the young man was looking, really looking, at Ben Ivey.

"In your own country," the king said, "you are like me, a leader, and yet you ask questions like any fool in the street."

Ben gave Julie a short glance, then said dryly, "I'm not a leader in my country, Your Majesty. I am merely the servant of a leader. I do his bidding as, in happier times, your servants do yours. I ask you to excuse a servant's foolish question and answer it: Why won't you cross the channel tonight?" The young man did not answer. Ben said, "Is it because you are afraid?" He waited, but still there was no answer. Ben said quietly, "I am not sitting in judgment, Your Majesty. I am seeking an answer." He gave Julie another glance and added, "It means a great deal to me, personally." The young man turned away. Ben walked up to him, seized his arm, pulled the boy around, and said angrily, "God damn you, you were born with it. It was handed to you for free, on a silver platter. Without lifting a finger. You've got it. The seat up on top. Why don't you act like the man who belongs in it?"

"All I can tell you is what it is like to get out of that seat," the boy said. "I never knew what it is like until my people made me go from my country and come here to England and I was presented with the identity of a simple Polish schoolmaster. It is like the sudden cessation of pain," the boy said. He paused again, and a look of concern crossed his face, as though he had suddenly been assailed by the fear that he was not being understood. "Life holds many pleasures," he said. "You are older. You have had more time than I to savor them. But unless you have sat in my seat, the seat to which as you say I was born, you cannot know the joy of getting out of it. It is the joy of pain stopping. The pain has been gone for almost a year. You are asking me to go back to it. I cannot. I have learned what it is like to live without pain."

"Then you *are* afraid," Ben said, and he shifted his scowling, thoughtful glance to Julie. "It's as simple as that."

429

"Yes, it is as simple as that," the boy said. "I am afraid to go back where I will once again cease to be a human being and become a symbol. I am afraid to go back to being adored and revered and bowed to and honored and touched by the reverent as though I were a god. I am not. The accident of birth has made a certain number of people think I am a god. They are wrong."

"So are you," Ben said.

The boy suddenly smiled, as though the professors, to whom he had patiently conveyed his piece of special knowledge, had demonstrated that they had known it all along.

"In what way am I wrong?" the king said politely.

"You *are* a god," Ben said. "Not in your own eyes, perhaps. But the image that exists in the eyes of all those people cannot be destroyed. You may think you're a Polish schoolmaster. You may even fool yourself into believing it for a while. But the masquerade will never be more than that, and it can never be permanent. You're right. I don't know what it's like to sit in that seat. But I do know this: once a man has sat in it, he can never sit in any other."

"But how can you know that?" the king said with what Julie could see was genuine interest. "You have never sat in it."

"Because until a man has suffered pain," Ben said, "he cannot enjoy what Your Majesty calls the joy of its cessation."

The boy shook his head. "It's not worth it, Mr. Ivey."

"I have only the word of a frightened man for that," Ben said and then, slowly, deliberately, like an assassin placing the muzzle of a gun to the temple of his sleeping victim, he added: "Cowards, I have found, make notoriously unreliable witnesses."

"I am sorry," the king said gently. "You have not understood me. Now I shall make it clear."

All at once, in an unexpected flash of comprehension, Julie understood a phrase she had been hearing and reading all her life but had never even bothered to examine: *noblesse oblige.* All at once she saw the years of careful study and self-discipline, the hours of work and training, the lifetime of relentlessly imposed and unquestioningly accepted drudgery, out of which had

430

come this patient, thoughtful, appealing, dignified boy who had not only been born but had been raised to be a king.

"I have no wish to cross," he said, "because I have no longer the wish to be responsible. You have, Mr. Ivey. This is your plan."

"God damn it!" Ben said. "This is no time for dialectics. We're trying to save a world."

The boy nodded. "In your opinion," he said thoughtfully, "this plan could do that?"

"It is the first big step," Ben said.

The boy nodded again. "In that case," he said, "let us take it together. I will accompany you tonight, Mr. Ivey." He moved toward the door, paused, smiled again at Ben, and said, "I will await your orders."

He walked out. Before the door could slam shut, Colonel Uxbridge pushed it open again.

"Mr. Ivey," he said. "London is becoming impatient. They say—"

"I don't care what they say," Ben said. "I need a few more minutes."

"Yes, sir," the colonel said, and then, after a moment of hesitation: "But what are your orders, Mr. Ivey?"

Ben tugged his lower lip for a moment as he stared down at the floor. Then his head came up, and he brushed the yellow cowlick back from his forehead, and he turned toward Julie.

"I won't know, Colonel," he said, "until I've given Miss Sarno a chance to retract hers."

Colonel Uxbridge also turned toward Julie. His face was impassive.

"I'm not retracting anything," she said.

"When you know all the facts," Ben said, "you may change your mind."

"No," Julie said.

"I think perhaps I'd better wait outside," Colonel Uxbridge said.

"No," Julie said again, but the door had clicked shut before she finished uttering the single syllable. She and Ben were alone once more. The memory of other such moments caused her to say quickly, "Don't, Ben. Don't even try. It won't work. I've told you—"

"I know what you've told me," Ben said. "On the whole, it was a pretty good job. I couldn't have done better myself. The window dressing was impressive. Pasteur, Einstein, Churchill, appropriate quotations from the textbooks, even a few casual paraphrases of Freud. Very impressive indeed. I'm sure it could fool anybody. But I'm not just anybody, Julie. I'm the man who taught you how to do it. I'm probably the only man in the whole damn world who could detect the great big hole in the argument, the thing you left out."

Julie shook her head wearily. "It's not going to work, Ben. You can't do it any more. Not to me. I haven't left out anything."

"You left out the human being," Ben said, and perhaps because her head moved involuntarily, indicating that once again, in spite of all her precautions, he had taken her by surprise, Ben Ivey's lips twisted with a touch of gentle mockery. He said, "All you left out was me."

He came toward her slowly.

"Sure I'm a leader," Ben Ivey said. "But so is the foreman of a construction gang, and so is the starter in an office building with a lot of elevators, and so is the girl in charge of your steno pool in the BEW office. You've got to have leaders. Without them civilization can't function. If to want to *be* in charge makes you abnormal, then remember this, honeybunch: there's just as much weight on the side of the argument that what you want is also perfectly normal. The man who *doesn't* want to get to be foreman of his construction crew is the one who's got something wrong with him. The girl who *doesn't* want to run the steno pool is the cripple. If you condemn me for wanting as you put it to run a piece of the world, then you've got to condemn that foreman for wanting to run his crew and that girl for wanting to run your steno pool. It's a question of degree, beautiful, not kind."

Julie shook her head. "No," she said. "The girl in charge of my steno pool wouldn't do what you did to get where she is."

"Do you know what she actually did do?" Ben said.

432

"I assume she took a civil-service exam for a higher grade than mine," Julie said.

The glint of mockery flashed again across Ben's eyes. "I know people," he said sardonically, "who assume I got where I am today because I did so brilliant a job in Oregon, where I outshone my boss Arnold Brahmin, that I was summoned to Washington as a reward."

"Those people don't know you as well as I do," Julie said. "And even I don't know how you covered the lie you planted about Brahmin."

"If you knew me as well as you think you do," Ben said, "you wouldn't have left me as a human being out of the bill of particulars in which you indicted what you think I am."

"I told you it won't work any more," Julie said. "I didn't leave anything out. You're not a human being. You're a machine geared to reach the top, and no amount of lying is going to change my—"

"A machine wouldn't collapse at the prospect of facing a Tyler Crispin in front of a settlement-house Board of Governors," Ben said in a low voice. "A machine wouldn't fold up because it was told it would have to sit across from an Arnold Brahmin at the Secretary of the Interior's breakfast table."

Ben paused, and perhaps he understood that once again—as when she had first realized the night before who it was that had set in motion the machinery that had brought her to Claridge's —the desire to run from the room had crossed Julie's mind. At any rate, Ben stepped between her and the closed door.

"If I'm a cripple," he said, speaking with great care, as though he wanted no nonsense about inattention or inaudibility to interfere with her comprehension, "then so is every man who ever tried and failed to get what I was groping for when I first met the Sarnos down on East Ninth Street."

Julie shook her head angrily. "That's not true," she cried. "When it happened, both times, before you had to face Crispin and then Brahmin, when you collapsed, both times, you didn't know about Celia and Frank Prohst. Both those times you thought you'd got what you wanted. Both those times you were not standing alone. Both those times, Ben—and no amount of lying is going to change the facts, because I was there, Ben, both times—both those times you still believed it was you that Celia loved, only you, not anybody else."

Ben nodded and said quietly, "Except that she didn't."

Julie shook her head again, desperately, like a fighter who has heard the referee utter the final count of ten over his opponent, then suddenly hears behind him the disquieting approach of the man he thought he had just knocked out.

"But you didn't *know* that at the time," she said. "*Both* times you didn't know that."

"Not up here, maybe," Ben said, and he touched his temple with a forefinger. "But I knew it where it mattered. I must have known it in the same way yesterday, when without knowing why I was doing it, after all these years, I finally sent for the right Sarno."

In the silence that suddenly enveloped her, Julie could hear the sounds of her own labored breathing.

"You see, honeybunch," Ben said quietly, "this has been just as educational an evening for me as it has been for you." He paused and added, "Do you still want me to cross the channel tonight?"

Julie made an effort, turning to face her inexplicably revived antagonist. "Why should I change my mind?" she said. "Even if what you've just told me is true—"

"You don't believe me?" Ben said. He sounded genuinely surprised.

"What difference does that make?" Julie said inpatiently. "Why don't you do what you're always asking the rest of the world to do? Why don't you stick to the root of the matter? Even if what you've just told me is true, why should I change my mind?"

Ben suddenly looked puzzled. For several moments, while his long, restless fingers burrowed through his yellow hair, he stared at Julie with a small frown. Then the restless fingers came down and his face cleared.

"I see that I've learned more tonight than you did." His voice grew gentle. "I don't expect you to change your mind, Julie, because we've both just learned I love you," Ben Ivey said. "You're quite right. That doesn't make the slightest difference. What does

434

make a difference, however, the reason I don't think you'll want
me to take that boy across the channel tonight after all, is something I've suspected for a long time, since that day the banks
closed and I gave you what I intended to be no more than a
brotherly kiss." Ben Ivey paused and, even more gently, he said,
"You see, Julie, what I've just learned tonight is that you love me,
too."

He put out his hand, like a priest conferring a benediction, and
he touched her cheek lightly, and then Julie saw his eyes and her
heart seemed to lurch under the sudden thrust of fear. Ben Ivey
was not conferring a benediction. He was looking at her with pity
as he turned, went to the door, and opened it.

"Colonel Uxbridge," he said to the white-haired man waiting
on the other side of the threshold, "I've got your orders."

"Yes, sir?"

"Tell London we're going across," Ben Ivey said.

"Yes, sir," Colonel Uxbridge said.

"I'll be along in a moment," Ben said, and he pulled the door
shut.

Julie took a step toward him and, without thought, out of the
unphrased but deeply felt awareness of what she had finally won
and was now because of her stubbornness about to lose, she said,
"Ben, no!"

The intensity of her outburst caused him to look at her in surprise. "No, what?" Ben said.

"I—I—" Julie said, but that was as far as her voice would carry
her along the path she knew she could not take. Ben seemed to
know it, too, because he shook his head, as though he were chid-
ing a little girl about a piece of information which, because of her
tender years, she couldn't know but which it was nevertheless im-
perative that she learn at once.

"It's too late," he said. "You should have thought of that before you took away my crutch and made me into a whole man."

Standing close to him, Julie was suddenly reliving the moment
in front of the Small Mammals House when she first discovered
Ben Ivey's eyes were blue, and in the moment of rediscovery,
which was for her the moment of rebirth, she was aware of the

435

stab of panic that lurks in the depth of all fulfillment. Ben was right. The long journey of exploration was over. They had both finally reached the harbor of truth. This, she knew at last, was what she had always wanted. Had she, however, in forcing Ben at last to face his future, doomed her own? Which, in the long run, did she want: the flawed man, who would always need her courage, or the flawless leader of other men, who needed nobody's help?

"Ben, I didn't know," she said. "I didn't understand."

"Neither did I," he said. "But it seems pretty clear now, doesn't it?" He gave her a small smile, but the look of pity did not leave his eyes. "It looks like we're stuck with each other," Ben Ivey said, and added, "Forever."

"But if you go across on this—" Julie paused, and she drew a deep breath, but all at once she knew she lacked the energy needed to mask her terror, and she allowed the words to emerge in all their naked desperation. "Ben, if you go, forever could be only a few hours, or even less. It could mean—"

He nodded, and she grasped with a sense of despair that the small movement of his head had already started him on the journey of which tonight's trip across the channel, even if it succeeded, was bound to be merely the first stage: the journey to which both their lives were now committed: his journey upward, and away from her.

"I know what it could mean," Ben said. "But that's both our tough luck, honeybunch."

"Ben," she said, and knew that she was incapable of saying the words that would ask him to remain behind, "you might not come back."

"On the other hand," he said, "I might."

The words seemed to echo in the room, because they had been released by a voice that had always, for Julie, seemed to echo. And she saw at last why no matter what Ben did, he had to be forgiven, and no matter what course he chose to reach the place from which he could do it, questioning the steps he had taken along the way was irrelevant: the son of the debt-ridden Methodist minister from Cleveland had been granted at birth a great gift.

436

Probably, Julie thought, from the standpoint of those like herself who were its beneficiaries, the greatest. Ben's boss in Washington had it. The man who now held in his hand the fate of England had it. Every man who from the beginning of time had been able to turn the eyes and thoughts and feet of other men in the direction he chose, Julie saw, must have had it: the ability to do with a glance, a gesture, a sound, with his mere physical presence, what Ben had done for her in the past and now, in this tangled moment of unexpected completion and imminent bereavement, he was doing with his voice for Julie again: the ability to restore another human being's belief in the future.

Ben reached for the doorknob. Julie stepped forward and took his hand and pulled it away.

"I can't bear it," she said. "Not now. Not after all these years. Not when I've just learned—" The rush of words stopped. He was watching her sadly. "Ben," she said, trying to control her voice, "I said a lot of things . . . I didn't know what I was talking about. Now I do know. You were right. There must be those at the top who can see the whole picture." She paused, hoping he would say what she could not say herself, knowing now that the hope was vain. Almost wistfully, Julie said, "Isn't it wrong for one of those at the top to take unnecessary risks?"

"Unnecessary?" Ben said. "Julie. You showed me. You told me. Don't you see? I have to go."

Not because she needed an answer, but because she wanted to hold him for one last, lingering moment, Julie said, "Why? Why?"

"I was never cut out for Iberian villages," Ben Ivey said quietly. "I'm going to Rome, honeybunch."

ABOUT THE AUTHOR

JEROME WEIDMAN, novelist and short-story writer, was born in 1913 on New York City's Lower East Side. At the age of twenty-four, he was studying law at New York University when his first novel, *I Can Get It For You Wholesale*, was published in 1937. He quit law school at once to devote all his time to writing, and has been doing so ever since, except during the war, when he served with the Office of War Information in this country and overseas. He has traveled extensively in America and the far corners of the world, from which he has brought back raw material for a dozen novels and approximately two hundred short stories, published in almost every magazine in the United States as well as in Canada, Europe, Australia and Asia. His books have been translated into eight languages. His first play, *Fiorello!*, written in collaboration with George Abbott, was awarded the 1959 Pulitzer Prize. BEFORE YOU GO, his seventeenth book, was finished in New York City, to which Mr. Weidman, his wife, and his two sons have returned after living in Westport, Connecticut, for a dozen years.